REVOLT

LONG MAY SHE FUCKING REIGN.

K.A. KNIGHT

Revolt.

Written by K.A. Knight:
Edited By Jess from Elemental Editing and Proofreading.
Proofreading by Norma's Nook.
Formatted by The Nutty Formatter.
Cover by Emma at Moonstruck Cover Design & Photography.
Art by Dily Iola Designs.

For every girl who wanted to be a rockstar—or simply fuck one.

author note

PROLOGUE

"*The world exploded into chaos last night. If you didn't see it, you must have been living under a rock. Last night, the world of rock was, well, rocked at the reappearance of our beloved rock princess, Reign.*"

I snort at that as I sip my coffee, idly bending over the kitchen island as I watch the news report. My phone is blowing up next to me —a phone I haven't looked at in months until this morning. Beloved rock princess? Priceless. These are the same reporters who, not five months ago, were calling me a slut, a whore, and a money-grubbing attention seeker.

Figures.

"*Putting on an impromptu show in a seedy club called River's, she sang a brand-new song.*" The footage cuts to me singing, just me, on stage with the music I composed. The lyrics were torn from my very soul, my eyes hard with anger as I spilled my heart into the song.

"*But you'll never know.*

The vultures circle for my soul, ripping me to shreds for my secrets but I hold them tight.

Hold them to me and run.

Oh, you'll never know, not until I sing it on stage.

They will never get any more.

Not from me."

My smile twists into something downright sinister as the footage pans back to the reporter. *"After a four-month hiatus, during which no one has seen or heard from the infamous singer after her rumored split from long-term boyfriend and fellow rockstar Tucker, not even her friends knew what happened or where she went. She disappeared overnight, and it left a lot of fans worried, us included. Now, she seems to be back and rocking a whole new look."*

"Bullshit," I sneer as I sip my coffee, holding back the venom on my tongue, not wanting to be that vile creature who lashes out anymore. They will never see me like that again.

I will protect my peace and my heart.

"Fans went crazy, and speculation has already started. Did you hear the accusations in the lyrics, Ted? It all hinted at the suspected and rumored infidelity of rockstar boyfriend Tucker. Could that have been the reason for her sudden disappearance? Was our rock princess nursing a broken heart while her ex went on to a sold-out, worldwide tour?"

Of course he did. It didn't stop him from searching for me though, but like everyone else, he didn't find me, just like I wanted.

"The world, including other celebrities, are expressing their relief and happiness at her return, with many siding with her online against her ex."

I snort. Where were these celebrities or friends when I needed them? Nowhere. They were protecting their own image, but now that it suits them, they show their support.

Too little, too fucking late.

Once I was a foolish, naïve girl, spilling her secrets with hopes of creating friendships, but not anymore.

"We are left with more questions than answers," Ted responds, smiling insincerely at the camera, and then at his costar who has done most of the talking, the shit stirrer herself, Diandra.

"Where has she been for months? And the most important question of all: is she back for good?"

Smirking, I down my coffee and turn the TV off as I stare at my empty mansion.

Lyrics run through my veins, never to be stolen again.

Not by anybody.

The rock princess is back, that's for sure, but they will definitely be shocked.

Gone is the bubblegum, try-too-hard girl, and in her place is a fierce, no fucks given woman who's ready to spit venom at those who stole her innocence.

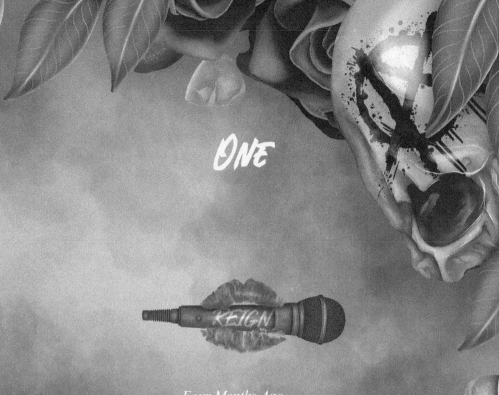

ONE

Four Months Ago . . .

The car speeds to the one place I feel safe, my solace, my home, and the man who holds my heart. The silence is too loud, leaving me with my turbulent thoughts, so I turn on the radio and instantly regret it.

"—she is basically asking for it. Did you see what she was wearing? And she's supposed to be an example for our kids. No thank you!"

With a sob, I skip to the next station, my heart hammering and body shaking. Fear and pain fill my soul, blotting out the music that never comes.

"She's a wannabe, nothing more. She hasn't made any good music in months—"

Skip.

"I'm just saying, a girl like her fucked her way to the top—"

Skip.

"If it weren't for her boyfriend, no one would care about her—"

I smash my fist into the radio, silencing it, then look at the rock on my finger. At least they have that wrong. It's fiancé, not boyfriend, and as I park in the underground garage, I practically sprint into the elevator that will take me up to his penthouse in the city—one of his many homes. He's not expecting me, but I need him. I flew overnight to get here and feel the safety I only find in his arms.

When the doors to the elevator open, I rush inside, not even bothering to kick off my heels or drop my bag or even remove my coat. I ignore the stunning view and familiar sights, heading straight down the corridor to the bedroom.

He'll be sleeping, but I can wake him.

At the door, I almost giggle before silencing myself, wanting to surprise him, but something cuts through the silence. I freeze, unable to place it for a moment, and then the sound comes again, a familiar one.

My mind screams at me to back away, to run, but instead, I open the door and get my first look at what's making the noise. I stare at their joined bodies with sweat glistening on their perfect skin, and everything in me aches.

The final blade of betrayal has sunken in, but this one goes right into my heart and something snaps within me, breaking permanently.

I slowly shut the door. They don't even hear me, their moans increasing as I wander through the apartment I once thought was a sanctuary but now feels like a cold prison. I stop before the empty island he never uses, since he doesn't cook, realizing it's all for show, just like our relationship.

Before I know it, I have the ring from my finger curled into my palm.

I stare down at the rock and know with certainty it was another game, another publicity play.

He never loved me, not like I deserve to be loved.

None of them do, and enough is enough.

A person can only take so much before they break, and I refuse to give them the satisfaction of letting them see that.

They want my life, but they can't have it.

Not anymore, no one can.

Clarity curves a smile onto my trembling lips, and I know that's the right move.

I want to scream and cause a scene, but that's exactly what they are expecting.

Never again.

Opening my fist, I let the ring clatter to the island, where it sparkles under the lights, and then I step back into the darkness, seeking sanctuary in it.

The clank of the ring is the final nail in the coffin as I turn and leave, heading out to my car and driving away from the city.

Away from it all.

I don't look back, not once, as I abandon everything I worked so hard for, and for the first time in a year, a truly grinning from ear to ear.

I didn't cause a scene, nor did I spread rumors or start a fight. I just disappeared and let the rumors swirl. I didn't act on my anger, jealousy, or pain, I simply left his life like I had joined it—quietly and all too quickly.

TWO

Present day . . .

My once short blonde hair is now long and blue, falling in waves to my sides. I change the color when I feel like it, exploring and experimenting in ways I was never allowed to before. My image was to be protected—hell, every inch of me was insured, and my management made damn sure I stuck to their carefully cultivated image, even when I fucking hated the diets, tans, boring makeup, and fake blonde hair. I'd risen to success through hard work at a young age, but it thrust me into a spotlight I wasn't prepared for, full of lions and vipers all wanting a bite, and bite they did. I changed everything for them.

Too fat? I lost weight, becoming obsessed with it.

Too skinny? I binge ate until I was sick.

Too boring? I indulged in drugs and alcohol.

Too scandalous? I donated my money.

Each move was calculated, from being secluded so young to gaining an audience to being told who the hell I could and couldn't date. Not anymore. Long gone is that scared little girl who depended on everyone else. It was only in my pain and isolation when I realized the truth—they needed me more than I needed them, and that tipped the power to me. I had been alone all along, but now it was time to thrive.

First things first.

Staring up at the sprawling skyscraper that houses Willow Records, I straighten my shoulders and push my sunglasses up my nose, then I stomp into the building in my shit kickers, my short leather skirt rustling with the movement. My fishnets expose the tattoos on my legs, which they will hate, while my leather jacket hides the others. I ignore the calls and astonished looks as I scan my badge and head into the elevator, turning my back to the stunned employees inside and hitting the button I need. Humming to the music in the elevator, I look at the guarded expressions of the people surrounding me, and when the doors open, I step out and grin at them.

"Reign, it's you!" a shocked employee named Todd exclaims. He's the office runabout, not that he will ever tell anybody that with his inflated sense of self-importance.

He's shorter than me, but he spends forever in the gym to make up for his lack of height. With short blond hair and a scary dark tan, he's a prime example of everything I hate in this world.

He stands there with his phone in hand, probably to call security. "I, um . . . We were . . . I . . . I don't think—"

"Oh, I know you don't, Toddy boy." I pat his cheek condescendingly as I pass and head to the office I need. Opening the door, I meet the shocked and angry eyes of William Waler—my manager.

"Reign, we were not expecting you." It's the polite way of saying, *what the fuck?* "Would you like me to schedule a meeting?" It's another veiled rejection. That's the music industry for you; no one ever says what they mean.

"Yes, for now." I wander to the meeting room. "As fast as possible." I never issued commands or used the substantial pull I had as one of the world's biggest rock stars before. I hated it, but now I embrace it and utilize it. This time, the games are in my favor. Others might not get away with that shit, but this record label needs me.

In the next five minutes, they will file into the room to see me sitting at the head of the table with my legs up and a cigarette in my mouth.

"There is no smoking in here," one admonishes. I forget his name, but I forget most of them.

I ignore his words and blow a ring right at him. "Sit, gentlemen. We have some things to discuss."

Reluctantly, they follow my directive. I don't even bother to make introductions to the new faces.

"Reign," William starts, spreading his hands. "Where have you been? You can't just disappear—"

"I can and I will," I snap. "Now listen, this is how it's going to go—"

"You can't just come back without returning our calls and waltz in here like you own the place, not to mention that stunt with the new song. What were you thinking?" Willow, the head of the label, roars.

I arch an eyebrow until he sits back down. He's the one to look away first, but I remember when I could barely meet his eyes. He was like a god to me, but not anymore. He's just a man—a man I handed my power to. "I needed time, and now I'm back. I have new music, and it will be produced exactly how I say. There will be two albums this year and a tour announcement. I will do interviews"—I hold up my hand when William opens his mouth to speak—"when and with whomever I want to, no others. Everything that has to do with me will be run by me. If not, I will walk out of that door with the rights to my music, which I bought back, and you will never see me again, apart from in the news when I win award after award."

They share a confused look as I sit back and light another cigarette, giving them time.

"You're back for good?" William asks.

"I am, with better music than before, but this is my life, my music. I will consider your input, but you will not ever control me again. I am not an asset, I am a person, and you will respect that. Embrace the change, boys." Standing, I stub out my cig on the table as they wince. "I will await your decision." As I head to the door, I see the shocked expressions on their faces and know they have never had this happen before.

They control the narrative, the music, and the artists.

Not this one, not ever again.

"Oh, and hire some fucking women, will you? Sexist bastards." Leaving in a cloud of smoke, I make my way out of the building and into the waiting piranhas outside—the ones I called. Paparazzi scream for me as their cameras flash. I smile and wink, ignoring questions as I reach my car.

It's all planned and staged. My manager would be proud.

"Reign, is it true you're back?"

I lift my sunglasses and stare right into the camera. "It's true. I'm back and you aren't ready for what I have up my sleeve." I slide into the car, laughing as they chase me for the final money shot.

Picking up the whiskey in the back, I down a gulp, hating when my manager's voice slips into my mind. "Don't be seen drinking too much during the day." I down another gulp out of spite.

Fuck him. Fuck them all.

It's the dawn of a new Reign, baby, and this time, I'm doing whatever the fuck I want, whenever the fuck I want, starting today.

I know I was photographed during the shopping spree yesterday, and the images went viral within minutes. My arms were laden with designer bags as I was chased by store employees holding more. Then again, more pictures were taken last night after dancing and drinking the night away in an exclusive—but not too exclusive—club and chasing mayhem, then again in the early hours this morning as I entered a hotel with three men—a drummer, a bassist, and a singer from a rock band I respect.

Hours later, I left and waved to the cameras, and I can't help laughing as my phone blows up. My face is plastered everywhere. I lie on the sofa in last night's dress and makeup, sucking on a lollipop, with cum dripping from my ass and pussy, and I can't help but claim victory, especially when my phone rings.

"Speak," I answer, knowing that the tone is for William and William alone, but instead, Willow's voice answers.

"We will not be played, but we accept your conditions. We will . . . work together"—I bet it killed him to say that—"starting with this new music. The studio is yours. Produce it and we will come up with a plan. Reign, I'm glad you're back." Surprisingly enough, he actually sounds like he means it.

Hanging up, I twist my tongue around the lollipop once more as my face flashes across every channel on the television.

Oh, it's good to be back.

THREE

"**S**hit. I mean, shit, Reign, this is good," Jack remarks.

He's the only person I feel bad about leaving months ago. I would call him a true friend. Despite being one of the most successful songwriters and producers in the business, he never let it get to his head, and when he first heard me, he instantly aligned himself with me. Throughout the years, we created magic, until my lyrics dried up.

It pained him when I would come into the studio drunk or angry and I couldn't even get anything out. It led to more than one argument, and when I disappeared, we weren't even speaking. He only wanted the best for me, and he told me more than once that he saw the industry swallowing me up and he hated it. I thought about him a lot when I was gone, about how I treated him, and I knew when I came back, he was the only one I could trust with my new music. More than that, I want to prove to him that I'm okay.

When I turned up this morning, I was nervous and prepared to apologize, but he hugged me like no time had passed and without waiting, he told me to show him what I had been working on. That's Jack for you. You can go five months without talking, but once you are together again, it's like no time has passed at all. No excuses or apologies are necessary; there is just understanding.

Eight hours later, I've sung every song twice and explained the arrangements and my ideas.

He leans back on the sofa in the room opposite the recording studio. "This shit is . . ."

I wait silently because his opinion is the only one I care about. He's a genius, an actual genius who belongs in the Rock & Roll Hall of Fame. His way with words can rip you apart or put you back together again, and I know I wouldn't be where I am without him. I silently promise to get him where he belongs—up on those walls with the greats.

"The best shit you have ever written."

"Really?" I almost leap to my feet.

He grins and rubs his head shyly. "Shit, Rey, it's better than my stuff."

"Not a chance." I laugh, and then he sobers.

"I'm glad you're back. Don't get me wrong, kid, I'm even happier to see your excitement for music again, but are you okay? I'm your friend above everything else, Rey. Fuck the producers and the label. Are you okay?"

"I am." It's true. "I wasn't before. I'm sorry about leaving without a trace—"

"We do what we have to do to protect ourselves. I'll admit I was hurt, but I was also proud of you."

"Proud?" I repeat, picking up my Chinese food once more and crossing my legs under me.

"Very." He grins. "You fought back and stopped letting them walk all over you. Jesus, Rey, in the last year, I could tell I was losing you. You were so lost. You weren't Rey anymore. You were going through the motions, but seeing you alone in here, grinning and excited, is better than any music you could ever compose. You're alive again, Rey, and I'm so glad."

My heart melts. "Soft bastard." I chuck an egg roll at him, and he laughs as he catches it and shoves it into his mouth.

"You know it! Now, let's produce the best album of all time, shall we?"

"Let's."

I changed inside the studio, making Jack laugh. Over the six years I've known him, he's become like a brother to me, thank God, so he's used to my shenanigans, but as I'm leaving, he calls my name—my real name. He's the only person I have ever given it to since that dark night ten years ago.

"Give them hell," he says.

"Oh, I plan to." I can't help but laugh. Wearing my red, eight-inch stilettos, laced-up leather pants, and a bustier, I walk out to the waiting cameras, ready to play the part.

Gone is the soft, innocent girl.

Gone is the up-and-coming rocker.

Gone is the worldwide crush.

Gone is the heartbroken girl.

In her place is a woman on a mission, with music in her veins and purpose in her step. I slide into my brand-new Bugatti La Voiture Noire with personalized plates.

I laugh as I wind around the traffic in the city, heading out to the hills above and the mansion where the party is being hosted. At the opened gates, I wave at the security guards and park outside, tossing my keys to a drooling attendant before stepping inside to a different world.

I am crashing the rock and roll party of the week.

I have no doubt my ex and all my old friends are here.

Taking a flute of champagne off a passing server's tray, I down it and put it back as she grins at me. I wink then run my eyes down her body and she blushes. I take another and toast her before plunging back into the life I walked away from.

The music is loud as I wander through the mansion, noticing the looks and whispers and ignoring them. Outside, the pool is filled with partygoers, as are the areas around it, with people fucking, drinking, or doing drugs. There are no cameras here, or so they think, but everyone here has sold someone else out for fame. Nothing is ever truly safe or a secret in Hollywood, and it comes out eventually.

"Reign." The dark, sensual timbre used to bring me to my knees. The first time I met Tucker, I was starstruck. He was famous and one of the sexiest men in the world, and he wanted me, craved me. He made me feel like I was his everything. He blew me away with dates in Paris and dinners in Italy. He gushed about me, displayed me proudly on his arm, and worshiped me, or so I thought.

Once, that voice would have been enough to rip apart my defenses, but now, I feel nothing.

Turning, I sip my champagne as I look him over. He looks good, as good as always, wearing nothing but low-slung black jeans and boots, which are no doubt more expensive than this whole party. Every inch of his skin is covered in tattoos, and his black hair is shaved on one side to show more. His bright blue eyes are still showstoppers, and he still has a ring pierced through his lip. His hands are decorated with his usual rings, but it's the one on the chain around his neck that almost makes me falter.

Almost.

It's my ring.

"Reign, it is you." He steps closer, and I see others bring out their phones as they text and send pictures around the world. They want gossip.

I simply smile. "Tucker, nice to see you again." I sip my champagne like I have no care in the world, even though I almost choke on the bubbles under all the scrutiny. "You look good."

"You look incredible. God, babe, where have you been?" he asks, almost sounding contrite and wounded. I swallow my snort. He's a good actor. I'll give him that.

"I know I do," I reply, "and I had some shit to do, but I'm back now."

"I heard you were back, but I almost didn't believe it. I didn't hear a word from you for four months. God, I was so worried, babe." When he used to call me that, it made my knees weak and my pussy flutter, but now? Nothing. I almost pity him.

Almost.

"Why?" I cock my head.

His jaw hangs open before it snaps shut. "Because I love you. I was planning our lives together."

I can't resist. I know everyone is listening, but I don't care. He doesn't get to act like the heartbroken, abandoned lover. Not after what he did. He isn't an innocent victim, even though he wants to paint me as the villain.

"Between her thighs? That's an odd place to plan a wedding." I laugh, and his face turns beet red. "Don't worry, *babe*," I mock, "it's all in the past. Now, I better mingle. We wouldn't want gossip columns to start spreading lies, would we?" I kiss his cheek, seeing the flashes of cameras and hearing his sharp inhale. For a moment, his familiar scent calls me home before it's twisted by all the pain he caused.

He used to smell like home, but now his scent is just bitter and painful and makes me sad.

"It's good to see you, Tucker. Enjoy your night."

I leave him staring after me, calling my name as I step into the crowd.

FOUR

I wake up way too hungover. My head pounds, and my body feels shaky and hot. I take a quick shower, and without bothering to dress or dry, I head downstairs. I need fresh air, and when I see my pool filled with sunlight, I grin. Heading outside, I stop at the edge of the pool and dive in, letting the slightly warm water wake me up and wash away the night before.

The looks, the lies, the drinks . . .

Those who knew me pretended to be my friends in an attempt to get answers with carefully veiled jokes and questions. I was the center of attention, and it was draining to keep up the facade. The "Oh, let me get your number and keep in touch" remarks, fake smiles, and dumb acts were exhausting.

The booze was good though, so there was that, and seeing Tucker sullenly watch me all night made up for it. There was hunger in his eyes, as well as regret, and I must admit, it felt good. I didn't come back to hurt him or to get revenge, but damn if I didn't eat it up. It was the closest he would ever get to my body and heart again, and when I went upstairs with the rapper who had been flirting with me for years, I felt his eyes on me.

He was angry and jealous.

Oh yeah, I had a good time alright. My pussy still aches from that good dick, but I knew better than to stay. I got what I wanted and then I left them high and dry, waiting for a meltdown or a show. They got nothing other than pictures of me drinking, playing, and flirting.

I haven't checked the news or my phone this morning, but I know the images will be everywhere, and it makes me smile as I dive deeper and then swim back to the surface, pushing my hair back. I leave my eyes closed as I let the sun wash last night away before doing laps. While I was away, I learned that swimming centers me and my mind. I didn't have my fancy pool then, just a lake, but my heart aches for it for a moment as I remember the trees swaying around it and the slightly uneven wooden dock I spent hours sunbathing and creating music on. It was just nature and me.

Nothing else.

No expectations, no eyes, no judgment.

Just peace.

This is as close as I can get it now, so I push myself harder in the water, sweating out the alcohol. My mind clears as I swim, until my muscles finally begin to ache, and I slow before diving down once more. When I break the surface, it's at the far end of the pool, facing the house, and I blink.

Standing there are four muscular men dressed to the nines, and they definitely weren't there when I dived in.

Wiping the water from my face and slicking my hair back, I cock my head and run my eyes over each of them.

The one on the left is literally the biggest bastard I have ever seen in my life. He's easily over six feet and stacked with muscle, so he either has to be a gym junkie or some sort of military personnel with the way he's standing, but his hair, which is almost black at the roots but fades to a soft blond at the edges, is longish and tousled wildly around his head, giving him a roguish appearance. His eyes are a deep, dark brown below thick eyebrows. His full lips are framed by a neatly trimmed beard, and he has a nose that's been broken one too many times. He's fucking stunning in a rugged sort of way. Wearing a black shirt that clings to his huge pecs and arms, black jeans, and boots, he shouldn't stand out amongst those dressed in expensive, designer clothes, but he certainly would, and when his eyes run over me and heat, I quickly look away before I get lost in those bottomless depths.

The guy next to him is tall, but not as tall as his friend. Unlike the dark, rugged man, this one is all sunshine. He has bright emerald-green eyes that remind me of the ocean I swam in last year, with vivid red hair and a matching beard. His hair is longer on top and shaved on the sides, and he has tattoos crawling down his neck into his suit jacket. He's also muscular, just like the first man, but he's wearing a gray suit that molds to every perfect line of his body. His wide grin shows his straight white teeth and perfect pink lips, and the small scar dissecting the top only enhances it. There's a playful air about him, and I find myself smiling back.

The man next to him watches me carefully, his face blank and almost cold, but that coldness only adds to his sexy aura. Did I accidentally get drunk and stumble into a house belonging to models? Jesus fucking Christ. His deep, inky black hair is perfectly styled, and his black eyebrows enhance his deep brown eyes, which are surrounded by thick lashes. Unlike the other two, his face is freshly shaven and perfect, with a sharp jaw and cheekbones. Korean maybe? His lips are pursed and so thick that I'm actually jealous. Everything about him is perfectly pressed and sharp, down to his pinstriped shirt and shiny dress shoes.

I drag my eyes to the last man and swallow hard. This definitely must be the wrong house. His olive skin is proudly on display, and he wears a crooked smirk on his thick lips. He has stubble on his jaw with perfect, clean lines, and his dark hair is slicked back. I briefly catch a glimpse of his bright brown eyes with amber flecks before he slides some shades on to cover them before running his hand through his hair. Cocky fuck. I have to admit, though, he's hot as hell, and his body is perfectly encased in a black button-down, with the buttons undone to expose his chest, and snug blue jeans. He also easily has to be the second tallest.

My eyes run back over them again as I wonder what the hell they are doing in my house. Don't get me wrong, they are pretty to look at, but I still don't know them.

The east asian man steps forward.

Rolling back his sleeves with deft, quick fingers, he exposes thick, muscular forearms as he reaches down and offers me his hand. Grinning, I place my hand in his and let him tug me from the water before he steps back. I see him gulp as his eyes drop to my very wet, naked body. I don't hide myself as I look them over, hearing the olive-skinned one groan.

"God damn, I'm going to love this job," he mutters.

"Do you greet everyone like this?" the ginger-haired man asks.

Water sluices down my body as I bring my hair over my shoulder and ring it out, still looking them over until the huge one steps forward. "Miss Harrow—"

"Reign," I correct, pushing my hair back and propping my hands on my hips.

"Reign," he says, though he seems reluctant. "I am Raffiel, head of your new security team, and this is Cillian." He jerks his chin at the redhead who winks. "Dal." The Korean man nods. "And Astro."

"Hello, beautiful," Astro purrs, making me grin, and then my mind screeches to a halt and I jerk my gaze back to Raffiel, who's patiently waiting with his eyes very properly on my face.

That's when I realize he's a bodyguard, and a good one, since he's trained to be discreet. Oh, this one will be fun to crack.

"I didn't hire a new security team. I already have one." I don't mention that I let some of them go, but there are a few around here somewhere.

"Who didn't even notice us waltz into your house," Astro says. "We are the best."

"We were hired by your management. You didn't answer your phone when we tried to alert you of our arrival. We tested your security on the way in, and changes will be made," Raffiel begins.

Rolling my eyes, I saunter past them, making sure to add an extra sway to my step. I feel their eyes burning holes through me, and when I reach the door, I glance back to see all their eyes locked on my ass.

Even Raffiel's.

Victory.

"Well, are you coming?" I call as I step inside.

"Oh, I will be, in my hand at the memory of that," I hear someone mutter, and then there's the distinct sound of flesh meeting flesh. I chuckle as I grab a container of strawberries and bend over the counter, reaching for my phone. I hear their boots as they follow me, then they spread out before the island as I suck on a berry.

"Jesus, I'll never be able to eat strawberries again without getting hard," Astro mutters, and I meet his eyes as I suck it into my mouth and swallow, making him groan.

"Don't taunt him, Miss Harrow," Raffiel says.

Ignoring that and the shiver it sends through me, I dial the number and wait, leaving it on speaker as I drag another one across my lips while staring at Astro. His eyes are narrowed and filled with desire, and I take sick satisfaction in winding him up. His reaction is so raw and unfiltered. It's not for show or to use against me.

He just wants me and isn't afraid to show it.

I like that.

"Can I have one?" he murmurs, reaching across the island and sliding his upper body closer.

Just because I can, I lick one and hold it out to him. He has to bend to reach it, but he keeps his amber eyes on me as he sucks it from my fingers and groans. "Sweet, so sweet."

Smirking, I lick my fingers clean. I'm certain he has a big dick.

"Astro, go patrol and cool down," Raffiel orders.

Winking at me, Astro steps around the room, purposely passing me. "Worth it," he whispers, and I grin.

I lick my lips and watch the others, who watch me back. Raffiel wears a stern expression, Cillian smiles broadly, and Dal seems unsure.

William finally answers the phone. "Reign, it's nonnegotiable," he states.

"Why?" I ask my manager curiously. He was obviously expecting the call since he didn't even ask.

"It's the boss's stipulation for your . . . um, new contract."

"He didn't mention it," I reply, eyes narrowing. "I laid out my conditions. Full control—"

"Over your music and public life, yes." I see the guys share a look, but I ignore them. "We will no longer make demands on how you choose to live, but your safety is not negotiable."

Gritting my teeth, I glare at the phone. "More like he's doing it to lord some power over me. Are they here to report back to you on what I get up to?"

"That is their job."

"Great, I have fucking spies in my house again," I mutter, hanging up when he tries to speak, and then I glare at the men I was smiling at just a moment before.

"Miss Reign, we are only to report back on matters that affect your safety." Raffiel spreads his hands in apology. "I swear that we will never tell them anything else. They hired us, but we do not play games or participate in power trips." He watches as I run his words through my head.

"We will see." I shrug, grabbing another strawberry as I head past. "Better make yourself at home then." I feel them following as I head to the foyer and start to saunter upstairs.

"Oh, since you are supposed to know my every move, I'm going out soon," I call, stopping to look back.

"Where?" Raffiel stands at attention.

"Who knows?" I smirk, and his eye twitches in annoyance.

"Reign, I can't do my job—"

I roll my eyes and head upstairs, ignoring his annoyance. He can suck my clit for all I care. Nobody, and I mean nobody, gets to control me again.

That includes sexy bodyguards with eyes deep enough to fall into and bodies strong enough to ride.

Five

I stare up the winding white stairs the naked rock star princess just ascended. Fuck. Scrubbing my face, I turn to the others. "Check the car situation." I tell Dal, and he wanders off to do as ordered. "Cil, check on Astro and begin making a list of updates we need."

Smirking, he salutes me and takes off, leaving me alone. I look at the top of the stairs again, wondering what trouble we got ourselves into now.

That's what she is, trouble, and I knew it from the first moment they told us her name. You'd have to be dead not to know about the playgirl rock princess who's known for being slightly crazy. Now, with her tight, curvy body imprinted on every fiber of my being, I know they underplayed just how much trouble she would be. Fuck, my dick is ridiculously hard, not that I would ever let the others know that. We are the best at what we do, and we never draw attention to ourselves, but I knew that would be hard the moment I saw her swimming laps naked, the sun caressing her incredible body.

She changes everything, and I don't like it.

I don't like change. I like rules, and I like knowing every single step of a plan. I am clearly the opposite of the nudist rock star singing upstairs. I saw her pictures on the news, but they did not do her justice, not one bit. Obviously, she was younger back then, more innocent, and there was something fragile in her eyes, but not now. Oh no, her eyes are hard, and she's full of sensuality.

Her long hair was made to be fisted, her pouty little mouth was made to be fucked, and her perky ass was made to be marked.

Fuck, those tits tipped with rosy nipples would look fucking incredible above me while she rode my dick. No. Stop. Don't even think of that.

It's too late, and I just fucking know Reign Harrow, the rock princess, has ruined me forever with just one look at her naked body.

Turning away before I follow her bratty ass upstairs and teach her not to talk back to me, I leave to find the others and check in on their progress, knowing she is going to fight us every step of the way.

The house is fucking massive, but also very tastefully done. Some rooms are still empty or being decorated, and that makes sense since she just reappeared. The outside is my favorite though, like an oasis. It has the pool, a bar, a teepee, and feels homey with cushions, rugs, fire pits, and an incredible view.

The seven empty bedrooms on the second floor are where we will live to be close—not that she knows that yet. They are all plain but furnished enough for us to live in. Hell, we've lived in sand before, so that won't matter. Her floor is all open plan, and I won't go up there until later. The first floor has a massive kitchen with doors that lead outside, a dining room, two living rooms, and a cinema room. There's even an elevator, as well as so many other rooms, I lose track. Strategically, it's a nightmare, but we can make it work.

I have a long list that I start phoning in while we wait for her. Her management said they wanted the best, so that's what they'll get.

Astro appears. "Captain."

I hold up my finger and he patiently waits while I finish my text to my guy who takes care of cameras, and then I raise my eyes to his. He doesn't even look shameful. "Reign is our job. Do not cross the line."

"You know I won't, but I can flirt."

"No, we'll keep it professional," I retort, and he laughs at me.

"Good luck with that, captain." He grins.

"I mean it. She is our job and one of the biggest names we have ever protected. This isn't the military anymore. We are under scrutiny, so there is no leeway for a fuckup. Get it in check. It doesn't matter that she's the most beautiful fucking woman on the planet. You think with your head, not your dick, understood?" I know my tone is commanding and sharp, the one I used to use in another life.

"Got it, captain." He has the grace to look chastised, but then he grins and I follow his gaze to Reign.

She has on a black, skintight, V-neck shirt or bodysuit that molds to her incredible tits, her nipples pebbled against the material, little shorts that mold to her ass, and knee-high boots. Her hair falls over one shoulder, her lips are bright red, and her eyes are darkly lined. She looks fucking incredible and way too expensive for us to ever stain with our touch.

She winks at me. "I'll take it as a compliment. Let's go, boys."

I walk before her and open the door. "Let us get the door and go out first, even in the car, understood?"

"Sure," she responds, dragging her hand along my side as I head into the garage.

For some reason, I don't believe her, nor do I think about the way her touch burns my skin, causing me to ache. Ignoring it, I stride over to the huge SUV, where Dal sits in the driver's seat. Opening the back door, I gesture for her to get in and she slides inside. Usually, I would put Astro in the back, since he's good at keeping our marks comfy and happy, but I want space between them, so I get in with her and he gets in the passenger seat.

"All good?" I ask Dal.

He meets my eyes in the rearview mirror. "No IEDs, trackers, or issues."

Reign looks up from her phone. "Bombs? Really?"

"I take my job very seriously, Miss Harrow," I tell her, using that to keep some distance between us as I stare out of the window before glancing back to find her watching me. "Is now a good time to discuss the updates and upgrades to your security systems?"

"Do I have a choice?" she asks, crossing her long, supple legs.

"Of course. We would appreciate your input—" I grunt as she presses her foot into my thigh, spreading it wider. Giving her a warning look, I carry on. "It is your house and life, Miss Harrow," I say as she presses her booted foot against my cock. I grip her ankle and squeeze, showing her a little of my strength as I try really hard to ignore the flare in her eyes as I lift her leg and place it down on the seat next to me. "As I was saying—"

"Fine, read me the list." She sighs and settles back, but I know she hasn't finished messing with me. I see the mischief in her eyes and the tilt of her red lips. For a moment, I get lost in them, imagining them wrapped around my hard cock. The tinted windows would stop anyone from ever knowing that I had their precious rock princess on her knees, begging for my cum.

Shifting, I try to ignore my dick and my dirty thoughts, but it's like she knows because she chuckles and drops her gaze to my very obvious erection. "Need a hand?" she teases.

"I'm thinking cameras." I hope that by focusing on my job, my stupid fucking hard-on will go away. I have never had this issue before.

"Like watching, do you?"

I actually choke on my own words. "Miss Harrow, this is very inappropriate," I say, and she rolls her eyes.

"Fine, I'll behave . . . for now. So cameras?" She easily switches to business mode, and I find myself missing her sass, but it does make it easier to focus on what I need to do.

"Boss, I need to know where we are going," Dal says.

"Miss Harrow?" I inquire.

"I want a new car." She reels off an address.

I don't comment on that. Instead, I continue, "Cameras. We won't have blind spots except for your bedroom and bathroom to give you privacy."

"I don't mind the bedroom." She smirks.

I ignore that and the jerk of my cock. "We need to hire new guards for security detail, those we trust and know are up to scratch. I want some new alarms in place as well as a security officer. We will put together an approved list of visitors."

"No one," she replies, her face hardening.

"Miss Reign?" I ask, confused.

"My house is my sanctuary. They will not defile it again. No one will be allowed at my house except for me and you guys. Is that a problem?" She dares me to comment, but I just nod, and she looks out the window. "Do whatever you think is best."

I don't like the closed look on her face. I don't even like that her eyes aren't on me anymore. In fact, she seems to be trying very hard to ignore us. Suddenly, all joy is sucked from the car, leaving it cold and sterile like our normal jobs. She shut down on us, and a part of me hates that.

"It's your house, Reign," I say, dropping the title. "We will make sure it and you are safe."

For a moment, her eyes come back to me, and I feel like cheering in victory. "Good, now let's pick out a new car." She smiles, and although it's small, it's there.

I nod, okay with whatever will make her happy.

I'm beginning to realize I would do anything so I wouldn't have to see that look again, but some things start to click into place in my mind. Is that why she left? Her peace was taken, or defiled as she called it?

For the first time, like the rest of the world, I wonder what happened to Reign Harrow and where she went.

SIX

"Miss . . ." The man hesitates as I climb inside the Rolls Royce and stroke the leather. He's the manager here.

The sales associate panicked and bolted when I bent over to check out the trunk of the car. It's clear the manager hates me; it's in the distasteful way he watches me moan as I touch the car. It's not meant to be pornographic, I promise, but it's just so sexy. I'm imagining all the ways I could fuck in it when he steps closer. His stern lips are tilted down, and his small eyes narrow farther. His receding hairline isn't hidden by the comb-over, and the slight beer gut can't be disguised by his designer suit.

"We would prefer if you didn't sit in the car just yet. As I was saying, we have a waitlist on vehicles at the moment. Maybe we should sit and talk. I'm assuming you're using your daddy's or husband's money? We would need their permission before we continue."

My hand stills on the leather, and anger flows through me at his assumption and the cocky way he watches me.

I see my new guards frown. Dal even steps forward as if to deal with the threat, so I gracefully climb from the car. I've been looked down on a lot in my career, called names, and treated like trash, a whore, a child, and a fuck toy. I've taken it all in the name of my career, but it's clear this man doesn't know who I am, nor does he care. He saw what he wanted to when he looked at me and assumed that a man must be buying because obviously, women can't earn their own way, especially enough to buy his fancy cars, which he probably can't even afford himself.

The prick.

The old me would politely explain then feel angry and scandalized and rant when she got home, but not the new me. The new me wants to cause chaos and see this chauvinistic, fuckwit meat sack on his knees, begging for my forgiveness.

"You assume wrong," I reply slowly, straightening to my full height. There's a flare of annoyance in his eyes when I tower over him in my heels. Men tower over me all the time, using their height and weight to their advantage, so I use it now on a man who no doubt comments rude shit about women online. He seems like the keyboard warrior type.

He sniffs, eyeing me in disgust.

I slide my hand down the car, making sure to leave a handprint, and then I slip past him, purposely hitting him so he stumbles back a step, and then I turn and take in the brightly lit dealership. There are ten or more cars here. They are all perfectly placed on pedestals and polished to perfection. The glass lets out onto the main road filled with expensive sports cars of the rich and famous, since we are in the classy part of town. Champagne mixed with fancy food sits to one side, ready to be served, and there are screens everywhere, showing dramatic footage of the cars in action. There are men milling about in suits, but only one female, who sits at the desk, watching the man I'm talking to with anger in her eyes. Clearly, she doesn't like the sexist pig either.

This place is too flashy, too showy, and I want to fuck some shit up. I want to paint the walls, turn on some music, get drunk, and dance on the cars, but I'll settle for embarrassing this asshole.

"How much for all these cars?" I question, propping my hands on my hips. Others are staring now, mainly workers. Some are whispering, and one has his phone out, showing someone else a picture—no doubt it's of me.

"Look, miss, maybe you should leave."

"I said, how much?" I demand, and then I point to the woman working behind the desk. "You, I bet you know. I am sure you have to do the work around here anyway. How much for all of them?"

She hesitates, looking at her boss, so I step in front of him. "Don't look at this pompous idiot. Please, could you find out how much?"

She grins, hiding it as she ducks her head and types. I wink at my guards. Astro is grinning widely, and Dal is glaring at the man. Raffiel is near the door with his arms crossed, watching me with a blank expression, but I see his lips twitch, and I want to scream in victory. Cillian is covering his smile with a fake cough.

"Ninety-nine million," she calls. "Give or take a few numbers."

"Good, I'll take them all," I tell her with a grin and look back at the manager. "Make it happen."

"I don't think—" He sputters, and I narrow my eyes.

"No, clearly not," I finish for him, watching him turn even redder in embarrassment. I stroll over to the champagne and tip a glass back before shoving an hors d'oeuvres into my mouth and feigning gagging. "Fuck, this shit is nasty." I look at Astro, who's moved closer. "Have you ever tried overpriced fancy food?"

He shakes his head, and I shove it into his mouth.

He stills but chews slowly, wincing thoughtfully. "It's rank," he comments when he swallows.

Turning to the manager who is just gaping, I snap my fingers. "I don't have all day. I'm a very busy woman. Do I need to call your daddy or husband to get the work done?" His mouth snaps shut. "No? Then get me my fucking paperwork and cars."

"I—" He tugs on his suit as I take another sip of champagne and wait for him impatiently, but he just continues to stutter.

"I want all the commission to go to her." I point and then narrow my eyes. "Understood?"

He flounders and flushes as I turn away once more and slide into the nearest car, stroking the steering wheel as I grin at Dal. "How do I look?" I strike a pose.

"Magnificent," he murmurs, and I flush under the compliment, even as I wink at him in thanks.

"Want to fuck on the hood?" I tease, watching his eyes flare. Why is teasing them my new favorite pastime?

"Miss Harrow?" another sales associate says nervously. The young man treads closer, shooting Dal a worried glance. "Could I have an autograph?"

"Sure." I slide from the car and take the paper he hands over. "Who else wants an autograph while I wait?"

It seems like everyone does, and while fuck nut works on the cars with the female who I learned is named Amy, I sign autographs and smile for photos, laughing and joking with his staff while he glares at me. I purposely leave litter around the place and squish some fancy food under my heel, watching him almost have a heart attack.

"Clean that, won't you?" I tell him as I pass and sit at Amy's desk, crossing my legs on top of it. She simply smiles at me nervously, but it's clear she's loving this. I grin wider at that. She's cute, with short, bobbed blonde hair, sharp blue eyes, a stern face, and a beautiful smile. She's clearly young and trying to work her way up in this job, and she deserves the commission for putting up with the meat sack currently picking up my fallen food with a pinkie finger.

"Um, where would you like the cars delivered?" Amy asks.

"Those three to my house." I point them out. "The others will be placed at these locations as giveaways." I quickly scribble them down. "Here's my manager's number. Organize the deliveries with him."

"Of course." She quickly types and then glances up at me. "That was amazing, by the way."

"Why, thank you. What can I say? I can't stand stuffy assholes— oh, speak of the devil."

He stops at our side, his face flushed with anger. "And how will you be paying, Miss Harrow?" he asks, his arms crossed.

"I could do cash if you like, but here." I toss the black card at him. "And grab yourself a better fitting suit while you're at it. There's enough on there to cover it."

His nostrils flare, and I ignore him, leaning back to grin upside down at Raffiel.

He stares the man down, his eyes hard. He's a weapon, and right now, he looks like he's ready to strike. "Is there a problem here?" he demands, his voice low and deadly. "Do we need to step into your office and have a word?"

Aww, I might melt a little at him trying to protect me, but I pat his chest. "I've got this, hot stuff. Why don't you go lean against a car for me and take your shirt off for my new wallpaper?"

He raises his eyebrow at me. "Miss Harrow." He sounds both resigned and amused, and I love it.

"No? Fine, keep the shirt." I look at Astro. "Hottie, you'll do it for me, won't you?" I purr.

"Astro, if you take your shirt off, I will use it to strangle you," Raffiel snaps without looking away. Leaning down, he gets in my face. "Now behave, Miss Harrow, please." It's almost ground out.

"Why? Worried you'll snap?" I purr, scraping my nails down his chest.

He shudders, his nostrils flaring. It's heady to see his reaction to me. "If you do not behave, Miss Harrow, I am within my rights to . . . punish you."

"Well, don't you threaten me with a good time." I turn in my seat. Pinching the bridge of his nose, he breathes slowly as if looking for the patience to deal with me. "But I'm far too busy torturing tiny dick here, so I'll get back to you later and we can discuss the types of punishments you are into."

I hear him groan as I look away, and I don't hide my grin even as Amy ducks her head, giggling but blushing. "I will just need your signature. I can handle anything else with your manager, Miss Harrow," she says, pushing some papers across.

I quickly scribble my name and date it, and she scans through it with a nod before quickly and efficiently typing in something and then handing my card back.

"Everything else will be taken care of. Delivery will be as soon as possible, and as an apology for the horrible treatment you have received in this store, I have okayed some apology presents that will arrive with them."

"You did what?" the dick manager roars.

She ignores him, folding her hands demurely on her desk and smiling at me. "Directly from the head office." The manager blanches, and she shoots him a dirty look. "I'm sure your phone will be ringing soon, sir."

Laughing, I get to my feet. "I like you. Make sure you get that commission, Amy, or call me and I will." I put my card away, and with a wave at the other associates, I start heading to the door while the manager scrambles after me like a bad smell.

I stop before him, straightening his crooked tie for him. "Maybe next time, you shouldn't assume anything. You clearly aren't good at it. Oh, and if you want, you can call me Daddy now since it was my money." I pat his ruddy cheek, slip on my shades, and head back outside, smiling and waving at the cameras.

I pose and wave and sign the autograph pages that are thrust at me. My new guards converge around me, keeping the crowd back as I slowly make my way to the car, trying to sign as many as I can.

When I reach the car, though, I hear a disappointed voice and quickly turn, scanning the crowd of men and women to see a small, teenage girl huddled at the back, trying to get through to me. One of my first ever albums is clutched in her grip, and her hopeful expression drops.

Ignoring Raffiel, I step around the open door and toward the crowd, fighting my way through.

"Move!" Raffiel barks, and I hear him pushing his way through behind me. When I glance back, I see he's created a barrier with the others between them and me so I can stand alone with the girl.

"Hi," I say. "Did you want that signed? I'm sorry I didn't see you at the back."

Her mouth opens and closes as she stares at me, clutching the CD so hard. I gently pry it from her grip. "What's your name?" I ask softly.

"I—" She clears her throat nervously as cameras flash, so I move closer to block them. "Dily, my name is Dily."

I scribble her name and a message with my signature and notice her necklace. It's a microphone. "Are you a singer?"

"One day, I hope." She finally seems to come to and smiles at me. It's so bright and beautiful, I can't help but return it. There is power in that smile, magnetism, and I have no doubt she will get everything she wants. "I hope to be as good as you. You are my inspiration, my role model."

"I haven't been a very good one recently," I admit quietly.

She shakes her head. "I love you more now. You looked so sad before, not like when you first started. You connected with the music, you know? It was in everything you did. I think you just got a little lost along the way."

"You are completely right," I reply, eyeing this girl who sees into my heart when even my own friends and fiancé couldn't. "But I think I found my way back."

"Good." She grins, looking at the CD. "Thank you so much. I will treasure this forever."

I pluck a card from my bag. "Here. When you're ready to be a singer, as long as you can get used to this madness"—I gesture around us—"call me. I'll help in any way I can."

Her mouth drops open again, and she flings herself at me, laughing. I squeeze her back, ignoring the shouts and questions. She pulls away, embarrassed, and I see tears in her eyes. "I'm glad you're back and that you're happy again."

"I'm getting there," I tell her honestly as I slide my glasses back up. "Keep working at it, and I'll see you when you're ready," I promise as Raffiel approaches me.

"Time to go. The crowd is getting restless." Nodding, I let him escort me through the surging people. At the car, I wave at Dily. "Don't forget to rock it, kid!" I yell as I duck inside and sit in the back seat, smiling at her through the window. She stares down at the card and CD as if I gave her a lifeline. I know that feeling. I've been there before, and I had my own helping hand. It makes me feel like I'm finally doing something right and making a difference in the music world. It needs people like her who are honest, true, and strong.

Dal and Cillian sit before me, and Raffiel and Astro take the front. "What?" I ask as they all look at me.

"You are not what I expected," Dal comments carefully.

"No? What were you expecting?" I scoff, stiffening in my seat. I expect an insult and for them to be like everyone else, but when he smiles, it's a slow, bright smile that steals the air from my lungs. It transforms his entire face until I'm entranced, unable to breathe in the face of such beauty.

"Trouble."

It breaks the spell, and a rare but real laugh slips free. "Oh, I'm definitely that. You have no idea." I glance back out of the window to see the manager at the door to the dealership, watching us go, and I laugh harder. "None at all."

SEVEN

I can't help but watch Reign. She is not what I was expecting at all. Not only did she go out of her way to sign a CD for that teenager, but she also talked to her. I saw the hero worship and the hope in that girl's eyes. She gave her a dream, a chance, and she doesn't even seem to notice it. More than that, though, the way she handled that stuck-up, rich prick in the dealership made my cock hard. I wanted to bend her over one of those cars and show her she might not need a daddy to buy shit for her, but I'd make her scream it as I fucked her.

The news portrays her as this untouchable, perfect rock princess or the heathen whore they all hate. There is no in-between, but she's human. That's all. She's bratty, stubborn, hilarious, beautiful, rich, and talented, and she seems to be tired of being treated like shit. I can't say I blame her. I have my own suspicions about why she left the spotlight, but that's her story and hers alone. We are here to keep her safe, which means being privy to her private business. We are new to this as well, but I'm finding I like seeing this other side of her.

I like seeing the flawed creature and the life she has built, and I want to know more. I want to know what put that sharp look in her eyes and what made her lock down her house. I want to know it all, but more than that, I want to hurt everyone for upsetting such an angel.

That's what she is.

She dresses and acts like a devil, but inside, she's our angel.

Music fills her soul, and she dances through her life, leaving her mark behind. I know she's left her mark on me.

My ma always told me that there are some people who are so filled with pure energy and life that it pulls you in and sucks you up. Being near them is like being in the presence of a god. I now understand what she meant. Reign Harrow is pure life, raw and unfiltered. She is as close to a god as people can get, and not just a rock one, as they call her. I've spent one day in her presence and I'm already a changed man. I can't imagine a day where I'm not standing at her back, watching her take over the world and correct every person who gets in her way.

Once we're back at her house, she waits for me to get out first. I scan our surroundings, and only then do I help her out. She rolls her eyes but heads toward the house. Raffiel snarls and hurries to be the first one inside, only for us all to slide to a stop in the entryway.

We all just stare.

Covering every inch of her entryway and far as we can see are roses in every color and size. Huge boxes and bouquets are placed everywhere with a tiny path through the middle.

"What the fuck?" she whispers.

"I want to know how this all got in here," Raff barks angrily, furious at security being breached so easily. He storms away to interrogate the gate staff while I step inside and grab a card I find. I want to be nosy, but I hand it over.

Eyes narrowed, she rips it open and snorts before tossing it at me. I can't resist. I tell myself it's so I can learn of any threats and report back, but it's pure curiosity.

I love you. I miss you. Come home to me.
—Tucker

Her ex? I look around. This is a bold move, apart from the fact that she seems angry rather than impressed.

Raffiel storms back in. "The gate staff apparently didn't know they weren't allowed to let deliveries in," he snaps. "Miss Harrow, I apologize for this oversight."

She shrugs, looks around, and pulls her phone out. We watch her delete all her messages and peer around again. "What a waste." She sighs. "Get rid of them." I start to move to do just that when an evil grin curls her lips. "Actually, send them to every hospital in the area. Someone should get some use out of them."

I can't help but grin, and she glances back at us.

"And I agree with the new security measures. Nothing from him is allowed to be let in again. Understood?"

"Of course, Miss Harrow," Raffiel responds, something unknown in his eyes.

She looks around again and shakes her head. "Idiot. If you need me, I'll be in the studio."

We watch her go, and then Astro lets out a whistle. "Oh, he really fucked up. How much do you reckon this cost?"

"Too much," I say. "Plus, her favorite flowers are clearly peonies." They all turn to gape at me, and I roll my eyes. "They are in her studio and her bedroom, and she has one tattooed on her skin, idiots."

"Well shit," Dal mutters, grinning at me. "I suppose we better get to work."

EIGHT

I lose myself in the music. My notebooks are spread around me, my guitar sits to the side, and the piano is open. I drum my fingers over the keys, trying to work through the problem in the melody. I know what I want to sing, but I can't seem to figure out the arrangement, and I don't want to show it to Jack until I'm sure.

Sighing, I scribble through the line and stretch my arms above my head. My back aches and my eyes are blurry, which tells me it's been hours. I have a tendency to lose myself in my work, sometimes for days at a time, barely eating or sleeping. It's a bad habit, but if I stop, it breaks my creativity and I struggle to get back into it.

Humming the melody I want, I pick up the guitar and rest it on my thighs, my comfy shorts riding up as I bend one leg under me where I'm perched on the stool. I close my eyes as I strum the chords, trying to fix the composition, and words flow as I play. Sometimes, just throwing myself into it is how I get the best songs. There is no thinking or second-guessing this way, and I can always make tweaks after.

"I guess I fell in love with a lie, nothing was true. Just some pretty lies spread from the lips I craved more than air in my lungs . . ." I break off and try again.

"Such a pretty liar, love was just another game to you. I saw the future, immortality held in your arms only to be buried away in your past."

Humming the next few notes, I strum more chords before turning to the notebook and scribbling down some rough lyrics with the melody.

I choke on your lies,
tears like fire tearing me apart,
devouring me with my mistakes.
With my regrets.
Wrap me in your arms, make it okay.

It's then I sense eyes on me. I don't know how long they have been here, but someone is watching me. Lifting my head, I spot Dal. He's leaning against the doorway. His suit jacket and shirt are gone, leaving a rumpled tank covering his torso, and his hair is slightly out of place. It must be late.

"Sorry, I didn't mean to disturb you," he says, his voice slightly rough as if from misuse. I'm already sure he doesn't speak a lot unless he feels the need to, and when he does, it's succinct and well thought out.

"No, it's okay. I need a break anyway." I carefully place the worn guitar away. It's the one I've had since I first started. I saved up to buy it from a secondhand store when I should have been buying food. I went hungry for a week, but it was so worth it. This guitar has carried me throughout the years and become my safety net. It's what I create every song on and always will. It's one of the only possessions I have from my past. My name and his are scratched into it. I run my fingers over the etchings we did under a tree, the sun shining down on us.

"You'll make it big, Rey. If anybody can, it's you," he promised solemnly.

My fingers catch on the uneven words—Rey and Kai.

"Hmm, sorry?" I ask, my head jerking up. He was speaking while I was lost in my past.

He watches me carefully, glancing from the guitar to me, and seems to hesitate. Smiling, I lift my knees and sit cross-legged, but instead of asking the questions in his eyes, he simply comments, "Your phone rang a million times."

"Ignore it," I tell him. "You want to ask me something, so ask." I shrug, uncaring about the outside world but curious about what he'll ask.

He hesitates a little more, looking over his shoulder before observing me and seeming to come to some sort of conclusion. "Where did you go for all those months?"

I want to offer something noncommittal, like exploring or traveling, but I know that would disappoint him. I don't know why I care about what he thinks of me, but I realize I do. Something about him implores me to give him the truth, even just a sliver. He could report it back to my manager or sell it to the tabloids, but I have to give him something. "Someplace no one would ever find me," I say, glancing back at the guitar before raising my eyes and meeting his cautious gaze once more. "I needed to find my peace again . . . to find myself again." He blinks, and I laugh self-consciously, rubbing my tired eyes. "I suppose that doesn't make much sense."

"It makes perfect sense," he says, and I look up to smile at him. He smiles back. "There is food upstairs. You should eat before you get back into it. I liked the last song by the way. It was . . . raw." He turns, and that's when I see the scar from a bullet on his shoulder and his words come back to me.

It makes perfect sense.

Maybe I'm not the only one who ran away. Maybe I'm not the only one struggling with my past.

Now, I'm even more curious than I was before about the four men who barged into my life.

Who are they really?

More importantly, can I trust them?

I spend a few more hours in the studio, pouring over my lyrics until my brain can't take anymore, and then I shut down the equipment, but I can't bring myself to go upstairs. Instead, I curl up on the sofa and trace the scratched leather. So many memories are coming back, happy ones of rehearsing and writing in here with Tucker.

He infected every inch of my life, and every room of my house has memories of him, both good and bad. There was the time when I came back and he was drunk in the studio. He ended up throwing a glass bottle near my head. There is still a dent in the soundproofing to remember it by. There was also the time we made love on this sofa after writing a best-selling love song for him.

Always for him.

Sighing, I close my eyes and stretch out my legs, trying to forget the memories. It was easier when I was just mad at him, and I am, but part of my soul still misses the connection we had. I thought we were forever, which was probably naïve of me, but when that was shattered, it was easier to be in a place without memories of him. I don't want him back. I don't even want what we had back. I'm still mad and hurt over it, but it doesn't mean part of me can't still grieve.

I've had enough grief in my life, though, so I know how to handle it. My eyes open and lock on the guitar, pain clutching at my throat until I choke on it.

Lyrics form in my head, lyrics more familiar than my own voice. They are bitter and filled with so much pain, I can't speak them out loud. They float around my head, filled with childish love and hope which is now nothing but dust.

Run, little one, the lost boys are coming.

No. I cover my face, refusing to sing those out loud ever again. I can't. It hurts too much, yet as if by conjured by the words, his face floats in front of mine, and before I do something stupid like spiral like I used to, numbing myself with drugs and alcohol and earning the nick-names they call me, I close the studio and head upstairs, trying to outrun my past like I have been since the day the coffin was lowered into the ground.

NINE

I'm trying to outrun my thoughts so fast. I skid to a stop in the kitchen at the sight of all four of my new security men sitting there, food spread between them as they eat. They all glance up. Astro smiles widely, Dal watches me with an odd expression, and Raffiel nods while Cillian shoves more bread into his mouth. "We cooked. Hope you don't mind."

I raise my eyebrows, hesitating. At least I don't see any flowers around anymore.

"You told us to make ourselves at home," Raffiel comments carefully. "If you would prefer us to eat elsewhere, we can also do that."

I've been quiet too long. They sit straighter, and I pry my lips open, grateful for the distraction from my own darkness. "No, it's fine. The kitchen should be used. Sorry, it's just been a long night and a long time since . . . Actually, I've never had this." I wave around to encompass them all.

They don't comment on that, thank fuck, and my cheeks flame at my admission. I sound lame. I have friends, after all, but they aren't the type to sit around and relax together with a meal. They are the party, where are the cameras type, where everything has a purpose or is a PR move. This is normal and homey, and I feel like I'm an intruder even in my own home. I start to slip back into the darkness when Dal's voice comes, calling to me like a lifeline.

"Join us."

If it had been from any of the others, I would think it was out of pity, but from him, it feels like a genuine invitation. He wouldn't ask if he didn't want me here. It's clear he has shocked the others because they shoot him a look but nod, and Astro kicks out a chair.

"Sit down, beautiful. Dal is an incredible cook. You have to try this."

I hesitate for a moment before sitting down, pulling my feet under me like I always do when I'm nervous. I use the excuse that I don't want to go to bed and lie in the dark, remembering.

Astro and Cillian work together to make me a plate as Raffiel watches me carefully, his eyes narrowed.

"What?" I ask.

"You need to sleep more," he comments.

"Jeez, is that a nice way of saying I look like shit?" I scoff, but it makes me smile.

"No, you always look incredible." He seems to realize he said that out loud and grits his teeth as he clenches his fork. "But you look tired. Sleep is important to function at full capacity."

"Or you will be slow and sloppy. Sleep, eat, drink properly, and take care of your body and it will take care of you," the others repeat in unison like they have heard that speech a million times. Raffiel huffs, looking down at his food, and it's just too cute not to poke.

"Adorable, do you have that on a sweatshirt? Or should I feel honored that I was included in the club?"

"Totally honored," Astro mutters. "One of us."

Cillian bangs his spoon and fork on the table in time with their chanting. "One of us. One of us." Raffiel just sighs as Dal carries on eating like their antics are typical.

Grinning, I grab a forkful of the chicken, and after biting into it, I moan, my eyes shutting in bliss. When they snap open, all four men are watching me intently. Covering my mouth, I mumble, "This is fucking amazing."

Astro grins. "Told you."

"Eat it all," Raffiel orders.

I roll my eyes and dig in since it's so good. Usually, I try to cook for myself, but it never goes well so I order from restaurants. I can't remember the last time I had a home-cooked meal this good. Before I know it, my plate is empty and a second one appears. I pick at it as I eye them.

"So how did you four meet?" I ask.

It's Cillian who answers. "We all served together, and when we decided to get out, we just kind of stuck together. We were used to working as a team and functioning as one, so it made sense."

"Exactly, then Raff had the great idea to use our skills to make money. We couldn't exactly become businessmen or some shit." Astro smirks.

"Utilizing the skills we had seemed smart, and it turned out there was a market for them," Raff responds.

"Bodyguards, security . . ." I nod. "Smart plays on what you know, and not many of them are actually skilled at all."

"We are the best, baby." Astro winks.

"Lucky me," I deadpan, making Dal smirk as he eats.

"What about you?" Dal asks when I push my plate away and lay my head on my knees, watching them. It's almost . . . nice. There are no judgments or expectations, just four friends eating and me.

It's clear how close they are. They anticipate each other's needs and work through them. Astro passes a drink to Raff when he's done, and Dal passes the sauce before Cillian can even ask. These are four men who have been together for a really long time and it shows. I've never had that, and for a moment, I wish I had that kind of connection, one of friendship and love, where I can depend on the other person wholeheartedly.

"What? Sorry," I say when I realize they are all watching me with confused expressions. Who knows how long I was lost in my own thoughts? It's a bad habit, but it served me well as a kid. Before I went to sleep, I would create elaborate worlds and stories to escape to, and more often than not, it spurred songs afterwards, but it was my escape, my happy place, where I felt safe, and I often find myself daydreaming.

I guess that's the downside of being an artist. We never truly shut off.

"What about your friends?" Dal asks, and I stiffen.

"I don't really have any." Their eyebrows rise, and I laugh bitterly. "Not the way you guys do. My friends, or my old friends, always wanted something. It wasn't a friendship just because they enjoyed my company. It was a business deal. They wanted to be friends so they could get things out of it—money, publicity, deals, men, climb higher in the industry, you name it. It took me a long time to realize that, so I guess I don't have any friends, not really."

"I'm sorry," he says sadly, or at least it looks like he's trying to change his expression into one of sadness. Dal's facial expressions are always a little off, as if he copied them from someone else.

"It's a cutthroat industry. You get two types of people—those who want to use you or those being used," I reply truthfully, my bitterness winding through my tone, but I can't stop it. It took me far too long to realize that and it left its mark.

"Which are you?" Raffiel asks, watching me carefully.

"Well, I refuse to ever be used ever again so . . ." I shrug.

"Maybe there should be a third category," Astro suggests softly. "Those who want to be neither, just like you."

"Maybe, but that isn't the way the world works, is it?"

"We've seen some of this life before, not necessarily the music industry but the rich and famous. You're right, everyone is out for themselves. It breeds a lot of selfish people, and even those who seem nice and wholesome on the surface are usually playing that angle," Cillian responds. "But I don't think you are. Astro is right. You are in your own category, at least to us."

"Thanks." I smile, suddenly feeling very exposed and uncomfortable so I stand. "I'll clean up. You guys can get back to work or relaxing or whatever." Luckily, they don't call me out on my lame excuse.

"We need to fit the cameras. She's right, back to it," Raff orders, and as I'm putting dishes in the sink, I feel him stop near me. I don't meet his eyes, too afraid of what I'll see there.

"Shame on them for using you, not the other way around, Reign. They are immoral and not worth your pain. We promise not to let anyone do that to you again. You're not alone now." He wanders away, leaving me staring after him.

He's wrong though. I am alone, and eventually, they will leave like everyone else . . . or use me to get a better job. They are already getting paid to be around me, but at least that's out in the open and not a secret. They seem like nice guys, but I've been fooled before.

I won't make that mistake again.

After washing up, I head upstairs to relax, falling into bed and staring at the ceiling. Silence fills this house now, and a clawing sense of emptiness and loneliness surrounds me. When I hear Astro's bright, booming laughter, my lips curve up of their own accord before I can stop them. I guess I'm not totally alone, and as I cuddle into my bed and listen to them chatter away, I don't feel as lonely.

Maybe this won't be so bad after all.

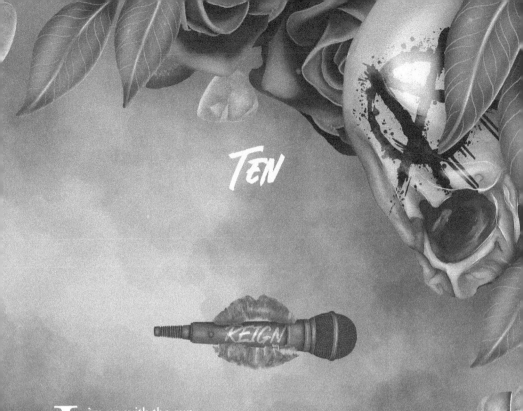

Ten

I'm up with the sun.

I never used to be. I used to sleep most of the day, either sleeping off a hangover, a night of bad decisions, or drugs. Now, the sun hits my face and I do a quick round of yoga and meditation before jumping into the shower and getting ready for the day. I find I like this new routine. I discovered it during my time away, wanting to better myself and change. Although it was hard to get up so early at first when I wasn't used to it, it made me more productive, and I feel like I can truly make the most of my time rather than waste it. Don't get me wrong, I love sleep, but there is always time for naps later.

I plan on heading to the studio today, so as I stare into my giant walk-in closet, I debate what to wear. Usually, I go with comfy clothes, but I have the insane urge to dress up again to see the guys' reactions, living for the desire in their eyes. It boosts my confidence and I'm weak, so instead of my usual comfy attire, I pick out some high-waisted, black cargo type jeans that flare toward the feet and a black crop shirt with a square neckline, showcasing my ample cleavage but covering my shoulders and arms. It shows off my underboob tattoos and stomach, and I make sure to hoist my jeans higher to cover the writing I never show anyone. That tattoo is just for me, no one else. I add some high-heeled boots and mismatched gold jewelry with a million rings. Curling my hair, I pin some of it back before putting on my makeup—my signature red lip and pink and purple winged smoked liner. Checking myself out in the mirror, I realize I look really good, and I feel good too.

I'm almost excited as I head downstairs, anticipation filling me at seeing their reactions. They don't disappoint as I head into the kitchen to find Astro, half asleep, sipping coffee and Raffiel checking over what seems to be camera angles. Both snap their heads up when I enter, their mouths open to wish me a good morning, but neither speaks as they stare at me.

Astro seems to take a drink out of habit.

"Well, do I look okay?" I smirk when no one responds.

He chokes on his coffee, and I watch as he coughs and splutters until Raff smacks him on the back, and Astro gives him a thumbs-up.

"You look . . . better than okay," he finally gets out, his voice hoarse.

"Are you sure?" I bat my eyelashes at him.

Raff smirks at me. "Behave. Don't be mean to him."

"Me? I'm always nice." I pout and purposely bend over the table and take his mug, sipping the coffee as he watches me. He glances at my breasts. Victory. Returning the coffee, I lick my lips as I lean back. "Mmm, good coffee."

"Is it?" Picking up the mug, he places his lips purposely where mine were, keeping his eyes on me the entire time, and sips it. "You're right, very sweet."

Astro groans. "Jesus, you two are going to kill me. I can't protect shit with a hard-on."

It breaks our stare off, and I move to the cupboard and pick out a to-go cup and pour myself coffee. "Time to go anyway." I glance back and tell them the truth. "I'll be at the studio all day. It can be long and boring for anyone else, so you don't all have to come. You can drop me off."

"Where you go, we go, and I'm betting it won't be boring." Raff stands, buttoning his suit jacket. "Let me get the others." He runs his eyes down me. "And warn them to hide their dicks."

"Or maybe pluck out their eyes." Astro groans, pouting at me. "My throat hurts now."

"Poor baby, want me to kiss it better?" I taunt.

"Would you?" He smirks, leaning back in his chair, all charming smiles and big, round eyes. I see a dare in his gaze, like he thinks I'll back down.

He should know one thing about me by now—I never back down.

Placing my coffee down, I saunter over to him. He watches me come, parting his legs to give me room. He pats his thighs, and a pulse of desire goes through me, but I ignore it. It's fun to mess with them.

Laying my hands on his thighs, I dig my nails in as I lean closer, almost touching my lips to his. His breathing picks up, and his eyes blow wide with lust. At the last minute, I lower my head and tug his shirt down, pressing a red-lipped kiss on his throat.

There's a groan, and when I lean back, Astro watches me lustfully, clenching his hands, and on his throat, hidden partially by his shirt, is a bright red lipstick mark.

"Miss Harrow," Raffiel chastises from the doorway as I move away from a dazed Astro.

"I was kissing his throat better," I tease as I pick up my coffee.

Cillian's hand shoots up. "Uh, I have something you can kiss better!"

We manage the drive with no incidents, although Astro looks like he's ready to jump me so Dal sits between us, watching him carefully. I blow him kisses just to wind him up further. Once we're at the studio, they exit first before helping me out. There are only a few cameras here today, hoping to catch someone, so I wave but walk straight to the door. The guys spread out around me to keep the paparazzi back, and when we get inside, I relax. Ignoring the looks and whispers from others, I head straight to the elevator and hit number fifteen—my lucky number. Once there, I open the huge studio we are using for the time being and kick off my shoes.

Jack is already here, playing with some background music, so I sneak up and cover his eyes. He startles and lets out a little scream before grunting. "Goddamn it, Rey," he grumbles as I release him, and he spins toward me, grinning. "How are you always so silent? I told you that I'll tie a bell around you."

"Kinky." I wink, and then I lean over and hit play. "What's this?"

The beats play again, a mix of drums and cymbals, and I listen to them twice, nodding my head as I do and tapping out the beat. "It's good. That would be good for the intro of track two."

"That's what I thought!" He perks up and spins, hitting something else, and more music plays, a softer melody. "And I thought this would work for track eight. We can add in vocals and maybe even some sirens."

I listen to his vision and sit in the chair next to him, tapping out the beat and imagining what he's saying. When he starts to put the track together, I murmur out some lyrics and see how they fit, then rearrange them to the beat.

Before I know it, an hour has passed and we have most of a song put together, and Jack finally comes out of his trance. He's like me when he has music on his mind. He can't stop until it's done, until it's perfect. It's why we get along so well, not to mention he often flows with my vision and rather than just agreeing. He challenges me to be better.

"Who are the hunks?" Jack asks, looking at the guys spread around the sofas, watching as we work. I offered for them to go home, but they seemed genuinely interested in watching us in the studio. I enjoy it here. It's the best part of creating music, but my ex or my friends would often get bored and end up leaving when they realized they couldn't film it or join in.

"My new security team." I nod at them. "The stern-looking one is Raffiel, the smiling goofball is Astro, the hot redhead is Cillian, and the model one is Dal."

"Nice to meet you," Jack says. "I'm Jack Standish. I've been working with Rey for years on her music."

"You're her producer?" Astro asks conversationally.

"Sometimes, and sometimes I'm just her bitch," he jokes, making me grin as I put my keys, phone, and coffee down before I stand to stretch. All their eyes go to me, tracking my movements, and Jack huffs.

"Oh, this should be fun." I smack him on my way by.

"Let's play it and test," I offer as I step into the booth. It doesn't take me long to get set up. We can add instrumentals later. I just want to test the rightness of the lyrics with the melody, so I pop on the headphones, make sure they are adjusted properly, and tug the mic down.

Closing my eyes, I focus on the steady beat of my heart. The music begins, and I shift focus to the notes, working my voice to fit and amplify them, creating more than just a match but a fucking symphony.

I lose myself in the one place where I am free—music.

ELEVEN

Goosebumps rise on my arms as I lean forward. Reign's eyes are shut, and her body sways with the music. Even with the glass separating us, I can sense the raw emotions and talent in her voice as she moves easily from note to note, and each lyric hammers home until I'm barely breathing.

We could be attacked right now and I would gladly die, trapped by her song.

She's not even done yet. When she tells Jack to replay the music, she changes it slightly, playing with how it sounds. She makes it seem effortless, but it leaves us all gobsmacked. I glance at the others to see that they feel the same, all their eyes locked on her, unable to speak or move.

We are transported away with her song, until my eyes actually sting with tears and my heart aches with her. It's impossible, but it's her. I've never heard of anyone who was capable of what she's doing. It's like she reaches right into your mind, pulls out every happy and sad memory, and forces you to relive them, all while she's a melody for it. She makes you feel and see what she wants until the music stops and frees you.

No wonder she's a rock star. No wonder she rose so quickly to fame. I've heard a song or two of hers before, and they are really good, some of my favorites, but seeing it in person is totally different. There's just something so intimate about watching her face as she sings from the heart, and that's exactly what she does.

She sings from the very depths of her heart. This isn't club music; this is deeply emotional. It's raw, it's real, and I can't stop myself from standing and drifting closer. When it finishes again, Jack grins at me knowingly.

"She's amazing, isn't she?"

"She's . . ." I don't even have words. I glance back to see her mouthing something to herself, frowning as she works through it.

"I know. It's why she's so in demand. It's why she's the best. It's not just because of her talent, but her ability to make you feel it with her. She creates more than music. It's an experience, a story, and she is the author. It's why I work with her. I've never met anyone else in all of my years in this industry who has the same capability, nor are they so humble and kind."

"How is she not everywhere?" I ask, confused.

"To an extent, she is, but people used to assume that her talent, her songs, were partly associated with her ex, that he or someone else wrote them, and he never corrected it, no matter what they said about her. She was too kind to say anything, even though she gives everything to her music. Not to mention a lot of people look down on rock and say it's just angry music, but when you listen to the lyrics? It's all her. It's the truth, her soul, her story, her passion. It's the world, and now that she's back and the deadweight is gone from her life, hopefully the world will see that. She is the woman they looked down on, the woman they were jealous of, and she is nothing but pure talent and heart. She deserves it. She's worked damn hard to get here and had to put up with a lot of shit from both the press and her own people."

"What do you mean?" Raffiel asks.

Jack frowns, looks at her, and then sighs. "The road to musical fame is not easy, nor is any road to fame, I presume, but even more so for women. There are men in this industry who take advantage of women, especially those trying to break out. Every singer I've ever worked with has their own story, and I have no doubt Reign does, but she will never tell. She will never give them the fame and press they so desperately want from her."

I read between the lines and almost growl at the implication. Someone took advantage of her. I know it happens, and I've seen a lot of shit in my life so I know the evil people in this world are capable of, but Reign was young when she broke into the spotlight. Why did I think that would protect her when it probably put her in more danger?

I want to go in there and demand names so I can hunt the fuckers down and show them they aren't untouchable, but it's her past, it's her truth, and I won't steal that from her. If she wants to tell us, then we are here and we'll listen. It's clear she hasn't even confided in Jack, and unlike those in her past who only took and demanded, we won't do that. We are here to help and make her life easier, and after meeting Reign, I want to.

Yes, she's beautiful, and I want her badly, but it's more than that. I saw an aching loneliness in her eyes last night, the same kind I carried until I met my brothers. I saw the same wandering soul, and it made me want to wrap her up and keep her safe.

No, this is more than desire.

This is something completely different that I can't even admit to myself or it will mean that I'll have to leave my job—my honor is all I have, after all—and I am reluctant to leave Reign when it's clear she needs us. She needs people to protect her, to stop the world from hurting her again.

She might not say it out loud, but it's in her song, in her heart.

She has been hurt badly over and over again, and it's obvious how close she is to giving up on the world.

I won't let her. Nobody with her soul deserves to give up.

The music turns on again and her voice fills the air once more, so I pay attention to the lyrics this time.

> *People hurt those they love the most*
> *Broken promises, scattered across wealth*
> *Heartache, broken heels, and mascara drips*
> *Lines in the bathroom, trying to forget you*

. . .

I ache with her. I seal them to my soul, and when she comes out of the booth, she blinks when she finds me standing so close to the door. I want to tell her everything, so I step closer.

"I see you," is all I tell her.

And I do.

I see Reign.

I see her struggling.

She isn't alone.

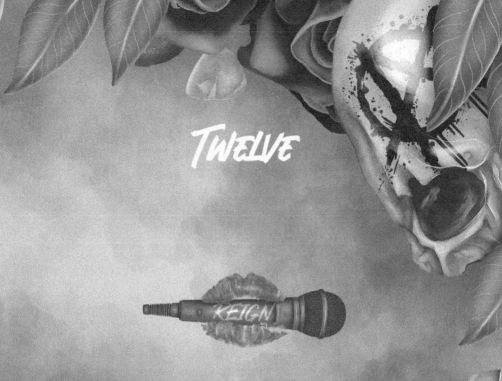

TWELVE

The rest of the day is a blur of new music and locking down melodies and compositions. At some point, Raff brings us all food, and Jack instantly gets along with them, talking to them like they are old friends. I'm quiet, my eyes on Dal as I think about what he said.

I see you.

What did he mean? I know deep down, and that scares me, so on the ride home, I'm silent, staring out of the window. I feel Cillian's eyes on me where he sits on the opposite seat, but I don't make conversation, worried I gave too much of myself away today. If Dal read me that easily, did the others? Do I care?

I don't know.

My phone rings, and I answer without looking, glad for any excuse for a distraction. "The team is here, Miss Harrow," the gate guard says. "Should I let them in?"

"Team?" I frown.

"Um, makeup, hair, clothes . . . One second, Miss Harrow." I hear him talking to someone while I frown. "For the premiere? Uh, of the movie you did the songs for? The action one?" he continues when I'm quiet.

Shit.

Kill List.

Fuck, fuck, fuck. I forgot I confirmed that I would attend when I came back—mainly because it was fun to work on and I get along well with the director. Fuck a duck, I'm not in the mood for all the questions and cameras, but it seems I need to be. Plastering on an old, fake smile, I reply, "Of course, let them in. We will be home soon to get ready."

"Ready for what?" Cillian asks.

Putting down the phone, I meet their eyes. "Have you ever been to a movie premiere?"

Once we arrive, I'm rushed upstairs to my formal dressing room. Luckily, the team has been here before and has everything set up. I take a quick shower and shave before sitting in the chair to let them work their magic. Hair and makeup are done at the same time, so I simply sit like a doll being pampered.

Cillian brings me herbal tea, and I thank him as I sip it and tell him to inform the others that they need suits. I give them a number for someone who I know can help if they need it, and then I'm forced to concentrate. I'm slathered, plucked, poked, and primped before being told to move over to the dressing area. My shoes are put on first, seven-inch sparkling stilettos, showing off my brand-new chrome toenails.

The dress bag is hung before me, and I can't wait to see it. My hair has been slicked back with curls on the edges, my ears are decorated with several earrings, and my fingers and neck are adorned with numerous pieces of glittery jewelry, which makes me think the dress will be similar.

Usually, I work with the designer I pick to come up with a custom gown, but I've worked with this one enough to trust the options he sent. He gets noticed when I wear his designs, and I get to wear a beautiful gown. He's a newish designer, and when I first started, he was a nobody sewing from his house, but I love his style. Everyone kept pushing big names on me, but I chose him. Every single time, I work with him nearly exclusively. He gets my style, and our partnership works well. He became a big name from dressing me, and I still work with someone who believes in their craft and passion.

When they unzip the bag, I almost cry. Gone are the puffy, beautiful dresses from before, and in their place is a sleek, sexy number. It seems Orita, my designer, has picked up on the change and is very happy. After all, he always wanted to push the boundaries, but my manager rejected it.

Not anymore.

The dress looks like a diamond, all long, sleek lines, and it glitters with a disco ball effect. It takes two people to help me into it. The cupped bodice enhances my breasts and leaves my shoulders bare, where they sparkle from the cream that was smoothed on me. It tightens at my stomach, showing my curves, and then flows down past my feet. When I drag my hand down the dress, it feels like silk covered in thousands of diamonds. I glance up, and when I look in the mirror for the first time, I feel like me—the me on the inside that I see, not the perfect girl they always promoted.

My tattoos are on display, my eyes are smoky and sexy, and my body is worshiped by the dress, encased not covered.

I look beautiful, but it's more than that. I look confident and put together, something I'm going to need tonight. This will be the first time I've attended an event since I got back, red carpet and all, not to mention going alone. Oh, don't get me wrong, I attended some alone in the past, mainly because Tucker was busy, but I was never single and now I am. All eyes will be on me, looking for my reaction. The questions will be sharp and shouted, wanting to rip me apart, but I won't let them.

As I head downstairs, holding up the gown, I realize that I won't be alone and the four men standing in matching black suits at the bottom will never let anything get to me. I never thought much about a security team, but I already feel better, not to mention they are some serious eye candy. Their suits might be meant to make them blend in, but the way they fill them out is anything but, not to mention they look like models themselves. People won't know if they are actors, stars, or security, and I like that.

The only thing that stands out on their suits is a silver pin they wear as if to match me.

At the base of the stairs, Raff steps forward, offering me his arm. His eyes run down me hungrily, and when he meets my gaze, he smiles. "You are breathtaking. They won't know what hit them. You'll be the star."

"I hope not." I laugh, and he grins.

"Sorry, there's no way you're blending in, beauty," he purrs as he helps me out the door, only to frown. "Wait here."

I stop, wondering what he's doing. He drives the car closer, the gravel crunching under the tires—ah, the gravel.

"It's fine!" I call, about to step forward when he points at me as he gets out.

"Wait, Miss Harrow," he barks.

He's gone for a moment before he turns with the plain board I used when painting the pool house. He lays it in a path to the open door and then comes back for me, taking my hand and walking me to the car.

My team swoons. "What a man!"

I silently agree.

What a man. My ex wouldn't even open the door for me, worried about getting out first and greeting the paps, and here is this man, who is only employed to protect me, who's so worried about me falling or tugging my dress on the gravel that he goes out of his way to help me. If I asked, I bet he would have carried me.

They all would.

Once inside the car, I meet Dal's and Astro's eyes. They are sitting in the back with me, while Cil and Raff sit in the front. "You look great," I tell them.

"Nope, we are just here to make sure you shine." Astro winks. "And baby, you shine so fucking brightly, no one will be able to look away."

I blush under the heavy makeup, and the appreciative glances Dal shoots my way make me sit up taller.

The drive to the premier isn't long, even with traffic, but when we pull up, I can see the red-carpet walk has already started. The bright lights of the cinema proudly display *Kill List* posters everywhere. The stars of the movie pose for pictures before the cinema, talking to reporters and mingling with each other. We have to wait as cars move slowly to let out more actors, directors, and staff, and I use the time to collect myself. It's almost quiet in the car, but as we stop and the door opens, the screams, questions, music, and people interrupt that, rocking me back to my past.

I glance up, and Dal leans forward. "Do not let them see you hesitate. You are better than that. Show them."

Nodding, I suck in a calming breath. They slide out, and Dal offers his hand to me. Cameras turn, and questions on who it could be are shouted.

Laying my hand gently in Dal's, I let him help me out. I want to cover my eyes as numerous flashes blind me, but I smile with practiced charm and step onto the carpet. Dal releases me, and my guards spread out as I pose and wave and slowly begin to move down the carpet, stopping every now and again to pose.

"Here, here, look here!" Some even snap or yell, making me feel like a dog, but I do as I'm told, turning to get my good angles and showing off the dress and my new look.

"Reign, here! Look here! Reign! Reign!" My name is chanted, and I straighten my spine confidently.

"Please, one question, Reign!" I simply wave and move on, stopping farther down to pose for more cameras and live footage. The dress almost tangles between my legs and feet before it's suddenly released.

I glance back to see Astro fluffing the back of my dress to make it perfect, and I grin at him in thanks, knowing he's working to show me off. On his way past, he whispers, "Show them what they are missing." I can't help but laugh and cameras flash. My every movement is documented and ready to be analyzed.

"Reign, who is he?"

"Reign, where's Tucker?"

"Reign, did he really cheat on you?"

"Reign, are you angry? Who did he cheat with?"

"Reign, are you seeing anyone else?"

"Reign, who are you wearing?"

There are so many questions, they blend into one. Clearing my throat, I smile politely into the cameras, trying to form a succinct response. "Thank you for welcoming me back so warmly," I joke, making them chuckle. "I have missed you all so much, and I'm honored by your attention, but tonight, I'm here to celebrate the incredible talent that is overflowing from the film *Kill List*. That is all. They are the stars this evening, and they deserve every moment. The director, Anthony, is beyond talented, and it was an honor to be invited to work on the scores with them. Enjoy the film." I wink and then wave as I walk away, heading to the double doors and the safety they provide.

The paps and piranhas might be outside, but the sharks circle inside. The rich and famous are here and watching everyone, waiting for them to trip up.

The doors open for me, and I smile as I lift my dress and climb the stairs, heading inside. The world instantly transforms. Gone is the madness of outside, and inside, glitz and glamor are ever-present. Stars, directors, and producers mingle. They talk and laugh as champagne and hors d'oeuvres are served on trays. Snippets of the film and trailer play on screens all around us, and posters of the stars are on every wall. The architecture of the old cinema is beautiful, decorated in white and ornate gold, with two open, winding staircases leading up to the balconies.

I accept a glass and force myself to mingle. I smile and make small talk that I really don't give a fuck about. I accept congratulations for the amazing music on the film and praise the filmmakers, all while waiting for it to end. I smile for pictures and social media videos. I'm the life and soul of the fucking party, but deep inside, I'm bored.

My guards see it. I notice their sharp eyes scanning everything, and when anyone gets too close, they move in, but it's in their knowing gazes as they look at me. They truly see me.

I sneak off to the bathroom, fixing my makeup in the mirror. Taking a deep breath, I head back out, only to run right into a chest.

A familiar chest.

I step back, gaping at Tucker. He blinks at me nervously before smiling. "You're here. I was hoping I would run into you."

"What are you doing here?" I demand. We are in a side corridor and all alone.

He tries to back me into the door, and I try to slip around him. We don't need more rumors, not to mention I don't want to be alone with him.

"I asked to come as a plus one with one of my friends who's in the movie. I had to see you. We need to talk, Reign, please. You won't answer your phone—"

"There's a reason why," I scoff, stopping my attempts to get around him when he moves closer. Panic claws at me when I see the intent in his eyes and smell the alcohol on his breath. "Are you drunk?"

"A little. Please, baby, I miss you."

"Step away from Miss Harrow," comes a sharp command.

I almost slump in relief at Raff's voice. I look over to see they are all there and they look furious. "Sir, I asked you to step away from Miss Harrow."

"We are busy, muscle," Tucker snaps, looking back at Raff. "Watch our backs, won't you?" He tries to grab me, but I duck under him. Dal pulls me behind them, and they form a shield between him and me.

"Are you okay?" Raff asks.

I nod, glancing at Tucker to see him glaring at Raff. "What the fuck, man?" he starts.

"She doesn't want to talk. You were cornering her—"

"Do you know who I am?" Tucker demands.

"Yes, and I don't care. Our job is to see to Miss Harrow's well-being, and that includes every part of her, including her happiness," Raffiel growls, getting in Tucker's face, and I realize Raff is both taller and bigger than my ex. He's also scarier and sexier. "You threatened that. If you come near her again, we will have a problem. Do we understand each other?"

"What the fuck, Rey?" Tucker barks, ignoring Raff.

"Let's go," I say, tugging on Raff's sleeve. He's tense and ready to throw down right here with Tucker. "Please, I don't want a scene."

"You're lucky she's here," Raffiel warns. "Next time, she might not be. Heed that warning, Mr. Tucker. Fame and fortune have no bearing on me or my actions. Yes, I know who you are. Now let me tell you who I am. I'm the person with the gun. I'm the person with the training and a file so blacked out by your government that you wouldn't even know where to start." He steps closer as Tucker steps back. "I'm the man at her back, so remember that."

Holy fuck.

THIRTEEN

Raffiel glares at Tucker for a moment longer before taking my arm and leading me out of the corridor, away from him. I smile at the partygoers still lingering about, but Raff steers me away. Instead, we go upstairs to the box we are using for the night. I showed him where it was earlier, and no doubt they all checked it out. I keep my relief from my face until we are in the box, and he helps me into one of the five seats. There are two in the very front, facing the screen, the velvet, dramatically draped curtains held back to give us some privacy. Three walls protect us from prying eyes on either side. Those below can see our heads and shoulders and not much else, with the wall before us preventing it. They shut the curtains quickly and turn me in the chair to face them so everyone else has my back.

"Are you okay?" Cillian demands, serious for once.

"I'm fine. Thank you for the save," I murmur.

"It's our job," Raff snaps. "I'm sorry we left you alone. We got caught between the door and the crowd. It won't happen again."

I nod, leaning into him, taking comfort from him for a moment. He opens his arms, allowing me more contact, as he takes off his suit jacket and quickly wraps it around my shoulders, rubbing my back, and then I realize I'm shivering.

"Let's get out of here," he suggests quietly.

I want to give in to the promise in his eyes, but I told myself I would never walk away because of a man again, not even Raffiel.

"No, we'll stay for the movie. I'll be okay, I promise." I will be okay now that they are here.

It was just the shock of seeing Tucker. I'm okay when I'm prepared, but seeing him practically beg? Yeah, it hurt.

Once, that would have been everything I wanted. Once, I would have given in, even knowing we were doomed to experience the same toxic cycles.

He relents, letting me turn back to the screen as everyone starts to take their seats. As time goes on, I begin to shuffle, inhaling his scent on his jacket. An uncomfortable desire pours through me as his scent wraps me up like I wish he would. The dark only makes it that much more intense. He protected me; he faced off with my very famous ex. I know it is his job, but it felt like more.

It felt personal. There was a flash of possessiveness in his eyes when he stepped up to Tucker.

And that? Yeah, it's hot as hell and leaves me wet and wanting. I always get what I want, and usually I flirt and we fuck. With this, with him, I flirted and he drew the line, but fuck if I don't want to cross it. Maybe it's because I know he's off-limits, or maybe it's just because he is sexy as hell and powerful and so unlike every other man I have been with. Raffiel is real. There are no pretenses, lies, or carefully practiced PR speeches. Clearing my suddenly dry throat, I focus on the movie. There will be a speech after, and I almost groan out loud. I need to go home or find someone to fuck to get this desire out so I can think clearly again.

I feel my neck burning from their stares and hunch, wondering if they know just how badly I want to fuck them. They are attractive, but it's more than that. It is the power they wield, the way they carry themselves, and the way they barged into my life and seem to fit so perfectly. It's the way I laugh when I'm with them, and the way I feel with them looking at me.

I want more.

I want them more than just for a game. I want to know what it feels like to have all that power aimed at me. No fake muscles, no drinks or drugs between us. There would just be pure fucking need, and the thought leaves a wet patch on my chair as I wiggle to get some friction.

I've never felt this strongly before. I've fucked a lot of people and sated my needs. I'm a sexual person, after all, but this? It's never been this intense, this strong, and I'm tired of fighting it.

When a hand lands on my thigh, I realize they are as well.

Thank fuck.

FOURTEEN

I glance up, meeting Raff's eyes where he sits next to me, the sleeves of his shirt rolled back to his elbows. His thick, veiny forearms are visible, even in the dull lighting. His dark eyes meet mine, turbulent with his own desire. I glance down, seeing his slacks tented, his hard dick pressing against the zipper there. His hand tightens on my thigh to the point of pain, and desire flashes through me once more.

"Sit still, Reign," he orders with an edge to his voice. "Please."

"I can't," I murmur.

"Reign, please." His eyes close as if he's in pain. "I'm trying really hard to be a good man, but if you keep looking at me like you are imagining me buried deep in your cunt . . ."

"You'll what?" I flirt.

His eyes snap open, and there's a tick in his jaw. "I'm a man with excellent control, Miss Harrow, but even I can be pushed too far." His tone is lethal as he leans in, almost pressing his lips to mine. "And you push that control every second, every single fucking day simply by existing, especially right now, looking as sexy as you do, so eyes on the film. Watch it and sit still before I forget every reason why I shouldn't touch the pussy begging to be petted."

"Then pet me. You want me, Raff, and I want you. Fuck your job, fuck who I am, and touch me."

His hand slides away, gripping his chair as he averts his gaze. "Miss Harrow—"

"Fuck the Miss Harrow shit." I slide closer, unwilling to compromise on what I want. "Do you want me, Raffiel?"

His eyes snap back to mine, black and filled with a hunger so strong, it steals my breath. "More than you could ever know."

"Then why are you fighting this? No one has to know in the dark," I purr. "I suppose Tucker could fulfill this need."

His snarl makes my nipples pebble against my dress, begging to be touched and sucked by this powerful man, and my thighs are slick with my own need. It's an empty threat, we both know that, since I would never let Tucker touch me again, but it gets me what I want.

"Such a brat, Reign. Eyes on the movie," he demands as his hand lands back on my thigh. Turning back to the movie, I almost slump in disappointment.

His hand slides up my dress, the box's edges obscuring his actions. I bite back my gasp as he leans in, looking to everyone else like he's whispering about the movie. "Keep your eyes on the screen, baby, and let your new security help you with that little problem." I shiver as he chuckles. "Be a good girl and open your legs wide for me. Let me touch what you have so desperately been flaunting at us."

I sit back in my seat, parting my legs. In the dark, it's naughty, and my heart thumps. Desire spirals through me, even as I control my expression like nothing is happening. I keep my eyes on the screen as if I'm watching the movie as my bodyguard slides his hand up and cups my wet pussy.

I hear the others groan. I know they are watching, and it only heightens my need. This desire has been building since I saw them outside of my pool. These beautiful men are so willing to protect me, to help me shine, and to worship the ground I walk on. They give me the confidence I need to get back out there.

"Fuck, you are so wet for us, Reign, you're practically dripping. If we didn't care who was watching, I would drop to my knees right here and lap up the pretty juices you made just for us." I shudder, widening my legs farther. "I might just do it anyway. They wouldn't see me on my knees, would they, baby? Even if they did, they would just be jealous, wishing they were getting to taste you."

"Raff," I beg as he strokes my folds teasingly, not giving me what I need.

"Yes, baby? What do you want? You want me to make you come? You have flaunted that tight little body since the moment we met, with your pouty lips begging to be fucked and a perky little ass begging to be spanked."

Fucking hell.

My eyes slide shut, and he stops touching me. "Eyes on the screen, Reign, or I stop. You are here to watch the movie, after all, and I'm here to take care of you, and I will if you are a good girl."

"Fucking hell, man, you trying to kill us?" Astro asks, and I flinch, almost forgetting they were there. For a moment, I worry what this will change, what everyone will think. Shit, am I reverting back to my old ways by seeking sex to make me feel better? But when Raff grips my pussy possessively, all those thoughts fly away, leaving nothing but desire.

"Focus on me, baby, and only on me. You will know exactly who is touching you, exactly whose fingers you are going to come all over, and then you will stand and clap when this movie finishes just like everyone else, smile, and be polite with your cum sliding down your legs. If you're good and behave, I'll let Astro clean you up with his tongue back in the car on the way home. He's wanted to since the first moment he met you, isn't that right?"

"Fuck yes," Astro growls behind me. "Please behave, Reign. I'd die to taste your cunt."

"Raff," Dal warns, but he's just as far gone as I am. It seems we are all giving into this thing between us, uncaring what tomorrow might bring. Life is too short to fear the consequences enough not to act. I want someone simply because they want me, and I love it.

"How does she feel?" Cillian asks. "At least let us live through you."

"How do you feel, baby? Tell them," Raff demands, his long, talented fingers expertly parting my folds.

"Wet, so wet," I whisper, lifting my hips to get his fingers where I need them. "Dripping and begging to be touched. Soft, so soft. Tight."

They all groan, and Raff flicks my clit, making me moan. It's hard to focus on the screen, but somehow, I do, even though my attention is fixated on the way his fingers touch me until I'm moaning softly.

"Good girl, that's a good girl. Eyes on that movie, don't let anyone else see. This is just for us, isn't it?" I nod, and he rubs my clit in praise before his fingers slide inside of me, stretching me. Finally.

My head falls back, but a hand grips my hair, using it as a handle to force my head back up.

Dal, I realize. He forces me to look at the screen as Raffiel starts to fuck me with his fingers, thrusting them inside my channel and curving them to rub the spot that almost has me shattering embarrassingly fast.

"I've got her," Dal whispers in my ear, but it's aimed at Raff. "Make her come."

"Don't you dare scream, baby, or I'm going to have to let them all see my fingers buried deep in this pretty pussy because there's no way I'm stopping now."

It's torture trying not to move, but I do as he grinds his palm into my clit with each thrust, fucking me harder until the chair creaks. I lift my hips slightly, riding them. "Fuck, she feels so good. I'm going to fucking spill in my pants like a fucking chump just from fingering her greedy little cunt."

"I'm not even touching her and I'm going too," Astro complains.

"She's close. I can feel it," Raff murmurs. "Aren't you, baby? You're so close to coming on my fingers, surrounded by the rich and famous, and not one of them knows their precious rock princess is being serviced by her bodyguard, dripping onto the chair and ruining her million-dollar dress."

"Raff," I whisper, biting my lip. He's right. I'm so close, so fucking close, and when he adds a third finger, curling them to hit that spit at the same time he grinds into my clit, I see stars. A hand covers my mouth, capturing my scream, while Raff's fingers still work inside me as wave after wave of pleasure slides through me until I slump.

Raff slowly pulls from my pussy and moves my panties and dress back into place like nothing happened. I'm shaking and so dazed from the pleasure, I almost slide from my chair. I glance at him, and he waits for me to meet his eyes before licking his glistening fingers clean.

"So fucking sweet, Miss Harrow."

Reality abruptly comes back with the music in the movie.

What have I done?

Do I even care?

FIFTEEN

R eign is quiet, the first sign that she is overthinking what happened. No doubt Raff is too, but it doesn't stop him from watching her hungrily. I've never seen him cross a line or break a rule before, but I get it. She is worth it. Me? I think rules are meant to be challenged and broken, and I will relish every single second of breaking them to have her. And I will have her, just like he ordered. She can stand there primly, clapping for the movie all she wants, but all of my brothers know her cum is running down her leg from us.

Only us.

My cock is solid in my pants, and when I stand, I have to shift it with a wince to be able to walk. I might want her badly, but I will not compromise her safety. Not for anything. Raff is the same as he guides her from the box, even if his hand on her back is a little more possessive than it should be.

Her cheeks are flushed, her eyes are filled with pleasure, and her legs are a little shaky as we head back downstairs. Satisfaction practically rolls from Raff, even as he scans the area, intent on protecting her. When we come out into the reception area, the party is in full swing, and I can tell from her quiet sigh and wince that she doesn't want to be here.

It's our job to protect her, both physically and emotionally.

"Bring the car around," I murmur to Dal, who quickly takes off to do just that, his own need blasting from him. Cillian is positioned before her, clearing a path.

"I need to mingle," she begins.

"It's time to go home, Miss Harrow," I inform her primly, but there's no mistaking my leer. She swallows, her eyes heating as she watches me. We both know exactly what is going to happen when we get in that car.

This beautiful, million-dollar dress will be ripped up, and my lips will be planted on that pretty, famous pussy for all the paparazzi to see. Her lips part, her tongue darting out.

"Don't tease, Miss Harrow," I mock. "Now smile for the pictures." She jerks her head around, wearing a perfect, practiced smile once more, even as she hurries with us to the car.

She might deny that she wants this, and she might worry about the repercussions like all of us, but none of us could stop this if we tried. We were foolish to think we could. There has been an electric connection between us all since the first moment we met.

It's time I act on it and take what I want.

Her. The people's rock princess.

Their idol.

Their icon.

Little do they know, their pretty, talented role model will be screaming in the back seat in moments.

"Say your goodbyes, Miss Harrow, like a good girl," I purr in her ear, pretending to whisper important things. She shivers next to me, that fake smile faltering for a moment, but it's enough to nearly make me cheer in victory.

She waves and says her goodbyes, and once she steps out on the red carpet, she poses for more pictures. I lick my lips, debating throwing her down right here and diving into that pretty pussy.

I bet she would let us because she would love it.

She's only had a taste of Raff, but I see her tracking him like her next prey. We thought we were in control, but she's ready to show us that's completely wrong. Nobody controls Reign.

She's ready to revolt.

"Reign, why are you leaving early?" a pap calls.

I smirk, covering it by turning to check behind me. I want to mock, "Yes, Reign, why are you leaving early? Is it because you're so desperate to get your cunt licked?" but I don't. I keep my gaze sharp, scanning every inch of the crowd. There's movement that catches my eye—a man slipping back into the masses from the front—but I quickly move on since he's not a threat.

She doesn't answer, continuing to wave and sign autographs on the way to the car, making sure to stop for every fan who calls her name. They even have shirts with her face and logo on the front, and pride fills me. Our girl is a fucking rock star.

We finally reach the car, and Cillian helps her inside before climbing in after her. Smirking, Raff takes the passenger seat, winking at me as I slide in and shut the door.

I sit opposite her with my knees spread. She watches me carefully, wondering if I plan to follow through. I'll teach our girl that I'm a man of my word and there is nothing more in this world that I want to eat than that pretty pussy so our girl will fall asleep satisfied, dreaming of me.

Taking off my jacket, I roll my sleeves back. She watches every move as the car pulls out into traffic. The windows are tinted, but we can't be too careful. I might want her and want everyone to see, but I would never put her in jeopardy like that.

"Part those pretty thighs for me," I tell her. Her eyes narrow as I grin. "I'm waiting, Miss Harrow." I lower to my knees as we come to a stop sign. Crawling across the small space between us, I grip her heeled feet and throw them over my shoulders. "Didn't want the suit jacket getting in the way."

"Astro," she warns.

I slide my hands up her silken thighs and almost come on the spot. I can't even see them because of the dress, but they are the softest motherfucking things I've ever felt.

It's like touching goddamn silk.

"I've wanted to taste your pretty pussy ever since you teased me with that strawberry and flashed it at me in the pool, so be a good girl and part them," I tell her roughly. I need her cum more than I need to breathe.

I need to taste her on my tongue or I actually might die.

Someone could come up behind me right now and shoot me in the back and I still wouldn't stop.

I push her dress up and to the side so I can get a clear view of that pretty, dripping pussy. It's ripe for the picking and begging for my tongue. Her hand comes out to slap me away, but I catch it, kissing her pulse as she breathes raggedly.

"You can slap me if you want, darling. I promised to clean this wet, greedy pussy and that's exactly what I plan to do. After all, we are here to serve you," I purr.

Leaning back, she finally parts her thighs enough for me to scoot closer, and my hands grip her thick thighs, holding them prisoner. "Then serve me," she demands haughtily.

Chuckling, I lean down and run my lips over one thigh. "Oh, I plan to. Let the others hear your screams, beautiful. Let everyone passing by hear you and wonder what's happening in here. Fuck, let them call them cops, thinking you are being murdered."

"You'll have to make me, and right now, you're all talk," she retorts, but there's a tremor of need in her voice that makes me smirk against her velvety skin.

Licking her tattoos, I slide my hands higher, pushing her thighs wider until I get my first look at her exposed clit and her pulsing, greedy hole, wanting to be filled. She's so fucking wet for it, she's practically already coming.

"I've never eaten rock star pussy. Let's see if this is why you are so famous," I purr.

The moan she lets out goes straight to my balls.

I drive my cock into the seat, grinding as I drop my mouth to her pussy, unable to resist any longer. I drag my tongue from her pretty little asshole to her engorged clit, making her groan loudly.

"How does she taste?" Cillian asks, his voice rough with his own need. No doubt he's watching us, his cock hurting, but she won't get any of ours tonight. Not here, not like this. I won't make her regret this or worry about how this will change the dynamic. We are her body-guards first and foremost. It just so happens to be that we want to fuck her as well, and if she lets us, we will make sure she's never needy or hurt again. This body is ours to protect and pleasure.

But never tame.

I like her wildness. Her hand comes down and grips my hair, her nails digging into my scalp until I grunt, lashing her clit with my tongue in warning. Her heels dig into my back in the very best way.

Dragging my tongue across her pretty cunt, I almost spill at her taste. She tastes like fucking strawberries. Grinding my cock into the seat, I dip my tongue inside her, making her moan, and it feels like a victory so I do it again. I won't give her my fingers or my cock. No, she gets my mouth. I want her to ride my face. I want to struggle to breathe. I want to be able to see and taste only her.

"Every single one of your fans either wants to be you or fuck you. I wonder how jealous they would be to see your bodyguard between your thighs, getting what they only dream about." I groan, making her whimper and grind that pretty pussy into my face. Her clit hits my nose as I circle her hole, causing her to fuck herself against me.

"Good girl. Use me and ride my face. Make yourself come for us. Let us serve you," I mumble against her skin, lifting my head a little so she can hear me. Her head is thrown back and her eyes are closed. She's so fucking beautiful, it's like looking at a movie or a painting, and my heart stops for a moment until her eyes snap open and look down at me. She's in a gown and covered in expensive jewels I wouldn't be able to afford in ten lifetimes, yet when she smiles, I feel like I've won.

"Get that tongue back to work," she orders.

"Do as Miss Harrow says," Raff chimes in.

"Yes, sir." I grin as I drag my tongue across her clit, flicking it until she grinds harder and moans loudly, but I want her screams. I thrust my tongue inside her, and then into her pretty little ass. My hands slip under her to lift her higher for better access, and I feel her plump ass cheeks in my palms as I fuck the seat through my pants.

Her hands grip me, dragging me back and forth across her pussy. She reaches for her release as I lap at her ass and pussy, cleaning up every inch of her just like I promised.

"Astro," she begs.

Her voice is wobbly. She's close.

We stop for a moment, and I see flashes of cameras as paps try to see into the car. They won't, but part of me swells with pride for getting her to come as they try to get a picture of her. I simply focus on her demanding little clit like she wants and let her grind against my tongue. Her panting breaths fill the car as it rocks, her nails tear into my scalp until her breathing hitches, and I speed up.

I want her release and need her cries.

"Astro," she begs, "don't stop. Right there, please—fuck." Her words end in a yell as her thighs clamp closed on my head, making me grin against her sloppy pussy as I lick her through her release. Her cream coats my face, and she writhes and then slumps back.

"Good girl, Miss Harrow," Raffiel praises, but I refuse to move. I lick every inch of her pussy clean just like I said I would, drinking down her cum. Strawberries will forever remind me of her, of this moment, and make me hard. My own pants are messy, filled with my release since I came when she did, unable to help it.

Reign Harrow is dangerous, but I can't seem to care when I sit back, seeing her smile at me in satisfaction. Her body shines with jewels and sweat as she slips down and crawls into my lap.

I get hard again.

Grabbing her before she'll regret it, I move us back into my seat, holding her in my arms as she relaxes. She fits perfectly in my hold, her head on my shoulder. She fits like she was always made to be in my arms.

Glancing at Cillian, I see him digging his nails into the seat. His gaze is locked on her, and his nostrils flare in need. We've never shared before, but we've never wanted to. There have been women, faceless ones from our past between deployments and missions, but none of us ever wanted to settle down. We never introduced any women to each other, and we never even cared enough to get their names, yet Reign Harrow is fucking seared into my heart and soul with just one meeting.

I don't know how that's possible, but my heart pumps in fear because this woman is guarded. She's determined never to be weak again, never to trust anyone again, and I know it will wreck me. I know she is going to break our hearts, yet I can't seem to care when she glances at me with a wicked smile.

"What does she taste like?" Cillian grinds out.

"Strawberries," I reply, making him groan. "Fucking perfection."

She laughs in my arms, not the least bit ashamed. I glance around the car worriedly, not wanting anyone to know what we did—not out of shame, but she would hate it. She doesn't want her life publicized, so that means she's keeping us a secret, but I don't care. Not as long as I get her in the shadows. It does mean we need to be careful, though, especially to keep our job, and leaving a wet patch of her cum behind is very telling.

"You want a taste, man? Here, clean up for us. We can't have any of her staff thinking anything, can we, princess?" I wink as she curls into my lap like a sated kitten, and I feel like a fucking king.

Her eyes remain open, though, widening as Cillian moves over. The big redhead drops to his knees and licks up every drop of her cum from the leather seat. "Shit, he's right. She tastes like strawberries." His eyes swing to her hungrily. "Next time, you are riding my face all fucking night, sweetheart." Without waiting for her reply, he goes back to cleaning the seat.

"Crazy, you're all crazy."

She doesn't know the half of it because with just one taste, I'm already hers.

She doesn't have a fucking clue how dangerous that is.

Once we reach the house, I rearrange her dress, and when we get out, I grip her tighter. "Astro, I can walk," she grumbles, but when I tighten my hold, she shrugs and lays her head on my shoulder, clearly tired.

"Let's get you to bed, Miss Harrow." Raff holds out his arms to take her, but I pull her closer.

"I've got her," I tell him, and his eyes narrow. No doubt he can see that I'm already attached. I don't care. Fuck them all. This girl is mine. She just doesn't know it. I'll play this slow because she's been hurt. She's been in an industry where it's celebrated to be stabbed in the back, but I will never let that happen again.

Ignoring them and happy there is no staff around, I follow them into the house and straight up the stairs to her room. We had to check out security while she was in the studio so I know the layout, but it never fails to surprise me how there are no pictures anywhere. There is nothing personal from someone as raw, emotional, and artistic as Reign, and that makes me sad.

It makes me angry that she feels so detached and alone that she doesn't even have anything to celebrate within her personal space. I will change that.

When we reach her room, I slide her down my body and turn her, carefully stripping her from the dress and helping her remove her jewels and shoes, laying them out for her crew to pick up later. When I turn back, she's on the bed and under the covers, and my heart pulses at the vulnerable look in her eyes as she glances at me.

"Thank you," she murmurs.

"It's my job." I instantly regret saying it. I meant to say that it's my pleasure to look after her every need as her man, but she winces.

"Of course." She rolls over, and I feel like I've lost her. Needing to recover some of the ground I lost, I head over to her, brush back her hair, and kiss her forehead.

"Sleep well, Reign," I whisper, "and know that there is nowhere else in this world I would want to be, job or no job." Leaving her with that, I head out and shut the door. When I get downstairs, my brothers are waiting just like I knew they would be.

"We need to talk," Raff snaps, glancing at the bedroom, and then he jerks his head. I follow him into the room he claimed and flop onto the bed, a goofy smile on my face at the memory of Reign tonight. Cillian sits near me, and Dal stands near the window.

"Do not get attached," Raff orders. "I see you."

"I wasn't going to deny it," I respond without even looking up.

"This is a job," he growls.

I sit up and glare at him. "Keep telling yourself that. Keep lying to yourself and us if it makes you feel better, but we all know the truth. This became so much more the first fucking moment we laid eyes on her, then again when we found out just how fucking alienated that poor girl has been, and once again tonight when you made her ours. You can lie to us all you want, Raff, but I see it. Keep calling it a job, but it's more, and you know it deep down."

"We can't cross the line—"

"It's a bit late for that." Dal is always the calm one between us. I'm the hothead, and it is usually Cillian whom I'm arguing with, but Raff is glaring at me. No doubt he's pissed that I called him on his shit.

"Fuck, this is so bad. We should tell them we can't protect her anymore."

"No." Cillian's voice is sharp and angry.

"He's right, she needs us. They hired us for a reason, remember? We need to protect her. The fact that we are getting attached only means we will do our job that much better." He sighs. "Raff, being emotional in our old jobs was a weakness. I know that, and it made us second-guess everything, but here? It only makes us better and more determined to protect her. We aren't at war anymore, man. It's okay to enjoy life. Maybe you should take a lesson from Reign on that."

I can't help but laugh, and Dal does as well. "He's right," Dal says once more. "I suggest we let this play out. If she doesn't look at us after tonight, then we can still do our job and not have to worry about the intimacy of our bond."

My heart pulses in pain, and I stand and begin to pace. "And if she wants to explore this? Wants us?"

"Then I don't see the harm." It is my turn to stare at Dal in shock. "I don't," he murmurs. "Like you said, there is something here. This is more than just a job, but we've never backed off before, so I say we don't start now."

"Fuck, this is all fucked," Raff snaps. "Fine, but you, get out of my sight. I'm annoyed at you," he orders me.

That's fine by me. I have something to do anyway.

SIXTEEN

S tanding near the pool, I stare out at the city. It's an incredible view, but I've seen many in my life. I've traveled nearly the entire world with my family, my brothers, who are spread out inside after our discussion, yet nothing compared to the first time I saw Reign Harrow. The great wonders of the world and true natural beauty most only dream of seeing has been all washed clean by the woman who has taken over my thoughts and life.

I was tongue-tied, looking at true beauty for the first time ever, and as we got to know her over the last few days, her beauty only increased because she's real. Sometimes, you see beautiful places, but they hide horrible pasts and secrets or never live up to the hype, but she does.

Because she's flawed.

Because she's real.

I want her more than I've ever wanted anyone else. There haven't been many, being so exposed to another person never really interested me, but I took part as rites of tradition and after bad missions to try and forget.

It never worked until her.

One look into her eyes and I don't remember the bad things I've done to get here. I don't remember my nightmares. I feel alive. I feel seen. I feel whole. She's just so full of life, where I am drained of it from the lives we have led and the lives that stain my soul. She shines a light on me, though, and when she smiles at me, I feel a spark of humanity seeping back into me.

It's a spark I'm beginning to crave. I only feel alive, feel human, around her. Raff is right, this is dangerous, but I have my own selfish reasons for wanting us to keep this job and be close to her. I might never get to touch her like Raff or Astro, who is already smitten, but that doesn't matter. Being around that much life is addictive. I've never thought about love or relationships. Astro is different. He loves women, he loves happiness and the idea of love, but me? Not so much. I'm considered too evil for that.

But that doesn't mean I don't understand it through her lyrics.

Another of my secrets.

I'm her biggest fan. Her music got me through some very bad times, and now I've met the woman behind the lyrics. She was reaching out into the world and calling for me, and now I'm here.

I'm not leaving.

Turning, I spot her standing in the window of her room. She clearly hasn't seen me yet. She's wrapped in a sheet, her eyes sad as she stares out at the city. She looks so alone, so isolated and lost that my heart aches. Didn't I used to see that look in my reflection every single day?

How can a woman so full of life, who can produce such raw and honest lyrics that it makes my ruined heart beat, feel so alone? She deserves everything—the perfect life, happiness, friends, and lovers— yet here she stands alone.

Just like me, another lost soul is reaching out into the darkness.

Her eyes drift down, and when they land on me, she freezes. I let her know with just a look that I see her. I see her struggle and I under- stand. For a moment, her eyes soften before they shutter, becoming guarded.

She drops the sheet, turns, and struts away. It gets the reaction she wants, igniting my desire, but my heart aches for her. She's so used to needing to turn her emotions to desire to hide the truth that she doesn't know how to be real unless it's in a song. She hides her fear of trusting anyone with her heart behind her incredible body, but I see it.

I see her.

"Dal," Raff calls from inside, standing in the light.

The man might be our leader, but we chose to follow him, and no matter how dark he thinks his soul is for the things he has done in the name of our country, it doesn't compare to the things I have done. I follow him out of respect, out of brotherhood, or the name of it. It never really meant much to me until now. I'm starting to understand it and the attachment others have to me.

Is this what it feels like to care?

Heading inside, I stop before him and wait for him to explain what he wants. Once, there would have been a slice of unease as he looked at me. Out of all of them, he's the only one who truly knows even half of what I am capable of.

"Are we right for doing this?"

"In what way?" I respond.

"For staying. Should we report that we can't do this job anymore and move on?"

"Why?" I can tell he's worried, but I won't understand why until he explains it.

"Because I'm worried that by staying, it will pull us apart. Astro is already attached, Cillian too. If we stay, will it ruin us? I don't want them to get hurt or for our unit to be fractured."

Ah, I understand. It's tactical. He needs us to be a unit, but if she comes between us, we can't be that. "I think she might be good for us. We have been working without truly caring for a very long time. Astro may be attached, but it's good."

His eyebrows rise at my response. Grinning, I slap his shoulder like I have seen the others do, copying the movement since I know it conveys friendship and relaxes him. "It will be fine. We are smart, and we've been in much worse situations. How about we simply play out the mission, day to day, for once?"

"You know I hate doing that," he grumbles.

"I know, but sometimes, sir, you simply have to roll with it and expect the unexpected, and Reign Harrow? She is the most unexpected thing in this world. You will never control that, so don't even try." I start to walk away when he calls out to me. I planned to lurk outside of her room, simply needing to be close to her.

"Dal, I have to ask . . . Usually, you are with me. Usually, you don't give a fuck what we do as long as it's following orders. Why now? Why do you care enough now to argue their case?" I can hear the censure in his words as he tries to figure me out. He shouldn't bother. The doctors couldn't, so he'll never be able to.

"Reign Harrow brings me to life," I tell him.

I hear him inhale. "Is that a good thing or bad thing?" he asks carefully.

"I guess we will see," I reply as I move back into the darkness to stalk my prey.

SEVENTEEN

I've painted my nails, colored my hair, changed my piercings, and I even dressed, and now I'm fiddling with the buckles on my knee-high boots. When that's done, I look around my room for something else to do to keep me in here. I'm not avoiding seeing them —it's my house, after all—I just want some time alone. That's all. I am totally not hiding to avoid seeing my bodyguards after I crossed a very hard line with them. I haven't fucked someone after playing around, and for some reason, what we did felt more intimate, never mind the fact that I usually slip out of the door and can avoid them. This time, I can't.

I realize I'm hiding.

I'm such a pussy.

Closing my eyes, I blow out a breath and get it together. This is my house. I'm Reign fucking Harrow. I do not hide. I own that shit. I own my mistakes. I own my nature and my sexuality. So what if I let them touch me? They wanted it, I wanted it, and we are adults. Nothing else matters.

It's also just a job for them.

No, we can't go there again. They are bodyguards; they can't be anything else. I remind myself of that as I head downstairs, but then I get a look at a sweaty Cillian coming from the gym, running a towel across his sweaty, bare, perfect abs. His red hair glistens with sweat and sunlight, sticking up, and my mouth goes dry, and I forget every reason I shouldn't play with these men.

Hey, I'm only a woman after all, and they are damn good-looking, not to mention they give some of the best head I've ever had, not that I'll tell that cocky fucker that. Shit, it's already embarrassing and far too intimate that he carried me to bed and tucked me in.

No, behave, Harrow, just this once.

"Morning," I call, and he stops, tilting his head as he grins at me.

"Morning, Reign—Miss Harrow," he amends. "There's breakfast in the oven if you're hungry. Raff is out on a run, Dal is on the perimeter, and Astro is still asleep."

I like that he gives me a report out of habit, or maybe it's because I look ready to bolt. "Thanks," I say as I head past him, trying not to sway when his sweaty, masculine scent reaches me. Fuck, I'm practically begging for him to fuck me and he knows it. He chuckles as he heads upstairs, and damn me, I watch him go, my eyes locked on that perfect, tight ass until he's out of sight.

So much for that.

Heading to the kitchen, I plate the food and pull my phone out as I start to nibble on the full breakfast one of them made for me. How sweet—no, stop. I focus on the phone, using it to distract me from my turbulent thoughts, and I open a thread of spam messages from a number I don't recognize. All the others have people's names, but not this one.

I change my number a lot, usually when it gets leaked, but I've had this one for a while now and I haven't really given it out. One of the guys maybe? I quickly realize it's definitely not when I get a glimpse of the messages.

Unknown: You looked beautiful tonight.

Unknown: I can't take my eyes off you.

> Unknown: But you didn't even notice me, did you? So lost, but I'll find you.
>
> Unknown: I missed you.
>
> Unknown: I'll see you soon.

Ew, it's probably someone I hooked up with. I instantly block it and drop my phone, reminding myself this is why I don't look at it. There are some downsides to being a celebrity, and privacy is one, but so are the types of messages you get—creepy ones, threatening ones, I see them all. I learned to ignore them after a while, otherwise it would get to be too much, but sometimes they cross a line.

Not often, but sometimes.

A knock on the door makes me drop my fork. I expect one of the guys to get it, but when no one does, I shrug and head to the door. I told them not to let anyone else in, so it has to be someone they approved.

As soon as I open the door, I have regrets. She tries to sweep past me as if I'm beneath her, but I put my boot in the door and block her entry. She stumbles back, her perfect, fake nose wrinkling before she smooths it out. Her sunglasses block her bright blue eyes, and she's dressed to the nines in a perfect designer dress and heels. Her makeup is perfectly done, and her blonde hair is immaculately styled. She looks cool and collected.

Serena was one of my old best friends before she decided not to give a shit when I disappeared. "Reign." She leans in and kisses my cheek. "So sorry for not visiting sooner. I've been so busy. First Paris, then Milan, you know how it is . . ." She trails off when I still don't let her in. "Oh, do you have company?" She slides her shades down, wiggling her eyebrows. "Tell me everything."

Ah, there it is. She wants gossip to sell since she's a failing model. She was once a supermodel, but as she aged, she has been looked over time and time again for younger models. It's sad really, because she's truly beautiful on the outside. It's the inside that's the problem. She aligned herself with me for my status and to get more jobs. I didn't believe it back then, but she used and discarded me when there was nothing I could offer her rep but bad publicity by association.

"What are you doing here?" I ask, my voice cold.

"Darling, are you going to let me in? Surely we aren't to talk out here." When I raise my eyebrow, she sighs and rolls her eyes. "Always with the dramatics. I'm sorry, Reign. You know how this world is. I would have been by sooner, but—"

"You didn't want the bad press that I got, only the good. Am I right? That's the only time we're friends, like now."

Her mouth drops at my curt barb. I let her walk all over me before, humbled someone like her was my friend, and I told her everything only for her to use it against me. I'm pretty sure she was the one who sold a story about me as soon as the media started attacking.

It wouldn't surprise me.

"Reign, I have my image to protect, you know that. You did the same thing. It's very rude not to let friends into your house so we can reconnect." She's good, I'll give her that. She has the *truly worried* look down to a T. She should have been an actress. All she needs is a tear and it would be convincing.

"Oh, I'm sorry I gave you the impression I wanted your opinion on who I let in my house, which I bought with the money I earned from singing songs you called trite and childish. I don't give a flying fuck what you think about me."

"You're being loud," she hisses embarrassingly, looking around as if people might overhear us.

I glance around dramatically and cup my mouth. "How about now?" I yell before dropping my hands. "It's my fucking house. I can be as loud as I fucking want."

"I see I won't be getting anything out of you today but anger." She slides her shades back up her face. "Call me when you are ready to apologize. It's a very lonely life without friends, Reign, you know that."

Nice, a threat, and then a perfume cloud of flipped hair as she strolls back to the gate. She gets in her car, pulling out her phone before driving away. I'm positive she's telling everyone about me being crazy, brash, and rude.

Let her.

Slamming the door, I turn to see all four of them there, and all my anger comes back.

"Do not let anyone else into my house ever again," I tell them. "Is that clear? I informed you of my wants. Make sure someone is at the gate at all times." I storm off, knowing I'm being a bitch, but I'm still irritated about her visit and need to take it out on someone and unfortunately, they are the closest.

I might regret it later, but what good do regrets do?

None, in my experience, so fuck it.

Do what you want and make no apology.

You want respect? Earn it. You want money? Work hard and make it. This world is made for the strong and it crushes the weak. I know that all too well. So fuck apologies, this is who I am. If you don't like it, then get the fuck out of my life.

I spend hours in the studio, but I'm in a foul mood. I can't even look at the guys. I'm annoyed about my reaction to them and how easily I gave in and fucked them despite my protests, and then add seeing Serena on top of that. Jack eventually tells me to go get this mood out of my system.

It's not a bad idea.

I'll get this anger and the guys out of my system all at once.

It will be a palate cleanser, just like with Tucker, only they will have to come with me. I'm not theirs in any shape or form. I'm Reign, and I do whatever I want. Just because they touched me and made me come doesn't mean anything.

Nothing.

"Where to?" Raff asks carefully, sensing my mood as I stomp toward the car, leaving them no choice but to follow. They scramble to open the door, but I ignore them as I climb in.

Better to end this now.

Pulling out my phone, I shoot off a text and wait for the response before answering. "Downtown, Mycroft Hotel."

His eyes narrow and search mine, but I give him nothing, and eventually, they begin to drive. I don't tell them whom I'm meeting there. I don't tell them I plan to go screw the brains out of the bass player who's good with his fingers—good but not as good as them—all to forget the way I felt when they touched me.

The true reason I'm angry.

They don't seem bothered by what we did, yet I feel different. I can't even breathe around them without being filled with desire, and they are calm and collected. There are knowing looks, but they haven't tried to touch me once.

So like the brat I am, I'm going to push them.

I'm going to make them pay because fuck them. They don't want me, then fine. There are plenty who do.

I don't need them for anything. I don't need anyone.

As soon as we stop at the back entrance to the hotel, I slide out, ignoring their calls, and head through the familiar back labyrinth. I met Tucker here more than once when we were both on tour, a little rendezvous that felt private and loving but now makes me think he just didn't want to be seen with me.

I know my way.

Trav waits in the lobby, leaning against the wall near the elevators with his phone in his hand. Wearing black jeans and a band shirt, he looks every bit the rock star he is. He's good-looking, tall, and lanky but with some muscle. He gets a lot of women and men, but he's like me, never wanting to settle down again after he got his heart broken, something I found out while Trav was supporting me on tour with his band.

He's great in bed, and that's all that matters, and he won't tell. I trust him.

We might not be besties, but I consider him a friend. He's probably one of the only ones. He and his band defended me after I disappeared and still support me now.

"Reign." He grins warmly when he sees me, putting the phone away and wrapping me in a familiar, warm hug.

I relax into it. "Hey, sweetie." I lean up and kiss his cheek. "You got a room?"

Nodding, Trav tucks me under his arm, and when the elevator opens, I look back to see all four of my guards glaring at the arm around me.

"I'll be down later. You can watch me from here." The door shuts, cutting off whatever angry words Raff was about to say. It was probably something about protecting me, but it's bullshit.

I saw the jealousy, anger, and hurt in their eyes.

Shit, I can't think about it. I push him against the elevator wall and kiss him, fisting his shirt. Laughing, he kisses me back before pulling away. "Almost there. Eager tonight, aren't we?"

"Yup." *Real sexy, Reign.*

Arm in arm, we head to the suite where he lets us in, and before the door is even kicked shut, we tumble into bed, tugging at each other's clothes in that familiar way only people who have fucked before can. We kiss hard and fast, but I barely feel or see him, trying to lose myself in his taste so I don't think about whom I wish it were instead, but he pulls back.

"Reign, stop," he demands, frowning. "Are you okay?" *Fuck.*

Rolling over, I cover my face. "Not into it tonight."

"Me either," he admits as I start to spew an apology.

We both laugh as we look at each other. "Trying to forget someone?" I ask, realizing he had been just as hard and heavy, as if chasing the taste of someone else away.

Sighing, he closes his eyes. "Maybe. You?"

"Maybe," I admit, and we share a knowing smile.

"Want to order room service, eat our weight in food, talk, and then go home?"

God, that sounds amazing. He's a great man and sexy as hell, yet all I see when I look at him is a friend.

His touch even felt wrong. How fucked is that?

"Sounds good to me."

He nods, looking relieved. It's clear neither of us felt right doing this. Usually, it's electric between us, but after Astro and Raff, it felt pale, like a cheap imitation, and knowing they are out there right now, protecting me while knowing exactly what I'm doing, I feel a little bad.

I also feel dirty and guilty, but not enough to walk out for a while. Let them sweat over it a little.

After eating, we end up sprawling on the living room sofas, comparing new music. I laugh at his jokes, genuinely happy. I forgot how well we get along. He is such a good guy, which is hard to find in this world. Like me, he is in it for the music, not the money or the fame.

"I think you better go before your guards come up here and drag you out." He smirks when I look at the door once more. I'm always expecting that.

"I don't know what you mean," I tease.

"Sure thing, Reign." He winks. "Your secrets are always safe with me. Just be careful, okay? Don't get hurt again. You're a good woman. You deserve better."

"Thank you." I kiss his cheek. "And whoever this woman is you're pining after, man up and tell her. You're a good man, Trav, and you deserve to be happy."

"It's complicated," he mutters.

"Isn't it always? That's when it's the most fun," I say and stand, slipping on my boots once more. I wrap my jacket around me and wish him a final goodbye before I head down to face my guards and the music.

Excitement and nerves flow through me at what they might do.

What I hope they will do . . .

EIGHTEEN

I'm pacing, as is Astro. I'm pissed and jealous as hell. We all know what's happening up there and we hate it, but Astro, fuck, he looks both devastated and furious. We've had to stop him from storming up there more than once, but we're so focused on him and our own anger that we didn't even notice Dal slip away.

"Shit," Raff hisses. "That's bad news, really bad fucking news."

Raff has been just as bad despite his words. He's been ranting, checking the guy out, looking for anything to use on him, and he told us a hundred reasons in the last hour why we should check on them.

It all stems from jealousy.

She isn't ours, but we all wish she were.

She can fuck whoever she wants, but it doesn't mean we don't hate it and wish it were us up there with her, tasting her sweetness and hearing her screams.

Disappointment fills me because I thought we had something, but maybe I was wrong. Maybe this is simply who Reign is. She never promised us anything, and she's more than welcome to do this, but it hurts.

"Raff?" I question. If Dal is gone, then there is only one place he'll be. He wouldn't abandon his post, and he wouldn't leave us without a

117

word, so that means he went after her. Raff looks very worried, though, his face clouded, like he knows something he didn't tell us.

"Cil, stay here in case someone comes down. Astro, you're with me." He stomps toward the stairs with Astro in tow. I shoot him a raised eyebrow, asking him if he knows what's going on, and the only response I get is a shrug, so I guess not.

I watch them disappear and glance around. I hate waiting. I want to be there with them. I want to find out what's happening.

More than that, I want to confront her.

I'm angry because whatever this is between us is fun and electric, and I've never felt anything like this before, yet she can easily toss us aside like we're nothing and fuck someone else?

I thought I knew her, but maybe I was wrong.

The elevator dings as it opens, and I whirl to see Reign. All of my good intentions, my professionalism, and sense of duty goes out of the window with one look at her.

The others aren't here to stop me, and her eyes widen as I march toward her. She tries to back away before tilting her chin up and holding her position. That's my girl. Grabbing her arm, I haul her from the elevator, barely able to even look at her without exploding with jealousy.

Her hair is mussed, her lips are swollen and bruised, and her shirt is askew.

She looks like she's just been fucked, and I hate it.

We are the only ones she should be looking at like that. It's stupid, impulsive, and unprofessional, but I don't care anymore. She came here tonight to either prove something to us or herself, and I plan to find out what.

I don't care that she's a rock star and earns more in a minute than I could in a lifetime. To us, she is just Reign, and right now, she's pushed me too fucking far.

"Cillian," she starts, but I ignore her and the looks thrown our way as I drag her down a corridor and into the first room. It's a fancy-ass powder room, and I quickly lock the door behind me. I release her arm like she burnt me and pace to the stalls, quickly checking that they are empty and alone, but even then, I don't turn back to her.

My control is hanging on by a thread. She might think I'm the nice one, that I'm funny and relaxed, but she's about to find out that I'm anything but when it comes to her.

"Cillian," she demands, her voice haughty.

I spin, knowing my hands are fisted, and her eyes widen as she backs into the door—not of our fear, but out of shock. I advance on her, unable to resist. Had she just stayed silent, I might have resisted these urges inside me, but no, she had to push like Reign does.

Well, she wants a reaction, so she's going to get one.

Slamming my hand above her on the door, I watch her jump and ignore the tiny bit of guilt I feel. It soon dissipates anyway when her eyes narrow and she crosses her arms in front of her chest.

"Was he good?"

Her lips part as I lean down, getting right in her face. I watch her bright eyes drop to my lips, her tongue darting out to caress her plump bottom one. Rubbing my thumb along the path it took, I breathe in her exhale.

"Well, Miss Harrow? Was he a good fuck? Did he make you scream like we did? Or are you still wet and you want me to take care of it? That's what we are here for, remember?" I sneer.

I don't care if I'm being mean, not when her pretty eyes flash with fire, making me hard. My cock jerks at the fight as her hands slam into my chest, trying to move me, but I don't budge an inch. I watch her breasts rise and fall rapidly, close to spilling from her shirt.

"Fuck off," she hisses.

Laughing, I reach down and flick one of her hard nipples. "Really? Is that what you want? Because I'm thinking you want me to fuck *you*, princess."

She tries to slide past me, and when that doesn't work, she turns to open the door. I slam it shut again and turn the lock, grinding my cock into her tight, little ass while my other hand wraps around her hair.

I pull her back and turn her to the mirrors, caging her in against the counter so she has nowhere to look but at me as I tower above her.

"Look at your hard, little nipples, practically begging to be sucked. He might have touched you and got inside your little cunt, but he left you wanting, didn't he? Otherwise, you wouldn't be here, rubbing against my dick like a good little slut, begging for me to make you come."

I see the truth in her eyes. No one has ever spoken to her like this and she loves it. She fights against me before realizing it's no use and switching tactics, rubbing her ass against my cock and making me groan. "Maybe I'm just greedy and want you as well as him."

Jealousy stabs through me so my grip tightens, making her smirk as I pull her head back, digging my teeth into her neck in punishment. Her moan rattles around the tiled walls as my other hand slips around her and rips her top down. I bare her pert breasts, her nipples tight and begging for attention. Our eyes lock in the mirror in a battle of wills.

"Well, maybe I'll get you all riled up and make you beg for my cock until you drip down your pretty thighs. I'll make you walk out there in pain and unsatisfied with tears running down your face," I snarl against her pulse as she groans, rolling her hips back to urge me on.

Fuck, she's magnificent.

Even with his smell and taste on her, I want her more than I've ever wanted anything.

"I don't think you will," she purrs.

"No?" I retort, sliding my hand up to circle her throat and squeeze, watching her eyes dilate.

"No," she whispers.

"Why not?" I ask.

"Because you want to fuck me too much," she retorts honestly. "Look at you, practically growling like a beast simply because I went up there and rode his cock and you wish it were yours. You wish it were your cum dripping from me and that I had your handprints on my ass."

Snarling, I shove her shorts and panties down, making her gasp as I kick open her thighs and bend her over. My eyes go to her round ass, and I smirk as I meet her eyes in the mirror once more. "No handprints. He obviously doesn't know how to fuck you well enough or how to give you what you need, does he, Miss Harrow?" I slam my open hand down on her ass, and I watch it jiggle as she cries out. A red handprint appears on her cheek.

Possessiveness and satisfaction roars through me.

"I bet if I reached between those pretty thighs, you would be wetter than you ever were with him. I bet he had to work to even try to make you come, all the while I could wind you up like this and have you coming without even touching you, couldn't I, Miss Harrow? You are desperate for me to touch you, taste you, and fill you with my cock." I bring my hand down again, and her hands grip the edge of the sink. Tears form in her eyes, even as she pushes her ass back for more.

"Words, Miss Harrow. We know you are good with them, it's your job after all, so sing me a song, pretty bird, and tell me exactly what you want or I'll slap this pretty ass, mark it all up, come across it, and then leave you here like the dirty cum slut you are."

"Fuck, what do you want? A sonnet begging you to fuck me?" she demands.

Chuckling, I rub my hand into the sting of the last slap, watching her pretty hips twist, searching for friction. "Maybe, but that wasn't very nice, was it, Miss Harrow? Ask nicely. Say, 'Cillian, please fuck me and make me come since that tiny-dick man I tried to use to forget you couldn't. Pretty please, Cillian.'"

"Fuck off." She pushes me away and tries to step around me, but I catch her and slam her back against the sinks, forcing myself between her thighs. She gasps as the cool porcelain hits her spanked ass.

"How did he taste, Reign?" I purr. "Did you kiss him and wish he were me? Every time his hands pulled you closer, every time you looked into his eyes, did you see us and wish it were us and not him you were fucking? Did you pretend it was us to get off? When you screamed, was it our names?"

She struggles in my grip, even as I reach down and cup her dripping pussy. "All this fight, all this fire, and you are putty in my hands, dripping for me." Sliding my fingers through her messy pussy, I slam them inside her cunt, watching her eyes roll back and her chest thrust out. I drop my lips to her breasts and attack her nipples. A whine leaves her throat, and she grips my hair to tug me closer, her cunt tightening around my fingers. I pop her nipple from my mouth and lean back, lifting my hand. I eye her cream on my fingers then meet her eyes.

"I don't see his cum, Miss Harrow," I snarl. "Did you make him wrap it? Well, I'm telling you here and now, I won't. I want deep inside that pretty cunt bare, and I want my cum so deeply inside you that it drips from you for days. Every time you try to look at someone else, you'll remember it. You'll remember what I'll do to you if you try to let them touch my pussy."

Something flashes in her eyes for a moment before she leans forward and captures my fingers, sucking them clean.

"Naughty fucking girl." My cock jerks at the sight, and when she tries to lean back, I thrust my thumb into her mouth, watching her suck it greedily. "Shit, those pretty lips are going to look so good around my cock, aren't they, Miss Harrow? Maybe I'll make you drop to your knees and apologize to my cock right now. You can suck it really good until they all know what we're doing in here and that the rock star loves to suck me off and drink my cum. They will know their perfect fucking princess is on her knees in a dirty bathroom, desperate to be fucked." I thrust my thumb in and out of her mouth, watching her eyes flare with need at the picture I'm painting.

Pulling free, I slap her pussy and pull her off the sink. She stumbles, and I push her down with my hand in her hair. "If you won't use your words, then fine. You can use your mouth for something else. Suck my cock, Miss Harrow, and make it nice and wet, and if you're a good girl, I'll fuck your tight cunt and give you what you want but couldn't find with another man."

She resists as I reach down and unbuckle my belt, moving my gun around and unzipping my trousers to free my cock. I stroke it as she watches, licking her lips as she struggles in my grip as if trying to get away when we both know she's dripping onto the tiled floor.

Painting her lips with my precum, I watch her moan and lean closer, her eyes rolling up to mine as she gives in. "Good girl, suck me deep. Suck me really good and show me how badly you want us."

Her tongue darts out, tracing the head of my cock. I don't hold back my moan, showing her my appreciation. I show her how much I want her since this goes both ways. Pleasure surges through my veins, demanding I thrust forward and bury myself in her mouth, but I know she needs to choose this or I'll walk away. I won't force her. I want her so badly, I can barely breathe, but I won't be another person who uses her. She's either with us or she's not, and I will go back to maintaining a respectful distance, even if it will give me blue balls.

From one breath to the next, she sucks the head of my cock into her hot, little mouth, swallowing me down. I thrust forward, sliding down her throat, and she opens her mouth wider. Her eyes water, but she takes me all the way back.

I almost unload then and there from the sight, but I grit my teeth and force back my release, pulling from her mouth before sliding back in. The sight of Reign Harrow on her knees for me with my cock in her mouth is almost enough to undo me.

She takes this urgency between us, this need that neither of us saw coming but can't resist, out on me. I know that's why she did it. She was tied down and she ran away to escape it, and now she's back for a fresh start and then we appeared and there's this pull between us. She's trying to resist it and fuck away the need, but too fucking bad because if I have to feel it, then so does she.

She can't run from this.

"Fuck, look at you, princess," I growl. "So fucking good. Your hot, little mouth is perfect, just like I knew it would be. You look fucking beautiful on your knees for me. Seeing my big cock in your mouth . . . Shit, Reign, just like that. Suck me hard, baby, please."

She wraps one hand around my cock and tightens her grip, punishing me. I let her. I give her everything. I let her taste this insane need I have for her.

Just when I'm about to come, I yank her off me. I want to unload in her mouth so badly, but I won't, not this time. She took that step and admitted without words that she needs me, and she gets a reward for that. If our girl wants to come, then that's what she'll get.

Spinning her once more, I bend her over the sink, slamming my hand onto her ass cheek as she moans. "Cillian, please," she whimpers, her eyes defeated as they meet mine in the mirror.

The door opens, and Astro stands there. He takes one look at us and shuts the door, leaning against it. "Don't let me stop you." He smirks at Reign.

I tilt my head in question, and he nods to let me know Dal and Raff are fine. I focus on Reign, who's rubbing her wet pussy all over my cock.

Astro needs his own revenge for what she did, so I wrap my hand around her throat and drag her up for him to see.

"Was he good, Reign?" he demands cruelly before he looks her over, seeing my marks but probably thinking they are the other man's.

Astro's expression drops, and he almost appears heartbroken. She glances away, unable to help it. I can see her thoughts, though, as she reminds herself that she doesn't owe us anything, least of all an explanation, and she doesn't, but I want her to know the consequences. She played with us, and now she has to deal with that.

"I didn't fuck him," she finally says, and I freeze.

"What?" I ask, pulling back.

She grinds her teeth, glancing between us. "I didn't fuck him. I couldn't."

I hear the truth in her words.

All this time, I've been punishing her because of my own jealousy and she said nothing. She didn't fuck him. She couldn't. She wanted to but, just like us, we're the only ones who can take this edge off. No one else. I haven't even thought of another woman since I saw her. It's pointless. There is only Reign.

"You said nothing," I snap.

"I don't owe you anything. This is my body," she retorts.

It's true, but I also think she likes our game, likes me punishing her, but that's an issue for another day.

"Fuck, Reign." I crowd her even as I see Astro's eyes ignite with need. "And I've been edging you. I'm sorry. Let me take care of you, princess. I'll give you what you need. I'll take care of you."

Dropping to my knees in apology, I lift her onto the sink and force myself between her thighs. I look up at her to see her glancing at Astro hesitantly. Gripping her thighs, I slide them wider apart, groaning at the sight of her dripping pink pussy. She's so fucking needy. I love how she reacts to us.

"Kiss her, As. She wants your lips. Don't you, princess? You want him touching you while you ride my face." She glances down at me, licking her lips. "You want him to replace the taste of that rock fucker up there. When you walk out of here, you want them to know who's been fucking you. You want them to see just how well your guards take care of you."

"Do you, beautiful? Do you want me to kiss you, to touch you while he licks your pretty pussy?" Astro murmurs.

"If you fucking don't, I'll find someone who will," she snaps, done with our games.

Chuckling, I swipe my tongue across her pussy, making her groan. Her perfect thighs tighten around my head and it's the best fucking pressure. This should be my full-time job, on my knees licking my girl's cunt. She tastes like fucking strawberries and it drives me crazy.

Her moan cuts off, and I glance up to see Astro gripping her chin and pulling her to him. Their lips meetnd my cock jerks at the sight. I love watching her come apart for us. This big, important rock star is falling into our arms and trusting us to take care of her. In reward, I circle her clit, feeling her legs jerk as cream gushes from her tight, little hole.

Humming, I wrap my lips around her clit and suck. I hear her scream into Astro's mouth as I thrust two fingers inside her, curling them to rub along those nerves that have her writhing against us. I don't relent, not until she comes around me. Her cunt tightens on my fingers as she cries out. Her thighs shake around my head, and I lick her clit as I thrust my fingers in and out, looking up to see Astro twisting her nipples as he dominates her mouth.

Lipstick covers his face and her clothes are gone.

The door rattles, so I lift my head. "Busy, come back later." I wink when Reign groans.

"Don't stop," she begs. "Please, I need you." No doubt whoever is beyond that door can hear her, but I don't care.

"I don't plan on stopping, princess. Now, come for me again, cover my face with it. Let them all see how well we fuck you." Dipping my head down, I return to torturing her clit as Astro takes her mouth and nipples. She shatters once more for us with a scream, her thighs clamping on my head until she slumps.

Sitting back, I lick my lips clean, loving her taste. I squeeze my cock to stop myself from coming and press to my feet. I nod at Astro and lift her shaking body, then I watch her eyes flutter. He sits back on the counter, and I place her on his lap.

Astro's hand comes around to cover her lips. "Shh, beautiful, we can't have anyone breaking down the door, thinking we're hurting you, because I promise we won't stop even then. They will get a good look at your guards fucking you while you beg for it."

Smirking, I move between her thighs, pressing her back as her eyes flutter shut. "Nope, eyes on me, Miss Harrow." She snarls at that, her eyes snapping open. "Good girl. You'll see exactly who is fucking you. You'll know exactly whose cock you are drenching and coming around. Do you understand me?"

She nods angrily.

"Good girl. Good girls get rewards," I promise. "But remember what I said, Reign? Bare. So open that pretty pussy and take my big dick."

I hear a scuffle outside but I ignore it. Nothing could make me stop now.

Not even Raff or Dal.

Astro spreads her thighs wider for me as she leans back into him. "Then fuck me already." Turning, she captures Astro's lips, biting them as he groans. "And then you fuck me. I want you both. I want to be unable to walk out of here. I want you to have to carry me, your cum dripping from me. That's an order."

"You heard our boss." He smirks. "You first, Cil. Fill her good and hard. Make her wet and wide for me." He nips her ear. "He's big, but I'm fucking massive, baby, and you're going to take every hard inch.

You're going to feel everything you do to me and you're going to love it."

Smirking as she groans, I drag my cock along her pussy. "He's not wrong, pretty girl, and next time, you're going to take both of us. I want to see you completely filled, every fucking hole."

They both groan as I press into her pussy, feeling her try to take me. "We are your bodyguards. It's our job to guard your body, beautiful, and to do that, we have to know every inch of it. Next time, I want you naked under the sun like the first time I saw you."

"Only if I get to see every inch of you too," she replies, rolling her hips to take every inch inside her, both of us moaning. "I want to ride you while they watch and see your red hair glistening in the sun."

Fuck.

I slam inside her, unable to resist. Astro covers her mouth as she screams, and my head falls back in ecstasy, unable to stand it. She's so fucking wet and hot, wrapped around my cock. One fucking thrust and I'm undone, nearly coming. I've never felt a more perfect body, especially one so meant for me. We fit together like a jigsaw puzzle, and I plan to use that to my advantage.

If Reign Harrow wants to see me, then she'll fucking see me.

Ripping open my shirt, I take her hand and slide it down my chest. She watches lines of red appear as she drags her nails along my skin. "Shit, you look so good with my nail marks," she purrs, clenching around me.

I've never felt more attractive than I do with Reign right now. She's one of the most beautiful people in the world and is constantly surrounded by beauty and perfection, but she looks at me like I'm the most perfect being she's ever seen. I pull out and slam back into her, watching her push back onto Astro who groans.

Her nails dig into my abs, leaving their mark, so I lean closer. "Mark me, pretty girl. Mark me all up so that when I'm not at your back, protecting you, I'll know your mark's on me, only me, only us."

Groaning, she digs her nails in harder, making me moan as I slam into her. Astro holds her tight for my assault.

"Cil," she mumbles around his hand, lifting her hips to take me.

"Shit, she feels so good," I say. "I'm not going to last."

"Look what you do to him," Astro murmurs in her ear.

I watch her eyes close in bliss as I tilt her hips higher and ram into her, making sure to hit that spot that makes her cry out.

"He's feral for you, Reign. You might have everyone on their knees, worshiping the ground you walk on, but not like us. No one would fuck you like we will and give you exactly what you need. That's what you need, isn't it, dirty girl? To be fucked hard, fast, dirty, and possessive. You want someone who's obsessed with you. Well, you got it, Reign. Now be a good girl and come for him. Make him fill you so I can get in this tight, little pussy before I say it fuck it and take your ass."

She groans. "Oh, she likes that," I say. "She's fucking clamped around me. You want him in your ass, pretty girl?"

Her channel squeezes me so tight, I can't hold back any longer. A roar leaves my throat as I slam into her so deep, she cries out. I come, filling her to the brim as she cries out, her eyes rolling back in her own pleasure.

"Fuck, Reign," I rasp when I can speak. My cock still jerks inside her tight, wet, fluttering cunt as I lean into her. "Such a good girl. Such a good fucking girl, coming for me like that and taking my cock and cum. Open your eyes."

When she does as I command, I pull from her even though I want to stay buried there forever. Her eyes drop to my glistening cock and the cum running out of her.

Grinning widely, I slide my fingers through the mess and lift them to her. "How do we taste, baby?"

She sucks on my fingers and shudders against Astro. "So good," she mumbles around them. The sight makes my softening cock harden once more. Shoving my other hand into her cunt, I force my cum back into her, not wanting to waste a drop. I want it so deep inside her, she can never get me out.

Only then do I pull my hands away from her. I smirk at As, knowing he's at the edge of his patience, trying to wait his turn and failing.

He slides her from his lap and nods at me. "My turn," he says. "Let's see how much cum you can hold."

Leaning back, I watch as Astro turns her. She faces him in the mirror, looking so fucking sexy I start to get hard again. He kicks her legs apart and grips her pussy. "Shit, he made you nice and wet for me, baby. Hang on because I need you too much to play with this pretty pussy this time." His hands grip the sink, and with his eyes locked on hers, he slams into her.

His palm covers her mouth once more, catching her scream as he fucks her. Both of them moan, her fingers gripping the sink so hard, her knuckles turn white. I turn her head and kiss her, swallowing her moans as he hammers into her. It's sloppy but fucking perfect, and when she screams into my lips, I swallow her sound of pleasure, kissing her through her release.

Astro powers into her, his face contorted in bliss and agony. I know the feeling. Nothing feels as good as Reign, and you never want it to end. Dropping my mouth to her pretty, flushed tits, I suck her nipples as she pushes back to take him. The slap of their skin is so loud, anyone outside could hear.

"Shit, I can't," he growls. "I can't hold back. Watching you fuck him and now being inside you? It's too much, Reign. I need to come."

"Then come," she commands breathlessly, rolling her hips to take him deeper as her hand anchors in my hair, shoving her breast deeper into my mouth. "Let me see you come. Please."

How could anyone deny her?

Astro can't. He slams into her with a yell, his hips jerking. His face is locked in a haze of pleasure, and she watches him the entire time, even as she shatters once more. Her eyes stay fastened on him until they both slump, her body covered in our sweat and cum.

I want to give them time to recover, but we don't have it as someone knocks on the door.

Holding her between us, I grin as I push her hair back.

"Shit," Astro mutters, making me laugh as he pulls from her body and she whimpers. Turning on the faucet, I wash her face and brush her hair to tame it. After I fix her clothes, I wash my own face. I might want to wear her lipstick marks, but I know I'm not allowed to.

It's her life. I won't upset her or use her for anything.

Once we are as acceptable as we're going to get, I lean in and kiss her softly. "Let's take you home, pretty girl."

Astro smacks her ass, making her whimper. "You can tell Raff you seduced us."

"Me?" she scoffs. "I'm innocent."

"Not a fucking chance." I laugh as I head to the door. "You don't even know what the word innocent means, Reign Harrow."

NINETEEN

I head to the floor I know she got off on. I even know the room. I wasn't letting Miss Harrow disappear without knowing everything. I also know the man she's with.

Despite my jealousy and anger, I keep my expression calm, but Astro, not so much. We stop at the door to the suite, and I know Dal is here. I should have watched him more closely.

He basically told me how he feels about her. The fact that he feels anything at all is shocking. Unlike the others, I know Dal's true depth and coldness. He would be classed as a psychopath, yet he feels with her and that makes him dangerous, especially toward a threat like Trav, who is with Reign.

The door is slightly ajar, and I step inside with my gun out as I head into the bedroom. I take in the scene in a second, my training kicking in as Astro protects my back at the door.

The bed is a mess, and I ignore my flare of fury and focus on Dal. He has a knife to Trav's neck, and I see a drop of blood as well as a black eye, but he's not dead yet so that's good. He's scared but also angry. If he knew just who Dal was and what he was capable of, he would be fucking terrified. Even I would hesitate to go up against Dal, but I have no choice. Reign would never forgive us, and for some reason, I don't want to hurt her, even if she was up here fucking this rock star instead of us.

"Astro, go back down to Cillian," I order without sparing him a glance.

He hesitates, looking between Dal and me before moving away as silently as we slipped into the room. I know Dal won't react well if Astro hears what I have to say, and this is between Dal and me. I'm in charge, and if Dal can't remain professional and calm, I will remove him or all of us from this job. I won't let Dal kill innocent people simply because of these new, confusing feelings. I will always protect him, even if he doesn't understand why.

"Dal, release him."

The man is smart. He kneels with his hands on his head, and although his eyes are wide and terrified, he stays silent and doesn't move, as if he's facing a predator, which he is. Dal glances at the rumpled bed, his nostrils flaring, and I swear internally as I shift to block his view of it.

"Dal," I warn, "if you do this, you will lose her." I try to appeal to his careful side, but it seems to have fled when faced with these new, intense emotions. "She will never forgive you. She clearly likes this man, and from what I've read, they are friends. If she finds out you killed him simply for touching her, she'll kick you out of her life for good. Right now, you have access to her, the access you need. Do this and you'll be in jail. Not even I can protect you from the consequences of killing a rock star."

The man glances at Dal. "Look—"

Dal presses the knife firmer against his skin, drawing more blood.

"I wouldn't speak," I hiss. "Dal, think about it. Do you want to lose her?" I know he doesn't care about prison—hell, we have all been in worse places than some cushy cell—but he'd be trapped without access to the one person he clearly wants. I see him hesitate, thank God.

I don't drop the gun, but I won't kill him. He's my brother, even if he never admits it or feels the same way, but I can wound him, knock him back, and give the man time to escape. I'd have to bribe him not to speak on this and get Reign up here to calm Dal down, but it's the only plan I can come up with.

"We didn't have sex," Trav says very carefully, and we both look at him. "She called me to hook up like we used to sometimes."

Dal snarls and I wince.

"But we didn't. We kissed, but it felt wrong. I'm . . . I'm in love with someone else, and she likes someone else too—obviously you since you're here threatening to kill me for even being near her. Reign is my friend, I would never hurt her, but I promise I didn't touch her. Our clothes stayed on. We kissed once, and then we had food as soon as we realized how wrong it felt."

"Are you lying?" Dal says calmly, too fucking calmly.

He shakes his head. "Check room service, check the bed or even my phone."

Dal hesitates but slowly releases the man.

"You move, you die," he whispers, and Trav nods as Dal moves away.

I watch as Dal walks to the bed, stripping it back and searching for any signs of sex. When he finds none, he moves to the trash to check for condoms, eyeing the man's shoes on the floor. Dal calls down, checks room service, and then picks up the man's phone. "Passcode," he demands.

"2325," he mutters. "Spells Beck."

Dal raises a brow but types it in and seems to scroll through something. "The same Beck you're texting here?"

He nods.

"Who is she?" I ask. If he's cheating on our girl, I'll kill him, even if they aren't together.

"She's our new lead singer," he answers. "She's totally off limits, but it doesn't stop me from wishing though. That's why I agreed to meet Reign tonight, to try and forget. It didn't work."

"She's jealous," Dal tells him as he drops the phone. "She likes you too. Fine, you won't die tonight." He puts the blade away, and I relax. "But if you try to touch Reign again, I'll hunt you down, understand?"

Dal crouches before him. "I've killed many people, Mr. Wright, and I won't hesitate to end you. Not even Reign could protect you from me. Do we understand one another?"

A pale Trav nods, and Dal moves over to me. I put the gun away and start to follow him out, unsure how the hell to deal, with this when Trav calls out, "I might not have your skills, but if you hurt Reign, I will make you regret it. How do you know Beck likes me?"

"It's a Saturday night and she's at home texting you and jealous you aren't with her. She likes you, idiot," Dal mutters. When I shut the door, he nods at me. "I like him. He's protective of Reign." That's it. That's all he says as I gawk, unsure how the hell to proceed. He makes that decision when he heads to the elevator.

"We'll talk about this later," I snap.

He simply faces forward as if he didn't hear me. "She didn't sleep with him."

"And?" I mutter.

"That means something." He nods. "It means she's in this as much as we are."

Fucking hell. I can't even believe I'm having this conversation with him. "Later," is all I say, knowing I need time to come up with a reasonable argument to explain why he can't do that kind of shit. Usually, he would just follow my orders unless he thought it would get us killed, but this time he's fighting me and I know why.

Reign fucking Harrow.

I knew she would be trouble, but even as I think that, a smile curves my lips. He's right though. She didn't sleep with him, and that means something. I just don't know what.

I can't stop the satisfaction I feel, knowing she's going to have to come to us for relief if she wants it. I might be hired to be her security guard, but I'm only a man.

A man who wants Reign Harrow more than I want my next breath.

Storming downstairs with Dal in tow, I curse when I see the empty lobby. The paparazzi are mingling outside the hotel, no doubt alerted to her presence, but I don't see Reign, Astro, or Cillian.

Where the fuck are they?

I search the lobby before hurrying to the reception desk, where a woman sits primly in her suit.

"Have you seen Miss Harrow?" I ask the receptionist, panicking. Astro and Cillian are gone too, but anything could have happened. Dal is searching behind me.

She blushes and lowers her head. "Um, I saw her go into the bathroom with one of her security guards. It was a while ago."

Fucking hell.

I pull out some bills and hand them over. "There was a threat. It was for her safety," I lie, and she nods, clearly not believing me, but she takes the bills. "If this gets out to anyone, I will remember your name, Caitlin," I warn, reading her tag, and she pales.

I move away from the desk and follow the signs for the restroom. There's a men's bathroom at the beginning of the corridor, but farther down is a wooden door for females.

I twist the handle, but it's locked.

"Busy!"

There's a giggle and a moan—one I know better than my own voice.

Reign.

Motherfucker. I try to slam it open, but Dal stops me, yanking me away. "This is how we keep her. You stopped me up there, and I'm stopping you here. Get over it."

I have no choice but to turn my back to the wall and protect the door. He's right. I can't stop this. They are consenting adults and it's her choice. Instead, I have to stand there and listen to her moans and the slap of their bodies. My cock is hard, and I glare at anyone who comes too close.

I'll protect her from out here. I won't let anyone see this.

I can't even be too angry about it. She's a siren and even I couldn't resist her, so how could they? A part of me knew when I left them alone that this would happen. It was inevitable. I just wish it were in private without so many prying eyes. It's our job to protect her reputation.

Time passes slowly, and my cock is uncomfortably hard the entire time as I hear them fucking until it's finally over. I hear water running, laughing, and mumbling, and a few minutes later, the door unlocks.

I turn as they open the door. All three have wild hair and are breathing heavily, and they all look way too fucking satisfied. "Have fun, Miss Harrow?" I snap.

She smirks, not the least bit bothered, and shuffles out. Astro and Cillian look far too smug, not even unsettled by my glare.

"Out back so no one sees you," I mutter.

"Nope, front door." She goes to walk away and I grab her.

"You look freshly fucked, Miss Harrow, and there are cameras," I warn.

She smiles, lowering her voice. "They will think it's from him, but we'll all know it's from you." Patting my chest, she steps past once more. The woman is going to drive me to madness, even if I feel a twinge of satisfaction from them seeing our girl and knowing it was from us.

"Get in formation around her, straight to the car." I don't let her argue with that. I press my hand to her back and guide her out the door, gritting my teeth against the flashes that instantly blind me. She smiles and waves, winking at the shouted questions.

"Reign, who did you meet here tonight?"

"Reign, are you seeing someone?"

"Reign, some think you're dating Trav from Dead Ringers. Confirm or deny?"

I elbow some of them out of the way, and Astro runs to the car door, opening it before she slides inside. I follow after her. Astro slides in after me, while Cillian and Dal get in the front, and then we are off.

I open my mouth to reprimand them for being so careless when it comes to her security, but she crawls onto my lap. "Miss Harrow—" I begin, but then her lips are on mine and I swallow my words, gripping her hips and kissing her back. When she pulls away, she smirks. "Reign."

"Have you noticed that I'm always Miss Harrow when you're trying to be professional, but then I'm Reign when your dick gets attention?"

I try to remain professional. "Tonight was reckless—"

"Kind of my whole vibe, big guy," she purrs, leaning into me. "We locked the door."

"And if someone got in and took a picture?" I challenge.

"There are worse pictures of me out there." She shrugs, and I grip her tighter.

"I don't care, not on my watch. You want your privacy, Miss Harrow, Reign, then I will give it to you. We will protect you from everything, but you have to listen to us."

"If that means not having fun or fucking where and when I want, then I won't listen, Raff. When are you going to realize that? Plus, we both know you are an exhibitionist and love watching me be fucked." She reaches between us and grips my hard cock, proving her point.

"Miss Harrow—"

She leans in, rubbing me to distraction, and my eyes almost cross. "I wonder if you would call me that with your cock in my throat."

Fucking hell.

She's enough to tempt the fucking devil. "Reign, I'm trying to keep you safe. Your mental health as well," I admit weakly, thrusting into her hand.

"And I appreciate that, but I'm a big girl who can make her own decisions. This isn't my first rodeo, Raff. I can take it. I know what to do and when to do it. I will make mistakes, but you will be there, so stop being so uptight and learn to have some fun."

"He doesn't know how. Why don't you show him, beautiful?" Astro suggests.

"Reign," I rasp, not sure if I'm begging for her to stop or for her to continue.

"Raffiel," she mocks, gripping my cock tighter. "Enough talking. I'm bored and want to play."

She drops to her knees in the moving car. I should stop her, and I had things to say, but it all disappears when she unzips me and pulls out my hard length, sealing her pretty lips around my cock.

I should have known that Reign Harrow always gets what she wants, and that includes me.

My careful control flees at the sight of her big, bright eyes locked on me while her pouty lips carefully wrap around the thick head of my cock.

Fuck.

I slide my fingers into her luscious strands, gripping them tight and pressing her down my cock as she whimpers. "Fine, you want to make it up to me? You want to suck me? Then do it, baby. Show me what you did to my men that made them forget their duty. Show me how much of a good slut you are for me."

She moans loudly around my length as I relax back into the sea. I lift my hips to bury myself deeper in her mouth, trying to take over and remain in control. She grips my base harder, to the point of pain, as one of those stunning eyes winks at me, and then she shows me just how out of control I truly am when it comes to her.

She seals her lips around my tip until I groan. My head hits the seat, but even then, I can't take my eyes off her.

She's just so damn beautiful.

Smirking, she pulls back, lapping at my precum with an appreciative sound before sliding my cock along her tongue as I watch.

Fuck!

My baby teases me, tortures me, and I'd tell her anything she wants to know in this moment as long as she never stopped. "Please," I whisper.

She hears, her eyes tightening in pleasure, and then she drops all the way down my length, taking me to the back of her throat. She hums around me as I shudder, pleasure exploding through me. My hands tighten in her hair and pull her up and off. I try to shove her back down but she resists, and only when I stop tugging does she carry on.

My heart races, and my breathing is loud in the silent car as her head bobs up and down. She takes my length all the way back with expert sucking, her tight, hot cavern making me lose control until I fuck her throat wildly.

"Shit, she's insatiable," Astro growls. "Aren't you, beautiful?"

She pops her mouth off my cock, licking at her lips as I groan, thrusting into her hand. "When it comes to you all? Yes. I want you everywhere I can get you."

"Don't stop," I bite out, the order harsh.

She looks up at me, arching one eyebrow, and waits patiently, fluttering her eyelashes.

"Please, baby," I ask, not ashamed to beg when it comes to her.

"Good boy," she purrs, leaning down and swallowing every inch of my length as I cry out.

"Fuck," I shout as I hammer into her mouth. She lets me. The pleasure becomes too much, and it washes through me like a tidal wave as I come, hollering her name.

My cum splashes down her throat as she whimpers.

I try to pull back, but she doesn't let me, sealing her mouth around me and drinking every single drop as I groan. When I slump, she finally relents, sliding her mouth up my cock and licking me clean as I watch, slumped in my seat.

How the fuck am I supposed to survive Reign Harrow?

"Shit, you can do that anytime. It stopped us from getting told off." Cillian grins at her. "Using your body against him? Why didn't I think of that?" he teases.

"It wouldn't work," I mutter, swallowing since my voice is hoarse. "Only for her."

That makes her grin as she sits back, sucking on her thumb as I watch.

Grunting, I force myself to focus. "Miss Harrow—"

She groans. "Raffiel," she counters, making me smirk.

"Just, next time let me protect you, okay?" That's what it comes down to, and it's more than just my job. It's a need to protect her from the world, from the vultures that circle such an amazing soul and peck it clean. "At least let me do that? I'm not asking you to change, but to let me in enough to be at your side. Can you do that?"

She eyes me, probably reading more into my words than I would like. "I'll try," she replies, and I feel like shouting in victory.

I've been to war, and I've assassinated people, but I have never felt such a victory as getting Reign Harrow to trust me, even if it's just a little.

I don't know what that says about me or us, but I couldn't care less. Not with her smiling at me like I'm her savior.

TWENTY

"So what is the schedule for the day?" Raffiel asks.

I had been so exhausted when we got back last night, I climbed into bed and slept the full night through, all alone, but then again, I'm not alone, am I? I can feel their eyes on me through the cameras they installed. One day, I'm going to ask them if they watch me change, but not right now in front of my team. They flutter around the dressing room, getting my stuff organized.

"We'll head to the studio. Hair, makeup, and clothes will be done on-site." Sometimes I forget they haven't been around me forever, since they simply just fit so well. I'm used to these kinds of appearances, but for them, it's an unknown, and I'm learning they hate unknowns. They want to control everything from start to finish. It's sweet. "We'll be escorted to the set, where taping will take about an hour or two, and then we can leave. There is a live audience there as well. It will be interview style so you can't be there."

"And security?" he questions, his eyes narrowed as I lean back, sucking on my lollipop. He's probably angry because I only told him I had this interview booked an hour ago. Oops. Old habits die hard, I guess.

"Plenty." I shrug.

"Miss Harrow," he admonishes.

"Mr. Raffiel," I mock, making Astro chuckle as he watches us argue.

"You two argue like an old married couple," Cillian remarks, and we both turn to glare at him. He holds his hands up with a grin. "Just saying."

"We can't protect you—"

"If you don't know every detail," I finish for him, and he glares at me harder before stomping away, muttering about annoying women.

"I think that means he likes me." I wink at them as my team takes everything to the car.

"Oh, baby, he more than likes you," Astro says as he puts his mug in the sink. Leaning closer, he drops his voice. "If he didn't, he wouldn't care. We've had plenty of celeb jobs, and not once did he give a shit about changing schedules or unknown factors. Not like this. He cares, Reign." He winks as he wanders away.

Well, shit.

Now I feel bad. Leaving them to clean up, I head out to find Raff, my slippers sliding easily across the floor. I'm warm and comfy in my matching sweats and sweatshirt set—the best type of outfit to get ready in—but when I step into the room, he eyes me like I'm wearing nothing. He has his phone to his ear and I wait, leaning against the door after I shut it, giving us privacy.

"Thank you." He hangs up, eyeing me as if he's waiting for a fight. We haven't known each other long, but we always butt heads. It's our way and I love it, but I don't want to piss him off when he's only trying to protect me. I was in the wrong, and I'll own it.

"I'm sorry." I pout my lips. "I should have told you and given you time to prepare." His eyes narrow as if he's searching for the trick.

I walk closer, dragging my hand down his suit and stopping just above his cock. His eyes flare and his mouth parts. Fuck, I love the effect I have on him, even when he's angry and in work mode.

"I truly am. I'll try to do better. Want to have angry sex?"

He barks out a laugh, seeming surprised at the sound. "You never have to be sorry, Reign." He sighs, and every time he calls me that instead of Miss Harrow, I do a victory dance inside. "It's my job to know everything. I called the studio and informed them of our arrival and spoke to them about security logistics. Everything is taken care of so don't worry." He cups the back of my head and kisses me softly. "If I didn't worry about you being late or them overhearing, I would have bent you over that kitchen counter and tanned your ass red for being a brat."

"Don't promise shit like that. I'll be wet on national television," I purr as he groans.

"Trouble, you are so much fucking trouble," he growls, brushing his lips along mine as there's a knock on the door.

"Time to go." It's Dal.

"Behave today," he murmurs against my lips. "If you're a good girl, I'll reward you later."

"Promises, promises," I tease as I slide my hand over his hard cock. "When you're watching me on TV, remember you could have had me screaming this morning but didn't." I wink and head to the door, but he catches me, slamming me into the wood.

"Don't taunt me, Miss Harrow." His voice is a growl. "Next time you want me, just tell me. I'll slip into that ridiculously big bed and wake you with my tongue in your cunt."

"Now, I can get on board with that," I murmur, pushing my ass back to tease him. His hand slides between me and the door, slipping beneath the waistband of my pants and lower until he cups my bare pussy.

"You're not wearing underwear," he hisses in my ear, his hand gripping me harder as I move my hips.

"Nope." I grin.

"Fuck, now I'm going to walk around all day knowing that. I won't be able to concentrate."

"Maybe you should fuck it out of your system."

"What did I say about behaving, Miss Harrow?"

"I am. You're the one who has me pinned to the door, feeling me up," I purr, rolling into his hand.

"True, I can't seem to resist around you," he mutters, but he doesn't stop touching me, thank fuck. "Maybe you're right. Maybe I should take the edge off. We can't have you this wet all day. It wouldn't do well as your bodyguard to know you want something and I haven't provided it." His voice is silky. Shit, he's flipped the switch and I'm helpless.

No one plays my body like Raffiel.

My head bangs against the door and I'm lost for words, just like every time he touches me. His fingers stroke my wet pussy as he speaks.

"Raff?" Dal murmurs through the door.

"I'll be a few minutes. Miss Harrow has something to discuss regarding very important things. Isn't that right, Miss Harrow?" His fingers slam into me, making me moan. "Oh yes, I won't be long at all," he calls.

The bastard.

"Miss Harrow, the time," one of my team calls.

Raff twists his fingers inside me, adding a third and making me swallow back my scream. "Better answer them, Miss Harrow, before they open the door." He licks the shell of my ear then bites down. "Because I won't stop. I'll let them see me giving this bratty pussy just what it wants. Isn't that right?"

"Yes!" I cry out before clearing my throat as he laughs. I try to kick back, but he pins my leg, thrusting his fingers in deeper. "I'll be right there."

My voice is off, but I don't care.

I bite down on my lip as I tilt my hips, taking his fingers as he fucks me with them. "Good girl," he growls, turning his hand until he's rubbing my clit. "Good girls get to come, so come, Miss Harrow. Stain my fingers so I taste you all day."

Fuck!

I detonate, flying off the edge with his words and touch. I come so fast and hard, he reaches around and covers my mouth, muting my scream as my cunt pulses. He strokes me through it, barely even breathing heavily in my ear.

"Good girl," he purrs. "That's it, ride out every last drop. Give it to me. I want to drip with your cum."

Fuck.

I slump into the door with a thud, and I feel his grin against my neck as he pulls from my body and deftly rights my pants before patting my ass. Turning on shaking legs, I eye him as he steps back.

His face is cold and empty, businesslike. "Are you ready now, Miss Harrow?"

The satisfied gleam in his eyes has me straightening.

I glare at him and open the door, smiling sweetly at my waiting team. Some have knowing looks in their eyes but I ignore them. They are loyal, or as loyal as you can be in this industry.

"Ready?" I ask as I pull on my shades and head outside to the car.

As soon as we're inside, I look out of the window, ignoring them all. A noise has me glancing over to see Raff looking at me, and when I meet his gaze, he sucks his fingers into his mouth. I flip him off, and he grins smugly.

It's a good thing he's pretty.

Luckily, there were only a few paparazzi and fans waiting outside of the studio. It hasn't been announced who is on today so I quickly sneak by. Once inside the dressing room I'm escorted to with my name on a plaque on the door, my team gets to work.

Raff stations himself and Dal outside, while Astro and Cillian are in here with me, watching the team's every move. I aimlessly scroll through my phone as my makeup and hair are done. We're going for a wavy hair look, with pieces braided back and charms hanging from them. The makeup will be everyday glam. I already picked my outfit, and as usual, they are working around it.

I'm on Instagram, replying to comments and messages from fans, smiling widely at their enthusiasm. They probably think it's my social media team, and it usually is, but sometimes I love to connect this way with them to remind myself that this is why I do it. I love feeling their support and hearing their stories, like the ways I've helped or touched them.

Dramatic, but music can save lives.

It saved mine, after all.

I accidentally slide to the message request section and groan at the hate I see there. Usually, the team is good at blocking it before I see it, but some messages still slip through. I don't even open them anymore. I instantly delete them. I don't have the time or energy for hate anymore. I'm determined to enjoy my life and not let anyone bring me down. Anyone who is willing to send hate messages or emails, hiding behind a keyboard, is not worth my time. It also usually has more to do with them than me. Remaining silent sometimes speaks louder than words so I delete hundreds, only to stop at one.

It's from two days ago, and I don't know why I open it, but the messages are weird.

I LOVE IT WHEN YOU SWIM AT NIGHT.

I MISSED YOUR FACE SO MUCH.

THEY SHOULDN'T BE IN YOUR HOUSE. WHO ARE THEY?

THEY ARE KEEPING YOU FROM ME.

Fucking weird. I instantly delete and block the account, but a shiver goes through me. I don't have much privacy in my life, but it mentioned my home, my swimming . . . I mean, yeah, they could have seen it in interviews. That has to be it.

Not reading too much into it, I drop the phone, done responding for the day, and ignore all other messages, especially those lingering texts from my old friends who want to reconnect.

"All done."

I nod in thanks as I check over their work. "I love it, thank you." I smile at Mindy who did my makeup and Sam who did my hair. When they slip away, I step behind the privacy curtain and change into the jumpsuit. It's black with red paint splattered across it, and the high neck is covered in a fur trim. My heels complete the outfit. It leaves my arms on display, so I add lots of rings and bracelets before stepping out to eye my work.

The lights are bright in the dressing room, with four mirrors at the dressing tables and big, comfy chairs that can be lifted or lowered. There are two sofas and a small table, along with some paintings and plants to make it look homey and a mini fridge with a TV above it to watch the audience and other guests. It's nice. I remember when I first started and was interviewed in some kid's basement. I guess I've come a long way. Sometimes, I forget, others I'm just so grateful to be here.

Not for the money or fame, but because it means I get to do what I love most—make music and get it out there to people who need the melodies in their hearts to take them away, even for a moment.

Good and bad, they feel it all with me, and that is why I perform. The rest? The rest is icing on the cake.

The door opens and I turn to see Raff, and beside him is a runner with a clipboard and a headset nervously smiling at me. "We'll be ready for you in ten minutes, Reign. I'll come back to escort you."

"Thank you." I smile, and he stares as if dazzled before mumbling out, "Thank you," and backing away.

"Stop bedazzling the workers, Miss Harrow," Astro teases.

I wink at him and face forward, adding some hoops to my ears and looking over the outfit. It's lowkey for me. This is my first public interview since I reappeared, so I wanted to show the changes without making it look like I was pushing it in their faces. Usually, my manager would be here, but I think he's genuinely scared I would turn him away. It's nice not having him here, reading off my schedule for the next ten years.

I'm almost free.

"You look stunning," Cillian says, and I look myself over once more, searching for anything they can use against me. Any stray hair or misplaced word will be picked apart. It's all a carefully crafted game, but luckily, I'm the master at it now.

"You think?" I ask, suddenly feeling a little nervous.

He and Astro get to their feet and stand behind me in the mirror. The big bastards make me look tiny and overdressed, but the heat, want, and desire pouring from them make me stand up taller. I don't know why I care so much about their opinions, but I do.

"I know," Astro replies. "You look . . ." He trails off, running his eyes over me. "You look like every person will either want to be you or fuck you. I know which one I'd pick."

Laughing, I hand them my bag just as the door opens again. "Are we ready, Reign?" the blushing runner asks.

"Absolutely." I smile brightly at him and head into the white hallway that will lead us to the studio. The runner hurries to catch up, directing me even though I've been here before. The guys surround me until we reach the wings.

"Got it," the runner says into his mic and then smiles at me. "Okay, Reign, the music will cue you in. Wave and smile and walk, and then sit in the chair and your interview will begin. We'll ask you the questions you approved and then you mentioned performing a song."

I nod, and he claps in excitement.

"Awesome, everyone will love it. Have fun."

I blow out a deep breath and school my features into a fake smile.

"Knock them dead, babe," Astro murmurs, and when the music starts, I step onto the stage. The lights blind me, but I flutter my lashes and wave and smile at the audience. Their cheers blow my eardrums. I guess they are a little excited. Laughing, I wave harder, trying to remember every face, every fan, but there are just too many of them. Once at the sofa, I wave once more before sitting.

Jim, the presenter, grins at me as they let the crowd continue, and I laugh, crossing my legs and waving and winking into the camera. The music and crowd finally quiet enough for us to talk.

"Well, Reign, quite the welcoming committee." He laughs, sitting behind his desk next to me.

I throw back my head and fake laugh. "Quite." I nod. "I guess you guys missed me?" I cup my ear, urging them on, and they call out to me and Jim, and I laugh.

"Alright, alright, Reign, thank you so much for coming today. I know everyone is very excited to see you once more, and we can't thank you enough for sparing the time to talk to us."

"I always have time for you, Jim," I purr, and his grin widens. Out of all the interviewers I've met, I genuinely like him. He's nice, he never crosses boundaries, and even though he asks prying questions, I know it's his job, and he always does his best to make everyone comfortable.

When I was underage, he never once touched me or took advantage, not like some interviewers who would manhandle me. That's why I chose him.

"Well, I'm very grateful for that and so are the fans, aren't you?" The crowd cheers again. "Okay, Reign, I have to ask . . . Where have you been?"

"Ah, that would be spilling secrets." The crowd boos as I laugh. "But I can say I took some time away for myself." The crowd sighs. "I think I needed it," I admit honestly and look out into the crowd. My fans deserve some form of an answer. They are the reason I am where I am, after all. "It was good to be alone without cameras or expectations. I got to be me again, not the rock star or the woman the reps were promoting. I got to be Reign, and in doing so, I found myself again. I found my peace, and with it, I found my music."

The crowd cheers.

"Does this have anything to do with your breakup with Tucker?" Jim asks, and I can clearly see that he doesn't want to.

"I mean, it was at the same time, I'll be honest." I wince a little. "But I wish Tucker nothing but the best. His band is doing amazing, and I'm very proud of him. I hold no hard feelings. Sometimes, things happen and people grow apart. People you thought would be forever disappear. It doesn't mean I'm not grateful for our relationship and everything we shared. I still care for Tucker."

"Any chance of you two getting back together?" he asks.

I simply laugh as the crowd boos and cheers.

"Okay, moving on, you mentioned your music. I think we all saw the impromptu show you held, which put the world into an uproar. Does this mean there is going to be a new album?"

I appreciate how quickly he moved on, giving me what I want to talk about—my music, not my relationship. After all, I don't want to be known for who I am and what I am capable of, not just for who I date or fuck.

"It does. Two, actually." I grin at the audience who screams.

"Two?" Jim asks, gasping.

"Two. What can I say? I've been very busy. There will be some amazing collaborations with other artists whom I respect and look up to, and I've found my sound again. Back to my roots. Rock and roll. Love and passion."

"We can't wait, but a little birdy told me that we might be able to have a sneak peek today?"

"I mean, would you like one?" I ask, hamming it up for the cameras.

"What do we think?" Jim asks the crowd.

The crowd goes wild, and I sit back, playing it on. "I don't know. You don't seem sure."

The screams echo through the building as Jim and I laugh. "I think that's a yes," he says.

Standing, I head over to the little stage on the left. It's just me, the band, and my microphone. Clearing my throat, I smile at the crowd. "All the songs in my new albums are about falling in love with yourself. They are about pain. They are about my life and situations everyone has been through, and I hope by ripping myself bare, you can heal with me too."

The music starts and I close my eyes. Jack and I have finished most of the first album, and we have the other artists confirmed and coming in over the next few weeks, but this song was the first one I wrote when I left. I actually scribbled it on napkins at rest stops on my drive.

It has my whole heart in it.

Every flawed emotion.

Every wrong thought I can't control.

It's me.

"Headlights bounce across my face, tears going to waste, there's no one here to see me cry. I guess that makes it not real. My heart is gone, left behind, but as the road stretches out, so does my hope. My anger. I miss you like a child misses a toy, but I can't love you and love me, so I said goodbye. I walked away from my life . . ."

I pour my soul into the song, and I let myself grieve for what could have been, for the woman I was.

As the lights come back on, the last note dragging out, I open my eyes. "Thank you," I murmur as I step back, and for a moment, the silence is deafening. I'm nervous because this is the most raw my music has ever been. Look between the lyrics and you'll find my truth, my story.

The crowd suddenly surges to their feet, clapping and screaming, and I smile the first real smile of the day. I take my seat once more, feeling more relaxed and happier.

Today, I was reminded of why I do this, why I sing. It's not for the applause, but that connection—the tears I saw in people's eyes and the truth in their actions.

It resonates with them.

It connects us, and for a moment, as music filled the room, we were one person.

The rest of the interview goes fairly quickly. We play some games and I answer more questions, and then I head into the audience to take pictures and sign autographs before waving and heading backstage. As soon as I do, I drop my shoulders, but my smile stays in place.

The last interview I did was like a rapid-fire inquisition, trying to trip me up and make me the bad guy. Clips still circulate of edited footage, trying to make me into a horrible person, but this was good.

It was great.

Another fear conquered.

Another challenge completed.

Now it's time to finish the music.

TWENTY-ONE

The dressing room door shuts, and I slump back on the sofa. I left the guys outside, needing a moment. Interviews like this take it out of me and I never know why, other than I feel like I'm pretending to be another person. It used to eat me up, but now I know better, and I can't let guilt rule my life. If I were a man, they would call me smart, a forward thinker, a boss, so fuck guilt. I'd rather enjoy the time I have on this earth, and I know better than anyone how quickly it can all be taken away.

My hand drifts to my hip, but I quickly snatch it away when the door opens. I expect Raff or even someone from the show, but Dal stands in the doorway. He shuts it behind him and stares at me. The intensity of Dal's gaze always puts me on high alert. Even without words, I can see what he's thinking.

He's all raw masculinity and strength, and right now, it's all directed at me.

"Everything okay?" I ask, my voice breathless.

Without a word, he heads my way, not stopping until I tilt my head back to meet his eyes. A gasp leaves my lips when his hand darts out and grips my chin. His thumb sweeps over my lower lip as I swallow.

"Dal?" I whisper, watching his eyes blow at hearing his name on my tongue.

"Your song," he murmurs. "I heard every word. I felt every word. You aren't just a singer, Reign; you're a master. You have a way of reaching into someone's head and heart and ripping them out. You make them feel everything. How do you do that? How do you make me feel anything at all? Every breath you take is like a hammer against the organ in my chest. I worry about you every moment of every day. Are you hungry? Are you tired? Angry? Sad? Are you lonely? Is that crack going to trip you? Are you going to fumble? It's exhausting, but I can't seem to care, not with you looking at me like that."

"Like what?" I ask.

"Like I am everything you have been waiting for, because, Reign, you are everything I didn't even know I was searching for and I'm tired of trying to figure out why. You sang for them, for you, and now you're going to sing in here for me."

"I—"

His hand covers my mouth and my eyes widen. "I don't want you to fake it, not with me." My heart stops at the truth in his eyes. He sees into me. "When you sing in here, it will be because you can't do anything but."

I don't even know what to say to that. Luckily, he doesn't expect a response. Something links Dal and me together, and he knows without words what I'm feeling. My exhaustion quickly turns to desire for him. I've wanted him since the moment I saw him standing above me, when he hauled me out of the pool. Unlike the others, whom I can laugh and joke with, there's always a knowing look in Dal's eyes, one I avoid because he sees too much, but right now, I couldn't prevent this any more than I could stop the music in my soul.

Maybe it's time to start feeling again.

My tongue darts out and licks his thumb, and it's the only response he needs. He drops to his knees before me.

His eyes feast on me as his hands slide my outfit up, exposing my legs. His gaze drops to my skin, and it's only then I realize I was holding my breath, and it comes out in a pant as I suck in much needed air.

Dal has this magnetism about him, an air of danger I can't help but crave, and with it all directed toward me, I'm helpless.

"Do you know how many times I have imagined you spread open for me?" he murmurs, his voice soft and reverent. "I have never given anyone a second thought, but you drive me crazy, Reign. You're all I think about every waking second. Every time you speak, I imagine what your lips feel like. Every time you move, I imagine how you will move with me buried inside you." My eyes widen. "I can't sleep, can't eat. All I can do is think about you. My whole world revolves around you. You own me completely. My body is yours, but first, I want to enjoy you. I want to do all the depraved things I have imagined."

Jesus fucking Christ.

My pussy actually pulses at his words, leaving me wet just from a dirty promise.

"Will you let me, Reign?" he purrs, dragging his nose along my thigh, down my calf, and up my foot until his eyes meet mine once more. "Will you let me act out all my depraved, sick fantasies on you?"

"Yes." I clear my throat since it's just a whisper. "Yes, fuck yes."

He could ask me to bend over in the middle of the stage and I would. I would do anything to have him.

His tongue follows the path his nose took until his teeth dig into the thick edge of my thigh. The sharp pain makes me cry out, even as I throw my other leg over his shoulder, waiting to see what he will do next.

He licks the bite mark before moving lower and striking again, biting so hard, it makes me whimper, and when he pulls back, his teeth imprint is very clear to see.

Dal is always hard to read. He's so cold and calm, but right now, his eyes blaze with a fire that leaves me burning. How someone could contain such desire is beyond me, and it's all aimed at me.

"I wonder if you would cry if I made you bleed," he muses. "But that's for next time." My heart stutters, but he doesn't notice as he cuts my jumpsuit away and then settles back between my thighs, leaving me open and bare as the expensive outfit falls in shreds around us.

I didn't even see a knife. He was that quick, and the sharp edge of danger only has me pulling him closer with my thighs, wanting what he's offering.

His tongue sweeps up my thigh again until he reaches my pussy, and his teeth close around my thong. He jerks his head to the side like a feral animal, and I gasp at the sharp sting as it snaps. Continuing to watch me, he stuffs my panties into his mouth, groaning as he licks them before pulling them away and grabbing my thigh and arm. I blink in confusion as he moves deftly, and when he sits back, my left thigh is tied to my arm, leaving me spread for him.

"Keep that up there, Reign," he commands. "Otherwise, I'll be forced to punish you."

Biting my bottom lip, I lift my hips, needing attention. When his eyes drop to my exposed, wet pussy, he makes a feral noise that has me moaning. I know he's going to fuck me so dirty, and I can't wait. The anticipation is driving me crazy.

There are no words after that, his usual silence filled with grunts as he holds my thighs prisoner, spreading them so wide, it hurts. My cream drips to the leather below as his mouth finally touches my cunt.

He isn't hesitant or loving—no, Dal fucking attacks me, using his tongue as a weapon. He shoves it inside me, making me moan before he lashes my clit. His feral, erratic attacks leave me on edge, unable to predict what he will do next.

His thick, scarred fingers thrust into me, splitting me open as he forces three in. The sharp pain turns to a burn of pleasure as he rubs my throbbing clit, until I'm lifting my hips and forcing them deeper. My eyes close and my head falls back at his attack.

Pleasure burns through me, and I'm panting so hard, I feel my heart thundering. Dal forces another finger deep inside me before I feel his other hand prodding at my ass.

I open my mouth to protest, but a scream slips free as he shoves two fingers in my ass. "There won't be an inch of you I leave unclaimed, Reign, just like you have claimed every inch of me."

It's a threat, a promise that I can't even deny as he fucks both my holes mercilessly, his saliva from his open mouth dripping to my pussy and sliding down. He seals his lips around my clit again and sucks, and I come so hard and so unexpectedly, I seize up with a yell.

My entire body shakes and contracts as I squirt around his fingers. He fucks my ass and pussy the entire time, stretching them to the point of pain until my leg kicks.

When I slump, he pulls his fingers free, making me mewl at the pain. With his dark eyes on me, he sucks his fingers from my pussy clean, shoving his pants down and circling his cock like an offering.

My eyes widen at the sight of him. "No! No fucking way!" I try to scoot backwards and get away, but I'm still weak from coming so hard. He captures my kicking leg and drags me down the sofa until I hang off it.

"This is yours," he tells me, stroking his cock as I stare, wide-eyed. "Don't fear it. I'll make it feel good."

"Dal," I whimper. "Please, you're too big, and the piercings . . . It will hurt."

"Good." He grins. "Let me hear you scream again. You scream so fucking beautifully."

His cock is the biggest thing I've ever seen, and with the eight piercings running down its length, it looks mean as fucking hell.

Most want sex to feel good, but not Dal.

He wants pain and the oblivion you find in darkness.

He climbs up my body, sliding his hand up until he reaches my breasts, and then his teeth clamp around my nipple. I cry out, wrapping my legs around his waist.

"Dal," I beg.

"I'm going to buy clamps for these," he says, biting my other one. "I want to see them hurt for me."

Oh my fucking god.

My eyes almost roll into the back of my head as he licks them better before sucking on them. His fingers twist my other nipple until I whimper below him. Finally, he releases my tortured breasts, his tongue laving over my chest and up my neck to my ear.

"Sing for me, rock star," he commands, and in one smooth move, he buries himself deep inside me.

I scream so loudly, I'm surprised the others don't beat down the door.

He's so fucking big, it actually hurts, but he doesn't care. He forces me to take every hard inch. "Look what you do to me," he says, biting my earlobe. "You drive me crazy," he snarls, pulling out and hammering back in, even as I wince, trying to escape. "You make me fucking feral. They've always wanted a beast, and they've got one now because of you. Reign, fuck, take it. Fucking take it. I want you to hurt as much as I do from wanting you."

He pulls back, and when he sees the tears sliding down my face, he wipes them away. "That's it, take me deep. Cry, scream, and use me, just don't make me stop. You're doing so well. I know it hurts now, but it will feel so good." He wraps his hand around my throat, anchoring me as he hammers into me.

Like everything with Dal, it hurts so good, I can't take it.

His piercings drag along the nerves inside me, but he's right. The pain fades to a burning pleasure so strong, I can't breathe, can't move, locked in a tidal wave. He sees me struggling and bites my ear.

"I've got you."

His hand grips my throat, and his grunts fill my ear as he licks up and down my neck, biting and licking as I cry out. He hammers into me so hard, it hurts. "Fucking perfect," he snarls in my ear. "Good, so good. How can you feel this great? It's like the high of a kill but ten times better. Fuck, Reign, I think I'm finding religion in your cunt."

His dirty words spew right in my ear as he holds me prisoner and rams into me so hard, it sends me spiraling. I scream as I come, my nails clawing at his back.

He doesn't stop, fucking me like an animal in rut.

We actually fall from the sofa, but he doesn't stop, hammering me into the floor as he bites and sucks my lips. I hold him, taking it and wanting the pain he demands.

I hear the door, and when my head lolls to the side, I meet Cillian's wide-eyed stare. "Are you okay?"

Dal snarls, and when I jerk my head back, I see his gun pointed at Cil, yet he doesn't stop thrusting for one fucking moment. Cil must see the truth written across Dal's face. He would kill his brother right now.

Hands up, Cil glances at me, and I nod to let him know that I'm okay. He backs away and shuts the door, then Dal turns those beastly eyes back to me.

"Again," he demands. "Come again. I want to feel you squeeze my cock."

"I can't." My words are hoarse, and with a snarl, he reaches between us, pinching my clit until he makes me a liar. I come so hard, I actually black out for a moment, and when I come to, his voice is in my ear.

"So good. So tight. Like a fucking vise, silken fucking torture. You fuck me so good. You're mine. Mine. Every inch of you, and I'm going to spend years marking every single hole you have, filling it over and over with my cum until it's all you crave and you fucking need it to survive."

I try to lift my hands but they flop to the floor, exhausted as he powers into me. He lifts my hips so he hits deeper inside me, and I cry out.

"I love the way you scream, like music to my ears. My very own personal song I want to listen to forever," he growls, dragging his mouth across my cheek to my lips, biting and sucking them before I open. His tongue slips inside, tangling with mine as he kisses me as hard as he fucks me.

My pleasure starts to build again, bordering on painful, and I know I need to make him come or he will never stop—not until he's fucked me to death.

His hand slams against the floor by my head. "I can't. Fuck, Reign, I can't take it."

"So let go," I say, licking and nipping his chin as I rip his shirt open, clawing at his skin, and when I catch his nipple, he roars.

Smirking, I bite his neck hard and twist his nipple until his back bows and he yells his release.

I drink in his twisted expression of ecstasy, his eyes closed as he lets go. It's fucking beautiful, and when he slumps over me, I wrap my arms around him, kissing his neck.

"Thank you," he murmurs into my ear, making me shiver at his dark, sexy voice. "You're mine, Reign."

I have no issue being Dal's.

I'll be black and blue tomorrow, but it was so worth it.

TWENTY-TWO

I know they have all had my girl, and she is my girl. This is a job, and there are lines, but all of us have crossed them. I can't even blame them—not when she looks and acts the ways she does. She's the only person who has ever made me doubt my conviction and lose focus, and I'm tired of fighting it.

It seems they are as well.

She heads upstairs as soon as we're back, and I watch her go, knowing my gaze is hungry and determined. "I want you on watch tonight," I tell them. When I glance at them, there is a knowing look in their eyes, which makes me narrow mine. "I mean it. Get the system updated, and I want that report I asked for," I snap, ignoring them and their leers as I head upstairs.

I go to my room first where I strip from my suit. I can't go to her in it because I want to go as me, not as her guard. No lines, no job.

Just us.

It's foolish, and we could get fired or cause her to be hurt. There is so much that could go wrong, but I can't stop myself as I head upstairs, crossing that last line, because once I've had her, Reign Harrow will be mine forever.

I'm lying to myself, though, because she already is—she just doesn't know it yet. Whether she's been under me or not, every inch of

161

her is mine. I care for her happiness and safety more than anyone else in the world.

This started as a job, but now it's a necessity, a constant drive to keep her safe, satisfied, and happy.

I step into her room. Her bed is made, and her room is spotless except for her clothes, which leave a trail to the bathroom. I can hear the shower running as she sings to herself and I smirk. There is no better sound than her voice—well, maybe her screams. Lying down on her bed, I spread out and wait.

I have a promise to keep.

A few moments later, the shower cuts off, and after another few minutes, she emerges followed by wafts of steam from the shower. She's wrapped in nothing but a tiny towel, showing off her shapely legs, thick thighs, and tats. She freezes when she sees me. Her hair is wet, and her face is clear of makeup. This is as vulnerable as you will ever see Reign.

"Raff?" she asks, confusion lacing her tone as she tilts her head.

The shortened version of my name drives me crazy, but if any of the others called me that, I would kill them. She could fucking call me her pet and I would answer, as long as she keeps those pretty eyes on me.

I lift my arm, and she tracks the movement as I grip the top of her headboard. "Getting shy all of a sudden, Miss Harrow?" I tease, knowing she gets all riled up when I call her that. Just like I expected, a spark enters her eyes and her lips tilt up in a mischievous smile. With a fanatic flair, she drops the towel. It slides to the floor, leaving her completely naked.

Her body is what songs are written about. I understand her ex's obsession with love songs now. She's made to be fucked and tasted. She's made for dirty romps and hard sex. She's a walking, talking wet dream that drives me wild.

"Come here," I order. She watches me with a grin, and I arch a brow. "I said, come here, Miss Harrow."

"Or why don't you come here?" she flirts, sliding her hand up her side. I track the movement like a predator, wanting to feel that silken skin.

Sitting up slowly, I slide from the bed and advance on her. Her chin tilts up in defiance, and she looks so fucking beautiful. I love it when she stands toe to toe with me. Not many can, but this girl can and she knows it. I would never hurt her—fuck, I'd rather die first—but I fucking love this game between us, and so does she, as we try to make the other break first.

She'll soon learn she might give orders outside of this bedroom, but in here, she's mine. She'll beg for my orders and dominance before the sun rises.

I back her up with my body, and she hits the wall with a thud. Her eyes widen as I slam my hand to the wall above her head, caging her in place. "When I give you an order, you will obey."

"Or what?" she retorts.

"Or I won't fuck you. I'll leave you here, wet and wanting, desperate to be fucked," I purr, tilting my head down so she swallows the words.

"Then I'll go find one of the others and fuck them," she replies innocently, fluttering her lashes in that goddamn annoyingly perfect way.

"I'll order them not to. Here's the thing, Miss Harrow . . . You are used to getting your way, but in here, with me, you won't. You'll get what I give and you'll thank me for it."

Snorting, she tries to step past me, rubbing that delicious body of hers across mine. I circle her throat like one of her diamond necklaces and slam her back into the wall. She freezes from the force and the rough handling.

Oh yes, my little rock star likes to be dominated.

I knew she was a brat from the moment I laid eyes on her, and tonight, she will get all that's coming to her for teasing me for so long.

"Don't test me, Miss Harrow," I warn, tightening my hold on her neck. Her pupils dilate with desire as I cut off her air for a moment, letting her feel my strength. "You have been teasing me since the moment I met you, and before the sun is up, I will have you. It is your choice how." Leaning in, I lick her lips, smirking when they part for me. "I'll have you coming all night or I'll use this delicious body of yours for my own desire and leave you wanting. Choose." I let her see the seriousness in my gaze.

She shudders against me, her perky breasts plastered to my hard chest.

"I'm waiting."

I watch her swallow, her eyes looking between mine before she relaxes, giving me control. "Then have me, Raff," she offers. "Show me what lies hidden beneath those suits."

Releasing her throat, I step back. "On the bed, Miss Harrow."

She hesitates only for a moment before pushing away from the wall and stepping past me, rubbing against me on her way. She presses one knee to the mattress and then the other.

"Slowly," I command, coming up behind her. "Show me that delicious cunt."

She groans and slows down, crawling on her hands and knees across the bed until she reaches the middle and lies down, rolling onto her back. Her bright eyes stay on me as she parts her thighs, stroking them as I stare at her perfect, pink pussy.

She arches her back, thrusting her chest up for me, her hair spread across the white bedding.

Growling, I circle my length as I watch her, stroking myself. "Touch yourself," I demand.

"Like this?" she purrs, sliding her hand across her stomach and over her breasts.

I step closer, my own desire strong. "Touch that pretty pussy," I say, aware that she's pushing the boundaries.

Her hand slides down over her stomach and mound until her long, talented fingers part her pussy for me. She slides two down her center and back up, circling her clit with slow, sure strokes. Her cream glistens as she touches herself for me, and I match her pace with my hand, stroking my cock as I watch her.

"Taste yourself," I growl, my voice clipped.

Her eyes widen, but she lifts her fingers and sucks them clean of her desire.

"Do you taste good, Reign? Do you taste how badly you want this?" I jerk my cock, and her eyes drop to my length as she moans around her fingers. "Words, Miss Harrow."

"Yes," she says, sliding her fingers back down and caressing herself.

"Is this what you want?" I taunt, stopping at the edge of the bed as I touch myself to the sight of her sprawled for me.

"Yes," she answers without hesitation.

"Where?"

Sliding her glistening fingers down, she thrusts them inside herself as she gasps. One leg comes up and bends as her hips lift. The sight of her digits sliding in and out of her greedy hole almost has me spilling.

Gripping the head of my cock, I stop myself from coming from the sight.

She fucks herself as she watches me, her chest flushing as her breathing picks up. Her other hand plays with her breasts.

"Enough," I command when I see her leg start to shake, knowing she's close.

Whining, she stops, doing as she's told for once.

Just for that, she gets what she wants. Climbing on the bed like a dark shadow coming to claim her, I crawl toward her. Her tongue drags along her lower lip as she watches me, and when I stop above her, she groans, arching up to try and entice me.

"Raff," she whispers, and my nickname on her lips drives me mad.

"Say my name again," I order.

Smirking, she rubs her breasts against me. "Raffiel." The fucking sound burrows into my brain, replacing every other use of my name before now. I want to change it so only she can say it and it belongs to her.

"You're being a good girl," I praise, lowering myself and settling between her thighs.

"Because I want you to fuck me," she retorts, her eyes flashing.

"Oh, I plan to, Miss Harrow, all night, but first, let me taste that sweet little cunt that will be dripping with my cum by morning."

Sliding down her body, I place a worshiping kiss above her racing heart. I might be in charge right now, but only because she's allowing me to be. She holds all the power. She always has.

"Then taste me," she whispers, widening her legs.

Settling between her thighs, I turn my head to kiss each one, watching her teeth dig into her plump bottom lip. I press my nose to her pussy and inhale, groaning.

She smells like fucking perfection.

She is perfection.

I never craved beauty until Reign Harrow. I never knew softness. She has me wrapped around her little finger, and when she realizes that, this world will suffer because if anyone ever hurts my girl, I will show them the beast that hides within my heart.

A beast she has tamed.

"Watch me while I make you mine," I command.

Pressing an open-mouthed kiss to her pussy, I keep my eyes on hers, watching every single emotion in those glowing orbs. When I nip her clit, they widen, and when I slide my tongue down and thrust it inside her, they shutter. Smirking against her wet heat, I use her eyes against her like a weapon.

I lick and suck her throbbing clit while sliding my fingers inside her, working them deep all while torturing her clit. The taste of strawberries slides down my throat from her sweet cream until I lap at it, desperate for every drop.

Her hips lift as she moans, and she grips my hair, tugging at the strands until it stings.

I oblige and press closer, choking on her taste and scent.

Strategy is my strong suit, it's why I got this far in my life, and right now, my entire focus is on Reign Harrow.

My brain filters every different reaction until she's moaning and crying out as I attack her.

Her body locks up under my attack, and her pretty little cunt clamps on my fingers as her release rolls through her.

Reign Harrow comes just like she does everything else—completely and fully.

Her thighs clamp around my head as she screams, her back arching and head thrown back as she comes. I burn that sight into my mind as I lick her through her release. When she relaxes, I pull my fingers free and cover my cock in her cum while sliding my tongue across her hole to catch more of her taste.

Whimpering above me, she opens her eyes, and I'm lost.

I crawl up her body and toss one of her legs over my shoulder, opening her wider for me.

"Raff—"

I drive into her tight, wet cunt, letting her watch the play of emotions across my face. I look into her eyes and see her desire, need, and love there.

"They say a look can say a thousand words, but yours say a million, Reign. I don't even have to ask you. All I have to do is look into your eyes and know the truth. Do you want to know your truth, Reign?" I say seductively. "Your truth is that you crave this. You crave love, not just desire, and you hope it will be different every time." Sliding up her body, I cover her lips as she goes to speak. "You can stop hoping. This is it, Reign. This is forever, you and me, so save those looks for me, and don't you dare give them to anyone else. They are mine, just like you are."

Her hands come up to my shoulders. "Then make them just yours."

Chuckling, I lean down and cover her lips, swallowing her words.

I kiss her hard while I start to move. My slow, measured thrusts have her other leg tightening around my waist, her nails sliding down my back like claws. The sharp pain makes me groan into her mouth and slam into her hard.

She rips her mouth away, crying out as she closes her eyes.

Smirking, I slam into her again.

Her eyes suddenly open, and I see panic in them so I stop. "Condom?" she blurts.

"I'm clean. I haven't been with anyone in years, and I know you are too. You think I didn't check? You're on birth control, and there was no fucking way I wasn't having you raw, baby girl. I want you to feel every inch of what you do to me."

"Fuck," she murmurs. "Then fuck me raw, Raff."

"I wasn't going to stop anyway," I tell her as I twist my hips and make her moan.

Straightening above her, I pull out of her wet cunt and drive into her, watching her breasts shake with the force.

She wanted me, tempted me. Reign Harrow might be a sinner, but I'm the fucking devil, and she just realized that.

Her nails press into me as she lifts her hips to meet my brutal thrusts. I use one hand to hold me above her, while my other slides down her body, tweaking and twisting her nipple until she screams out for me.

Grabbing a pillow, I stuff it under her hips, lifting her until I slide in at an angle that has her head shaking and back arching as she claws my shoulders.

"That's it, baby, make me bleed. You are the only person I would allow to scar me, so cut me up good and leave your mark." I can't help but spill the truth as I hammer into her.

"Raff," she cries out as the bed creaks from the force of us joining.

The slick, dirty sound of me pounding into her makes me harder.

Red-hot acid pours down my back, drawing my balls up as I fight back my own release. Reaching between us, I pinch her clit and watch her shatter.

Her screams echo around the house as she writhes. I fight to fuck her fluttering cunt as she comes, gushing down my cock. I continue to drive into her, rough, hard, dirty, and raw—the way she likes it.

"Oh god," she cries as another orgasm hits her.

"Yes, Reign, I am your god now. I am your everything. Inside these doors, I'm your master, your pleasure, and pain, so show your god everything."

Rolling my hips, I watch her eyes roll into the back of her head. I've never cared about another's pleasure before, but with Reign, I do. I want it all. I want to drain her of it. I want her pleasure to be my own, more than even my own release.

I want to own every inch of Reign Harrow like she owns me.

The cry she lets out burrows into my chest and cock, making me growl above her, my hips snapping as I fuck her. Her nails slice me apart with her own pleasure until I feel blood trailing down my back, but I still don't stop.

My hips flex and my teeth grind as I hold back, but when she cries out my name, I'm lost.

"Raffiel!"

It sends me over the edge. I snap my hips so hard, she cries out, and I bury myself so deep inside her she could never be parted from me. My release pours from me as I bellow.

She cries out, her pussy clenching around my length, draining every drop from me as she finds her pleasure once more.

Groaning, I push deeper still, shoving my cum deep inside my girl, until it feels like all my energy has drained with my release, and then I slide across her, pulling her into my arms, our bodies still joined as we pant.

"You have five minutes, Miss Harrow," I warn as we lie tangled together. "And then I'm taking that pretty ass bare."

TWENTY-THREE

Waking with a gasp, I jerk upright, only to fall back with a moan. Pleasure slams through me and my legs shake. My eyes are still closed, and my body is caught between being asleep and awake, so it takes me a second to realize what's going on.

Hands grip my hips, holding me in place, as a mouth lazily licks my pussy. I open my eyes and glance down to see Raffiel's head between my thighs. Lifting his mouth, he licks his lips with a wicked grin. "There she is."

"Raff—" I groan as his mouth drops back to my pussy.

"Good girl, drench my face for me. I'm starving for my breakfast," he croons, lapping my clit leisurely. "I thought I was going to get you to come before you woke up, but there's always next time."

"Oh god." My chest arches, and I bring my hands up to tweak my nipples as I grind into his face. I'm so close to reaching my release, and it's like I've been slammed into pleasure since I wasn't awake for it.

"I can be your god, baby, or better yet, you can be mine, that way I can worship your pretty pussy all night long, just like you want. Isn't that right?" he murmurs, the vibration of his voice causing me to pull him closer.

"Stop fucking talking and make me come," I yell.

"So needy." He chuckles. "You get to come when I say you can come, not before, princess."

"Fuck." Panting, I have no choice but to lie back and take it as he licks my clit, building me toward my release without a hurry, only to stop as soon as I get close. How many times did he edge me before I woke up? The wicked glint in his eyes tells me quite a few and he's enjoying it.

"Raff, please," I beg, too desperate to care that I am.

"I love it when you beg," he murmurs. "I almost love it as much as I love being buried in this magnificent pussy. Fuck, I've barely slept. Every time I do, it's with dreams of this cunt and how it felt, and I wake up wanting you, so I figured you had to as well."

My head thrashes as his tongue dips inside me, and I see his hips grinding into the bed, letting me know he isn't as unaffected as he seems. "If you don't get me off right now—"

"You'll what?" he mocks, sliding up my body to cover my mouth, forcing me to taste myself before whispering against it. "Get one of the others? They wouldn't even get close to you. They might be my brothers, but nothing will get in the way of me and this pussy, not even you, princess." Sliding down, he stops to suck and bite my nipples, making me cry out before his mouth seals over my cunt again.

I scream, my legs jerking, but once more, he pulls back before I can come, leaving me angry, frustrated, and on the brink of tears. "Raff, please, please—"

"You want to come, princess? Say Raffiel, please make me come like a good girl."

Gritting my teeth, I glare at him before giving in, needing to come too badly to care. "Raffiel, please make me come like a good girl."

"That's all you had to say." He winks before dropping his mouth back to my pussy and attacking me. His fingers thrust into me and curl, and his lips wrap around my clit and suck so hard, I actually jerk.

Within seconds, I'm screaming my release, grinding it into his face as I come. The strength of the orgasm has me shaking and writhing below him as it rolls through me repeatedly until I finally slump. Chuckling, he laps up my cream, cleaning me before sitting up.

"The best breakfast I've ever had." He winks. "Now it's time to start the day."

He climbs from the bed and peers down at me with a sardonic smile. "Good morning, Miss Harrow." Without another word, naked and hard, he walks out of my room, leaving me drenched in my own cum and sweat and wondering what the hell just happened.

I fall back with a groan, covering my face. This is crossing so many lines. I never let anyone sleep in my bed, not after Tucker, yet here I am. I can't even be mad. They are in my house, and they are cooking me food. They have seen me at my strongest and weakest, and they are still here and want me.

They are paid to protect me, sure, but it's more than that. This is more than a normal, new relationship or whatever the hell this is. It's so much more. Living with someone lets you get to know them that much quicker, and it feels like I've been with them months instead of weeks. I'm never lonely anymore, and they are there when I'm worried or needy. They laugh and joke with me.

It's a true relationship, but with four people.

How the hell does that even work?

I've never been traditional, but fuck, and thinking about it is giving me a headache. Sliding from the bed and nearly falling on shaky legs, I stumble to the bathroom. I won't give him the pleasure of coming back to tell me they are waiting for me twice. The smug bastard.

I promised myself I wouldn't let anyone get close after Tucker, but it seems these four men don't give a fuck about that or any walls I build.

They are smashing them down, and I don't know what will be left once they do.

I shower quickly, washing my hair and feeling somewhat vulnerable without makeup. Wearing just an oversized shirt, I pad downstairs. I expect recrimination, judgment, or maybe anger since they all know what Raff and I were doing, but when I enter the kitchen, I'm met by nothing but happy smiles.

Music pours from the radio, smooth and soft, and bacon sizzles in a pan where Cillian and Dal are working together, cooking eggs, bagels, and sausages. Astro comes over, kissing my cheek as he hands me coffee. "Morning, beautiful." He winks as he heads back to set the table where Raff sits with a tablet before him, but his eyes are for me.

His gaze is hard, as if he expects me to run and is ready to chase me.

I remind myself that this is just sex, nothing else. Nothing more. Not even if they are in my house cooking breakfast. "Morning," I tell them, smiling softly as I head to the kitchen table. I can't remember the last time this kitchen was used for cooking before they arrived, never mind eating at the table, but here we are. They bring life into this home. Even when Tucker was here, it almost always felt empty, but not anymore, and I refuse to look too closely at why that makes me smile.

Bringing one knee up, I balance the coffee there as I watch Cillian and Dal work together. Astro moves behind me and starts massaging my shoulders, his big hands working into the tension there as I close my eyes and tip my head back to rest it against his chest.

I should tell him to stop.

I'll tell him after he kneads out the sore muscles. When I open my eyes once more, all of them are staring at me. Swallowing my need, I clear my throat. "I was thinking that I would work on my music in the downstairs studio today, then maybe go out for dinner, show my face and all that."

Raffiel smiles at me as if I did something worthy of his praise, and I shudder at the look, remembering the way it was between my thighs last night and this morning.

It's only then I realize I asked his opinion and I want to curse myself, but I can't take it back without making him realize I know what I did.

"Sounds great," Raffiel responds with that slow smile.

Since when did I start asking permission?

Fuck that, I won't make the same mistake again.

My anger quickly softens as they bring food over, and we tuck in. Unlike before, where I watched them with each other, I find myself joining in on the conversation and even laughing at their jokes. It's nice. I like this friendship dynamic, even though we aren't just friends, are we?

I have to admit, it makes my home feel like more of a home and less of a prison. What must it be like to always have each other? To always have someone at your back? I guess I'm finding out and I like it. They are always in my corner, ready to protect me and fight my battles, but also not trying to control or change me.

Tucker struggled with that, often telling me to calm down or to think through my actions and how they would reflect on him and his brand. Not them, they simply embrace who I am and seem to like it, even my extremes.

I'm still so confused. I promised myself no relationships, and look where I am. This isn't a one-night stand or even friends with benefits. This has other complications, but I can't seem to stop myself when it comes to these four.

I always did have impulse control issues.

Luckily, the doorbell saves me from my own thoughts and the eyes that see too much. They all frown toward the door as Raffiel stands. "If they let someone else through, I'll fucking kill the useless bastards. I'm interviewing for new guards, but they can't come quickly enough."

I watch him answer the door, his hand on his gun on the small of his back. It shouldn't be as hot as it is, but it has me licking my lips, and when he turns to me, his face thunderous, I even wiggle, getting wet. It's then I see the huge bouquet of pink roses. The anger on his face suddenly melts to amusement. "How about we send them to the hospital this time?"

"Go ahead." I grin, loving how he's enjoying this as much as I am. No doubt they are from Tucker, but I don't ask and Raffiel doesn't explain as he comes back to join us.

Astro stands and starts to clean up, but something on his neck catches my eye. Frowning, I tug on his shirt, and his smile turns seductive. "You want me naked, sweetheart?" he purrs.

"What's that?" I ask, tilting my head to try and see. His eyes follow mine, and he quickly blushes and stands up, moving away from me.

"Nothing," is all he says. "Now get your sexy ass up. They cooked, so it's our turn to clean."

I snort. "I don't clean."

"You do now." He winks. "Come on, beautiful, it's part of being a team."

Is that what I am?

One of the team?

I find myself moving before I can even think it through. I can't remember the last time I washed dishes—horrible, but true. It's just part of who I am, but I find myself standing next to Astro, covered in suds as he washes and I dry. I like the normalcy of it, and when he nudges me, grinning down at me, I grin back.

Is this how every day will be with them?

Waking to orgasms, food, and banter?

Maybe it won't be so bad after all.

TWENTY-FOUR

I spend all morning in my studio downstairs. The guys pop in every now and again, usually with snacks and drinks and to check on me, but they don't rush or bother me, and I find I like having someone worried about how I am at all times. After working through more lyrics, I look over the concepts I came up with for some of the videos and album artwork, selecting my favorites and sending them over to management for them to get started on. This is going to be a comeback, so I want everything to be perfect. I want this music everywhere.

I'm talking merch, videos with superstars you can't help but love, and artwork you want on your walls. After, there will be interviews, venues, and a tour to sort out, and I can't wait. I respond to Jack's texts about some confirmations of artists, almost squealing in excitement, especially pop princess Falcon. I knew I wanted to work with her on one of the songs from the moment I started to write it. She just fits the style so perfectly, and she's talented and capable of singing nearly everything. Unlike the boxes people put her in, she's dabbled in country and folk as well as rock and pop, so I thought she would be down, not to mention that poor girl has gone through her own shit. We've trauma-bonded at some award shows.

I think this might be the best album I've ever written, and Jack agrees. We set dates to record, and I figure out a few more details before calling it a day. My brain is drained and I'm exhausted, but excitement still courses through me. This feels big, good, and I'm happy about it for the first time in years. I'm not doing it because I have to. I'm truly excited for the music and what it will bring.

This is just me and my music, and I hope the fans see that. They are already developing theories online about the songs and the album from teasers I dropped on my socials, and I love reading their commentary. Some even got close to a few of my ideas for songs, and some inspired new lyrics.

Putting my phone away, I head upstairs and get dressed. There will undoubtedly be paparazzi, but I genuinely just need to get out. I keep it simple with some loose ripped mom jeans and a cropped band T with a leather jacket. When I come downstairs, they are already waiting, and they help me into the car.

"Where to?" Dal asks.

"Le Establa, please." I see him typing it in, and then we are off.

I slide my shades on as we head into the sun-soaked streets. Raff is in the front with Dal, Astro and Cillian in the back with me, but I avoid their eyes. I need some quiet time away from them to reestablish my boundaries. I can't afford to be weak or soft right now, not when the vultures will be circling. During the drive, I rebuild my walls once more, and when we stop, I get out with that familiar, fake, cocky smile. I see them eyeing me worriedly, but I ignore their looks and stop to take pictures with fans who notice me. This isn't a celeb restaurant. It's a hole-in-the-wall, mom-and-pop place I found when I first came to the city, and I always come here when I need some home-cooked healing.

"Thank you so much, Reign," a young girl says shyly.

"Of course," I tell her as I sign her arm and take a picture with her. I take as many as I can before ducking inside and pushing my shades up on my head. Although the paparazzi know I come here, I make it random so they can't follow me all the time to protect the owners as much as I can. They also have a policy in place to protect me, although it's not something I asked for.

The tables are spread out, all mismatched, and chairs are missing. My booth in the back is free and I grin, waving at the familiar cooks in the kitchen before I sneak up on Mom where she is filling drinks. It's not overly busy at this time, so I can get away with it without her telling me off too much.

Wrapping my arms around her from behind, I pop my head onto her shoulder. "Boo."

She whirls around, smacking me. "Rey, you are naughty!" she snaps, and then she pulls back, glaring at me. "And too skinny. Have you not been eating?" Without waiting for a response, she grabs my hand and hauls me to my booth, pushing me down. "Pop, give me Rey's order and sides! What do you want?" She looks at the guys, her eyes narrowed protectively.

"Rey's here?" Pop calls, looking around the kitchen. I wave as he smiles at me.

"That's what I said, isn't it?" she scoffs. "What do you want?"

"They will have what I'm having. Mom, this is my new security, Raffiel, Astro, Cillian, and Dal." I introduce each one, and they smile and shake her hand softly. Dal even kisses the back of it, and she practically swoons.

"Fine, I like them." She turns her gaze to me. "You eat, then we'll talk."

"Yes, ma'am." I nod, sitting upright. While she hurries to the kitchen, I giggle, watching Pop try to get around her to come see me, but she pushes him back in.

"Mom and Pop?" Cillian asks, his eyebrow raised.

I shrug. "It's what they've always told me to call them."

"How long have you been coming here?" Dal asks knowingly.

"A long time." When they just stare, I sigh, looking out of the window. "They were the only people who cared," I admit, looking around. "When I first came here, I couldn't even afford a meal, so I ordered a drink. I was hungry and cold, and they offered me a slice of home. They fed me and looked after me, and every time I've come back since, they do the same. It never bothered them how famous I became. To them, I will always be that skinny girl practically living on the streets, trying to make it."

I can see the questions in their eyes—after all, not a lot of people know about my past—but I smile and change the subject. "The food here is incredible though, all homemade and healing."

Unlike normal people, they don't bite.

"It smells amazing," Astro says. "You lived on the streets?"

Sighing, I pick up the napkin and cover my lap, feeling four sets of eyes on me. "For a little while, when I first came here."

"I didn't know that," Raffiel murmurs.

"Not many people do. I was a nobody then, trying to make it," I reply. "I did what I had to do to survive. I hardly had any money, and I spent what I had on recordings and sending out my music. It wasn't as bad as it sounds. You kind of get used to it. I started working two jobs to pay for a tiny, shared apartment, and I was eventually noticed."

"Wait, you were seventeen right when you started, right? So how old were you when you lived on the streets?" Astro questions.

I hesitate. I don't often share my past and for a very good reason. I'm not ashamed of what I did to survive, but some people in the industry don't understand, especially those who came from money and privilege.

"I just turned fifteen," I admit.

I ignore their swearing and scan the diners to make sure no one is listening to sell my story. A lot of it isn't public knowledge. I'm not ashamed, but my past is my past. Nobody else's. I don't want my pain dissected and reported on.

"What about your parents?" Raffiel snaps. "They didn't care that their daughter was on the streets?"

I flinch. They aren't a subject I like to talk about, but I know I'm not getting away with it. "Hard to care when they are dead."

"You had no family?" Astro starts.

Sighing, I meet their eyes. "No, I had no one, okay? I lost everyone I loved, and that's all I want to hear on it, alright? It's my past for a reason. Yes, I lived on the streets. It wasn't easy. Yes, it was scary and I was in some bad situations, but look where it got me."

"You don't have to be defensive," Astro murmurs, and Cillian takes my hand. I want to snatch it away but he won't let me, curling his fingers tighter around mine.

"We all have our pasts. We are just trying to understand," he says softly. I ignore their eyes, not wanting to see their pity, but when I spare them a glance, they seem worried and angry, and there's no pity in sight.

"So you're going to rip my past open when I know nothing about you guys?" I ask, knowing I'm being defensive, but it's true. They are learning everything about me, and I don't even know their last names. I see the hit land, and Raff opens his mouth when Pop appears.

He walks back and forth, placing down drinks and food, and when the table is covered, he leans in and kisses my head. "Mom says to make sure you eat it all or you're in big trouble."

"I always am." I grin up at him, watching his face soften.

"Glad to see you back, kid," he murmurs, leaning down to kiss my head again. "Now eat, all of you."

When he leaves, I focus on filling my plate, knowing they are both watching me, and Mom is scary as hell. If she thinks I'm not eating properly, then who knows what that woman will do, so you damn well bet I'm eating, especially since it's so fucking good.

I pile my plate high, and when I look up, I freeze. They haven't moved and are watching me carefully.

"You can know everything. You only have to ask," Dal says slowly. "About any of us. We won't hide or lie about anything."

"Look, it's fine," I start, but Astro leans in.

"He means it, beautiful. My full name is Astro Michael Vasileiou. I was born in Greece, and I lived there until my teens when we moved to the States for my dad's job in the military. My mother is a chef, and I have two siblings, both younger. I joined the military right out of school and was eventually moved into these fuckers' unit."

"Stop—"

"My full name is Cillian Walsh, no middle name. You probably guessed, but my parents are Irish. I lived there for a few years, which I don't remember, and then we moved. I joined the military after college and was put in their unit. No siblings, and I'm not close with my parents. They loved me, but they weren't meant to be parents, and we haven't spoken in a long time. These fuckers are my family."

"Seriously," I protest. "You don't need to do this."

"No, you're right," Raff murmurs. "We do. You should know who we are, who is protecting you and in your house." It's clear he wants to say more, but he can't in case someone is listening.

"Dal means moon. I was born under a full moon. My mother raised me alone as a single parent. She died when I was nineteen. I didn't have a good childhood, and that translated to being a bad adult. I found my place in Raff's unit."

I wonder what that means, but I don't have the balls to ask. There's something cold about Dal, something dark, and part of me recognizes it, even while part of me understands I probably don't want to know. I've seen that look in people's eyes before, usually from the streets and years of abuse and problems.

Without meaning to, I look at Raff.

"Raffiel Walker. I grew up in Australia, and I still have a house there. No family because I was an orphan. My family became my job. I loved being in the armed forces, but I wanted something else. I was searching until now. My favorite color is the color of your eyes."

Cillian grins. "Oh shit, that was smooth."

"You can ask us whatever you want, but know that opening up goes both ways, Reign. Now eat," Raffiel orders, and unsure what to say to that, I start to eat.

"My favorite color is black," I mutter.

"That's not even a color," Astro teases.

"Fine, what's yours?" I smile, but I feel better now that I know some of their past, just like they knew I would. They always know what to say or how to fix something if they fuck up. It's refreshing.

"Blue." He grins widely. "Like the ocean."

"Of course," I mutter. "What's yours, Dal?"

"Red, like blood." He shrugs as my mouth gapes, but none of the others seem bothered. I keep eating, wondering what the hell happened to Dal to make him automatically say bloodred.

"Cillian?" I ask, looking away.

"Green." He grins, making me smile back, and they finally start to eat. With the first bite, they groan.

"Shit, this is so good, maybe even better than my mom's—don't tell her that," Astro mutters, covering his mouth as I giggle.

"I won't." I scoop up more noodles and chicken and devour the whole plate, going back for seconds. I always feel better when I eat here. Once the table is clear, Mom heads over.

"I will have dessert brought out."

"Mom," I whine, but she glares at me, and I shut my ass up.

"Now." She sits and takes my hands, completely ignoring the guys. "Are you okay?"

"I'm fine."

"Do not lie to me, young lady." I snap my mouth shut as she stares at me, always seeing the truth. "I never liked that Tucker—"

"I know. He didn't like cheesecake, and you said it was a sign." I grin.

"Well, it's true." She huffs.

"I love cheesecake," Astro remarks, and she grins at him before looking at me.

"Do you want me to kick his ass?" she offers seriously.

"Nope, it's fine," I promise, patting her hand. "But thanks, Mom."

"Always, my girl. I don't know where you went, but we are glad to have you back, and if you ever disappear like that again, I will be very angry." She stands. "I'll bring extra cheesecake."

I watch her go, and when she gets into the kitchen, I hear, "I like the pretty one with the curly hair. He likes cheesecake. Let's set them up—"

"Oh god." I groan, banging my head on the table.

"She likes me." Astro grins proudly.

Save me now.

"I like cheesecake too," Dal grumbles.

I'm just heading to the car, where paparazzi are taking pictures after being tipped off, when I hear my name shouted. The familiar tone makes me freeze. I can't pretend I don't hear it, so I turn and scan the crowd. Emerging from her own crowd, Sal steps forward.

She looks as perfect as always. Her long, tan legs are exposed in her tiny skirt, and her skinny body is on full display. Her blonde hair hangs in waves over one shoulder, and her makeup is perfectly applied. She looks every inch the flawless celebrity, even though one of her biggest claims to fame was being my bestie. Before that, she wanted to be an actor, and now she's in films and she models and her name is everywhere.

It's all thanks to me and the games she played to get there.

She hurries over, grinning like she is excited to see me. I see the cameras snapping pictures, and the guys move closer as if to block her.

Shit, maybe it wasn't the fans that tipped them off to my presence, but her. It would be something she would do, wanting this on record either to use against me or for herself. There was a time when I never knew just how deep her twisted games and plans went, but that was before. I sidestep her half-hearted hug.

"Sal." The door to the car is still open, and I want to dive inside, but I refuse to hide. I give her my fake smile, pretending I don't give a shit, even as my heart rips open. How could someone I was so close to, who knew all my secrets, hopes, and dreams, turn into this? Was I really that blind, or has she changed that much?

No. I remind myself this was always hidden deep inside her. I was just too blind to notice. Her smile doesn't falter. She's a good actor, I'll give her that. "I missed you." She pouts. "I heard you were back. I can't believe you haven't called." She lets out a fake laugh as the paparazzi move closer to capture us. After all, we were inseparable before I left.

I simply smile, and she clearly wasn't expecting that.

"Well, I'm glad you're back." Leaning in like we are the only people present and they won't hear every word, she drops her voice and says, "I hope you've been better with alcohol and drugs."

This bitch.

"I never had an issue with them." I smile. "That was more your field."

Her smile turns brittle before she laughs.

"Can I get a picture?" a pap yells, and she turns to pose. "Reign!" he shouts. I take sick joy in posing for one as they ignore her. I guess she's not as popular as she wants to be. When she turns those cynical eyes on me, I know whatever she'll say next will be for the camera so she can get what she wants, just like always.

After all, she can't stand it when she's not the center of attention.

"I'm really sorry about what happened, Reign. You have to know that. I hope we can meet up and discuss Tucker and me."

And there it is.

I always thought that when I saw her again and her legs weren't wrapped around my fiancé, that I would smack that smug smile from her lips, but that wouldn't be enough. I won't make her a martyr. I won't be the crazy ex she wants me to be.

"No hard feelings, you did me a favor." I smile, even as I hear the chatter. "Now, I have to get going. You know how it is, places to be. Those acting classes must really be working. by the way. Brava."

"So we'll meet up?" she calls as I climb inside and shut the door in her face. I hold it together as we pull away, and then it hits me and I can't breathe. Tears fill my eyes.

How could someone I love be so cold?

So heartless?

I'm a fool.

"Baby, breathe." A hand rubs my back. "Shh, breathe, we're here. You're safe. They are gone. She's gone. Let it all out."

"Fuck!" I kick the seat, burying my face in my hands. "I thought I was fine. Shit, I should have known she would pull a stunt like that. I'm a fucking idiot." I laugh bitterly, straightening and wiping my eyes. I thought I cried it all out, but I guess not. "I'm fine, I'm fine," I mutter, trying to fake it until I make it.

I can feel their eyes on me as I slide my shades on and wrap my arms around my stomach, breathing slowly to center myself as I stare out of the window.

"Who is she?" Raff asks. "We'll make sure she never gets near you again."

I laugh bitterly once more. "She won't like that. Her name is Sal Warner. She was my best friend, my sister, until I found her fucking my fiancé in our apartment, and then she sold the story on it . . . or tried."

TWENTY-FIVE

"**S**al Warner, model and actor, born in 1986. Her true name is Kennedy Wise, but she changed it when she entered the modeling world. Her father is some big CEO who buys her way out of shit, with her mother being a socialite. She's as upper class and stuck up as they come, yet she's in debt for two houses she can't afford, or should I say, she *was* until a few months ago when she came into a large amount of cash. When I traced the payments, I could see they were from some local reporters and exclusive stories she sold on Tucker and Reign. It seems their sexual relationship ended that same time, and Tucker hasn't been spotted with her since." I glance up from my iPad to see Raff looking annoyed, Cillian impressed, and Dal . . . well, Dal.

"You learned all that in the space it took for me to check on Reign and make coffee?" Raff asks.

"Bitch, please," I scoff. "I learned all that and made myself a snack."

Cillian laughs and holds out his hand. I give him the iPad as he scrolls through the background check, bank records, and cell phone tap I made. "Impressive. She's a cunt. I can't believe she betrayed Reign that way. No wonder Reign disappeared. She couldn't even trust her fiancé and her best friend."

187

"Yup."

"So, we are killing her, yes?" Dal says slowly.

"What? No!" Raff snaps, leaning up before lowering his voice. Reign disappeared somewhere as soon as we got back, and she clearly needs her space, so we let her have it. "We can't go around killing everyone who insults or hurts her."

"Why?" Dall frowns, blinking in confusion.

"For starters, it's illegal."

"When has that ever stopped us?" I grin, making him glare at me.

"She also doesn't need us to fight her battles for her. She's a grown woman with her own strength and power. Do you think she would want us to wage her wars? No, she would be pissed as hell."

"Or flattered and suck our cocks," I comment helpfully.

Pinching his nose, Raff looks at the ceiling as if praying for strength. "Let me make this clear—nobody is to kill Sal Warner."

"Well, that's boring," comes a drawl, and we all turn to see Regin there. "Especially since I just realized I might be moving past this shit but I'm still mad. Turns out, the old rebel part of me still exists, and she wants revenge."

"Miss Harrow?" Raffiel frowns in confusion as I high-five Dal and lean over.

"Okay, you get the cameras, and I'll get the weapons. I'm thinking we'll make it look like an overdose—"

Reign laughs and kisses my cheek as she sits. "I never got any revenge, not against anyone. I'm all about penance these days. I might be trying to turn over a new leaf and do better, but it's clear Sal isn't. She won't stop until she gets the dirt she wants for another story. I know her. I know what she's like. She drove me out of my own home, my own bed, and my own fucking marriage, so yeah, I want revenge. Maybe not death"—she spares Dal and me a look—"but it's very sweet. Still, there has to be something we can do to get a little even."

"We are here for your protection, Miss Harrow, not to get involved in your battles," Raffiel says, his voice soft.

It's my turn to frown at him. "That's us protecting her."

"I'm not saying we are going to stop you or that we won't be there to protect you." He smirks as Reign laughs. "Just that we can't officially get involved."

"So, ideas . . ." I rub my hands together as I look around. "I say we shave her head and tattoo spunking dicks all over it."

"How about we put burning poop on her door?" Cillian suggests.

"Oh, my sweet summer child." Reign pats his hand.

"I still say we kill her, but fine. What about some torture techniques?" Dal offers.

"I like your idea, but I'm thinking something less breaking the Human Rights Act," Reign explains.

"We pay someone who looks like her to film a sex tape!" I shout.

She sighs. "We aren't about revenge porn, babe."

"The best ones are the simplest. You want to stop her from coming for you? Then scare her." Raffiel shrugs. "You want that revenge? Then look into her eyes while you show her what you're willing to do if she crosses you again. Make her remember why you are Reign Fucking Harrow."

"I like this idea," I say.

She nods. "Me too."

Top secret model espionage is kind of fun. It's not like our missions from before, so I'm almost enjoying it as we all dress in black and idle outside of one of Sal's houses up in the mountains above the city. The lights are on but nobody's in—talk about wasting power.

"How long do we have to wait?" I groan, shifting in the seat before turning to Reign. "Baby, come sit that pretty ass on my lap. I'm bored."

Rolling her eyes, she climbs toward me, and I perk up, but then she sits on Dal's lap, who wraps his arms around her and grins at me. Covering my chest with my hands, I feign dying. "The pain, the betrayal."

She licks her lips and I track the movement, insanely hard. "I have three holes—"

I push down my pants as she laughs and leans back. "Mean," I mutter.

"Lights," Cillian points out, and we sit up straighter and turn to peer out the front window just as a car pulls up to the gates. Sal gets out, waving at someone, before heading inside, teetering on her high heels.

"Mission Smack a Ho is a go," I whisper as Reign giggles at my side and climbs over me to get out, purposely dragging her perfect ass over my cock.

"No fair," I mutter as I climb out after her and pinch her nipple, making her yelp. "I'll kiss it better later."

"Easiest access is over the west wall. Dal and I will cut the alarm and cameras at the back door," Cillian says as he tugs his mask down, and I do the same. We can't be too careful. Reign might like going to prison, and it might be good for her reputation, but I can't be that far away from her. Not for too long anyway.

She pulls down a matching pink mask, her pouty lips tilted up in a grin in the hole. "Let's go, team every hole is a goal."

"Wait, I thought we were team slong-a-dong," I say as we hurry across the road.

"Nope, Cillian and I changed it," she replies as Raffiel holds out his hands to boost her.

"Traitors," I grumble at her back as she places one foot in his hand and he tosses her up and over before taking a running jump, pushing off halfway up the wall, and flipping over. "Well, shit, now we have to show off." I roll my sleeves back and crack my neck as she gapes, straddling the wall.

"Watch this, beautiful," I call quietly.

I take a few steps back before rushing at the wall. I manage to clear it, gripping the lip and flipping myself over, landing on my knees in the flowers next to an annoyed Raffiel. Reign claps softly just as Dal flips over and onto his feet on the ledge. Grinning down at her, he offers her his hand and pulls her up, lowering her down to us before hopping down casually.

"Wait, where's Cillian?" she hisses, only to find him leaning against a tree, watching.

"I give it an eight for a clean dismount, but I give myself a ten since no one even saw me get over." He winks at Reign. "Don't you think, babe?"

"For sure." She nods as he carefully rolls his sleeves back. She watches him, almost drooling at his arms, and he notices. No doubt the fucker will cut all his shirts now so she'll stare at his arms all the time.

Maybe I should. I have nice arms. Glancing down, I flex them, only to look up and see them all watching me. "What? Shouldn't we be moving?"

Sal saunters past the kitchen and upstairs, lights coming on deeper in the house as she goes.

"Okay, team, time to get serious." Raffiel crouches, and we all automatically copy him, falling into old habits even if we aren't invading enemy territory, just a spoiled brat's house. Reign copies us too, and I can't help but grin at our girl. "Okay, Reign is with me. We enter through the back door. Dal, I want you to enter through the second story, but stay out of sight for now. Cil and Astro, I want you to go in through the front. Is that understood? We enter low and slow. I want this tight and quiet, boys."

"Got it." We all nod, even Reign as she grins at us.

"This is so hot," she whispers and winks at Raff. "Remember that voice and use it later."

He tugs at his mask. "You got it, Miss Harrow."

Crouching, I lean in and kiss her. "See you inside, criminal." Cil and I rush through the trees and into position, ready to help our girl get her revenge.

Nobody fucks with Reign Harrow.

TWENTY-SIX

The back door is unlocked just like Cil said, and Raff slips through first. I'm really hoping they cut the cameras or we are going to be in a whole lot of trouble. I don't really give a fuck, though, because she has this coming. She needs to understand that she can't go around ruining lives and get away with it. There are some things her and her daddy's money can't buy—not just class, but safety.

She fucked my fiancé, but worst of all, she betrayed me. She hurt me and then sold my pain for everyone to use as fodder. The bitch deserves it, and I plan to make her aware of that. Raffiel leads the way through the house and up the stairs, silent as a mouse. I try to copy his movements, but he's like a shadow. I know these guys are some sort of prior military, but they are fucking good.

There's music playing—Tucker's of course—when we reach the upstairs. I've never been to this house, so it must be new, and there are photos of her everywhere. Nothing else. How boring. We find her dancing around in her pajamas in a dressing room filled with jewelry, perfume bottles, bags, and clothes. She's completely oblivious. I hear a whisper of movement and turn to see Astro and Cillian strolling down the corridor. Cillian is eating an apple, which makes me grin. They are so casual about breaking and entering, I wonder how many times they have done it before and why I find it so hot.

But where's Dal?

I turn to peek around the door once more and Raff points up. I follow his finger, and my mouth drops open when I see Dal casually sitting on a beam in the ceiling, his legs swinging back and forth. How the fuck?

A scream splits the air and there's a crash. I glance back to see Sal screaming and throwing her phone at us. Raff pulls me out of the way and stomps on it so she can't call the cops as they enter the room. I linger in the doorway as they cross their arms and take their positions.

"Get out! I'll call the police!" she yells, her eyes wide with fear. When they don't speak, she steps back. "Who are you? What do you want?"

It's now or never.

Who do I want to be?

Do I just want to walk away and be the bigger and better person?

I debate it before I realize the necklace I bought Tucker is hanging around her neck. Yeah, fuck being the bigger person. This bitch deserves it. They say those who seek vengeance should dig two graves, and I will. One for her and one for him.

Stepping into the room, I lean against the door as she looks around, debating running. "I wouldn't," I say.

She frowns, squinting at me. "Reign, is that you?"

Ripping the mask up, I grin at her as I ruffle my hair. "Guilty."

She covers her heart as she sags. "Jesus, you scared the shit out of me. What is this? Some sort of hazing for a new TV show?" She rearranges her tits.

"Fuck, you're dumb." I shrug as I kick the door shut, and Cil steps before it to block her from escaping. "This isn't a show, Sal. This is us having a little talk. No cameras, no recordings. Just you and me. It's a little overdue, don't you think? After all, you told me today that you wanted to catch up." I fake pout as she stiffens, glancing around nervously.

"Reign." She laughs anxiously. "We could have set up dinner or something. This is a little weird. How about we go and get a drink? I can call us—"

"Will you shut up?" I snap, and her mouth shuts with an audible click. "Fuck, you never stop talking. Is it to cover your insecurities? Be the loudest in the room and they'll never realize you don't belong?"

Her eyes flare wide. "Stop it," she snaps. "Get out right now. It's not my fault you had a mental breakdown or some shit. You know what, Reign? I'm glad you're back. I'm glad you get to see what everyone really thinks of you. You deserve everything that happened to you."

"Me? How the fuck did I deserve my best friend sleeping with my fiancé and selling the story?"

"You never even wanted him anyway!" she yells. "We both know that, so don't lie to me. He was just a way to make yourself feel better. You might have even loved him, but he wasn't for you and you know it, so don't come here, playing the victim. You forget that I know you, Reign. I know all the evil shit and games you played. I know all your dirty little secrets."

"Is that a threat?" I murmur.

"Need me to spell it out? I thought I was the dumb one."

Dal drops down behind her, and she spins, stumbling back. "Watch your mouth," he warns. "They told me I can't kill you, but if you insult her again, I will forget their orders."

"Reign, get your fucking dogs back in line," she snaps, looking over at me. "And get the fuck out of my house. The press will have a field day with this shit just like your shit show of a life."

"You aren't even going to apologize?" I genuinely can't believe her.

"For what?" she retorts. "We both do what we have to do to get on top. We play the game, Reign, and you can pretend all you want that you don't, but we both know that's a lie. If you're in this world, you've played the game. Fucking Tucker wasn't personal, so get the hell over it."

"You nasty bitch." I shake my head in disbelief, even as my wound rips open from wondering if she's right. Am I no better than her?

"Me?" She steps closer, looking down her nose at me. She's wearing the expression she perfected to tear down those she thinks are below her. "You're nothing, Reign. Just a has-been rock star who's too dumb to even capitalize on her cheating fiancé. You're still that scared little street girl."

"Stop it."

"You're still that country bumpkin with the dead little brother. I'm betting he's so happy he's not alive to see the mess you are now—" Her words cut off as Dal wraps his arm around her neck. "You can't do this!" she coughs out.

"She can't, but I can," Dal states coldly. "I've killed many people, Miss Warner. You would just be another name on a list I don't give a fuck about, but her? I give a fuck about her, and you have upset her. You are going to apologize, and you are going to beg for her forgiveness."

"Dal," Raff warns.

He squeezes his arm tighter, making her struggle as her face turns red. "You will get on your knees like you did for her fiancé, and you will beg her for mercy. She will decide if you live or die."

"Reign," Raff hisses, and I nod.

"Dal, let her go." His eyes go to me, and I see the question there. He would kill her, a famous model, simply for disrespecting and upsetting me.

I think I might be falling in love with this man, even if he is batshit insane.

"She's not worth it," I whisper, shaken at the mention of my brother. She's the only person I ever told, but I didn't tell her everything, and I'm glad for that now. Worry still gnaws at me. Will she sell that story too? Will she tell them all about the past I would do anything to forget? "Let her go, Dal." He promptly releases her, and she tumbles to her knees, clawing at the carpet as she coughs and splutters.

I crouch before her. "I like seeing you scared and humbled," I tell her. "You're right, I'm a mess. I play the game, and I play it well. I didn't get where I am without faking my smile and giving them what they want—the pretty innocent schoolgirl, the bad girl, the fiancée . . . I played them all, and I played them all well, so trust me when I tell you this. I can play the grieving ex-friend if you cross me again." Her eyes widen. "I saved your life tonight, but I won't do it again. If you dare speak another word about me, or we so much as find out you are even speaking to reporters, then I'll let Dal finish the job, understood?"

She nods, tears falling from her eyes.

"You're an ugly crier," I tell her sweetly. Standing, I smirk down at her. "Oh, and Sal? If you ever mention my brother again, forget Dal. I'll kill you myself." I look back at them. "Let's go."

"I don't know. It doesn't seem like it was enough," Astro comments, pushing from the door. "Are you satisfied, Reign?"

"Not at all." My eyes land on her glass jewelry box. I kick the podium, and it tumbles and crashes. Glass shatters everywhere as Sal screams.

"Now, Miss Harrow." I freeze at Raffiel's voice as he heads my way. "If you are going to do it, at least do it right." He pushes a vase over, and it smashes to the floor. "Get the rage out, baby," he whispers. For a moment, I thought he was going to stop me and realize they are bodyguards, not accomplices, but I should have known better.

Laughing, I grab a dress and rip it as she watches. Dal places his foot on her back, keeping her in place as she cries while he grins at me proudly. "Keep going," he urges.

I start to smash the room up, getting out all my anger, hurt, and betrayal. I rip seams out of dresses and designer clothes. I break heels off shoes and toss them into the pile before breaking jewelry. When I reach the perfume bottles, I sweep my arm across the top, shoving them all to the floor while I laugh. When it's done, I'm panting and grinning, and Cillian comes over. "Feel better?"

"Much," I admit. "Alright, time to go."

He nods, but I glance back to see Sal sobbing on the floor. Taking pity, I head her way.

"Oh, and if you report any of this, well, you get the picture." I wink as I pat her cheek. "I hope the house was worth it because I know for certain his dick was not."

I tug my mask back down and offer my hand to Dal. He accepts it, and we leave her crying in the middle of the mess, hurrying out the way we came, but instead of the back gate, I use the front one. No one will give a fuck, and we aren't hiding anymore. As we round the corner, barking reaches us, and we slide to a stop. Lunging on a metal lead, barking in fear and confusion, is a fluffy Samoyed.

"She left her dog outside. The monster!" Dal hisses.

"We need to go before she calls the police," I tell him.

"She won't," Raffiel assures me. "But we should still leave."

"The dog?" I frown at it. She never had a dog when we were friends. It's clearly a puppy and living outside. She hid it behind the wall so her paparazzi can't see it, and I have no doubt that she uses it for photoshoots. Poor little man.

"It's okay," I coo, and it stops barking, whining as it tugs on the chain to get to us. "Raff?"

"No." He drags me up, sparing the dog a sad look before hauling me through the gate and back to the car. Once inside, I pull my mask off and toss it away as Raff slides into the front seat behind the wheel. Astro gets into the passenger seat as Cillian tugs me onto his lap.

"Wait, where's Dal?" I scramble off Cillian's lap and peer out just as I see him running toward us.

"Dal, where were you?" I ask as he jumps into the car, only to turn to show the fluffy dog he stole. "Dal! Did you steal her dog?"

"If she can't look after him, she shouldn't have him," he says. "Drive."

Laughing, I pet the dog as it yips in excitement, crawling across our laps. "I wonder what he's called?"

"He doesn't have a tag." Dal shrugs. "Maybe you should name it."

"We can't keep him, can we?" I frown.

"Call it a gift." He grins as Raff sighs.

"What do you think, little buddy? Want to come home with us? We would walk you, love you, feed you. You can sleep on any bed or sofa,

I don't care, and you can have all the toys." He yips, licking my face as I giggle.

"Okay, buddy, but you need a name. What about Rodger?" he asks. "Okay, no Rodger. What about Raff Jr.?"

"Don't you dare," Raff snaps.

"What do you think, buddy? Raff Jr.?" He barks, and I cuddle him. "You like it? Oh, you're such a good boy, aren't you, little Raff?"

"Fuck." Raffiel groans while Astro laughs and reaches over to pet him. He wiggles forward and licks Raff's face. "Fine, you're cute, but if you shit on my clothes or eat my shoes, we are not friends."

Raff Jr. barks as I sit back, grinning.

Not only did we just get away with breaking and entering, destruction of property, and theft, but damn did it feel good to get out all that rage.

It wasn't the most mature, healing thing to do, but I don't give a fuck. I feel amazing, and I got a dog.

So bite me.

Or better yet, Raff Jr. will bite you.

TWENTY-SEVEN

I was wondering how long it would be before they asked about my brother. They are elite soldiers trained in every aspect so they miss nothing, and they certainly didn't miss Sal mentioning my brother. Surprisingly, they haven't brought it up yet. Cillian and Dal went straight back out and returned with everything a dog could need. I mean everything. I'm pretty sure they bought the store out.

I'm too pumped to sleep, so I show Raff Jr. his new house and he gets settled on one of the beds and instantly begins snoring. I leave him there in peace and go in search of the guys. They are surrounding what seems to be a doggy teepee, debating how to put it together.

"You could just read the instructions," I suggest.

"Instructions are for losers." Raff snorts, even as Cillian glances at them, winking at me as he puts it together as they struggle on the other side.

"When you're done with that, I have some other things I need you to do," I call.

"What?" Astro asks, biting his tongue.

"Oh, don't know, maybe work off some of this excess adrenaline?" They freeze, their heads swinging to me. "I guess if you're busy, though, I could always go work out." I turn away, and I hear the teepee drop before I'm scooped up over someone's shoulder.

Men.

"Living room, it's closer," Astro says, and Cillian turns and sprints into the living room, dropping me onto the floor in a heap as he grins at me.

Raff follows them in, and Dal shuts the double doors after us, leaning against them as he watches me with dark, lustful eyes.

We all know he likes to watch.

I lean back on my elbows and smirk at them, my tongue darting out to wet my lips. "Naked, now," I order.

"You heard her," Raff commands, prowling closer as he unbuttons his shirt. The sound of a zipper has me whirling around to see Astro yanking his jeans down. I glance at Cil to see him throwing his shirt over the sofa, while Dal unbuckles his belt.

I watch them all undress, their hard muscles on display for me as they wait for my next command. "You're mine tonight," I tell them as I get to my knees and push down the spaghetti straps of the simple silk dress I'm wearing.

It pools at my waist, exposing my breasts, and my nipples tighten under their gazes. My desire only grows as I move my thighs apart to tease them. "And I'll have you however I want."

"And how do you want us?" Dal asks.

Sliding my hands up, I squeeze my breasts. I watch Dal's eyes darken and know he's barely holding himself back.

"Baby," Astro growls, pacing before me.

I drop to my hands and crawl right to Dal, sliding my palms up his thighs as he shudders. I stop when I'm level with his huge, hard cock. Licking my lips, I blow out softly and watch him shiver. I grin as I wrap my hands around his length and squeeze. "I want you all hard. I want every hole filled. I don't want to be able to walk after." Squeezing tighter, I grin. "I'll leave the details up to you."

I gasp when a hand slides into my hair, guiding my head closer to Dal's cock as he leans against the door. "When he snaps, you'll have to pin him down, Miss Harrow," Raffiel orders. "That means I get that sweet ass of yours."

Opening my mouth, I swipe my tongue out, teasing Dal, and with a groan, he surges forward, slamming his cock down my throat. I gag a little, but I tighten my hand on his length, and Raff guides me, gently pulling me off and bobbing my head back down.

"Good girl," Raff praises. "Astro."

I hear movement, but I can't look away from Dal's dark eyes as I torture him, sliding him in deeper until I can't breathe or think.

"Pet that pretty pussy and get our girl nice and wet. She'll need it to take all of us."

Astro doesn't hesitate, and his mouth brushes across my neck as his hand cups my cunt. Rolling my hips, I grind into him as I suck harder on Dal, watching as he smashes his head back into the door.

Astro pets me, sucking on my neck as his fingers slide through my wet folds and thrust inside me, curling and finding that spot that has me moaning around Dal's dick.

The sound makes him jerk and he thrusts harder, taking my mouth brutally as Astro fucks me with his fingers until I'm dripping wet, and when he slides his fingers out, he trails them up, circling my asshole.

"Got to get this hole nice and wet, baby, if you are taking all of us."

My eyes shut as I push back, letting him fuck my ass, stretching me as I reach for my peak, but just as I'm about to come, he pulls away. I whine and shake, deciding to take it out on Dal as I clamp my mouth around him.

He bellows, gripping my head and yanking me off his cock. I fall backwards, and my back hits the carpet. I look up to see him glaring, his nostrils flaring and chest heaving.

He lunges at me, forcing himself between my thighs.

Just like Raff said, Dal snaps, so I roll us. I know he lets me, otherwise I wouldn't be able to, and I grind against his cock. I work myself on his length until he lifts me and slams me down, impaling me on it.

Moaning, I roll my hips and ride him as I dig my fake nails into his chest, pin him, and fuck him.

My very own trapped beast.

A hand hits my back, pushing me down, and my eyes widen as I feel the thick head of a cock at my ass.

"Be a good girl, Miss Harrow, and scream for me."

Raff drags his cock across my ass, all while Dal rocks into me from below as he tries to hold still. We all know he won't last long, so when Raff starts to push into me, I push back, forcing his huge length inside my ass as I scream.

The pain and ecstasy are too much.

The feeling of being stretched between them, with their hands sliding possessively over my body, sends me spiraling, clamping around them in my release as I cry out.

Dal roars, lifting his hips and forcing himself deeper, and Raf slides in the last few inches.

My head hangs as I wind my hips softly, riding out my release, but hands grip my hips and my shoulders, holding me between them, and they start to move.

It's not soft or even loving.

No, they move hard.

I love it. I can't speak. I'm just a dripping mess between them as they plunder my body. Raff snarls in my ear as he slams into my ass, my cheeks jiggling with the force. Dal works deep inside me, hitting that spot that has me seeing stars, even as he bites and sucks every inch of skin he can reach.

"Keep your eyes on him, baby," Raff growls. "Look at what you do to him, feel what you do to me." He brutally twists inside my ass and I whine.

A hand grips my jaw, their thumb and finger digging in until I open my mouth. "Turn your head," Raff commands, and I do as I'm told, opening my eyes to see Cil and Astro watching me on their knees. "Suck them."

He doesn't have to tell me twice. I reach for Astro first, wrapping my lips around his cock and sucking him all the way back. The feeling of being filled by three of them makes me clench before I pull my head off and turn to Cil, licking and sucking his tip before swallowing him and pulling back.

"Closer," I say, and they move closer, practically pushed together, and an idea comes to mind.

It's filthy, but I want it.

Trusting Raff and Dal to hold me, I reach out and push their cocks together. They jerk, but then I lower my mouth, licking and sucking them both. They touch, but it makes it easier for me to play.

Cil and Astro groan.

"Fuck," Raff snarls, his hips snapping against my ass.

Dal almost lifts me into the air with his feral thrusts. "Mine," Dal growls, his eyes wild, and I know he's close.

Turning my head, I lean down and press my lips to his. "Yours."

He kisses me hard, bruising my lips with force as they fuck me. With a roar, he jerks below me, and I feel him explode, pumping me full of his cum, while Raff works me on his cock.

"I'm so close," he says, and I sit up, my back pressed to his chest as I take him deeper.

"Then come," I order as his hand slides down and he pinches my clit.

I cry out as my own release slams through me. Biting my neck, he follows me into pleasure. He jerks, pushing his cock deeper into my ass as I feel him spill.

I slump in their grasp as they slowly pull from my body, making me groan.

"Our turn. Open your eyes, sweetheart, and watch us as we fuck you."

"Our dirty little girl," Cil praises as Raff lifts me and sets me on my knees before them. I crumple, my body lax in pleasure, and Astro catches me.

I'm rolled over and lifted, my ass yanked into the air as Cil buries his cock deep inside me, making my eyes roll back in my head. I've barely caught my breath when Astro, who is holding me from below, pushes into me, forcing his cock inside my cunt with Cil.

My screams bounce off the walls.

I can't breathe, can't think. I can't do anything but be fucked by them. Their two huge dicks slide in and out of my pussy, stretching me to the point of pain. The wet sound of us coming together makes me arch my chest out as I give myself over to them.

"Look at her," Dal comments. "Our fucking goddess."

"Ours." Cil nods, his eyes bright as he fucks me.

Astro's warm body heats my back, sliding against me as they fuck me, holding me captive between them, and there is nowhere else I would rather be.

"So beautiful," Astro croons in my ear. "Look at you, taking us so well. Our rock star, your pussy is our stage." He groans in my ear as I tighten around them. "Keep doing that, Reign, and I won't last. You feel too good as it is."

Cillian leans down, sucking my nipple into his mouth, making me cry out.

"I love the way you moan for us." Astro wraps his arm tighter around me. "There is no other sound like it." I do it again, unable to hold back as Astro's hand slips through my messy cunt and rubs my clit. "Now come for us, Reign. Let me feel it, sweetheart. Let me feel you explode for us and drench our cocks while we fill you with our cum. Forget drugs or booze, Reign, all we need is you, our addiction." His words are so sexy as they're whispered in my ear.

Cil bites my nipple, and I can't hold back anymore.

I give into the tidal wave, letting it swallow me, my body clamping on the edge of pain, and Astro groans in my ear, his cock jerking as he spills deep inside me.

Snarling, Cil slides in and out, fucking me shallowly before exploding across my pussy and stomach.

I can't open my eyes. I can't speak or move.

I guess I got what I wanted, and it was so fucking good.

"She named a dog after me." He sounds pained.

"And you love that dog, don't lie. I caught you teaching him push-ups this morning," I retort without even glancing at Raff as I pour my apple juice and turn to lean against the counter. Said dog, Junior, is currently on Astro's knee as he eats around him. It's seriously too fucking cute, not to mention how fluffy he was to cuddle last night, much to Astro's chagrin, who got jealous of the dog.

"He needs to be part of the team," is all Raffiel says. "And befitting of the name."

"Sure thing, big guy." Grinning, I head his way and plop down on Cillian's lap at the table, stealing his bacon. He simply kisses my cheek, moves the bacon closer to me, and eats the toast. My heart softens. They truly are right when they say a way to a woman's heart is through her stomach—or her vagina . . . or both. Definitely both with this lot.

"Are we committing any crimes today, or just the usual chaos?" Raff asks, sipping his coffee. The sunlight streams in, lighting the room brightly. The first thing I did this morning was check socials and news to see if Sal reported us, which she didn't. She's probably too scared to.

I almost can't believe we got away with it, but it sure did make for some epic sex.

Top ten easily.

"I'm going to work outside for a few hours. There are some lyrics I need to get right and nature helps," I reply. "Then we're going to the studio later. We played, now we need to work."

"Sounds good." Raff nods. "Then it's drill time."

They all groan, and Astro even looks at me pleadingly. "Show him your boobs! Distract him!"

"It won't work." Raff grins. "Okay, it might, but she needs to work and so do we. We need to protect Reign, which means being alert and in shape, so drills, soldiers. Outside in ten." He stands, kisses me, and leaves.

"I hate drills," Cillian grumbles. "I can never feel my legs after."

"Tell me about it. After the way you drilled me last night, I couldn't feel my legs either." He chokes on his toast, and I pat his back. "Better?" I ask sweetly.

"We better get ready." Dal stands, and with one longing look at me, he leaves too.

"Me too." I hop up, stealing more bacon before kissing them on the way to the studio. I'm not gone long. I grab my guitar and notebooks and make my way into the huge daybed outside, setting up. The guys are nowhere to be seen, so I plug in my headphones and listen to the beat Jack made, scribbling along to it. Sometime later, a grunting noise invades the beat, and I pull out the earbuds and turn, my mouth dropping open at the sight.

Glistening with sweat, and wearing nothing but shorts, are all four of my bodyguards. Forget writing lyrics. I lean back in the daybed and watch as they work through sets of grueling exercises that would put even the Rock to shame. I watch the play of their muscles, their veins, and the way their bodies move. In Cillian's case, I ogle the way his huge cock bounces in his shorts as he does his burpees. It's way better than porn, and I rub my thighs together to get some friction as my pussy pulses in need. They are completely oblivious to me watching them. My nipples pebble as the heat beats down on me, warming my skin as I roll onto my side to watch them better.

Unable to resist, I slide my hand down my stomach and into my denim shorts, rubbing my pussy over my panties. Dal is the first to notice. His sharp eyes lock on the movement, and he stills before leaping down and working harder. His eyes remain on me despite Raff's orders. It doesn't take the others long to notice what he's watching.

They all stop, their eyes on my hand as I lean back and slide my fingers past the barrier of my panties and across my slick center. My hips roll as I play with my clit, watching the pull of their muscles. "I need something to watch," I call to them.

"You heard Miss Harrow." Raff smirks, watching my fingers for a moment. His muscles stretch as he turns to press into a push-up. Astro purposely flexes as he leaps, Cillian grins as he jumps, and Dal copies them with elegant moves that almost look like he's dancing.

They are all sweaty and glistening, their muscles ready for me to explore and play with.

It's like an all-you-can-eat buffet.

Flicking my clit, I moan loud enough for them to hear as I roll my hips. My heart races, and my body overheats as desire roars through me, leaving me breathless and touching myself faster.

"Shit, I can't concentrate," Cil says, his eyes locked on me as I touch myself at the sight of them.

"Fuck this," Astro growls and heads my way.

Striding over to me like a blond Adonis, Astro does a push-up above me, blocking out the sun. "See something you like?"

"Absolutely," I murmur, rolling my clit harder and lifting my hips.

"Need a hand?" he flirts, watching my hips.

"No, I'm good. Go back to being eye candy," I reply, pulling my fingers from my shorts and sliding them across his lips. They part as he groans, his pink tongue darting out to lap at my cream.

"Shit, Reign."

"Back in formation," Raffiel barks.

Throwing me a glare that promises retribution, Astro stomps back over as they carry on with their drills. Raff pushes them hard, no doubt for my benefit, as I leisurely play with myself. I drag my pleasure out as I push two fingers inside myself, letting every noise of pleasure slip past my lips to give them motivation.

The sight of them and the feeling of my own fingers finally sends me over the edge with a cry, and I arch off the daybed, my legs shaking as I come. I pull my fingers from my shorts and open my eyes to see them all slack-jawed with tented shorts.

Sucking my fingers clean, I wink at them. "Back to work, boys. Got to keep those bodies prepared."

Astro smirks. "In case you're attacked?"

"In case I want to climb you," I respond as I put my earbuds in once more, grinning at their incredulous expressions.

TWENTY-EIGHT

"Y**ou never asked about my brother," Reign says randomly.

I turn my eyes from the horror flick we're watching and peer down at her where she's cuddled into my side. Her warmth invades my usual cold, and the numbness fades around her. I wonder if this is how most males feel all the time. It must be exhausting, not to mention the continuous hard-ons.

"It's your past, your story," Cillian murmurs, squeezing her hand and laying his head on her shoulder. We are way past caring about lines, and in this house, we can be whatever we want. "If you want to tell us, you will, and if not, we respect that. We don't get your pain just because your asshole ex-friend used it like ammo."

It's quiet for a moment, but I feel her tense.

"His name was Attie," she whispers. "He's dead now."

That's all she says, and it's clear she's swallowing anything else, but the fact that she trusted us with that shows how far she's come. "Thank you for telling us," Raff murmurs, leaning over to kiss her. "I'm sorry about your brother."

"Thank you," she says.

Just then, a cell phone rings loudly. Hers is usually on silent or forgotten somewhere, so it must be one of ours. Raff groans, pulling it out and answering.

"Yes?" he barks, and then he listens before handing it over to Reign. "It's for you," he grumbles.

"Hello?" she answers as I reach over and pause the film. "How the hell did you even get his—never mind. The answer is no. Fuck no actually. I told you, my life, my choice. I am not going on his show." She pauses. "Because he's a sexist fucking pig."

There's silence again as she listens, her eyes narrowing and brows furrowing. Her lips twist in anger—anger that has my cock jerking. "I don't give a fuck what the PR team or my contract says. We made a deal." She drops her head back, clenching her fists. "If you put me on that show, I won't hold back. You've been warned." She disconnects the call and tosses the phone.

"Want me to beat him up?" I ask, deadly serious. I heard his voice. It was her dickhead manager. I can't kill him . . . .At least, I don't think so.

She laughs, and I frown. Did she think I was joking? Patting my chest, she leans into me again. "Tempting." She's quiet for a while, and we trade glances, wondering how we can help. She was so happy and relaxed, and one phone call changed everything. No wonder she protects her privacy so much. Sighing, she grabs the remote and turns the movie off, making Astro groan, but she ignores him and puts on a talk show interview.

There's a middle-class white man behind a desk with celebrities on a sofa, although I couldn't name any of them. He's laughing and joking with a man in a tux, and next to that man is a young lady in a red dress, who looks distinctly uncomfortable. If you weren't looking at her body language, you wouldn't notice. She smiles and laughs at the jokes, even when they are at her expense.

"I fucking hate him," she mutters. "I remember being in her place. I cried after my interview with him when he insinuated I was only a good lay and not a musician. He's a sexist asshole, but he's the best in the industry. He can make or break careers, so you grit your teeth and smile. Most managers even prep you for it. Look at her." I do, frowning when I see a sheen in her eyes. "She hates it. She's embarrassed and upset. It shouldn't be like this. You shouldn't be forced to endure that for simply wanting to do something you love. Fuck it. Call them back and tell them to book me."

"What are you planning?" I ask since I can almost see the wheels turning in her head.

"Anarchy." She grins and then tilts her head. "Can you get me dirt on him?"

"What kind?" I murmur as the others straighten.

"Something I can use, ammunition."

"Be very careful what you're asking for," I warn, and she frowns, looking at Raff for clarity.

"Be very precise with what you want to happen, Reign. We are not private investigators; we are the best killers in the world. So, what do you want?" he presses.

"What do you want?" I repeat.

She gnaws on her lip, thinking it through. It's clear she doesn't like asking this of us, used to fighting her own battles, but I would do much, much worse than track down some dirt on this man for her. The things I would do if she simply asked would horrify her. I need to be sure what she wants so I don't upset her. She might like a little chaos, but she is not a killer.

Not like me.

"I want dirt. Nothing else. No one gets hurt; nobody dies," she answers, saying it like she can't believe she has to. "I want something I can use to embarrass him. He loves throwing people's pasts in their faces, so I want to do the same to him."

"Done." I nod and stand, kissing her swiftly. "I will have it in an hour."

"He's that good?" she asks as I leave.

"He's better than that. Just be careful what you ask him for, Reign. I have a feeling Dal wouldn't deny you anything," Raffiel warns her.

He's right.

Raff Jr. barks as if he agrees.

TWENTY-NINE

Dal got exactly what I needed. I don't ask how because part of me doesn't want to know. There's something unhinged in Dal's eyes, and it's clear I have no idea just what he is capable of. Raffiel basically implied he's loyal to me now and I can use him as a weapon, so I need to be careful how I wield him. It doesn't mean I'm scared of him—no, not the man who snuck into my bed and held me tight all night as if he couldn't bear to be away from me or listened to my lyrics and helped me work through the issues today. Dal is much more than a killer, but from the confusion in his eyes, it's clear he didn't know that.

Until now.

I stand in the wings, waiting for my turn. I've dressed the part of a villain in a low-cut, revealing black dress with slits up both sides. My makeup is dark and bold, and my piercings and tattoos are on display. I'm everything he will pick apart, which is just what I want. I want his focus on me. I want him to take the first shot. I'm ready this time. I still remember the first time I stood here, nervously chewing my nails. I was so young, so naïve, as my manager told me to smile more, to laugh at the jokes, and that this could make my career so play nice. Well, fuck him. It's clear he regrets it now. I see the panic on his face as he strides toward me.

"Play nice," he hisses. "Remember who he is."

"Oh, I do." I grin, and he groans.

"Why do I regret this?" he mutters.

"You should," I retort as I turn back to the stage as he lands another jab. I spent the whole day preparing while writing a new song. The release of my new single is coming next week. I understand the need for marketing and media, but this? This isn't it.

"Now let us welcome Reign Harrow to the stage!" he calls as the crowd goes mad. "The disgraced rock star recently made a reappearance, and I'm sure we're all dying to ask the dirty questions."

It's my cue, and his line sets the tone for the interview. He wants to make me out to be the villain. I can play that well. Smiling widely, I saunter onto the stage, winking and blowing kisses at the crowd. The others sitting on the sofa have already been interviewed, and they slide down to make room for me. There's a very famous, middle-aged male, an older female filmmaker, and a new pop singer. I nod at them in greeting, even though we met backstage before this. They expect me to sit and joke and smile. I sit smoothly, crossing my legs, and Gerald, the interviewer, frowns at me for not shaking his hand, but he sits behind the wooden desk as the crowd quiets down so he can talk.

"Welcome, Reign. It's nice to see you back, and with some clothes on this time!" he jokes, and the crowd laughs nervously with him. No doubt he's referring to those nude pictures that were leaked last year right after I came on this show.

"Well, I was told I could be arrested if I were naked on the show."

He laughs, as do those next to me.

"I don't know. It would be more comfortable than this tux," the middle-aged actor—James, I think his name is—jokes, and I grin at him as I lean back.

"Tell me about it. You don't have to wear a bra and Spanx," I reply, and he chuckles with me.

"Oh really? With the sort of dresses you wear, I always assumed you went nude underneath." Gerald smirks. "What about the one we saw the other day? How do you even wear underwear with that?" He displays a picture from the paparazzi the other day when I wore a tiny dress.

"You don't." I blink innocently as he leers and the others laugh.

"Okay, okay, Reign, we have some very important questions to ask you tonight." He becomes serious.

I'll give him one chance. If he asks about my music like he should, then I might let him off. It's his choice. I almost hope he takes it.

"Tucker . . . Is he good in bed? Did you get bored? Is that why you left? Rumors are he cheated on you. Can you tell us with whom?" When I don't respond, he carries on. "Or maybe there's a new romance? Planning to settle down and have kids, are we?"

Settle. Down.

As if a man will tame me. He made his choice.

He made me out to be nothing more than a vessel for a man's pleasure. He doesn't care about me as a person, just what I can give others.

I have a choice. I could bite my tongue, play nice, and be the old Reign Harrow, but fuck that. No one likes a revolutionary, at least not until they are dead.

It would be easy to go with the program, and I could play it safe, but safe is boring and overrated. I want to live big. I want to live so big that they never forget the woman they tried to destroy. He wants a reaction, so he'll get one. It's time someone took him down a peg, and I'm in the position to do so. I have an audience, and I can either use that for good or bad. I choose good, so no other girls who come after me have to go through the same shit. No more baby models, artists, and singers will have to suffer his degradation.

Dal called me an anarchist. Maybe he isn't wrong, but an anarchist isn't a villain.

No, they are fighters who are given no other choice.

I came back with the plan to do what I wanted, and I will do just that, starting here. This is about more than my fame and making money. This is about who I want to be as a person.

"You have no better question than about my ex or if I'm sleeping with someone else?" He blinks, and the crowd goes quiet. "Or when, not if, I will have kids and get married? As if that's all I am good for?"

"It's just a question." He holds up his hands.

I tilt my head mockingly. "Does anyone ever ask you that?"

He shifts uncomfortably. "No, but then again, I don't have the capacity to have kids," he jokes, and some laugh nervously.

"So, because I have the capability to produce children, nothing else about me matters? I'm more than my uterus. I owe no one anything, especially not my body or my life. Women are more than their ability to procreate. I'm so tired of women only having to be one thing. You wouldn't ask this of my male counterparts, so why do you feel comfortable asking me this? Is it because you think I'll laugh and look pretty? Yeah, fuck that. My life is whatever I want it to be, and I owe nobody, I mean nobody jack shit."

He laughs nervously. "You seem very angry tonight, Reign. Maybe you do need to get laid," he jokes, but it falls flat. Everyone is staring at us, wide-eyed.

"It's not anger. It's self-respect. It is me standing up for myself against you and every male like you. Call it anger to try and belittle us and make our intellect seem lower. You whittle down our confidence to an instinctive emotion. Too emotional. Too angry. No, Gerald, this is me tired of being treated like a piece of meat. Night after night, you do this to women. You don't ask them about their thoughts on what's happening in the world. You don't ask them about their passion or why they are here. No, you reduce them to a sex object."

"They do that by coming on here," he sneers as I see a manager rushing over, making a cutting motion across his throat.

"Let me get this straight. You're saying women deserve to be reduced to sex symbols and nothing else for simply wanting to succeed? Couldn't the same be said for you then? You want to succeed, and since you have no clear talent, you use others, dissecting their lives for credit and turning them into a joke. Tell me, Gerald, since you seem to love dirt so much, does your wife know you're sleeping with your assistant who's half your age?"

I hear the shocked gasps and whispers.

"I d-don't know what you're talking about. Obviously, you aren't here to enjoy the evening, so I think we'll move on." He turns to the cameras, pale and unsure.

"I don't think we will." I smile, fluttering my lashes. "I'm here to talk about my new music. It comes out next week for anyone who wants to know, and the very reason I wrote that song, which is filled with female rage, as you so succinctly put it, is because of men like you. You tell us to sit prettily, settle down, and behave." I peer down at the older actress. "Would you like to discuss the new film you shot that deals with sexual exploitation in Hollywood? I'm assuming he didn't ask you."

"He didn't." She smiles brightly at me. "I would love to talk about it."

I stand and move over to Gerald. "How about you sit on the sofa? I'll do the interview."

He hesitates before getting to his feet uncertainly. Sitting behind the desk, I lean over to speak with her. "Tell me all about it. What did it take to get the script approved? How did you secure your budget? How did the story come about? Tell me everything about the brilliant women acting in it, shining a light on the dark underbelly of Hollywood."

She explains it all. She's intelligent and incredible, and when she's done, I stand and walk over and shake her hand. "Thank you." She blinks up at me. "For every woman who came before and after. You are changing things for the better. I want to thank you as a woman who has been through those very same things."

She stands and hugs me, and when she pulls back, she's smiling brightly. "Thank you for taking over tonight. I worried I would only be here to fill their demographic."

James stands and glances at Gerald. "The film sounds incredible, as does your new song, Miss Harrow. I would like to apologize for Gerald's behavior. He doesn't speak for all of us. I personally don't care about your personal life. It's personal for a reason. You're right though. I did nothing to stop it. I sat and nodded with him, too scared to speak out. Thank you for calling me out on that." He glances at the crowd. "This, right here, is important. These women? They are the future, not him, not me. These are the role models you should look up to. Two very powerful, intelligent, and brilliant women, carving a path for others."

I take his hand and we stand side by side. Even the young artist joins us despite what it might do to his career. "Tonight, I invite you all to thank the wonderful, talented guests who stand at my side." I wink at the cameras. "Oh, and don't forget to revolt every once in a while."

They cut, and I turn to Gerald who's still standing in shock.

"You might want to call your wife. Oh, and if I ever see you tear down another woman on this show, I'll come back with worse dirt. Understood?"

He nods, and with a smile and a hug for the others, I head off stage to my men. They clap and whistle, and I see the pride on their faces.

Oh yeah, being a rebel feels good, especially with them at my back.

THIRTY

Reign's manager nearly passed out when she started talking, and now he's practically crying in a corner, his phone ringing nonstop. I ignore him, smirking as my girl heads toward us. She's so fucking sexy and strong, I want to drop to my knees and worship her. I don't, though, simply because I wouldn't want to undermine what she just did.

She just gave every woman, every girl, the ability to fight back and change the narrative.

Fuck, she's incredible.

I've craved control my entire life, but with her? I'm learning to love the chaos. "Incredible, Miss Harrow!" I murmur.

"You think so?"

"I think I just had babies," Astro says, making her laugh.

I see Gerald heading this way, and I nod, tugging her behind me. Dal steps into his path with his arms crossed.

"How did you know about my affair?" Gerald roars at Reign.

She ignores my insistent tugging and steps to my side. "You have your sources, I have mine," she replies innocently. "Were they wrong?"

"I'm going to ruin you," he hisses.

"Do not threaten Miss Harrow again or I'll take it as a sign of aggression, and as her bodyguard, I am within my rights to not only

221

disarm you, but make sure you could never follow through on that threat."

He blinks at me, paling when he realizes I'm very serious, and then he turns and storms away.

She takes Cillian's arm as we lead her through the building and out to the car, ready to get out of here since she just made an enemy. I scan the area around the car. We left it at the side, knowing we would need to make a quick getaway. We even paid someone to let it idle at the back where the other celebrities enter so we could avoid the cameras.

She hesitates and I stiffen, disliking that she put herself out in the open. It's like I feel eyes on me everywhere.

"Miss Harrow, get in the car," I snap.

She turns her glare on me, making me hard and so goddamn turned on it's difficult to breathe.

"I was just going—"

"Reign, get in the fucking car," I order, my need and worry for her safety mixing together.

Her eyes widen before she ducks into the car with a defiant hair flip. I climb in after her, the doors shut, and then we're off. Leaning forward, I grip her throat. "Good girl," I praise, and she melts. The sight is so fucking sexy, I can't help myself. "You did so good tonight, baby, so fucking good. I think that deserves a reward, don't you?"

"Absolutely," she replies breathlessly, her eyes locked on me. I love how I get to touch her and order her around when no one else can.

"I have a plan for when we get home, but for now, be a good girl and lean back."

She does as I command for once, leaning back in the seat.

Sliding to my knees in the car, I push her dress up. "You were so incredible tonight, baby. Let me show you how much I want you. I wanted to storm onto that stage and make you mine to prove it."

She groans, widening her legs as I settle between them, my hands stroking her skin.

It's not a long drive from here to the house, so I make quick work of her underwear so her pussy is bare before me. My cock jerks in my slacks, but I ignore my own need and focus on hers.

Sliding my hands up, I grip her hips and lift her to my mouth. She moans as I lick and suck her pussy, her sweet, fruity taste exploding on my tongue. She fights my hold, but I grip her harder, tugging her to my mouth so I can bury my face in her cunt as I lick her pretty little clit, torturing her. I slide two fingers inside her and work them deep, curling them and rubbing at the same time. I force her pleasure from her as she grinds into my touch and cries out for me.

Her hands claw at the seats and then my hair, and when I suck on her clit, she explodes for me.

I thrust my tongue into her alongside my fingers to drink from her, and as she slumps back into her seat, I clean her up before sitting back. "That will tide you over until we get home."

"What happens then?" she asks, her eyebrow arched.

"Then you're mine," I tell her.

She swallows hard, searching my eyes, but I see the lust in her gaze. Smirking, I sit back and wait, feeling her eyes roving over my body until we finally pull up outside.

I get out first, helping her out after me.

Lifting her into my arms, I carry her into the house and head straight upstairs. Once we're in her room, I lower her to her feet where she's safe from cameras or prying eyes.

"Take off your clothes, Miss Harrow."

"Make me." She tilts her chin up in challenge.

The outside world gets the strong rock star, but I get the bratty whore, and I love it.

"I said take your fucking clothes off, Reign," I order, rolling my sleeves back. "Now."

Meeting my eyes with that defiant tilt to her head, she reaches behind her back and drops the dress, leaving her in her black, sky-high heels and a red lace bra and thong. My mouth goes dry at the sight, and my cock twitches in my pants, making me forget who is in charge for a moment.

When she prowls over to me, swaying her hips, and runs her hand down my chest to grip my dick through my pants, I groan. "If I'm yours, Raffiel, then show me." Squeezing me tightly, she steps backward, smirking all the way.

I advance on her, watching her eyes flare in desire as her breathing picks up. My little rock star likes to play, likes to be my prey, and that's exactly what she is.

I'm a hunter, and I'm going to capture and breed her tonight until every inch of her drips with my essence.

"Run, little rock star, if you can," I growl.

She turns and takes off, heading out into the hallway. I watch her go, slowly unbuckling my belt and wrapping it around my hands before storming after her. Each step is deliberate and loud so she can hear me coming. I hear her gasp and giggle and I follow the sound, hearing her heels tapping as she races down the hallway. Smirking, I stop behind a decorated bookcase and wait. A few minutes later, it's clear she's tired of waiting and she storms past me.

I silently step behind her and wrap the belt around her neck, tugging her back as she screams. It turns into a moan as I press her against the bookcase. Her hands hit the shelves, sending books tumbling to the floor as I tighten the belt. I run my nose across her neck, feeling her pulse as I lick up to her ear. "Caught you, Miss Harrow. Now you're mine." Kicking my foot between hers, I force her legs open wider. "Be a good girl and scream for me. Let all those cameras outside capture you being fucked hard by your bodyguard. Let them all imagine how you taste and feel and how you look when you come."

"Fuck." She pushes her ass back into my cock and grinds. "Make me, Raff, if you can."

"So bratty," I snark, then I tighten the belt until she gasps and wrap it around my fist. I hold her there as I slide my other hand up and pull on her thong, making her groan. I do it again, knowing it's slapping against her cunt. Smirking, I slide my hand between her silken thighs, feeling the wet material clinging to her pretty pussy.

I rub the material into her clit as she moans, her heels almost falling off as she stands up, trying to relieve some pressure from her neck, but if she does, she loses the pressure on her pussy. Whimpering, she pushes down, choosing her pleasure and giving into my dominance.

"Good girl," I coo, rubbing the sopping wet material into her clit, forcing her pleasure higher until she's panting. I feel the heat rolling from her body as she winds her hips, her hand slapping against the bookcase and holding on. "You remember what I told you last time? Good girls get fucked, so come for me. Let me feel it, and then you'll get my big cock like you want."

Her head drops forward as she races for her release. I help her along, pinching her clit until she jerks.

Wave after wave of pleasure crashes through her as she cries out. I release the belt enough to hear it, all while rubbing her through her release until she slumps into the bookcase.

"I love the way you come, baby." I pull my dripping fingers away. "Taste your surrender. Taste the pleasure only I can give you."

Her lips wrap around my fingers and suck greedily, making my cock jerk. I can't wait anymore. I kick her legs farther apart and snap her thong off, shoving it in my pocket as I push my pants down. Stroking my length, I press it against her pretty ass as she groans, sucking harder on my fingers. I pull them away and slide them down her body, tweaking her nipple behind the lacy material as she cries out.

Gliding my hand down over her hip, I tug her leg up and press the high-heeled foot into the third shelf up, opening her cunt for me. "Stay like that or I'll stop," I warn.

Her head presses to a shelf as I run my cock along her wet pussy.

"Look at the mess you made for me, Miss Harrow."

"Raff," she begs.

Lining up with her entrance, I tighten the belt. "Scream, rock star," I command as I slam into her.

Despite the belt, she screams, her nails curling into the wood as I force my huge length deep inside her. I force her to take every inch as I settle one hand on her hip to control her as I pull out and slam back in. I'm unable to go slow, needing her hard and fast.

The bookcase rattles with the force of my thrusts, causing books to tumble to the floor as I fuck her. Her claws scratch the wood as I drag her head back, forcing it into a long line for me to lick and bite as she writhes, her pussy clenching around me.

She's close again. I can feel it in the tremor of her muscles and the tightening of her perfect cunt.

"Fuck, you take me so well, baby. This pretty cunt was made for my cock . . . was made for me to fuck and fill with my cum, wasn't it?" I snarl as I hammer into her.

"Yes," she gasps, rolling her hips as much as she can to take me deeper.

Jerking her head back, I thrust deep inside her until she whimpers, and when I reach down and pinch her clit, she shatters for me. Her eyes roll into the back of her head and her mouth parts on a silent scream. Her cunt clenches around me so tightly, I have to grit my teeth to hold back my own release.

She writhes on my cock, wringing out her pleasure until she slumps once more. "You didn't scream loud enough for me," I tell her. "Let's correct that, shall we?" Turning her to face me, I grip her chin and kiss her hard. "Clearly, you can't scream loud enough, so let's make them watch."

Dragging her by the belt, I throw her against the window in the hallway farther down. I know they are darkened so no one can't see in from the other side, but the effect is the same as I push her to her knees and use the belt to pull her head up. "Suck me, rock star. Let them see and take pictures of you on your knees as you suck off your bodyguard."

Her pupils are blown as she greedily wraps her shaking hands around my length and sucks me into her talented mouth, swallowing the taste of her pussy and my precum. I'm close from fucking her, but I want to make it last.

I squeeze my base, even as I slide to the back of her throat, my hips flexing as I hold back, but I should have known better. Reign's eyes narrow and she smacks my hand away, sliding hers down to cup my balls and squeeze until I can't take it.

My head drops forward as my chest heaves, my hips snapping with brutal thrusts as I use her like my personal fuck toy. She lets me, moaning around my length and swallowing me deeper until the sight has red-hot lava flowing through my veins, squeezing my balls dry.

"Fuck, baby, I'm going to come," I warn, but she slides my cock to the entrance of her mouth, letting me unload all over her tongue.

She opens her mouth wider, letting my cum drip down her chin to her chest before she curls her tongue in with a groan. "I love the way you taste. I want to cover myself in it." Getting to her feet, she presses me to the window. "I hope they saw," she tells me, pressing up on her tiptoes. "I hope they recorded me sucking you off. I hope they saw how crazy you make me." She leans in and kisses me softly. "Now take me to bed, Raffiel, and do all the wicked things you're thinking about."

She steps back and takes my hand. I follow, unable to do anything else.

THIRTY-ONE

T he sun shines through the window, hitting my face as I slowly wake up. There's a leg holding mine down and an arm slung across my back, and when I lift my head, I see Raffiel there, asleep. For a moment, I just soak in the sight of him. He's naked, and the scars littering his body are proof of his harsh life, but for once, he's not running into a situation or barking commands. No, he's sleeping in, something I've never seen him do. Smiling, I lay my head back on the pillow and just watch him like a creeper, cuddling deeper into Raff Jr., who must have wormed his way into my bed during the night. He seems to split his time between all of the guys and has complete run of the house, and we hired the best dog walker and trainer around to help. It's clear he's fitting in like he's always belonged here.

Just like them.

"It's weird to watch people sleep, Miss Harrow." Raff's voice comes out rough, and one eye opens as he grins at me.

I snuggle deeper into the bed. I didn't notice a change in him indicating he was awake, the sneaky bastard. "You love it," I purr.

Grinning wider, he tugs me into his arms and closes his eye again. "Uh-uh, go back to sleep."

"It's morning," I protest.

"It's too early." He buries his head in my neck as I grin.

"It's nine." I feel him stiffen and his head lifts. He's wide awake now.

"Nine? No, it's not." He looks at the clock in shock. "I haven't slept until nine . . . well, ever."

"Then you needed it." I lay my head on his chest, expecting him to run off and check on the others, but he simply holds me tighter. His hand caresses my body softly as he embraces me, letting me soak in his warmth. I haven't shared a bed a lot since Tucker, and even then, it was when he was exhausted or passed out.

I like this. It's nice. He's warm, strong, and comforting. I feel safe in his arms. It's as if none of the outside world could touch us here.

I have things to do and so does he, but right now, I don't care.

I just want this moment to last a lifetime. I'm happy.

We lie like this for a while, neither of us wanting to move. We don't talk, we just hold each other, his hand tracing my body like he's memorizing it, and knowing Raff, he is.

"This tattoo isn't like the others. It's older too," he murmurs, his hand stopping on my hip. I know exactly which one he means and stiffen, unable to meet his eyes. "Reign?"

"It was my first one," I admit. "I was underage, and it was done by a cheap tattoo artist who spent the entire time looking at my ass."

"Always a rebel," he murmurs. "Lost boys? What does it mean?"

I pull away and he frowns, searching my gaze. I've never told anyone, not even Tucker. I always lied or changed the subject. I could do that now or tell him to drop it and Raff would, but part of me wants to tell him. Part of me wants someone else to understand the pain I carry with me every single day of my life. If anyone could, it's Raff.

He would never judge me. He would simply be here for me because that's who he is. He's a protector, a shield . . . my shield. This might have started as a job for both of us, but we know it's so much more now. He's everything I never knew I needed. He's a control freak, and he's strict and surly and stubborn, but he makes me feel safe. He makes me happy. He makes me want to be a better person, and even when I'm doing fucked-up shit, he's there with me.

He's my ride or die.

They all are.

"It's for my brother," I share quietly. His eyes soften, and I glance down at his thumb caressing the script. "It's something we joked about. We called ourselves the lost boys. It was really just a way to fantasize and escape our lives."

"Escape?"

I peer up at him, wondering how much to share, but I'm so tired of secrets and being on guard all the time. Maybe he'll hurt me, or maybe he'll use it against me like everyone else has, but at some point, I have to trust someone. I'm realizing I can't do this alone. I might be Reign fucking Harrow, rebel and anarchist, but I'm also just a woman—a woman who wants to trust and be loved.

Maybe I need to learn to trust, and maybe that needs to start here, with a man who would willingly take a bullet for me. A man who carries me to bed when I've been working too hard in the studio. A man who makes sure I eat. A man who sees through my bullshit and calls me on it. A man, I realize, I'm starting to fall in love with.

"An escape," I murmur, covering his hand on my hip for courage. "I grew up really poor. My little brother, Attie, and I shared a room, and we often went days without eating since our dad couldn't afford it. My mom was in and out. She wasn't an addict or anything like most people thought. She was just absent and flighty. She often told us she never wanted kids. My dad let her come and go because he loved her, but then one day, she never came back, and that was when every-thing changed. He was really angry, overworked, and tired. I tried to keep us out of his way, and I tried to make it easier on him. I got a job after school and would clean the house, but eventually, his anger turned on us and he took his pain out on me. I never let Attie see. At first, it was just some punches or kicks when he was drinking or stum-bling in from a double shift, but it kept getting worse. He hated us, hated everything we stood for, and most of all, he hated that I looked like the woman who abandoned him." I laugh bitterly as Raff holds me tighter.

"It got worse. It turned into broken bones and black eyes. I was careful not to visit the same hospitals or clinics so nobody noticed. I knew no matter how bad our house was, it could be so much worse in the system—I had seen it myself—so I protected my little brother as much as I could. I saved up my money for him so when he was ready and I was eighteen, we could get out of there. I gave him my food and my clothes and held him when he had nightmares, but I know he saw the pain our father inflicted on me. One night, I thought that he was asleep and I went to the bathroom. My father was drunk and as usual, he took it out on me, screaming about how she never would have left had I not been born. I curled into the floor and waited for it to be over, but then I looked up and there he was. Attie held his stuffed wolf, and there were tears in his eyes. Something broke in me, but even more so when he ran to my father to try and get him off me. My dad smacked him so hard, he flung into a door. I remember that. I remember the sound his body made even now when he hit it. I remember the blood dripping on his dinosaur onesie. It haunts me. My father left to go to the bar, and I held Attie and cleaned him up. He didn't even cry, not once." My brow furrows, and tears well in my eyes. "No, he took my hand and looked me right in the eye and said, 'It's okay, Rey. It's not your fault.' He was a kid, Raff. He was a fucking kid and he told me it was okay. He told me not to blame myself even though I couldn't protect him after I promised to. He told me we protected each other and that he loved me. I cried myself to sleep as I held him that night."

Wiping my eyes, I look up at Raff to see his own are glassy. "I hated my father. I hated him so much, so yes, Raff, an escape. Now you know I'm nothing like these rich bitches who grew up in a loving home. I'm nothing but a pretender who doesn't belong here, who can still smell the faint whiff of alcohol and see the patches in her clothes."

Pulling me closer, he kisses my head. He doesn't tell me it's going to be okay. He doesn't minimize what I went through. He doesn't ask for more details. He just listens and comforts me, and in his eyes, I see that he knows how much it cost me to share. "Thank you for telling me, baby."

Resting my head on his chest, I let the tears fall. "I couldn't protect him, Raff."

"You were a kid, Reign. It wasn't your job to protect him, yet you did anyway. You loved him, and you did everything you could. It's time to stop blaming yourself, baby. It's time to forgive yourself."

"I can't. You don't understand," I whisper, pulling back. I feel too raw, too vulnerable.

He catches me before I can escape and pins me down, glaring at me. "Then make me understand, Reign," he demands. "Why can't you forgive yourself for your father's crimes?"

I try to look away to escape his all-seeing eyes, but he turns my face back to him. "Tell me," he orders.

"Because it got him killed!" I practically scream before covering my face. I feel him jerk, and then soft hands pry mine away.

"Tell me," he whispers.

"I can't." Sliding from the bed, I hurry to the bathroom, slamming the door. He tries the handle but it's locked. His hand slaps into the wood, making me jump.

"One day, you will tell me, Reign. One day, you will trust me enough. I will be here waiting, remember that. I'm always in your corner, baby. Always. No matter what you tell me. I won't let anyone hurt you, including yourself, but I'll give you this time you need, and I'll be downstairs. You haven't pushed me away. I'll be right there waiting." He retreats, and I slide down the door, placing my head on my knees.

The tears fall once more because I know he will be downstairs, waiting for me. He won't stop until he learns the truth, and I don't know if I'm ready for that. My broken heart never recovered from what happened, and I've spent so long running, I don't know how to stop.

Not even for them.

For him.

"Rey?" His little voice cracks, filled with pain. "Rey, wake up. Please wake up, Rey. I need you. It hurts, Rey. Please."

Leaping to my feet to escape the memory, I crank on the shower, adjusting the temp so it's the hottest it can get, and step under it. I let the sting wash away the pain and tears, my fingers covering the tattoo on my hip.

What I said is true.

It's my fault he's dead.

I can never forgive myself for that, so how could anyone else?

After showering, I wrap myself in clothes that offer comfort—an oversized band shirt from a friend and some soft leggings and socks. I hesitate downstairs, but Raff simply smiles at me. There are no hard feelings or calling me out for being a chicken. He simply holds out a mug of coffee, kisses me softly, and goes back to the stove to help Dal cook. I let out a relieved sigh, knowing I've escaped for now, and instead head into the living room where I find Cillian and Astro on the sofa, watching the news. I sit between them, needing their warmth and comfort, and they move closer and hold me tight. They do it automatically, and it makes me smile as I wrap my slightly shaking hands around the mug.

"Morning, beautiful." Astro kisses the top of my head.

"Morning." Cillian lays a hand on my thigh and squeezes.

"Morning," I whisper, unable to look at them just yet in case they see the ghosts in my eyes. When Raff sits heavily on a chair, his eyes on me, I avoid his gaze.

"Breakfast won't be long," Dal says as he enters, kissing me before he sits on the floor at my feet.

"Thanks," I murmur, taking a sip of the scalding hot coffee to avoid having to say anything else. It's only then I notice what's happening on the TV, and I almost groan as it shows an interview of Tucker from the night before.

"Shit, let me turn it off." Cillian reaches for the remote, but I cover his hand, frowning at Tucker's image.

"Wait," I say without looking, my eyes on the TV.

His eyes are bloodshot, and his fingers are clenched together and white. He's shaking and pale. He looks sick. He also looks horrendous, which is worrying because he's always so put together.

"So you and Reign are truly over?" the interviewer asks.

"She's made it very clear we would never get back together, and I respect that. I respect her." He looks at the camera. "Reign, I want you to know I'm sorry. I did love you, I still do, but I hurt you. I made a mistake, a big one. You were right. It's so easy to lose yourself in this industry, and although I'm suffering with an addiction, that's not an excuse for what I did to you. I'm going to get the help I need, and I hope you can forgive me one day for what I did to you. You deserved better, so much better."

"Mistakes happen," the interviewer interrupts. "Don't you think she is being overly emotional?"

"I just told you I'm suffering with an addiction and that I hurt someone I vowed to love, and your first response is to diminish her hurt by calling it overly emotional? No, I don't think she's being emotional. I cheated on her, and I betrayed her trust. I betrayed our relationship and everything it stood for, and not only that, she had to deal with the fallout with vultures like you picking apart her every move while she nursed a broken heart."

It could be PR, but the fire in his eyes is real. No social media manager would allow him to talk to an interviewer like that.

No, this is real.

I don't want to like Tucker, I really don't, but seeing him defend me while apologizing reminds me of the man I fell in love with, not the one the industry created.

"I made a horrible mistake, and a good person paid for it," he continues, looking at the camera. "Reign, if you see this, know that I hear you and thank you. If you had never . . . had never loved me and then left me, I wouldn't be getting the help I need. It took breaking your heart to realize how truly messed up I am. I'm sorry for that. I hope you find someone who is worth loving, and I hope I didn't ruin your trust in everyone too much. That's all I have to say." He takes his mic off, stands, thanks the flabbergasted interviewer, and walks away.

Sitting back, I stare at the screen as the anchor discusses and picks apart his interview, but I know he didn't do it for the public. He did it for me. He made his problems public so he could apologize.

I might never be able to forgive Tucker for what he did to me, but I realize I don't hate him anymore. We are both flawed people just trying to find our way in this world, and people make mistakes. His mistake led me here. I was able to find my identity, my muse, my happiness, and my strength. What he did was fucked up, but maybe it had to happen.

Maybe this is the best outcome for both of us. Some people are not meant to be together forever, and had I not walked in on them, I probably would have stuck by him and faded into a shell of who I was. Some people simply come into your life to teach you lessons. Tucker broke my heart, but he also showed me who I could be if I wanted to. He showed me what I don't want for the rest of my life, and just now, he showed me what it means to be brave.

THIRTY-TWO

Maybe I'm just feeling raw or extremely vulnerable after my talk with Raff and then seeing Tucker, but I find myself curled up on Cillian in my studio. We should both be working, but it's nice. I strum the guitar out of habit, not really paying attention. He's playing with my hair, and I can't help but smile. My eyes close as I focus on the warmth inside me and the bravery I feel.

That's when the lyrics start to form. "Shit, I need my pad," I grumble, not wanting to get up.

"Huh?" he asks.

"My pad, I have some lyrics to write down."

"Here." Without question, he grabs a pen and taps his thigh, which is on display in his shorts. "So neither of us have to move."

Giggling, I turn over, carefully laying my guitar down, and take the pen. I look at him to see him watching me, and he smiles encouragingly. Grinning, I hum the melody again as he lies back, and I scribble the words as they come to me. They are just feelings, jumbled and jagged, and although they aren't polished, they are real.

Home is his arms.
Safe, warm.
Just us.
Your eyes are just for me.
Sparkling like the fire you blaze through me.
Setting me alight, burning anew.
Remembering what it felt like falling in love
with you.

I pull back and nod. "There, thanks." Grabbing my phone from the table, I take a picture so I don't forget and snuggle back into his side, conscious of the writing and melody forming once more in my mind.

"Anything for you, Reign," he whispers.

I don't ignore the emotions in his voice, not today. I'm tired of being a coward. "Anything?"

"Anything," he replies. "You don't know that by now?" Tilting his head, he watches me openly with a soft smile. "I'm obsessed with you, Reign Harrow. Beyond why we are here, beyond the magic we make together, I am completely and one hundred percent obsessed with you as a person." I search his face, seeing everything he wants to say but isn't sure would be welcome.

"I'm obsessed with you too."

No more words are needed. They would cheapen the moment, so instead, I throw my leg over him, straddling his lap, and kiss him. I lick his lips until he opens with a groan, letting my tongue slide in and tangle with his. We kiss slowly, our bodies pressed together. His hand slides down my back to grip my ass and hold me closer, and then we break apart.

Something big lodges in my throat as I look into his beautiful face and peer into those green orbs I know better than my own. His pink lips tip up in a soft smile as he reaches up and pushes my hair back for me.

I see nothing but worship in his gaze.

I swallow hard. For some reason, I want to cry, but not wanting to seem crazier than I already am, I lean down and kiss him again, telling him everything I can't with words. He pushes my hair back and grips the back of my head, tugging me down and deepening the kiss. He dominates my mouth, showing me how much he cares for me.

Heat flares throughout my body, making me grind into his lap. My clit throbs in time with my racing heart as he builds my desire with each flick of his talented tongue until I'm on the verge of coming from a kiss.

Finally, I break away, my chest heaving as I stare down at him.

He grins, flashing his dimples, as one arm goes behind his head. He watches me, letting me make the decision. I could end it here and he'd be happy, but I don't want that. I want him just like this—spread on my studio couch with my words on his thigh.

My declaration of love written between the lines.

Sliding my shirt up, I reach between us and undo his jeans while meeting him halfway, our lips clashing with purpose. He pushes my hands away, taking over and pulling himself free of his jeans, only to groan into my mouth as I wrap my hands around his length. "Reign."

I swallow it like a prayer, like a sinner's confession.

His hard, huge length slides through my hands as his head falls back, his chest arching as I stroke him. The sight is so beautiful, it takes my breath away, and when his eyes open, they are dark with lust. He leans up, moving my hands away as he tugs my shirt and skirt off, leaving me bare. I tug at his shirt, and he reaches behind, pulling it up and off as I run my nails down his abs.

He slides his hand between my thighs, stroking me softly, but I lift my hips and press against the head of his cock. My lips find his once more as I sink down onto his length, needing him too much to wait. I take every inch until he's balls deep, and both of us groan as we press together and start to move as one.

Wrapping our arms around one another, we work together, our bodies moving in sync. Pleasure flows through us as our bodies slide against one another, and my head falls back as his lips slide down my neck, biting and licking before moving lower and sealing around my nipple.

The pounding of my desire makes me cry out as I clench

around him.

Punishing him in return, I press my hands against his chest and swivel my hips, riding him as he watches me with lustful eyes. His hands find my hips and help me, and seeing his hips flex up with his thrusts, his skin covered in my lyrics, is so fucking hot.

"Reign." He groans my name, our hips meeting in slow thrusts. It's a leisurely, building pleasure that flows through my veins like a drug as I move my hands behind me to his legs and roll my body while he watches. His eyes lock on my curves, and his cock grows bigger inside me.

"Fuck, sweetheart, you look like a goddamn vision from heaven right now."

His hands hold me tight, as if he will never let me go, and I don't want him to. They slide up my back, dragging me to him. Our lips meet in a frenzy, and I roll my hips harder, chasing the pleasure I feel building. Every nerve ending is alive, and my heart races in time with his heartbeat under my hand.

His name is on my lips when I finally tumble over the edge in a slow orgasm.

He groans into my mouth, his hips stuttering as I grip him, and then he finds his own release. Moaning into my lips, he holds me tight, grinding me down onto his length as he comes.

We kiss through it all while pleasure surges and ebbs through us until I pull away, panting and sweating. Gripping my cheeks, he presses a hard kiss to my forehead, to each eye, my cheeks, and then my lips. "I'm so happy we found each other."

"Me too," I whisper, letting him pull me down to lie in the circle of his arms.

His hand strokes up and down my back as I relax, a smile curving my lips.

I feel so happy, it can't be real.

Our bodies are still joined when I feel his cock harden again, and we come together once more.

Here, in my studio, with a melody in my heart and my lyrics on his leg, declaring what I'm too scared to say out loud, we make love.

We find our bravery.
We find our happiness.

THIRTY-THREE

I reluctantly leave Reign in the studio. She's playing the piano, and the sight is beautiful. I could listen to her all day. She has the ability to transport you into another world. You feel what she feels as she plays, and you see her story, just like when we made love. She is just so alive that others crave her, me included, and what we just did . . . I know it was more than fucking. It was us—pure, raw, and unfiltered.

I wanted to tell her how I felt, but I knew it would scare her away, so I showed her, hoping she would understand. This is real. This is something people search for their whole lives. It's a forever kind of thing.

If she will let it be.

I'm truly hoping so because despite what I said, it's not obsession I feel for Reign. It's love. I love her, and the more I learn, the more I love her. She is worth loving. She deserves love, and I hope she lets us feel for her. I don't care what anyone else thinks, and she never has either. We are just . . . us. She once told us that she didn't really have friends, but she does now. She has us, people who would fight in her corner to their dying breath and never hurt her, use her, or leave her.

No, it's not just obsession. It's love in its simplest and most brilliant form.

I'm just passing the security room to go check on Raff Jr. when the comms go off. "Yes?" I ask the guards at the gate. Usually, one of us mans this, so I'm betting they recently left.

"More flowers, sir," the new guard Raff hired replies.

"Coming." I head out to the gate, nodding at the guard who hands them over. Searching for a card, I head to the trash bin. I know she wants to donate them but it's only a small bunch, and that's when I realize they aren't roses.

They are peonies.

Frowning, I find a card and open it.

I'll be seeing you soon - your admirer.

Looking around, I head into the house. "Raff!" I call, not wanting to spook her. I go into the security room and put them down carefully. Raff hurries in, wiping his face, no doubt from the gym. "These were just delivered."

He frowns. "So toss them."

"They are peonies, and they aren't from Tucker." I point at the card. "I think this is what her management were talking about."

Frowning down at the card, he switches modes instantly. "Find out where they came from and who sent them, now. I want the guard at the gate interviewed, all cameras checked, and her management alerted."

"And Reign?" I look behind him. "Do we tell her?"

He glances at the flowers. "Not yet. It's our job to protect her from this. That's why they hired us. For now, we keep it between us. Understood? Send Astro to the flower shop to get what we need."

"Got it, boss." I text Dal and Astro as I speak.

"I'll stay with her," he says as he strides away, fully alert now. I'm thankful for the new security systems in place or she would have found them.

Astro and Dal hurry in. "What's up?"

I nod at the flowers and watch as they look at the note, their faces clouding. "Astro, use the card, find out what flower shop they came from, and go there. See if they can ID who ordered them, if they used a card or cash, and get the camera footage. I'm going to interview the guard at the gate. Dal, tell her management."

"Are we telling her?" Astro frowns.

"Raff says no, we handle this quietly."

They share a look, and I sigh. "What?" I ask.

"We should tell her," Dal murmurs. "It's not right that she doesn't know. I don't like keeping things from her."

"Neither do I, but this is for the best. It's not like we are lying to her. We are here to protect her, so let's do just that. They are clearly getting bolder, considering the letters her management intercepted. The quicker we handle this, the quicker it is over and we can tell her. Raff's orders."

"Got it." Astro grabs his coat and heads out the door, card in hand.

Dal grabs his phone as I head out, going to the security gate. I think the guard's name is Will. We handpicked them all ourselves, so we know we can trust them. They are the best, and although we upgraded all the security systems, we haven't put many guards inside due to her need for privacy. Maybe that was a bad idea.

I remind myself they are just flowers, but we all know how quickly something like this can escalate, and we won't let our girl be caught in this.

"Sir?" Will calls as he stands.

"I want to know everything about who dropped off the flowers."

He starts to outline the delivery, and I have no doubt Raff is already looking at the footage.

We'll get this bastard, and she will never know.

---

astro

I smile at the woman in the apron behind the counter of the small flower shop, leaning into her. "Please?"

"I can't give you their information." She sighs. "I truly am sorry."

"Come on." I look at her name tag. "Penny, help me out. My boss will kill me if I don't get it."

Gnawing on her lip, she looks around for customers or her

manager. My nose is stuffy from all the flowers in here, but I don't let it show as I flirt shamelessly to get what I want. "Fine, but don't tell anyone, okay?"

"You got it, cutie." I wink as she blushes.

She starts looking through receipts before plucking one out and handing it over. "Paid cash, ordered yesterday."

I frown. "Do your cameras work?"

"They do, but I remember this one. It was a sweet little old lady."

"An old lady?" I frown.

"Let me show you." I follow her to the back as she loads the computer and scrolls back on their camera system. "There." She points, and I quickly snap a picture on my phone, sending it to Raff to get her information.

"Thank you, Penny, you've been very helpful," I say as I turn. She catches my arm, and I glance down to see her smiling shyly.

"Uh, I finish at four," she says.

I take her hand and kiss it softly. "Enchanted, but I'm sorry, my heart is already taken." She smiles sadly, and I leave. Once I'm outside, I pull down my shades and take out my phone as I head to my bike.

"Speak," Raff snaps.

"Got my text?" I ask.

"Searching now . . . Ah, here she is. Seventy-five-year-old Lorraine Watson. I'll text you her address." He hangs up.

"Bye to you too, asshole," I mutter as I swing my leg over my bike, knowing he's annoyed and worried. As I wait, I snap a picture of me on my bike, flexing my pecs, and text it to my girl.

> Me: Gone for a ride, wishing it were you I was riding though.

A few moments later, a text comes through.

> Reign: Then hurry back ;)

Fuck, I need to find this old lady and fast. Yanking my helmet on, I check the address Raff sent and pull out into traffic. It doesn't take me long to get there, and I take the steps two at a time, about to buzz everyone to get in when the door opens and Lorraine herself steps out. She smiles at me as I hold the door and starts to head past me.

"Excuse me, Lorraine?"

She blinks, turning to me, bag in hand.

"Hi, you don't know me. I'm Astro."

She shakes my hand hesitantly.

"Sorry, the flower shop you used yesterday gave me your information. My girl got your flowers, and we were just trying to work out who sent them." I put my hand in my pocket and give her my sweetest smile.

"Oh gosh! Well, dear, it wasn't me. Some nice gentleman stopped me near the shop and asked if I could do it for him. He said he was in a hurry but didn't want his wife not to get them . . . .Girlfriend, you said?"

"I did." I grin. "You don't happen to remember his name or what he looked like, do you?"

"Hmm, well, he was tall, but it was hard to see much more under the hat he wore," she admits. "Sorry." She pats my arm as she passes.

"Lorraine, where was this?"

"Oh, just outside the dry cleaners next door. I must go now. I'm late for a date." Fluffing her hair, she hurries down the street as I pull out my phone, my smile fading.

"Yeah, it's me. I want all the footage from the camera on Wilcox yesterday. We are looking for a little old lady and the guy who stopped her." I hang up, knowing my friend will get me what I need. It's time to stop this bastard. Today it was flowers, but tomorrow, it could be anything.

He's getting bolder, and if Reign is going to marry anyone, it's me. Asshole.

THIRTY-FOUR

While we wait for the footage, I head out. I told Raff it was to chase a lead, but I lied. I hate lying to him, but this is important, and it's on a time crunch. I know Reign is safe with them, and in a few hours, we will have the information we need on her stalker, and then we can make sure she's safe for good.

When we were first hired, we scanned through the many threats she gets. Some are harmless, others not so much, and we put a stop to most of them, but her management was worried about this one specifically. This one kept sending her letters they intercepted and they were creepy, but we couldn't find out where they came from. Whoever it is, he's smart and clearly annoyed at being ignored, so he's stepping up his game, and now it's time to act.

When this fucker is taken care of, she'll be safe again.

Our jobs will be over as well.

I have to tell her the truth and just hope she keeps us around anyway. I hate lying to her, but it's for her protection. I know she'll be mad, but she'll understand, right? She already has enough to worry about without having this on her plate.

It's our job to protect her, and we'll do that.

I take my car, not wanting Raff to track me in hers. This is a surprise for her and her alone. Pulling up outside the tattoo studio, I turn my phone off, knowing they'll turn up if they want me. I head inside and grin at the big, burly biker. I've known Vaughn since our days in the service, and he does all our tattoos, including Astro's new one, which he thinks he's hidden.

"Sup, brother?" he calls.

"I need this inked." I slide my jeans down and he whistles. "Got the time?"

"I do. Are they lyrics?" He leans down. "They are good."

I grin proudly. "You bet they are. My girl's a rockstar."

---

dal

"He's not answering." I shrug at Raffiel. "His phone's off too."

"I'm going to fucking kill him," he snaps, pacing angrily. "And where the fuck is my footage of this loser?"

"It takes time," Astro says as he munches on popcorn, watching Raffiel lose his shit. He always gets like this on missions, especially if he doesn't like the results, but this is personal now.

"When we get the information, do you want me to handle it?" I ask carefully. He doesn't like it when I offer to kill people so openly, but why else would he be obtaining information on this asshole?

"I'll decide," he mutters, rubbing his face. "Astro, I want that footage, and I want it now."

We hear footsteps, and Raff narrows his gaze on us. "We say nothing," he orders just as Reign stops in the door. She freezes as we all swing our gazes to her.

"Uh, is everything okay?" She cocks her head.

"Everything is fine, beautiful," Astro replies. "Just a team meeting to sort out some new measures," he says, but I can see the tightness in his shoulders. He hates lying to her. I can usually lie without thought, but when she glances at me to see my reaction, I find myself unable to do so and betray her like that.

Raffiel's voice covers for me as I frown.

"Just work," he promises. "How's writing going, baby?"

"Fine." She shrugs, looking at me once more. She sees too much. "I just have to finish this verse and then I'll send it to Jack. I was thinking about going out tonight—not a club or even a party, but maybe for a nice meal. What do you think? I've been working a lot recently, and when the album comes out, I'll be on tour, so I might as well enjoy it while I can."

"Sounds great. Anywhere in particular?" Raff asks smoothly.

"I'll have a think. I thought you all might like to go. Not as work but . . ." Blowing out a breath, she smiles. "Fuck, as a date, okay?"

"Beautiful, I would love nothing more." Astro grins widely.

Date? That's serious, right? I have never dated, so I wouldn't know, but it seems important. However, if she thinks we are anything other than together, then she has another thing coming.

"Of course, baby," Raff purrs. "I would love to."

"Dal?" she queries.

"You're the boss."

She winces, looking away, and I want to kick myself. Fuck, I really can't lie to her, and it has messed me up. "Right," she drawls. "I forgot." She leaves.

Fuck!

Ignoring Raffiel and Astro, I head after her, refusing to let her be angry at me. I don't want her to think I don't want to go out with her either.

She's practically running down the hall, and I catch her between the stairs and the door.

"Reign."

She turns to me wearing that fake fucking smile on her face she uses for paparazzi photos. I hate that it's aimed at me. I never want that. I want all of her, especially the pieces no one else ever gets.

"Wait."

"No, it's fine, Dal. I'm sorry. I shouldn't have put you on the spot like that."

"Reign," I warn, advancing on her, needing her to shut up and listen.

"Seriously, it's okay. Just because we're fucking doesn't—" I slam my fist next to her head, watching her jump as I cover her mouth and get in her face.

"Shut the fuck up and listen to me, Reign Harrow. I have never been on a date, but if I were ever to go on one, it would be with you. I was simply distracted by work and didn't choose my words correctly, but understand me when I say this. You do not need to take me on a date for me to be yours. I already am."

Her eyes widen and her chest heaves, pressing against mine as my heart races, and I wonder if she can feel it. "Do you understand me, Reign? Nod."

She nods slowly, and I peel my hand away. She licks her lips but doesn't protest or move away. "You're kind of intense, you know that?"

"For you," I reply without shame. "Now, Reign, let's get one thing clear. A date is important to you, yes?"

"Yes," she replies shyly.

"Then we'll go on them every single day. Make no mistake Reign, we are . . . dating. We are so much more, but I have a feeling you wouldn't be comfortable with that yet. There is nothing I wouldn't do for you. Raffiel is correct when he says to be careful about what you ask of me, because I would deny you nothing. You want me out in public, then I'm there, even if I hate it. I am not a civilized man, Reign. I never have been. I'm a killer, a trained professional, and I can't change that, but I'll try for you. You want a date, then we'll go on one."

Her eyes roll up to mine, so big and innocent for a moment, and her soft skin rubs against mine. I know I should walk away because the blood that covers my soul should never touch this angel, but I would drop to my knees right here and now and beg her to never leave me, despite the fact that I'm a monster and I don't deserve her. She has ruined me. I can't go back to who I used to be. I feel everything in her presence. She brought me back to life, and if she walks away, I will never recover.

Reign Harrow is my salvation and my heart, and the fear of losing that leaves me breathless. Her words could be weapons for the way I wait for them to fall. I don't regret many things in my life, but I would regret losing her.

"Okay." She smiles and it's bright. "I like you being mine. No matter what you think of yourself, Dal, I like you. I like who you are. I'm not afraid of that. I'm also not dumb. I can imagine the things you've done and what you've seen, but it won't stop me. I can't let you go."

"Good, because I won't let you." It should scare her, but she grins wider, sliding her hands into my hair and tugging me close.

She's the only person I will let touch me.

She's the only person to ever see past what I'm capable of.

I wonder if she knows this killer's heart is hers. Wherever Reign Harrow goes, I will too. Never in my life have I followed another so willingly into destruction—not even Raffiel. Before her, there was just killing, but now I have her.

If she wants dates, then she will drown in them.

If she wants to rip out my heart and serve it on a platter, then she can have it. If she wants my soul, even dirty and stained, she can take it. I will give her whatever she wants as long as she keeps looking at me like she is now.

Like I'm hers.

Like I'm enough.

THIRTY-FIVE

REIGN

It's been a while since I've gotten ready for a date. Tucker and I went on many, but they were usually very public affairs, and more often than not, they were set up for the paparazzi. This is real, and I'm a little nervous, which is silly since I practically live with the guys and have already slept and bonded with them, but dating is so . . . formal. It's a huge step for me, since I never thought I wanted to be here again, giving someone the power to hurt me.

Raff Jr. barks happily as he chews on one of my expensive heels, watching me struggle.

Peering into my closet, I gnaw on my lip. Raffiel told me what time to get ready and that they would sort out the details. Usually, I use my name to get us in somewhere, so it's kind of nice not to have to think about it. They are taking care of me, which they seem to love doing, but it also means I have no idea what to wear.

The shelves overflow with dresses and pants, yet I'm standing in my black lace thong and bra, completely unsure. I'm always so confident, especially now, but they leave me like this, raw and unsure. I don't know if that's a good thing or not, but I guess only time will tell.

"Raff?" When there's no answer, I stick my head out. "Dal? Cil? Astro?"

Nothing. Fuck.

I'm just stepping out of the closet when Cillian walks in. He grins when he sees me. "Don't get me wrong, I'm good with that look, baby, but we don't like to share, so may I suggest clothes?"

"Can you at least tell me where we're going so I know what to wear?" I prop my hand on my hip as I pout at him.

"Nope, that face doesn't work on me, beautiful." He chuckles. "And I'm not telling. We worked hard on this. You will look beautiful in whatever you wear, but I would suggest a nice dress."

"Thank you!" I rush to him and kiss him softly, only for him to grip my hip and deepen the kiss. His hand slides low, gripping my ass and pulling me to him. I grip his shoulders as his other hand tunnels into my hair. He dominates my mouth before suddenly pulling back. He's breathing heavily as he grins, leaving me blinking and shaking.

"Get dressed, beautiful, and I'll see you downstairs." He turns and leaves.

My hand drifts to my mouth as I stand there, wide-eyed. Never have I been kissed like they do it. It's addictive, and every time they do it, I find myself weaker and desperate for more. I realize I'm just standing here, and so I hurry to the closet.

Cillian said a dress. Picking out a tame number, I slip it on over my head, letting the silk fall across my body. It has a low-cut, plunging neckline to show off my chest. It's also backless with a slit up the thigh, yet it remains classy. I turn in the mirror, watching the way the deep red shimmers black in some light. Pairing it with my black Louboutins, which lace up my thigh, I quickly style my hair so some hangs down while other bits are pinned up. I smoke my eyes out and add dramatic lipstick. I might dress up for them, but I don't change who I am, and they seem to like that. Popping a leather jacket on my shoulders, I call it good and grab a matching bag before I head down to see them.

I find them waiting at the bottom of the stairs, and my mouth goes dry at the sight. Astro winks at me, running his eyes up my legs with a groan. Wearing a deep green shirt with black slacks, he looks like a fucking supermodel, especially with his hair slicked back. Cillian is next to him, wearing tweed patterned slacks with a white shirt rolled back to his elbows, his red hair styled. Dal is in a suit, as always, but he has a red tie on, as if to match me, and looks absolutely incredible as those cold eyes rake over my form. Raffiel is waiting by the door, looking at a black watch, but when he hears the others, his head snaps up and his jaw actually drops. He holds out his hand to me, and I grin as I place mine in his and let him pull me closer. In a black suit, black shoes, and a gray shirt, he is totally sexy. His eyes eat me alive as he tugs me closer, his bare palm warming my back as he dips his head and kisses me hard. When he pulls away, his eyes sparkling, I giggle and wipe his mouth. "Lipstick."

"Leave it."

Grinning, I do just that as he leads me out to the car. Astro trips over himself to open the door and bows as I draw closer. "My lady," he says.

Shaking my head, I climb in, gasping when a hand snakes under my dress. I turn back to see him grinning innocently at me.

"Perv." I pout as I slide into the farthest seat. Cillian climbs in by my side, but then the other door opens and Dal slides in, picking me up and dropping me onto his lap without a word.

"Seat belt. Think of safety," Raff snaps, and I turn to see Dal staring at him, his gaze hard and cold.

"You think I would ever let anything happen to her?" Dal retorts. "I would break my body before she was ever hurt in this car."

Raff shuts the door and climbs into the driver's seat, while Astro takes the passenger seat. We drive out of the gate and cameras instantly begin flashing, but they can't see us in the back, so I relax into Dal's chest, resting my head on his shoulder as he slides his hand under my dress and strokes my bare thigh, gripping me tightly.

"You look ravishing," he murmurs to me. "If it were up to me, I would have ripped this off you and fucked you on the stairs, but I know this is important to you."

"Thank you." I blush slightly, meeting Cillian's sparkling eyes. He winks at me.

"Good choice, beautiful. You could wear a trash bag, though, and look incredible, but tonight? Tonight, I'll be thinking of nothing more than when I can get you home and to bed," he promises, licking his lips as he watches me.

I look away before I let them, my pussy clenching in need like it always does around them. "Later," I promise. "If you're good boys."

"Oh, baby, I'll be so good to you," Cillian flirts.

"I don't know. I'm starving," I tease, leaning into Dal.

"So am I," Dal rumbles, shocking both me and Cillian as we turn to him. He grips my pussy, making me yelp. "You'll be my dessert."

"See what you've done, Rey? You've made him make jokes!" Cillian booms, making me grin, but I freeze at the nickname. Dal feels it, even if Cillian doesn't notice, leaning around to tell the others about Dal flirting and making a joke.

"I'm not offended, if that's what's wrong," Dal whispers to me.

Without looking at him, I shake my head, and I feel him working through what Cillian said. He always sees too much. "Was it the nickname?" He sounds confused.

"My brother used to call me that. I just haven't heard it from many people in a really long time. It's okay. Was just a shock."

He watches me carefully, and I know he will probably have a word with Cillian later, but I can't find it in me to care. I move back into his embrace as I stare out of the window. Astro puts on music and sings along off-key until Cillian joins in, and surprisingly, so does Raff and Dal. It brings me out of my thoughts and memories and I laugh, which only makes them sing louder.

I know they are doing it for me, and my heart melts. Another wall cracks and falls, exposing me to them, and whatever they see, they smile at.

We pull up outside of a restaurant that's so exclusive, even I haven't gotten to visit yet. Astro runs around, unwilling to let the valet open the door. Cillian gets out first, checking the area, before they both offer me their hands. Laughing, I let them pull me out, and I wink at the valet whose eyes bug out of his head.

Raff slaps some bills into his hand. "Leave the car there. No one touches it. And if I find out that you post anything about her being here online, I will end you." The poor kid almost faints as Raff offers me his arm. "Shall we, Miss Harrow?"

"Let's." I let him guide me through the frosted black doors and into another world. This restaurant is brand new and has a great view of the city. There is no waiting area; you simply emerge right into the restaurant that has tables on different levels, with windows covering the entire outside that look out but not in.

Something is amiss though.

There is no one else here. "Raff?" I turn to him, and he grins.

"You wanted a date, my love, so you get one, but only the best for you. I wanted you to be able to be yourself without prying eyes or questions," he explains as he leads me through the restaurant like he knows the way.

"How?" I peer around with wide eyes.

"You're not the only one who knows people." He chuckles as we come to the middle table, which has been decorated with black roses and peonies. Astro hurries to pull out my chair, and when I sit, Cillian pushes me in, kissing my head. Dal lays a napkin on my lap before they all take their seats. All four of them look at me. It's unnerving but also so addicting. They watch my every move, my every reaction as I look around, and I can tell they are excited for this but also nervous.

"It's amazing," I say, and they all seem to breathe a sigh of relief. "I've always wanted to come here."

"Good." Astro reaches over and takes my hand, kissing the back of it.

"Shit, I should have sat next to her because then I would get her hand," Cillian grumbles. Dal is on my other side, with Cillian and Astro opposite. Grinning, I slide my legs under the table and lay them on Cillian's lap. He grins, gripping them as Raff shakes his head, but he's smiling at me lovingly.

"You can relax here, Reign. We made sure of it. No rules tonight. This place is all ours, and we plan to spoil you, starting now."

Two waiters in black tuxedos appear at my side. They don't meet my eyes at all. In fact, they don't even look at me, as if they were told not to. They pour me a glass of red wine, and the others have water, making me pout, but I understand. "First course will be served soon," one says before they disappear.

Soft, sensual music sounds through the speakers as I look around in awe, taking the wine glass with my other hand. I still wonder how they managed this. I know some celebrities who couldn't even get on the list for the next year, and somehow, my men managed to clear the entire place on the busiest night of the week.

Fuck, power is sexy.

Cillian's hand slides up my legs, and I meet his gaze with an arched brow.

"Behave, Miss Harrow," Raffiel admonishes. "We won't touch you until we have wooed you. You wanted a date, so you get the best one of your life."

My eyes widen when plates suddenly appear before us, and just as quickly, the waiters are gone again. I don't even know what's on my plate but I begin to eat, moaning at the taste that explodes in my mouth. It's only two mouthfuls, and once I'm done, I look up to see them all watching me. Instantly, four plates are shoved toward me. Laughing, I take theirs and eat them as well, moaning again.

"Can we negotiate on the no touching rule?" Astro asks, tugging at his collar.

"Miss Harrow," Raffiel says, but he's grinning.

"Whoops." I wink as the waiters come to clear the plates.

"Was that course okay?"

I look up to see a male waiter grinning down at me, with bright blue eyes and surfer boy hair. He's so very young.

"It sounded like you enjoyed it." He drops his voice an octave as he leans down to get the plates.

"Oh, it was magnificent," I respond, but when I look up, the guys' expressions are as hard as nails, and I slide back on the chair at the venom aimed at the waiter who seems completely oblivious to the tense atmosphere. His eyes sweep along my body.

I just stare, unsure what to do or say, when Raffiel drops his napkin on the table before him.

"Miss Harrow, could you close your eyes for a moment?" Raffiel instructs.

I peer up at the waiter then back at Raffiel.

"Reign, close your eyes now," he snaps, losing his patience.

I close my eyes and hear a thud. They snap open, and I gasp, seeing the now unconscious waiter being dragged away, yet none of the guys seem to have even moved. "What . . . Is he dead?"

"We are not animals." Astro laughs. "But he will have a really bad headache."

"He's lucky I didn't pluck his eyes from his head for daring to even look at you," Dal warns.

Raffiel nods like he agrees as I shake my head. "Insane, all of you are fucking insane."

"No, Reign, we are possessive. You are ours. Ours to guard, to fuck, and to love, and that's exactly what we'll do. Now eat your food."

Well, shit.

"He's right, you know," Astro murmurs, and I see a flash of red on his neck. Frowning, I tug at his collar to move it out of the way. He ducks, avoiding my touch, and I sit back.

"What is that?" I ask. "Are you hiding a hickey from me?"

"It's nothing." Astro lowers his head, and I tilt mine, watching him.

"She asked you a question," Dal says.

"It's nothing," Astro replies, looking around, his face turning even redder.

"Astro?" Raffiel prompts. All eyes are on him.

He turns to look at me and then sighs. "I'm not trying to hide anything from you, I promise. It's just something I wanted to show you alone." Still blushing, he tugs his shirt aside and my eyes widen, unsure what I'm seeing. On his shoulder, at the base of his neck, is a red lipstick mark, and for a moment, jealousy and pain hit me. He must see it in my gaze because he reaches for my hand, and when I tug it away, he kicks my chair back and presses his legs on either side of me, gripping my chin. "Look at it."

"Stop it. Why are you being cruel?" I snap, trying to tug myself away.

"Reign, look at it," he orders. I feel the others looking, but they are relaxed, as if noticing something I don't.

"Um, next course," a waiter says hesitantly.

"Not now," Astro snaps at the waiter without even looking. "Look at me, Reign. This is yours." He takes my hand and covers it. "One of the first days I met you, you kissed my throat better. Remember? That very same day, I got it tattooed."

Realization strikes me as I stroke the still healing tattoo, remembering exactly what he's talking about. It's even the same shade of lipstick. He got my kiss tattooed. My eyes meet his, searching them for answers—answers I'm not sure I'm ready for but probably need.

"Why?" I ask, peering into his eyes.

"You know why," he murmurs.

"Why?" I demand, my heart pounding.

"Because I knew from the moment I laid eyes on you what you would become to me." He covers my hand, smiling softly. "I know you're not ready for that, and I know you're still healing from the man who came before us, but I would never hurt you, Reign. I would never betray you. I'm all in, okay? All of us are. You never have to worry about that, and when you're ready, we'll be waiting. Until then, this is for me." He kisses my hand and then guides me back to the table. "Now let's enjoy our next course."

Swallowing, I stare at the plate that appears in front of me, barely paying attention to what I eat. I feel their eyes on me, but I'm unable to meet them, too busy working through my emotions. There's worry, as well as the need to run far and fast from something so serious, since my commitment issues are raising their ugly heads, but below it all is . . . glee.

He cares so much that he tattooed my kiss on his neck.

When have I ever felt such dedication and love from another person? I was with Tucker for years, and even moving in together was a carefully thought-out decision. It's not like that with them. It's real and almost feels like it was meant to be.

If I were a person who believed in destiny, I might even say these men were destined to be mine, which means I have a decision I need to make because Astro just admitted they are all in. I need to decide if I want that or want out, and now, before they get hurt. As I play with my food, my eyes go to them, and I realize I'm all in with them.

I want this. I want them.

Even if it terrifies me, I want what I see in their eyes. I want lazy mornings filled with laughter, I want to spend every night with them in my bed, and I want their comforting arms around me as I write my music. I want their strengths, and I want their pain. Wherever this takes us, I'm in.

"Okay," I say, knowing they are waiting.

"Okay?" Astro turns to me.

"Okay." I smile. "I'm in."

The grin he gives me makes it worthwhile, and I giggle as they all whoop. I know I made the right decision.

There are several courses but luckily, the portions they present are small so I don't get too full too early. I enjoy it, though, and they regale me with stories of their time together overseas. They make me laugh until it hurts. "I can't believe you actually let him get away with that, Raff!" I chuckle and glance up to get Raff's reaction to a story Cillian is telling, but my smile disappears when I notice he isn't paying attention. He's looking at his lap, and I realize he's on his phone, completely oblivious. Shaking it off, I smile and turn back to Cillian, listening to him weave the tale.

When they all laugh, I turn once more to Raff to find him still on his phone. Frowning, I sip my wine. "So, Raff, what about you?"

"Hmm?" he replies distractedly.

"Any funny war stories?" I ask, sliding to the edge of my seat. For some reason, I need his attention on me. When he just shakes his head, I realize why. It's what Tucker used to do to me. We would be out at dinner or on a date and he would spend the entire time on his phone, causing me to feel lonely and embarrassed. It made me feel like I wasn't good enough company, and once more, that insecurity grows, even if the others are here.

I remind myself that he's probably working, but as time stretches on and the others try to fill the gap his distraction creates, the worse it hurts and the angrier I get. Here's a man asking me to be all in, telling me he will never hurt me like those before him, and he planned all this, yet now he's on his phone like I don't even exist. Work or not, it lets me know where his priorities lie, and it fucking hurts.

"Reign." Dal tries to draw my attention away as they glance from Raff to me, but it's too late. My mouth tastes sour, and ugly memories raise their ugly heads until I feel like that scared woman I once was.

I hate that, and I've come so far, so I do something I always wanted to do in this situation.

I stand, making the chair scrape across the floor, and drop my napkin on the table. Raffiel's head snaps up, and he looks confused as he peers at me.

"I'll be back, and then we can go since you are so busy." I turn and walk to the bathrooms. I refuse to cry. I refuse to let them ruin all the progress I've made.

I push into the bathroom and slam the door shut, staring at myself in the mirror as I remind myself who I am. I'm Reign fucking Harrow. Fuck them. Fuck him. If he doesn't want to be here, then he doesn't have to be. He doesn't get to hurt me like that, nor does he get to ignore me. A date shouldn't consist of people being on their phones. Maybe that's an old-fashioned way of thinking, but it's what I want, and I refuse to accept any less, not even from Raffiel. Even if he was looking into my protection, it's not okay.

The door opens, and my head snaps around. Raffiel storms inside, kicking the door shut. Backing up, I hold my palm up between us, and it hits his chest as he advances on me.

"Miss Harrow," he begins, "you do not walk away from us."

"Oh, fuck off, Raffiel." His eyes widen. "I'm surprised you even noticed," I spit before I realize that doesn't help at all. I'm reacting, not explaining. "You were too busy on your phone."

"Reign." He sighs, reaching for me, but I duck under his hands and turn to him, refusing to let him smooth it over and make it all better like Tucker would. I feel what I feel, and I deserve that. I am allowed to be hurt. I am allowed to feel. No matter how pretty he is or how good he makes me feel, he doesn't get to brush this under the rug with excuses.

"No, I don't want to hear it, okay? Whatever your excuse is, it's not good enough. I spent years in a relationship where I felt alone and isolated, paraded on dates only to be ignored, and it took me a long time to come back from that, yet the first date I go on since him, here we are again, and I feel ignored like that woman back then. No matter what you were doing, no matter how important it was, it doesn't make it okay. This is my expectation in a relationship. I don't ask for much, but if you can't handle that, then fine. Good luck to you. I refuse to lower my standards for any man ever again. Not even you, Raffiel. Actions speak louder than words."

"Then let me show you," he snaps, angry now. "Let me show you exactly how dedicated I am and how goddamn proud I am of you for speaking up and setting your expectations. I'm sorry, and you're right. There is no excuse. I will never let it happen again." His expression is so sincere, and when he drops to his knees, my eyes widen.

"Raffiel, no." I push him away. "You don't get to just touch me to try to get me to forget. I'm angry, let me be angry. I need to consider if this is what I want."

Sliding up my body, he grips my neck and slams me back into the wall. "Let me make one thing very clear, Miss Harrow. You get time, you get your feelings, but you do not get to threaten me with walking away when we both know that's what it is—a threat. You said you are all in, and we are holding you to that. I made a mistake. It was in regard to your safety, but it was still a mistake. I am rusty at dating since I haven't been on one since I was sixteen fucking years old, but never think for one single second that you are not my priority. If you want to see my phone and what I was doing, then you can. I was checking in with the staff to make sure everything I planned for when we get back is sorted, and I checked the cameras. I will never keep anything from you, but don't ever threaten to walk away from me again. I don't like games of manipulation. I made a mistake, and I apologize. I will make sure it will never happen again, but I am not that idiot Tucker, and I will prove that to you every single day from now on. Now, what can I do to make it up to you?"

I search his gaze. Is he right? Was it a threat to try and hurt him like he hurt me?

Yes.

I relax into his hold. "I don't know," I admit. I reacted so badly. Of course he was checking on my security. I should have known. He isn't Tucker. I'm his entire priority, and he's shown me that time and time again. I simply jumped to conclusions because of my past. I'm still not happy that he was on his phone on our date, but I can tell he will never do it again. He truly is sorry. I guess we are both rusty at this, and our pasts make it harder to work through.

"I don't know," I admit.

"No?" he purrs. "How about I kiss it better? How about I show you exactly how obsessed with you I am?"

"Raff," I protest, but it dies on my lips when he drops to his knees, peering up at me with sincere, worshipful eyes.

"You are my everything, Reign, and something I didn't even know I was looking for, yet I found you, and I'm never letting you go. I'll spend my life on my knees for you if you'll let me. I've served before, baby, but never the way I'll serve you."

"Raffiel." I stumble back into the wall as his hands slide up my thighs and meet my hips, and then he stills, waiting for me to decide. I could say no and he would walk out of here holding my hand, willing to fight for us. Everyone makes mistakes, and I will probably make some too. I've been in relationships before, but never like this, and I realize it's how we deal with those mistakes that makes the difference.

Do I still want Raffiel? Yes.

Do I still want this? Yes.

Am I scared? Shitless, but I'm Reign fucking Harrow, and I don't let fear hold me back from what I want.

"Show me," I order. "Show me that you want me. Show me that you're sorry. Show me that . . ."

"That you're mine?" he finishes with a wicked smirk. "Gladly, Miss Harrow. Now be a good girl and scream so they all know that you're mine. I don't like the way they look at you. If you knew what I wanted to do to that man who dared speak to you, Reign, you would be terrified." He pulls my dress up, leaving me breathless. "It is not just Dal who would kill for you, Reign. I would as well. Remember that. I'm a weapon, and you are the trigger."

His hands keep my dress gathered at my hips as he leans in, placing a kiss over my mound. I reach for him, tangling my fingers in his hair and mussing it. Kicking one leg over his shoulder, I smirk. "Prove it," I taunt, still annoyed, but I know from the look in his eyes that I will be too tired to feel anything but pleasure when he's done with me.

His dark eyes consume me, drinking me down. His suit is perfectly pressed, and every inch of him is perfect until I mess it up, and he loves it.

The man who craves control loves the anarchy I bring into his life, and he shows me how much as his mouth covers my pussy. The sight is so dirty, so goddamn sexy, it has me clenching, wanting him to fill me. My clit begs for attention, and like the good bodyguard he is, he rubs his nose along my clit as I groan. I tilt my hips to give him better access, and that's when his hands tighten their hold, jerking me closer until he's buried in my cunt.

His tongue darts out and circles my clit, rubbing hard, and pleasure slams through me as I cry out. I grind into his waiting mouth as his tongue slides down and thrusts inside me, fucking me as I grip my breasts and tweak my nipples.

My anger turns to blazing desire as I ride his face, using him as he replaces his tongue with his fingers and laps at my clit, circling and rolling it in his talented mouth until I'm breathing heavily, needing to come so badly.

"Raff," I beg, everything else forgotten except his possessive touch and his dark eyes.

I will never escape Raff. It's a good thing I don't want to.

I can't look away from him as three fingers rub inside me while his tongue punishes me, reminding me why I should forgive him and that no one can touch me like they can. He uses the knowledge against me until my leg shakes and I scream his name, my release exploding through me.

When it's over, he catches me and places a kiss on my oversensitive clit as he pulls his fingers free, and as I watch, he rubs them across his lips. "In case you forget whom you belong to, you can look at me and know that I will be tasting you all night."

Jesus fucking Christ.

He climbs to his feet, straightening his suit except for his tie. I reach out to straighten it, and he captures my hand, kissing it. "I like it like this, mussed like you." I huff, and he grins, crowding me. "Forgive me?"

"I guess," I say, but I can't hold back my smile as my cum slides down my legs. "I might have overreacted."

"No, you reacted right. I was in the wrong. You are allowed to feel however you want, and I always want you to tell me when I've messed up or hurt you, but never doubt that you are the center of my universe, Reign. In this life or the next, I would find you. They could pluck out my eyes and I would know it was you. They could take away my senses and I would still know your body, your heart. They could steal my words and I would still find a way to show you how much I care. They could put a fucking bullet in my skull, Reign, and I would still find a way to come back to you. You are my everything, and I will show you every day."

I stare, speechless, as he leans in and kisses me, letting me taste my pleasure on his lips. "Now let's get back to our date—the first of the rest of our lives."

THIRTY-SIX

When Reign and Raff come back, they are holding hands and grinning. He looks ridiculously smug, and I've never been so jealous of the bastard before. I've been sitting here with Dal and Cil, eating this ridiculously small portion of food, while it's clear he's been eating or fucking her. Narrowing my eyes, I watch her giggle as he leans in and nips her shoulder before pulling her chair out for her, and when she sits, he kisses her head. When she glances back at us, her face flushed and lipstick mussed, jealousy flares through me.

I know we are sharing her, but for a moment, it almost rips at my heart and I want to snap. At her. At him. I lower my gaze, not wanting her to see that as I work through this. It's not right to be jealous. She cares for all of us, and she wants all of us. They clearly needed that moment, but fuck if it doesn't hurt. He got my girl when I've been dying to touch her all night, yet I behaved myself, wanting to give her the date she deserves.

"This looks good," she says, tucking into the food that was plated moments ago. I watch her mouth work as she moans, and my cock hardens.

I'm still mad and jealous, but I always want her.

A reckless idea comes to mind.

If Raff can take what he wants, then so can I.

It might drive back these irrational feelings if I touch and taste her and know she's mine as much as she's his.

Pretending to drop my fork, I crawl under the table.

She jumps when my hand slides up her leg. I sit back on my heels, forcing her legs wider, and press between them. I hear her breath stutter, and someone hands her a glass of water with a murmur. Chuckling softly, I run my lips up her leg, pushing her dress up until I expose her pretty pink pussy to my greedy eyes.

Oh yes, Raffiel had fun alright, and she's still fucking wet from it. The jealousy morphs into gratefulness because if he hadn't, I wouldn't get to touch and taste my girl. She's my favorite fucking meal in the entire world. Fuck these fancy dishes, I'm starving, and she's about to be my buffet.

"Are you okay, Reign?" I hear Dal ask.

"Fine," she says. "This food is delicious."

"So is mine," I rasp against her thigh, nipping the skin there before dragging my tongue up and across her pretty pussy, flicking her swollen clit. "So good," she says, making me grin against her. Her hand comes down, hitting my shoulder before dragging me closer.

Oh, my girl is so fucking naughty, and I love it.

I lap at her pretty pussy, and her taste explodes in my mouth, replacing the million-dollar meal we're having, and it's fucking better. She tastes like strawberries. Groaning, I tighten my hold on her thigh, widening her legs to give me better access as she slides farther down the chair for me.

Dragging my tongue over her clit, I lash it as she grinds into my face before thrusting it inside her. She clenches around my tongue, and my cock jerks. Releasing her thigh, I pull my cock out and squeeze, stroking myself as I lick her. Her breathing is heavy now, and she's trying to hold back, so I push her, licking her clit until she almost comes, and then I stop.

She moans in protest.

A waiter comes up—I see their feet—and places another dish down as I continue to tease her. "Thank you."

Stroking myself harder, I slide three fingers inside her with my other hand. She cries out as I stretch her and suck her clit.

"Are you okay, Reign?" Cillian asks, amusement lacing his tone, no doubt figuring out what's happening. What I don't expect is Raff's words.

"You look flushed, love," he teases. "Maybe we should get some fresh air."

"No!" she yells, making me grin and nip her clit in praise. "Yes, no, I mean."

"You seem unsure. Are you sure everything is okay?" he taunts.

"Fine, everything's fine."

Just fine? Oh, we can't have that. I spear another finger into her, stretching her pussy to the point of pain as I suck and lick her greedy clit. Pulling out of her wet cunt, I slide my hand down my cock, making me nice and wet, before thrusting them back inside her with my precum.

"Fuck!" she curses then tries to cover her mistake. "This meal is so good."

"I bet it is. Why don't you be a good girl and finish?" Cillian asks.

She shudders in my grip, knowing exactly what they mean. Tightening my hold on my cock, I stroke it at the same speed I thrust into her greedy cunt. Her legs shake, and when I suck her clit into my mouth once more, she cries out, her cunt gripping my fingers as she comes.

Releasing her clit, I slide lower and lap up her release as I slowly twist my fingers, fucking her through it. I grunt as my own release slams through me. I cup the end of my cock, catching the cum before pulling my hand out of her. I smear my cum across her pussy and push it inside her as she moans and quakes for me.

Grinning, I place another kiss on her clit, put my cock away, and close her legs before sliding out from the table and into my seat. Her eyes are narrowed as she grips the edge of the table. She looks at me, and I lick my lips clean of her delicious cream as I moan. "You're right, this is the best fucking meal I've ever had."

"I bet," Dal offers, making Cil chuckle.

Panting, she shakes her head. "You guys are going to kill me," she mutters.

"You'll die happy, baby," I promise.

A waiter comes and clears the dishes while more set down the last plates—chocolate strawberries. She laughs as I groan.

"Fucking strawberries, man. It's all I think about," Cillian mutters.

"Me too." Dal nods. "I went to the market yesterday and got hard in the produce section when I saw them."

"It's my favorite taste in the world," I mutter.

"Mine too." Raffiel nods as she flushes once more.

"I don't know, I prefer more salty flavors," she purrs, playing the game as she picks up a strawberry, sucking it into her mouth with a pornographic moan.

"We need to leave," Dal murmurs, "or I'm going to bend her over this table and fuck her."

"It's our table." Raffiel shrugs. "I'm eating my strawberries."

Taking that as permission, Dal stands, and Reign's eyes widen. She doesn't think he'll do it, but she should have known better. Kicking her chair back, he grabs her and tosses her onto the table. Plates fall and shatter, but Raff grabs his, not even bothered, and continues eating.

"Dal," she protests as he turns her so she's leaning onto the table with her ass in the air, her face pointed toward Cil.

Ripping her dress up, he slaps her ass hard, making her gasp and grip the tablecloth. Crossing my legs, I lean back to enjoy the show as she tries to stand up. "Anyone could—"

He pushes her down, making her grunt.

"Then let them see," he says, his voice calm, but his hand is almost shaking as he unzips his pants. She hears it and shivers.

"Dal," she whispers, but it doesn't seem like a protest. If anything, it's a plea, and when I lean around, I see him dragging his cock across her wet pussy, bumping her clit. She grabs the tablecloth, her head falling forward in resignation and need.

"Did you really think you could taunt me with everything I want all night and get away with it?" he asks her. "You've been naughty tonight, Reign, and it's time you were punished."

"Please," she begs as his hand comes down on her ass.

Crying out, she jerks on the table as Raffiel reaches over, grabs Dal's plate, and starts to eat his dessert too. That's fine because Dal has his very own in front of him.

Grabbing a flat-edged bread knife from the table, Dal brings it down on her ass, the sound audible. She cries out, looking at me even as she pushes her ass back for more.

"Good girl," Dal murmurs, and I move my chair to get a better view, watching as he slams into her greedy pussy. She screams, and he pulls out, slamming the knife down on her ass again. "Shh."

I thought I would be jealous, but seeing them together is better than the aftermath. There is no jealousy now, only need.

Grabbing a strawberry from Cillian's plate, Dal dips it inside her, fucking her with the fruit before bringing it to his mouth and swallowing it whole. "They are right, Reign, I'll live on strawberries now."

"Dal, please," she begs. "Fuck me right now or I swear I'm going to jump one of the others."

"I'd like to see you try," he threatens, his voice cold, but she flips her hair and pushes back.

"Try me," she hisses.

Gripping her chin, he bends over her, snarling into her face as he slams into her, watching as she writhes and screams for him, taking every inch of his huge cock. I scan the room quickly to make sure we have no spectators. They would be dead if they were watching, but the restaurant is completely empty. The staff is undoubtedly hiding in the back.

"Do not threaten me again, Reign. Not unless you are prepared for the consequences," he warns before leaning up and gripping her hips as he slams into her, pushing the table forward with the force.

"Take her mouth," Dal tells Cil. "We all know you want to. Silence our girl so they don't call the police and I don't have to kill them for trying to stop me from fucking what's mine."

"Glady," Cillian says as he stands. "Turn that pretty head, baby."

She does, her greedy eyes locking on him. Pulling his cock out, he strokes it as he watches her, and she licks her lips. "You want this, baby?" She nods, groaning when Dal slams into her. "You want to suck my cock? You want one of your men in your pretty pussy and the other in your mouth? Pumping you full of our cum?"

"Cil," she says, her eyes closing in ecstasy. "Please."

Fuck, she begs so sweetly.

Grabbing a strawberry, Cillian rubs it across her red lips before tossing it aside and sliding his cock into her mouth. She chokes as he thrusts all the way down her throat. Her eyes open, wide and watering, as he grips her chin and pulls out before pushing back in. He forces himself deeper as Dal hammers into her from behind, bringing that knife down and reddening her pretty ass.

Raffiel leans back, watching the whole thing with dark, glittering eyes. "She's still making noises, boys. Maybe she needs more persuasion," he remarks darkly with a chuckle.

"Can't have that, can we?" Cillian murmurs, slamming into her mouth until she gags.

Their grunts are loud in the empty restaurant, while Raff and I just watch. I smile as she looks at us to check in.

"Good girl," Raff praises, and Dal groans.

"Fuck, she loves it when you call her that. She almost strangled my cock," he snarls, fucking her so hard, she's forced deeper onto Cillian's cock. Her mouth is stretched wide as he groans.

"Is he right, Miss Harrow? Do you like to hear that you are our good girl?" Raffiel says leisurely. Dal snarls, and I know that's her answer. Grinning, I reach over and grab a strawberry, eating it as I watch them claim her body.

Her eyes roll back into her head, and she mewls around Cillian's cock. Dal groans, his eyes closing and hips stuttering, and I watch him shatter, finding his release in her. He runs his lips down her back as he groans, pushing his cum deeper as Cillian grips her chin and forces her mouth wider. He bellows, his hips stilling as he pumps his cum into her. I watch her throat swallow before he pulls out and leans down, kissing her softly.

"She is our good girl."

Damn right she is.

TWENTY-SEVEN

affiel sets his card down to pay, and something about that makes me want to cry. A waiter appears, and after he departs, Raff comes around, takes my hand, and leads me from the restaurant. I can walk, thank fuck, since they let me finish my wine as I recovered from them claiming me. I should be embarrassed, but I'm not. I don't care if the staff heard or saw the mess on the table. It was worth it. The car is right out front, and Raff opens the door. Cil climbs in with Astro, and I clamber in behind them, relaxed and tired.

There's no paparazzi, no reason to be on display, and I love it as I climb onto their laps as Dal and Raff get into the front and we take off, heading home.

Curling into Cillian's lap, I sigh and close my eyes in bliss.

"Did you have a good night, baby?" he murmurs softly, kissing the top of my head.

I love that they tried to be gentlemen this evening, keeping their hands off me, but I love it even better that they gave in.

"The best," I admit. "That's probably the best date I've ever been on." They gave me what I wanted without me even realizing it, and more than that, they gave me the chance to feel safe enough to explore myself and my actions. I know I am always safe with them, and it's heady.

"It was the best date I've ever been on. Well, the only one actually." He laughs above my head, and I lift it to meet his gaze.

"Really?" I look at Astro who shrugs.

"We had no time for dating, babe."

I turn to look at Raff, and he winks. Laughing, I lay my head back down, secretly pleased I'm the only one they have ever taken on a date. Cillian holds me as Astro rubs my feet. It's nice and relaxing, and I must drift off to sleep because I startle awake when a hand brushes my hair.

"Shh, baby, I've got you." It's Raffiel. He picks me up, and I open my eyes to see us heading to the front door. I didn't even know we were home. Curling into his chest, I relax as he walks inside—only to stop.

"Raff?" I lift my head as he turns.

"Dal, take her," he barks.

Dal takes me and slides me down his body, shielding me. I peer around him as Astro and Cillian move into the door.

Sitting in the reception of my house are ten bloody hearts—ten real-looking, dripping, bloody hearts placed in the shape of a heart, and blood is smeared across the white marble.

Gasping, I cover my mouth. "What the fuck?"

"Dal, with her," Raff orders. "We sweep the house now." His voice is quiet. "At the first sign of trouble, get her out of here."

"No, wait!" I try to help, but they are already moving.

They dive into action, hustling me to the side. Dal stands before me with his gun out as Raffiel points, and the others split up, heading into the house, while Raffiel goes upstairs, their weapons drawn as they move silently.

I cover my mouth, horror and fear surging through me. "Dal," I whisper.

"Shh, baby, we've got you."

My eyes go back to the hearts in terror. Who the hell did this? How did they do this?

Why?

Oh god, Raff Jr.

I have so many questions, but fear fills me, and I cower behind Dal, letting them protect me as they silently sweep the house. Every second they are gone, my heart beats harder, and when they suddenly appear, I jump.

"Downstairs is clear. I found Raff Jr. locked in a cupboard. He's fine," Cillian says, glancing at me to check me over, Raff Jr. snuggling happily in his arms, and I rain kisses across his head as I wait nervously.

Astro appears a second later. "Outside too."

Raff strides down the stairs, phone in hand. "Upstairs is clear, but they left a present. Get her into the kitchen. I want two of you with her at all times. I want cameras accessed and security spoken to. Find out how the fuck this happened," he roars.

"Raff?" He turns to Astro, speaking in low, hushed voices, and I clear my throat. "Raffiel," I practically shout. They all turn to me. "What's happening?"

He heads my way, cupping my chin. "Someone broke in, baby, but they aren't here anymore."

"Why?" I whisper, searching his gaze. Something slides across his eyes too quickly for me to identify.

"I don't know. We will find out who, and they will never do it again. I'm sorry, baby. Go relax with them while I take care of this, okay?" His voice is soft, but his eyes are hard and angry.

"Upstairs, you said—"

"Shh, go." He pushes me toward Dal and Cillian, while Astro goes with Raff.

I watch them walk away, feeling uncertain and terrified.

"Here." Dal places a hot cup of herbal tea before me. "Drink this."

I pick it up with shaking hands, sitting in a chair with them guarding me. Cillian stands at the back, his sharp eyes scanning everything, while Dal continually moves around the space. The others haven't appeared yet.

Raff Jr. is fine, we double-checked, and he seems unbothered as he sleeps happily on one of his many beds on the kitchen floor.

"What's going on?" I ask.

"It's okay. You're okay," Cillian promises before turning back to his duty.

"Tell me," I demand, my tone harder this time.

"We will once we know—"

I slam the mug down, cracking it, and wince. "No, now. This is my home, my life, and I want to know." They share a look over my head, which I hate. Snarling, I get to my feet, refusing to cower. I stomp to the stairs, and they scramble after me, but I'm fast and I make it up there before they can stop me.

They grab me when I reach my room, horror coursing through me.

Another bloody heart is sitting on my bed, and surrounding it is my underwear, which is ripped and covered in a glistening liquid—cum. Gagging, I turn away before forcing myself to look again. Written in blood above my bed is a message.

I've missed you. Come home.

"Who did this?" I whisper, turning to them. "Why did they do this?"

"Because some people are sick, baby. Come on, let's go back downstairs. The others will be back and we can talk then, okay?"

Nodding, I let them lead me back downstairs, and this time, I don't protest. I sit and sip from the chipped mug of tea as they wait for the others. My mind whirs. Who did this? Tucker? No, this is too insane, even for him. One of my enemies or Sal? No, this isn't a prank or even retribution. This is something more.

A crazed fan maybe?

How did they get in here?

I thought I was safe, untouchable, and now my castle is crumbling down around me, leaving me cold and unsure. The happiness from tonight fades.

Sometime later, a furious Raffiel and Astro appear. Raff crouches before me, eyeing Cillian and Dal before he glances at me. "Are you okay?"

"No, I'm not fucking okay. Someone broke into my house, Raffiel. They left a sick fucking message in my bed. My fucking bed. It feels tainted and wrong. This is my sanctuary, my safe space!" I yell, and he just takes it so I deflate. "Who did this?"

He glances away for a moment, and when he looks back at me, he searches my face. "We don't know." I go to pull away, but he doesn't let me. "But we will. I promise, Reign, we will. The cameras went down, so did the alarms, and it drew the security team's attention which is how he got in. It won't happen again."

"I don't care. I don't feel safe here," I snap.

"We will be here. You will never be alone—"

"No, I can't." I stand, swallowing. "Not here, not right now. It feels wrong." I try to explain, but it doesn't feel like my house anymore and I'm pissed. I'm pissed they took that from me. I want to argue and fight because this is still my house and they won't take it from me, but the message above my bed makes me shiver in fear. No matter how badass my men are, I still won't feel safe here.

"Okay," he says without fighting. "How about we go somewhere else for a few days and let them clean up? A team I trust will come in and secure everything, and when we come back, you can see how you feel."

Nodding, I peer at the others. "But where?"

Biting his lip, Raff seems to come to a conclusion before he stands. "How about we get out of the city for a few days? You have no appearances, and you can work from wherever we go."

I nod. Maybe getting out of the city would be good. We can get away from all this for a few days and the media frenzy that will undoubtedly come once they find out about this. Raff Jr. can stay with Emma, the boarder, so he'll be okay. It will get him out of the line of fire at least. "Okay, but where?"

Raff turns to Astro and grins. "How do you feel about going home?"

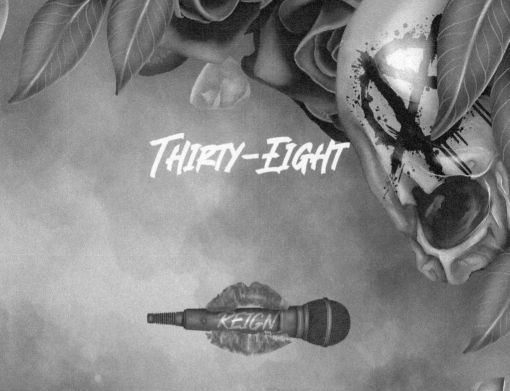

THIRTY-EIGHT

I 'm nervous as hell. We are going to Astro's family home and I'm utterly shitting myself. What if his family hates me? What if they judge me? What if someone recognizes me and we're mobbed?

I'm more worried about what Astro's family will think. It's obvious he loves them very much, and I care about Astro. Will he introduce me as his girlfriend or as his job? Will they care? I'm overthinking, and I know it.

Peering down at my outfit, I frown once more. I felt the need to be comfortable after what happened, and Cil packed my bags so I didn't have to go upstairs. He handed me the hoodie and legging combo, but now I worry what his family will think of that. I've never been this panicked before about meeting my boyfriend's family, so why now?

Is it because this thing we have feels right? Because I decided I'm all in and I don't want anything to ruin it?

Cillian covers my jumping thigh, smiling tenderly. "Don't worry, okay? The police are there now, and everything will be okay. We alerted your manager and Jack, so there's nothing to worry about."

"It's not that," I admit softly, eyeing Astro who's whistling as he fills up the car with gas. Raff is inside paying, and Dal sits in the front.

He follows my gaze to Astro. "Don't worry, his family is amazing. They took us in like we're their own. They are so kind and welcoming, and they will love you. Trust me, from a guy who never really had a family, I love his."

"It's different for you guys. What if they hate me?" I whisper.

"Impossible," Cil murmurs, kissing me softly. "It would be impossible not to love you, Reign Harrow."

"But what if—"

He covers my mouth and meets my eyes with a grin. "I can see you panicking. I know you are anti everything, Reign, but I promise they will love you, and Astro is so excited for you to meet his family."

"Isn't this too fast?" I mumble.

"Baby, what did you think all in meant?" He smirks. "Astro is already planning your ring." My eyes widen, and he chuckles. "Don't worry, we'll slow him down for a little while, but I'm not saying I won't get you one." He winks and I smack his shoulder, but I'm relaxed now.

"Thank you," I tell him quietly. "For always . . . well, everything."

"I'm yours, Reign Harrow, and you are mine. We are in this together. You never have to thank us." Wrapping his arm around me, he tugs me into his side as the door opens, and I jump.

"Here, baby." Raffiel places snacks and drinks near me on the seat and my eyes widen. He got all my favorite candy and drinks. He kisses me as he climbs in, not even noticing he did it or not expecting my shock, but it's the little things like this that make me so sure I'm doing the right thing with these men. They think of me, even with something small like that, and it makes me smile wider as I grab a bag of chips.

Astro slides in and turns back to me, grinning. "Road trip time! I get to pick the first songs." He hits something and "Man! I Feel Like A Woman!" comes on, making me laugh as he starts singing off-key as we pull onto the road.

I'm ready to head to Astro's family home and escape what lies behind us.

Astro's family home is . . . well, cute, to say the least. I don't know what I was expecting, but it wasn't this huge, white, blue window-framed house with a swing on a tree outside and rolling hills behind it. He told me he loves his family but he left when he was young. They were Marines, special forces, so I just didn't expect such a normal home and for a moment, I panic.

I'm worried they will be able to see the dirt-poor street girl hidden underneath all the money and call me out for it, but Astro is so excited. He yanks me from the car, hurries up the stairs, and walks right in without knocking.

We stand in a foyer filled with shoes and family pictures. In front of us is the hall leading to what looks to be a kitchen, and to the right is a living room with the TV blaring a football game.

"I'm home!" Astro calls loudly. I try to tug my hand free, but he holds it tight, winking down at me.

The scent of something delicious reaches me as a heavyset woman pokes her head around the hallway and screams, running toward us before she tackles Astro. "My boy!" she yells, gripping his face and peppering it with kisses before smacking him. "You didn't tell me you were coming."

"It's a surprise, Ma," he whines and kisses her cheek before stepping back. "The guys are here too. I thought we could stay for a few days. That's okay, right?"

"Of course, you know you never have to ask! Who is this beauty?" She grins at me. Her bright eyes match Astro's, and her hair, a faded gray-blonde, is pulled up in a bun on her head. She's shorter than me and wearing an apron with boobs on it, and she's just so fucking adorable.

"Mom, this is my girl," Astro declares proudly, beaming at her. "Reign, this is my mom, Gloria."

She turns to me and I stiffen, waiting for the questions and scrutiny, but she simply pulls me into a bear hug. "It's so nice to meet you," she gushes. "We have heard so much about you, Reign."

"Um, you have?" I hedge. I can't remember the last time a mother figure hugged me. Pulling back, she looks me over. "Of course! You look hungry. Come, let me get you something."

The door opens behind me and she grins. "Boys!" They give her one-armed hugs as they pass her, bringing in our bags. Even Dal accepts a stiff hug, and she tugs at his clothes. "You've lost weight."

"I'm fine, thank you," he says, but I see him relax a little, and I know why she did it. Whatever happened in Dal's past, it clearly involves his family and it messed him up, just like my own. She's being the mother I don't think he ever had to all of them, and when her eyes sweep to me, I realize that now includes me.

No questions, no complaints, no judgment—just a loving welcome.

I wonder what it must have felt like to grow up in such an environment. No wonder Astro turned out as amazing as he did.

"Your house is beautiful," I blurt, trying to remember my manners.

"Thank you, Reign." She loops her arm through mine and drags me to the kitchen, where she sits me at a wooden table. "Sit, I'll grab you all something."

"Oh, can I help?" I ask, starting to rise.

"Don't be silly!" She hustles into the kitchen, humming to herself as Astro kisses my head.

"Don't offer, it will offend her." He chuckles as he throws himself into a chair next to me. "Where's Dad?"

"Out tinkering," Gloria grumbles, "in that stupid workshop."

Raffiel and Cillian sit, and Dal hovers, but when Gloria turns her gaze to him, she points. "Sit now, boy." He quickly follows suit, making me giggle.

As quickly as we sit, plates appear before us, overflowing with food, along with water bottles, and then she sits, grinning at us.

"Well, eat!"

Astro plates me some and hands it over.

"Thank you," I tell him as I try to eat, not wanting to be rude but still feeling slightly sick from what I saw in my house. At the first bite of her food, though, I moan and dig in. I don't stop until the plate is empty, and I blush with embarrassment.

"Now that's my type of girl." She winks and eyes Astro with a knowing look as he quickly makes me another plate. Just then, the back door opens, and a huge, gruff man who looks like an older version of Astro steps in.

"I'm starving. I smelled—Astro!"

Astro gets up, and his dad bear hugs him. "Hey, boys, how's it going?" he calls and then looks at me. "You're not one of these heathens." He holds out his hand before wincing and wiping it when he sees there's oil on it. "Sorry."

I take it as I stand, uncaring about the oil. "Hi, it's nice to meet you. I'm Reign."

"Reign?" His eyes widen and he grins at Astro. "Is that right? It's nice to finally meet you. I'm Glein. Let me wash up."

I sit as he scrubs his hands before coming and sitting heavily.

"So, is everything okay?" Glein asks, getting straight to the point.

"Some sicko broke into Reign's house, so we wanted to bring her somewhere safe for a few days where she can lie low," Astro answers honestly, and I freeze, expecting Raff to be mad, but he just nods.

"Well then, welcome home, Reign," Glein says. "Are you all okay? This sicko didn't do anything?"

"No, sir, just, uh, left some things in my house, and I didn't want to be there," I reply.

"I don't blame you," Glein says. "But if my boys are on the case, they'll catch him and keep you safe."

"Nonna!" comes a yell, and we all look up to see a small head peeking around the stairs.

"Young man, it's way past your bedtime," Gloria scolds. "Off with you."

"Astro!" The boy runs in, aiming a dimpled grin at him, and then he turns to Dal. "Dal!"

Surprising me, Dal picks the little boy up and swings him around. "Hey, Theo."

I watch them with disbelief, and Cil leans in. "Astro's nephew. His sister lives here. Her husband was an abusive asshole and we got her away from him. I bet she's working right now. She's studying to be a doctor."

I look at the kid, wondering what he's seen or been through, and something twinges in my heart when he turns to me with a smile. "I'm Theo." He sticks his hand out, and I shake it softly.

"Reign."

"Are you that singer my mom says Uncle Astro is obsessed with?"

I laugh as Astro coughs and blushes. "Shh, don't ruin my rep, kid."

"Off to bed with you," Gloria says.

"But I can't sleep. Will you sing to me?" He pouts up at her.

Oh, this kid is good.

"Now, Theo." She props her hands on her hips. "We have talked about this."

"Yeah, she sounds like a bag of cats being hit by a wall." Glein laughs, and they all join in.

"Reign, you sing, so will you sing me to sleep?" Theo turns to me, so hopeful.

"Oh, um—"

"She's a guest, Theo, and tired. Maybe another night," Glein says, but I swallow, looking into those baby-blue eyes that remind me so much of my little brother, it almost makes me cry. Besides, singing always makes me feel better, and right now, I need some peace, and the guys probably need to talk to Astro's parents.

"Sure." I stand, offering my hand. "Show me to your room?"

"Oh, Reign, you don't have to," Astro's mom protests, wringing her hands in worry.

"It's okay, I promise." I grin as Theo tugs me down the hall and upstairs as they laugh. Once in his room, he leaps into a bed made with dinosaur bedding and shuffles down, patting the chair next to it.

Grinning, I sit. "What do you want?"

"A story or….a song!" he yells and passes me a book.

I freeze, staring down at the title. "*Peter Pan*?" I whisper, throat tight.

"It's my favorite. Do you like it?" he asks.

"I do." Biting my lip, I stare down at the familiar cover. Mine was a little more worn and stolen from the local library, and when my dad destroyed it in anger one night, I had to get creative. "It was my little brother's favorite."

"Really?" He sits up.

"Really. When he couldn't sleep, I would read and then sing it to him," I reply, stroking the cover.

"Was he scared of the dark too?" he whispers trustingly, and I jerk my head up and smile softly.

"Yes and no. He was scared of what hid in the dark in our house." He frowns, and I shuffle closer. "Your house is filled with good things, though. I can tell."

"He liked it though, so it helped?"

I nod once more. "I would sing him to sleep so he could dream of adventures and good things and be anywhere but there. It's why I became a singer actually, why I started to play—to give us an escape."

"You love him." He nods, peering up at me.

"I loved him very much."

"Loved?" He frowns.

"He's not with us anymore," I admit, heart clenching.

"The dark got him?" he asks in fear.

"In a way," I answer truthfully.

"The dark got my daddy too. I don't like the dark. Mom always said it infected him and made him bad. When it was dark, we used to hide from him," he says with tears in his eyes. "I don't like the dark now. I want to protect Mom from it."

"I'm sure you do, but there's nothing to be scared of now. Astro and your family made sure of that, and I'm certain your mom would say the same. You're safe, I promise." I take his hand as he wipes his face.

"That's what she says," he replies. "Sing to me instead?"

"Of course." Keeping one hand in his and the other on the book, I close my eyes and the lyrics that live in my heart and memories flow out, and when I finish, I realize I'm crying.

He leans up, wipes my face, and kisses my head. "You shouldn't be scared of the dark anymore either." He snuggles back into bed and closes his eyes.

"I'll try," I murmur and stand, carefully tucking him in before shutting the door behind me.

I press my back to it and breathe in slowly.

I feel pain in my heart, but also hope.

THIRTY-NINE

"She's so wonderful," my mom gushes, fixing my hair as I roll my eyes. "So kind, not to mention pretty."

"She's a keeper." My dad, a man of few words, nods.

"That she is and I plan on it." I grin, looking at the others before lowering my voice. "Which reminds me, while I'm here, can I have the ring?"

My mom's eyes widen before she squeals and slaps her hands over her mouth. "I'm just so happy," Gloria whispers.

My dad pats me on the shoulder. "Good man."

Chuckling, I ignore the others' looks, knowing I'm being very forward, but it's how I feel. I know she's the one.

"Let me go check on them." I chuckle as I stand.

I slowly make my way upstairs, only to freeze in the hallway to listen to my girl and my nephew's conversation. My heart aches at his admission that he is still afraid of the dark. His father was a piece of shit, but he never has to worry about him again. We made sure of that. As soon as my dad called me after they turned up in the pouring rain with black eyes, the guys and I came and hunted the fucker down, but it's Reign's answer that has my heart pounding.

Realization sets in as I listen to her.

I knew her brother died, but from the way she's speaking, it's clear Reign was abused when she was younger.

It explains so much, but I walk away quietly, not wanting her to know I was spying on her. She will tell us when she's ready and not a moment before, but her tattoo makes so much more sense now, and I have someone I need to kill for my girl.

———

Since it was so late when Reign came back down, Mom and Dad helped us with the bags and we made up beds in the guesthouse. Mom fusses over it, even though it's immaculate, and when they leave, we all collapse on the mattress on the floor in Reign's room. Raff explained it's for her safety, but it's actually so we can be close to her. She's curled up on her bed and her breathing is even, but I don't think she's asleep.

Turning over, I eye the others. Dal is under the window, Raff is near the door, and Cil is to the left of me. We made a barrier between her and the outside world to make her feel safe, but when she sighs, I get to my knees. "Want company, baby?"

"Please," she replies, her voice small.

I throw myself on the bed, and she bounces with a giggle before I tug her into my arms. A moment later, Cillian settles in on her other side. Dal sits up on the window ledge, watching us, as Raff sighs from the floor.

"You're just mad you didn't offer first." I stick my tongue out at him and snuggle into her. She grins, closing her eyes once more as we hold her between us.

I have so much I want to say, to ask, but I don't want to betray her confidence. I meet Dal's eyes, knowing he would understand the most. We don't know all of Dal's past, only some, and even that is enough to horrify us for life. He tilts his head, frowning at me.

"Your sister and nephew will be okay, won't they? He can't hurt them?" she asks softly. Despite everything, my girl is worried about my family.

"Not anymore," I promise.

"But what if he comes here—"

"He can't," I assure her, and she peers up at me.

"Astro—"

"He's dead," I say, and she stiffens. "I killed him for daring to lay a hand on my sister and nephew. The bastard deserved it. He'd broken her ribs, her arm. Her eyes were black and blue. He chopped her hair off and raped her. I made sure he never had the chance to touch her again."

I will never regret hunting that man down like a dog and breaking every single bone in his body to make him feel what he did to my sister, but I worry how she will react. Will she turn me away? I don't think I could continue to live if she did.

"Good," she finally says, and I slump. "I'm glad you did. I'm glad they are safe."

She becomes quiet then and seems like she's a million miles away, so I put my head down and just watch the rise and fall of her chest, each breath a reminder that she is here, she is safe, and she is mine.

"I killed someone," she whispers, and we all swing our gazes to her. She shrinks but keeps talking. I expect her to stop and close up. Reign is so tight-lipped about her secrets, but that's okay. I'll fight that much harder for her and her heart.

"I killed someone too," she repeats, and when she looks at me, I see tears in her eyes. She quickly glances away, and her voice rushes out as if she doesn't say it now, then she never will. "My father. I didn't take a gun and shoot him or anything, but I helped it along. He was a true fucking bastard. My mom was out of our lives at this point, and he was drinking every night. He would . . . He would hurt me. I tried to protect my little brother from it. I would hide him away, and even with broken bones, I would still climb in bed next to him and hold him tight through the night. I never wanted him to know, but he did. I saw the loss of innocence and it killed me. One night, I'd gone to an open mic night at Attie's urging. He always wanted me to sing for people and follow my dreams, and I spun us a tale of me being discovered and running away together where we would never be cold, hungry, or hurt." She hiccups as I stroke her arm.

"That night, I had a bad feeling so I rushed back, and when I did . . ." She closes her eyes. "He was dead. My father killed my brother in a rage, threw him down the stairs, and he was dead. The police came, but my father was friends with them and they ruled it an accident. They said he fell. He hadn't. I still remember curling over his body and begging them to take me instead." Tears fall as the others move closer. "The day his coffin was lowered into the ground, I made a decision. I didn't care if I lived or died, just that he paid. He killed the only good thing in my life."

Her face hardens and for a moment, I see fury in her gaze, and it's glorious.

"I spiked his drink. I watched him almost pass out and told him we had run out of alcohol. He got in the car like I knew he would, and I let him. In fact, I got in it with him. He was a good drunk driver, since he was so used to it, but when we got on the back country road, I grabbed the wheel and I told him the truth. I said, 'We all die today,' and then I jerked it. We flew over the ravine and flipped, hitting a tree. I was ready to die. I couldn't live like that anymore. When I woke up—" She shudders.

"I couldn't feel much of anything, probably shock. There was blood dripping into my face, my ears rang with the sound of the dying engine and screeching metal, and there was my dad. He was badly hurt. His phone was just out of reach, and I could move, so I grabbed it. He begged me to call for help, but I didn't. I watched him die. I watched him breathe his last breath and I knew I would do it again. It would never be enough for what he did, but I made sure he would never hurt another again, and then I called for help. I didn't expect to live, but I did. They said it was a miracle I only had some cracked ribs and a broken arm. I felt anything but lucky. I was dead inside. I discharged myself, and once they cleared me of all wrongdoing—since his alcohol limit was way over the legal limit, they assumed he crashed—I packed up the only things I gave a fuck about. Just one small backpack and the guitar I saved up to buy, the one with our initials carved into it, and I left. I left and raced toward our dream, but when I got it, it wasn't the same without him."

She turns to look at me. "Nothing's the same without him. I miss him so fucking much all the time. I don't know why I didn't die that night, but something in me wanted to live. Either way, I left my soul in the coffin where he's buried. I've never told anyone the truth about the night."

"I'm so sorry, Reign," I whisper, pulling her closer. My heart breaks for her, and the thought of losing my sister—no. I'd have done the same, maybe worse.

"You did the right thing, baby. I'm so sorry we weren't around to protect you," Raffiel says, jumping onto the bottom of the bed.

"You did," Cillian states. "He would be so happy for you."

She sobs in our arms as we hold her, and when she looks up to Dal, she freezes. His face is pale, and his eyes are wide.

"Dal?" she whispers.

"I killed my mother. What a pair we make, huh?" He snorts as she blinks. He looks out the window, scanning for threats before looking back at us, but his eyes are all for her.

"She was literally a psychopath. She was diagnosed. She never should have had kids. She hated them, but she had me as a mistake and punished me for it every second of every day since I was born. She would let people she was dating beat me and touch me, and one day, I had enough. I knew I could get caught, but I had to do something. I wanted her dead, and when she was, I felt nothing, not even joy. She ripped all emotions from me. I was numb, empty, and then you came along and I felt something for the first time ever."

"How did you—" Reign cuts off, two lost souls staring at each other.

"Kill her?" he asks calmly. "She did drugs, and one day, I changed out the doses. I measured it precisely and made it look like an OD, and I watched as she choked on her own vomit. I laughed like she used to when I did."

"Dal." She slides out of our arms, climbs from the bed, and pads toward him. He watches her approach, his face cold, but I see the truth in his eyes. I see his fear that once she realizes the true depth of Dal's madness, she will leave. Laying her hand on his chest, she steps between his legs, and he wraps his arms around her. "Fuck her. She got what she deserved."

He blinks, and then a slow smile curls his lips. "I would kill for you, Reign. Does that scare you? Does it scare you knowing I would rip apart every single person you asked?"

"No," she admits. "It makes me feel safe."

"It should scare you. They call me what they called her, a psychopath."

"Psychopaths don't feel, you do," she murmurs, taking his hand and leading him back to the bed.

"Only for you," he admits.

"Good." She grins as she lies down with us, tugging him into our midst and bridging the gap Dal always put between us.

She wraps her arms around him, and we wrap our arms around her, holding her tight. We will never let anything else hurt her.

Not ever.

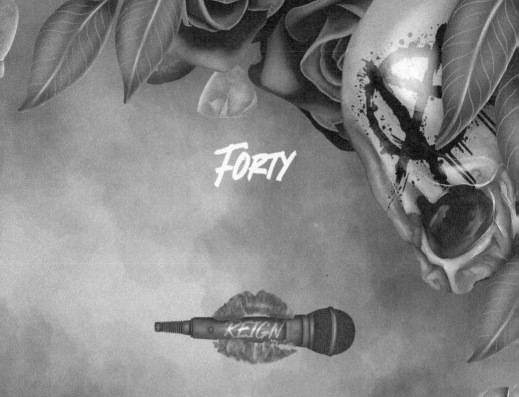

FORTY

I wake with the sun, wrapped in familiar, loving arms, and for once, I just relax. My mind wanders, worrying about what will happen when we go back. I'm sure there will be interviews, and press, and police everywhere. I still want to know who did it, but that will all be dealt with, so instead, I relax and enjoy this time with my men without cameras.

Slipping out of bed, I shower in the guesthouse and dress in some leggings and one of their oversized shirts. After kissing them good morning, I leave them to get ready as I head to the main house.

I step into the kitchen, smiling at Astro's mom. "Good morning."

"Morning, Reign!" She comes over and hugs me. "Did you sleep well?"

"I did, thank you, and thank you so much for letting us stay here. I know we didn't give you any warning—"

"Don't be silly, this is your home now too, and you are welcome whenever. Coffee?"

"Please." I slip into a seat as she pours two mugs and sits near me, enjoying the sunshine streaming in and the sound of laughter from the open guesthouse doors.

"You don't have to worry about cameras out here," Gloria remarks, sipping her coffee. I turn around to look at her, and she laughs. "I know who you are; we all do and always did. Don't worry, you're safe here. Your life is your life. All I care about is my son, and he has never been this happy."

"Really?" I ask. "He always seems so happy."

She smiles, but it's a sad one. "He is. He didn't used to be. He struggled a lot with his mental health growing up. I watched my happy little boy disappear and it killed me. When he enlisted, I cried for days and I thought that was it, but he met the guys and trained and seemed to find his purpose, and he got better. I never saw his smile again, though, not until yesterday. You gave that back to me. You gave me back my son."

Reaching over, I cover her hand with mine. "I didn't know."

"Oh, I shouldn't have said anything." She wipes her eyes.

"No, I'm glad you did," I reply. "I care about your son a lot. He makes me happy too, happier than I've ever been in fact. I didn't even know I needed him until he blew into my life."

"Fate is funny like that." She pats my hand. "How about I show you some pictures?"

When they come in, I'm holding coffee and laughing with his mom as she flips through books of photos from when Astro was a kid.

"Oh god, no, Ma!" He dives for the book, but I lift it out of his reach.

"Nope. Astro, do you still like to dress as a cat?" I tease.

His face blooms bright red. "I was four! Mother!"

"A cat?" Raffiel chuckles and steps up to my other side, peering over my shoulder. "Oh, such a pretty kitty, Astro."

"If you'll excuse me, I'm just going to throw myself off the roof," he mutters, stomping away.

Raffiel's phone rings, and he kisses my cheek before heading outside. I watch him go, and when I glance back, Gloria watches me with a knowing look. Ducking my head, I hide my blush.

"You know, I've known these boys since they were teenagers."

"Oh?" I reply softly, unsure what to say.

"They have never brought anyone here. They treat this like their home, and each one is my son, yet I've never seen them with anyone. Ever." Unsure what to say, I swallow, meeting her eyes. "I won't ask, since it's clear you don't want me to, but know this—those boys never would have brought you here if they didn't love you. It's clear you feel the same way. Just please don't hurt them, okay?"

"I don't want to," I murmur.

"Good." She pats my hand. "Look at this one. This was on Christmas—"

I listen to her stories from when Astro was a kid until Raffiel returns, his face thunderous. "What is it?" I whisper, a bad feeling blooming inside me.

His mom takes my hand, holding it tight. Raff wipes his expression clean, but it's too late. "Raffiel," I demand.

"There are no prints that match the one who broke in, which means they aren't in the system, and the cameras caught nothing."

"So they will just get away with it?" I whisper.

"No, not at all. We'll find them, I promise. The police are on high alert now, and we will be extra careful."

"What if they come back?" I ask as he crouches before me.

"Whoever it is won't get within thirty feet of you without my gun aimed at his head. I promise, baby." We both freeze at the slip, but Gloria just pats Raff's shoulder.

"Don't worry about me, I understand."

He winces but nods, looking at me. "We will keep you safe, Reign. Do you trust me?"

I search his gaze. "Yes, I trust you."

"Good, then we'll spend the long weekend here then go back. Don't let one nut drive you from your house and life. You have done amazingly well, Reign, and you have more left to do. You worry about the revolution you are creating, and we will worry about this. Deal?"

"Deal."

FORTY-ONE

I excuse myself after, leaving Raff to talk to Gloria as I go to hunt Astro down. I'm starting to feel bad about how embarrassed he was. It was nice to see him lose some of that cockiness, but after his mom mentioned his mental health, I don't want him to think my opinion of him has changed. After searching the main house, I head outside, spotting Astro's dad working through the open door in a work-shop. Curious, I move closer as he bobs his head to country music while he works on what seems to be an old muscle car.

"Morning," I call.

He clutches his chest as he spins. "Wow, girl, you are quiet."

"Sorry," I reply sheepishly.

Laughing, he wipes his face with a rag. "Don't worry about it. Morning, love, did you sleep okay?" His eyes sparkle knowingly, and I look away.

"Yes, great, thank you. Have you seen Astro at all?" I cock my head.

"Ah, the boy's probably off in the forest. He usually runs in the morning." He wipes his hands as he watches me. "Why?"

"Oh, I just wanted to talk," I reply hesitantly.

"Uh-huh. Can I ask you something, Reign?" He stands, leaning on the metal door. "Do you love my son?"

My eyes widen in panic, and he grins.

"Okay, how about, do you care for my son?"

"A lot," I respond without missing a beat.

He seems to sag in relief. "Thank fuck. Sorry, you're hard to read and I can tell my boy is smitten. He might seem strong, but he wears his heart on his sleeve, and I would hate for him to get hurt."

"The last thing I want to do is hurt him," I say truthfully. "He means a great deal to me, but he's stronger than you think. Truly, he is. I don't think I would have managed the madness that is my life without him. He always makes me laugh, even when I don't want to."

"He's good at that, always was, the class clown, but beneath that smile is the truth. He's good at diverting attention away with a joke but never talking about if he's okay. Just please don't hurt him. You're a nice girl, I can tell, and the others think the world of you, you wouldn't be here otherwise, but please don't hurt my son."

"I promise I won't," I respond. "He's lucky to have you."

"Oh, um . . ." He rubs his neck self-consciously. "I don't know about that."

"He is. He has parents who love him enough to protect him and want nothing but the best for him. That is something special, and he's very lucky. I would have done anything to have my parents love me half as much as you love your son and daughter."

He eyes me sadly, and I wince when I realize I revealed too much. It's my turn to duck my head in embarrassment, and I start to slide away. "Right, well, I better go find him. Thanks."

"Reign?" he calls, and I stop. "Your parents are fools. That isn't on you. It isn't your fault they didn't love you like they should have." He takes a deep breath. "And if you want, there will always be a place for you here. You've noticed we kind of adopt everyone, and that includes you. I'm not saying we won't be overbearing, and you'll regret the day you said yes. We'll call you when you are sick way too many times, we'll check on you way too frequently and criticize your decisions, but we will love you with everything we have."

"Why?" I ask, tears in my eyes. "All because I care for your son?"

"No, because you deserve it. You deserve to be loved, Reign. You deserve a family. My boys wouldn't have brought you here if they didn't think so. I love them, and no matter what, you're one of us now, kid." He kisses my head softly. "No matter where that road of fame takes you, we will be here." Squeezing my shoulder, he steps back. "Go find him, he's probably waiting for you. Just don't be too late for breakfast or they'll send out a search party." He whistles as he strolls back in, bending over the car once more like he didn't just heal some fractures in my heart.

Swallowing my tears, I turn away and head into the forest, searching for Astro. Now, more than ever, I want to make sure he's okay. I need to see him.

His family's laughter chases me into the brightness of nature, a welcoming sound that unlocks the tightness in my body and becomes the sound of safety and home.

"Astro?" I call as I duck under branches and carefully climb over roots. I'm not made for forests, not anymore, but as a kid, I used to spend hours playing under the trees with my brother. We would build whole worlds there, and as I smile up at the sun, I remember those good days now, not just the bad ones.

It's been so long since I thought of his laughter and smile that when Astro pops out, I almost scream, lost in my memories. "Shit, you scared me," I hiss, covering my racing heart.

Chuckling, he heads my way. "You were looking for me, baby?"

"Yeah, are you okay?" I ask softly.

He freezes, his eyes going to the house. "They told you?" He seems cold, and his face shuts down.

"Your mother just told me that you hide the same pain I have under all your humor. They are worried I'm going to hurt you."

He brings his eyes back to me, swallowing hard. "And now that you know," he whispers, "will you hurt me?"

I hate the distance between us so I cover it quickly. He steps back, hitting a tree, but I don't let him go farther, plastering myself to his front. "Never," I answer truthfully as I search his gaze. "I care about you a lot, Astro. I can't say the words to explain how much, which is ironic for me, I know, but I do. This changes nothing. In fact, it makes me think more highly of you. You're always so funny, so happy, Astro, but knowing you struggled and still struggle and fight every day to be that way . . . I'm in awe of you, you brilliant, kind, strong man," I murmur, sliding my hands up to his shoulders. "I'm glad they told me, and I'll never be more grateful for the day I met you. Don't you know that you changed my life? I was closed off and on a spiraling path to revenge. You saved me, all of you did, and if you let me, I'll save you every day. You'll never struggle alone again. Just let me, baby."

"Reign." He swallows hard, closing his eyes for a moment. "I hate the darkness inside me, so every day, I chose light. I chose laughter and love, but from the moment I met you, I chose you. You are what keeps me alive. You are what keeps me fighting. Maybe it's too soon, but I can't help it. I met your eyes and I knew I was lost. I don't believe in true love, Reign, but I believe in you."

"I thought I was supposed to be the one who's good with words," I reply, smiling, "yet you all leave me breathless and speechless for the first time ever. I don't even know how to put what I feel when I'm around you into lyrics." Grabbing his hand, I place it over my heart. "Know I'm right here with you. The moment you walked into my house, you changed the trajectory of my life, and I can't be anything but thankful for that."

"No more words." He covers my lips. I place my hand over his racing heart, feeling it beat in time with mine. Our two melodies are in sync, creating something magnificent.

Our lips meet in a flurry for what we feel when we are together. We've searched our whole lives for this, and I find it in his kiss, in his touch, in his presence. I'm not ever going to give this up. It makes a mockery of everyone who came before and they cease to exist. There is only Astro and his touch.

Groaning, he grabs me and turns us until my back hits the tree. His knee presses between my legs, and I grind down on it. "Baby," he murmurs, nipping my lip. "I need you."

"I need you too, so fucking badly," I admit.

He grabs my shirt and hikes it up, his tongue darting out to lick his lips while his bright eyes darken with lust. "Panties off, Reign, I want them in my pocket when we go back there."

Under his watchful gaze, I shimmy down my leggings and panties and hand them over. He meets my eyes and, with a wicked grin, licks the length of my panties with a moan. Shuddering, I lean back and part my legs, feeling my desire on my thighs.

One promising look from any of them and I'm wet.

It's annoying but great in this situation, since I need him too much to wait. He tries to drop to his knees, but I drag him back to my lips as he stuffs my panties into his pocket. "I need you fast and hard. Make me come, Astro. Show me how much you want me. Show me we are still alive despite everything this world has thrown at us."

"Reign—"

"Astro," I mutter, biting his lip. "Fuck me right here, right now. Don't make me wait."

"Never." He grips my hips and lifts, and I wrap my legs around his waist as he fumbles with his zipper. My head drops back as he drags kisses and teeth across my neck, making me shiver in want. I need him so badly.

Swearing, he tears at his jeans, and then his thick cock presses to my entrance. We meet each other's eyes as he drives into me. I cry out as he thrusts through my tightness, forcing himself all the way in, and then he starts to move.

He fucks me hard and fast like I wanted, forcing me to accept it. Our heavy breathing mingles as birds squawk above us. "Reign. Fuck, baby, I love this. I love being inside you. I love your taste. I love the way you look at me," he growls, and we both know what he wanted to say.

He loves me.

He doesn't, though, and instead, he shows me.

He drives into me hard and faster until my head falls back as I cry out.

Snarling, he pulls from my pussy, making me whine as he turns me. My face hits the tree, and I grip the bark as he yanks my ass back and slams into me. He covers my mouth and muffles my screams as I claw at the bark.

"Shh," he hisses into my ear before he groans as I tighten around him. "Be a good girl and stay quiet so my father doesn't hear my baby screaming her release. He might try to come and stop me, but baby, I wouldn't, not even knowing he was there. I wouldn't be able to. I'd be pumping into you even as you screamed your release, filling you with my cum."

Shit, shit, shit.

My eyes close as I push back, the smack of our hips loud in the forest. I bite his hand and hear him hiss in my ear, and in retaliation, he bites my neck so hard, my back bows and pussy clamps on him as he roars.

He hammers into me harder and faster. "Come for me," he demands. "Come for me right now, Reign. Cover my cock in your release."

How could I do anything but?

The words send me over the edge, screaming into his hand as pleasure explodes through me like a bomb, leaving me unable to stand. He catches me, fucking me through my release and straight into another, and yet he still doesn't stop. I whimper, and when he reaches down and tilts my hips so my clit hits the tree with his thrusts, I'm lost once more.

His hips stutter. "Shit, Reign, I can't hold back. You feel too good, baby. I love the way you come for me. That's it, take me." He groans loudly, slamming into me as deeply as he can and bellowing his release as I slump into the tree. Panting, he shifts his hips, forcing his cum deeper before covering me with his body, holding me up against the tree as we both pant and shake.

"So much." He kisses my neck. "One day, you'll let me say the word. You'll be ready to hear it and I'll be waiting. I'll wait forever if I have to because I plan on keeping you until we are old and gray."

"You better," I whisper, showing my weakness for once.

We get knowing looks over breakfast, and when Cillian picks bark out of my hair with a smirk, I want the floor to swallow me up, but I smile. Astro disappears into the garage with his dad, and Cillian and Raff are dragged off by a hyperactive Theo, leaving Dal and me alone.

"Why don't you take Reign to the falls, Dal?" Gloria suggests as we help her clean up. "It's going to be a nice day for a swim."

"Oh, that sounds fun." I peer at him, and he smiles at me, and Gloria gasps, covering her heart. When we both look at her, she turns away, but not before I see the sheen in her eyes.

"Go get ready. I'll make you a picnic," she mumbles.

I nod, and Dal takes my hand and leads me to the house. I look back to see his mom watching us with a wide, loving smile, and I swear I hear a whisper on the wind.

"Thank you, God."

I put on some tennis shoes and a hoodie, and by then, Dal is ready. He runs back to grab a basket, and then we are off. The silence between us is comfortable, allowing me to take in the views as we wander down a dirt trail.

It only takes us twenty minutes, and then we come upon a clearing with a waterfall. Rocks are built up on either side with clear marks from climbing, the water rushing down into a crystalline pool at the base. It's big enough to swim in, and there's grass surrounding it. Dal quickly spreads out a blanket from the picnic basket, but I kick off my shoes and shuck off my hoodie.

He turns to me then, his eyes darkening. "Do you want to explore?"

I grin. "No, I want to swim."

"Okay, sweetheart. Did you bring something to change into?" he asks.

"I don't have a swimsuit," I reply, tilting my head with a wicked grin, and as his eyes sweep down my body, I drop my dress and, with a wink at Dal, dive into the pool.

When I resurface, Dal is already naked and striding into the water, unwilling to leave me even for a second. I wait for him, and when he's close enough, I launch myself at him. He captures me midair and lets me climb his body until I'm wrapped around him. Grinning, he dunks us, and I sputter and giggle when we resurface. I brush my hand across his face to remove the water from his lashes, pushing his usually perfectly styled hair back with the water. He freezes under my touch, and I soon see why.

At the very edge of his hairline is an old white scar. "What happened?" I ask, peering into his beautiful eyes.

"One of my mother's friends tried to scalp me for my disrespect." He says it so casually, like one would discuss the weather, but my heart breaks for the little kid who suffered through that.

Taking his hand, I guide it to a tattoo on my side. "Feel that?"

I bite my lip as he carefully runs his calloused hand across the scar like I'm breakable. "What's it from?" he murmurs, anger in his eyes.

"My father stabbed me with a beer bottle. Took ten stitches to close it." He blinks, and I grip him tighter. "Your scars don't scare me, Dal. I have my own, and one day, I will know every one of yours and their story and I will kiss them all better. No matter how you feel now, you hurt back then and I'll make it better." I drag my lips along the scar, and I hear him inhale harshly.

Unlike the others, Dal feels differently. Emotions are deeper, more intense, and unsure for him. He hides it so well, but in moments like this, I know he feels. He calls himself a psychopath, but I think it's only because he had to become one to survive.

He was given no other choice.

We float in each other's arms, two broken, scarred beings with pasts so dark that shadows still haunt us today, but here is the thing about shadows—the sun always chases them away.

"I love you, Reign." My eyes widen and my heart stops. "I never knew what that word meant before. I should ask the others, but I can't explain these feelings any other way," he mumbles. "I think about you every waking moment, day or night. I can't sleep without knowing you are okay and happy. I wake up and my first thought is to check on you. I worry about you eating and drinking enough. I want to know every thought in your head and make every hope and dream come true. I see the sunrise and I think of you. I watch the moon and I hear your lyrics and laughter in my head. Everything I see reminds me of you, and when you're not at my side, I wonder what you are doing. When I see something beautiful, I want to take a picture and show it to you, so yes, Reign Harrow, I believe this is love. "

"Dal . . ." I don't even know what to say.

"You don't have to say it back. I just needed you to know. I refuse to wait another second without you knowing that you own me mind, body, and soul. You have my heart, something I didn't have until you. It's new and scarred, but it's there and it's yours. I'm a man who has done terrible things, Reign, and I will never be perfect, but one day, I hope you love me too because I would give everything to be loved by you. Until then, this is more than I thought I would ever have or wanted. I needed you to know that."

Before I have a chance to respond, not that I would know what to say, he kisses me softly, telling me with that kiss that it's okay and he understands. Tears slide from my eyes, mixing with the water of the pool, and when he pulls back, I bury my head into his shoulder and he holds me.

No expectations, no rushing me or getting angry.

He didn't tell me he loves me to hear it back. He told me he loves me because it's true, and that is what makes me start to fall more in love with him.

Yes, more. I can admit that they have my heart, but it terrifies me, so knowing they are willing to wait without rushing me makes me want to cry.

How could one person ever be this lucky?

FORTY-TWO

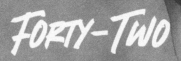

Reign fits effortlessly into our lives, especially here. Astro's family has always been like our own, welcoming us when ours abandoned us. They showed us love, comfort, family, and friends. They showed us what family should be, and now they are showing Reign. Gloria fusses over her, constantly handing her food and blankets and drinks. She asks her about her music, her friends, and everything in between. Astro's father, Glein, shows her around his land. He takes her shooting and even lets her sit in the car he's working on, something Astro is shocked about since none of us are even allowed to step one foot in the garage.

No, Reign fits, and it's clear they already love her. She belongs, and the radiant smile she gives me when she looks back from helping Gloria pound the cookies is all worth it.

This weekend away is good for her, for all of us. Here, we can be what we want. Here, we can be together, and by the way Gloria watches us, I know she knows. We should have known better than to think we could hide anything from that woman.

When Gloria goes outside to check on Raffiel and Astro, who are marinating the meat for tonight's BBQ, I wrap my arms around my girl, placing my chin on her shoulder. The sigh of contentment she lets out is pure bliss, and I can't help but turn my head and kiss her cheek.

"They look great, Reign," I murmur.

"I've never made cookies before," she admits.

"Well, you're doing amazing," I reply, "and Gloria loves you."

"You think?" She perks up. "I hope so. I want them to like me since they mean so much to all of you."

"I can assure you they do." I kiss her neck just as Gloria comes back. She gives me a knowing smirk, and I move away, leaving them to bake.

I'm just sitting down to go over the police reports when an exhausted, scrub-wearing Cherry stumbles in. Astro's sister blinks at Reign. "Who are you?" she asks.

I see Reign's eyes widen. Cherry has been known to scare off all of Astro's girlfriends, saying they aren't good enough, so I stiffen, shooting her a glare. I love her like a sister, but if she hurts Reign, I won't be happy.

"Hi, I'm Reign. You must be Cherry, right? Astro and Theo told me all about you." Reign wipes her hand and offers it to Cherry to shake, not backing down from the frosty glare. Just as I'm about to jump up and intervene, Cherry's whole expression changes.

"You're Reign? The Reign?" She smiles wide and yanks her into a hug. "Theo told me so much about you. Anyone who looked after my kid like that is good with me." She glances at Astro nervously as he steps inside, no doubt hearing her and worrying as well. "You did good, brother. Come on, Reign, sit with me and tell me everything, and let me spill all of Astro's dirty secrets."

Gaping in shock, we all watch as a giggling Reign and Cherry head outside to sit and talk. Even Gloria is covering her mouth. "That does it. She's a miracle, that one. It's definitely meant to be." She nods before rushing upstairs. I'm still staring when she comes back down, thrusting a box at Astro. "Here, take your grandmother's ring. If you don't marry that one, you are a fool."

"I plan to," Astro replies but then hesitates. "But what if she says no?"

"Boy, that woman is crazy about you. Don't let that darkness win, not this time." She cups his face. "You look it right in the face and

310

tell it to fuck off. It doesn't get to ruin your happiness or your future."

The smile he gives is wobbly. "I'll wait. She will run the other way if I ask now, but I promise I will, Ma. I know she's the one." His smile is blinding. "She hates mushrooms."

His mother whoops. "I knew it."

"Sorry, what?" I ask.

Chuckling, Gloria heads my way and kisses my head. "I've always told him about the mushroom law. I hate them, but your father loves them, and that's why we get on so well. Balance. Astro loves them."

"And she hates them." I grin. "I love them too."

"See?" She points at me. "Perfect."

It's only when she wanders away to finish the cookies that I realize what I said.

I admitted I'm in love with Reign in a roundabout way.

Fuck.

Gloria doesn't seem to care, though, and when Cherry and Reign come back in, she grins at us all. Cherry grabs her stuff and waves goodbye, while Reign gets back to making cookies.

"I hate mushrooms," Dal says. I jump in shock. I didn't even hear him come in. "Does that mean we aren't right for one another?"

I glance over at him and grin. "Nah, you've always been one to break rules and so has she. I don't think the rules apply to you two."

He nods, his gaze going back to her. "You're right, she revolts against any rules."

"That she does, our little anarchist."

---

raffiel

The cookies are terrible.

They are burnt around the edges and somehow underbaked in the middle. One bite and I want to throw up, but the pride and hope in my girl's eyes has me swallowing.

"Are they okay?" she asks nervously, twisting the tea towel she holds.

"They are amazing," I tell her, swallowing hard again. There is no fucking way I will let my girl be upset over some fucking cookies. The fact that she made them for us at all makes me want to roar from the rooftop.

I turn back to the guys sitting around the table.

I narrow my gaze on every single one of them, warning them not to say a word. "Eat every single one," I say when she looks away. When she comes back with more, I want to groan, but I shovel the cookies in with a big smile as Gloria and Reign watch, open-mouthed.

All four of us look like pigs, shoveling cookies in.

"Oh, can I try one before they are all gone?" Reign goes for one but I reach out, gripping it and shoving it in my mouth.

"Sorry," I mumble around the bite.

I can see Gloria giggling as Reign just stares at us. "Um, maybe I should make more?"

"No!" we all say at the same time before I chew and swallow, ignoring my gag reflex. "Or we'll eat them all," I add to smooth it over. "And we have to stay fit." I smack my abs, my stomach gurgling at the somehow overbaked and undercooked cookies.

"Oh, okay." She shrugs. "Let me get you some drinks." She watches us for another second before heading into the kitchen.

My girl is made to be a rock star, not a baker.

Chuckling, Gloria watches us. "Adorable," she whispers loudly so Reign doesn't hear. "Don't worry, I won't tell her." She winks as Astro shoves more in his mouth until nothing is left.

"I don't know what they are talking about. They are amazing," he says, and we all stare at him as he mops up all the crumbs. He genuinely meant it. That boy has a stomach made of iron.

"Your dad's grilling the meat for the BBQ," Gloria tells us. "Why don't you go help while Reign and I finish up some bits in here before we join you?"

Happy to escape, I down some water on the way outside, leaving Reign with Gloria.

The food is delicious, and I sit back and listen to Glein's stories with a grin, holding Reign's hand under the table the entire time. I need to touch her, surrounded by my family, and the knots in my shoulders unfurl. When I glance at her as she laughs, my heart skips a beat.

I promised myself that I would find a partner to traverse this world with one day, but only when I was ready. I wasn't ready, but she is right here, sitting at my side. Reign Harrow might be a rock star, but Rey is ours and so fucking beautiful, it hurts.

I love her more than anything in this world.

I wasn't looking for her, but I'm lost without her, and alongside that realization comes fear—of losing her, of hurting her. Reign is so strong yet weak at the same time. If we hurt her, that would be it. She would shut down for good and never forgive us.

I can't be the reason Reign Harrow gives up on love, so I keep those words to myself until I can prove to her that I'm not going anywhere.

"Right, kids, since we cooked, you clean. Glein and I are off for our date night drinks." Gloria stands and points at us. "Behave. Don't do anything we wouldn't do."

"So anything goes?" Astro grins, even as she hits the back of his head on her way by.

"Thanks for dinner, it was amazing," Reign says.

Gloria kisses Reign's head, and Glein winks at us as he follows his wife. We stay put for a bit longer. Reign nurses her wine while we watch nature and just find peace in each other's company.

"Right, washing up before we can relax." I sigh and stand. "Come on."

Reign slowly stands and stretches, and we all turn our eyes to her. She giggles when she catches us. "I'll fill my wine and get started inside." She hurries away from us like we might pounce on her, which isn't incorrect.

Grumbling, I start to stack the plates with the guys' help and carry them inside to find Reign wiping down the table and piling up more plates from earlier.

Reign bites into a leftover cookie we must have missed, even as we all dive at her. "Oh my god, these are disgusting." She spits it out and then turns to us. "You ate every single one."

When we just stare, she steps closer. "You ate every single terrible cookie. Why?"

"So you wouldn't know," I admit. "You tried so hard, baby."

"You're fucking nuts." She laughs, even as something blooms in her eyes. "Come on, Gloria said she and Glein are going out for the night and Cherry took Theo to a friend's. Let me show you all how cute you are."

With that and a wicked grin, she takes my and Astro's hands and leads us outside.

Fuck cleaning up.

My girl needs us.

FORTY-THREE

T hey ate them all to spare my feelings. Deep down, I know what that means.

Am I ready?

Can I admit it and embrace love once more? Am I ready to fall one more time? The truth is, I've already fallen. I'm lost in them. They've quickly become my everything, whether I want to admit it out loud or not.

I'm in love with them.

Unlike when I realized how I felt about Tucker, it doesn't terrify me. Instead, I'm elated because I feel safe and secure enough to know they will catch me.

I release their hands and turn, the stars shining down on me as we stand near the shelter of trees by the side of the guesthouse. All four of them watch and wait, always following my lead and letting me choose.

I drop the dress I'm wearing and step out of it.

"You keep saying I'm yours, so prove it." I tilt my chin up in defiance as I stare at the four men who stole my broken heart and put it back together. Their arms became my shelter, their souls my fire, and their touches my reason for living.

They move as one, and from one moment to the next, I am surrounded. My heart thrums as the stars shine down on us, and the sounds of nature echo through the trees.

I meet all four sets of eyes—green, blue, brown, and black.

They are mine, and I am theirs.

At least for tonight. I almost smirk at that thought, and a hand wraps around my throat from behind, making me gasp as I'm yanked against a hard body. I know it's Astro from his scent and the feel of his muscles. I would know him even in the dark. I would know each and every one of them from just the sounds of their hearts beating for me.

Raff steps before me, his dark hair shining under the moonlight, and as I watch, he rips his shirt open. My mouth waters as I drag my gaze over his chest. He sheds his jeans, and then he's as naked as I am. "You want us to prove it, my love?"

I nod, my eyes catching on his hard cock.

He smirks. "You heard her."

"Want us to fuck you in the dirt under the stars?" Astro croons in my ear as Cillian appears before me, naked. I feel dark eyes on me and know Dal is watching.

"Yes." I arch my chest in offering to Cillian, who moves closer, stroking down my body.

Cillian's hand trails back up, pressing to the top of my head and pushing. "Then get on your knees," he orders, and I fall under the weight of his hand, dropping to my knees. I feel Astro move with me, his lips dragging across my neck and then my back as he pushes me to all fours. His lips sweep all the way down to my ass and press there, and when his voice comes, it's hushed.

"Let's show her."

Cil drags my chin up, rubbing his cock on my lips as I gaze into his bright eyes. "Suck me, baby, make me nice and wet."

I part my lips eagerly, sucking the tip of his cock as he groans. With the moon shining down on him, he looks like a god—all hard muscles and glowing skin—so I worship him like one.

I show him how much I want him, sliding my mouth along his cock as hands slide along me.

A mouth seals on my pussy and laps at my cream. "Strawberries." Astro groans against my pussy before he kisses along my center, his fingers sliding into me to find me already wet.

I always am around them.

I look past Astro for a moment to see the shadow there. Dal's dark gaze runs across me as he lingers in the darkness, protecting me.

I suck Cillian harder as he groans, his hips snapping forward to fill my mouth with his huge length while Astro adds a third finger and sucks my clit before pulling away, making me whine.

Arms wrap around me, tugging me to my knees, as Cillian lowers to his knees and then his back. Without words, I go to him, crawling up his body as we come together, his hands guiding me onto his length as I widen my thighs and take him deeper.

Our lips meet in a slow, loving kiss as I sit on him fully, impaling my pussy. A moan reverberates between our lips, and then I start to move, making love to him, before more hands stroke my body.

I lean forward eagerly as I feel Astro's cock press to my ass, and he slowly works into me, inch by inch, as Cillian kisses me. They play with my breasts, making me relax, until they are both inside me.

Breaking the kiss, I turn my head and find Raffiel waiting. He feeds me his cock, sliding into my waiting mouth as his rough hand slides into my hair. "Look at you, our goddess," he croons, sliding deeper before pulling out. All three of them move in tandem, completely in sync as they make love to me.

I'm missing a piece of my heart, though, and I look around, trying to find him.

"Your girl wants you, Dal. Don't keep her waiting," Cil says.

"Never," Dal replies as he steps from the shadows.

Raff pulls from my mouth and Dal takes his place, surging inside as my eyes widen. He fucks my mouth before pulling out, and he and Raff set up a rhythm, one thrust each.

Their hands caress my body lovingly as they fuck me, claiming every inch of me in a way I didn't even know I needed until them.

Rain starts to spot across my body, the cool droplets making me gasp.

Every nerve is alive, and I fall into their waiting arms.

I cry out my release, my pussy and ass clamping around them. They fuck me through it, and as drool slides down my chin, Raff feeds me his cock once more.

"Good girl." Dal watches me with heavy-lidded eyes.

"Isn't she? Taking us all like this, our goddess. Now take us over the edge with you. The stars could fall right now and I wouldn't stop," Cil says.

"Me either," Astro adds.

"The world could end and I would die happy," Raffiel admits, his dark eyes blazing with love and want.

Fingers slide across my clit, making my gasp. It's all too much. "I can't . . ." Astro groans. "I can't last. She's just so perfect."

Pushing my ass back, I take him deeper, wanting to feel him come.

He buries himself deep, crying his release to the sky. Cil's eyes roll back in his head as I tighten around him, my own release building inside me once more until he bellows his pleasure, pumping me full of it.

Raff snarls, grips my chin, and hammers into my mouth until his head falls back and he gasps my name, his cum sliding down my throat. When he stumbles back, Dal slides in as I swallow.

Fingers attack my clit ruthlessly as I feel their cum seeping from me where their cocks are still buried.

As Dal snarls, shoving deep down my throat, I tumble over the edge once more, making him spill across my chest and body.

The heavens burst as I scream and rain lashes down on us, soaking us, but none of us care. I reach for them, dragging them down with me, needing their lips more than I need to breathe. Our bodies are slick with rainwater and sweat, and our promises are on our tongues as we come together under the stars.

We tumble to the wet grass, our bodies locked together like we will never part.

I'm not Reign Harrow tonight. I'm just theirs.

Forty-Four

Saying goodbye to Astro's parents is hard. I found safety and happiness here, something I haven't felt since I was younger. It was a paradise, an escape, but as we drive back into the city, the pressure, the cameras, and the break-in all come rushing back.

The peace of this weekend is forgotten, and when we pull up outside of my house, having to wade through reporters and cameras so thick that police have been called, I hesitate to get out.

I stare up at the big house I was so happy to buy. It was my first big purchase and it proved I was making it. It became my sanctuary on the hill, away from prying eyes. Inside these walls, I could be myself. I could be wild, sad, and happy. I could be in love. I could be greedy or lazy. Now, though, it feels wrong. It feels tainted.

"Are you okay?" Dal asks quietly.

Nodding, I get out before I can hide further, but at the door, Astro holds me back as Dal, Cil, and Raff surge inside. I wave at Havier at the gate, who nods and waves back. Standing in the sunlight, I hide behind Astro as I hear paparazzi trying to climb the wall to get a picture. I even hear a helicopter, so I almost breathe a sigh of relief when they come back to the door.

"Everything is clear and fine. Come in, Miss Harrow." Raffiel winks, and the familiar teasing makes me smile.

Before I know it, I'm inside, but I freeze in the entryway. The door shuts behind me with a resounding bang, making me jump.

It no longer feels like my home.

Someone entered my sanctuary and defiled it, and as I look around, I don't know if it will ever feel safe or like it's mine ever again. Maybe I should move.

Even that thought makes my mouth sour. That would mean the crazy person won and that I'm weak. I'm not weak. This is my house, my fucking house. Not theirs. I won't let them win.

Taking a deep breath, I step farther in. The guys' eyes shine with pride as the first thing I do is head upstairs. My bedroom is spotless, exactly as I left it before the break-in, except with new bedding, yet I feel wrong being in here. I head downstairs to my studio. Everything there is clean and safe and I begin to relax.

This is my home.

Mine.

I spend the rest of the day on the phone with Jack, going over plans and finalizing things for the album. The cover launches in a few days, and I can't wait for my fans' reactions. This is the first music I'm putting out since I came back, and although I'm nervous, I've never felt prouder of my work. It's me, it's raw, and as long as I'm happy with it, that's enough.

The guys are busy. They pick up Raff Jr. and I know he's happy to be home, and despite their protests, they missed him too. They speak to the police and my managers, and they report in and check on me all the time. I tell them I don't want to know anything. I trust them to look after me and do their job, so I let them do it. Instead, I focus on the million and one things I need to do, and before I know it, it's one in the morning.

Sighing, I drag myself upstairs, and after showering, I stare at my bed. I climb inside, wincing, but as I lie here, staring at the ceiling, it feels wrong and cold.

It's too empty.

Needing the safety I found in their arms, I climb from my bed and head downstairs to find them. I step into the first room I find, which just so happens to be Cillian's. He's sitting up in bed with Raff Jr. curled at his feet, the quilt pooled around his bare waist as he watches TV, but when he sees me, he smiles brightly, lifting the covers and welcoming me. I rush in, diving inside, and he wraps me in his arms. He kisses my head as I snuggle into his side, finally able to breathe . . . finally feeling safe.

"I've got you. You can sleep, babe," he tells me, always knowing exactly what's wrong without me having to voice it.

Looking up, I meet his bright eyes, his hair flashing with brilliant colors from the TV. "I don't know what I would do without you."

"You'd be fine. You're so goddamn strong, but luckily, you will never have to know. I don't plan on going anywhere, ever," he whispers.

"Promise?" I search his gaze, knowing my tone is soft and vulnerable.

"I promise," he murmurs, leaning down to kiss me. "Now sleep. It's been a long day, and you need your rest."

Nodding, I curl into his side with a smile, looking at the TV to see the news there. Just as I'm drifting off to the sound and the hum of his heart, my name catches my attention. Cil isn't fast enough to turn the channel, so I hear what they have to say about me.

One sentence rings in my ears.

Attention seeking bitch.

They think I'm a bitch?

Fine, I'll be a bitch.

FORTY-FIVE

I dressed with one purpose in mind today—a giant fuck you to the people on the interview last night and the person who thought they could take this away from me. When I head outside, I make sure to leave the car parked on the street as I wave. Taking center stage is a giant, sparkling, bedazzled diamond hair clip saying, "Bitch."

It's petty, but I don't give a fuck.

"Where to, Miss Harrow?" Raff smirks as we pull away, his hand snaking under my dress and stroking my bare thigh.

"The office," I murmur, opening my legs to give him better access.

He leans closer, his breath hot and heavy on my ear. "And after, do we get you all to ourselves tonight? No interviews or parties?"

"Oh, I see how it is. You are using orgasms and sex to get me to divulge my secrets and schedule." I laugh. "Tricky man, but very clever."

"Well?" he responds huskily, sliding his hand higher to cup my pussy.

"Cruel, Raff, real cruel." I groan, grinding into his hand. Cameras flash outside, but I know they can't see anything, and even if they could, fuck them. I don't care. "We have a party tonight, someone's album release after-party, but other than that, I'm yours."

"Good girl," he praises. "Just for that, you get to come."

"I fucking better."

He lowers to the floor of the car, kneeling in his perfectly pressed black suit and tie. He wears a wicked smirk as he rolls his sleeves back, pushes my dress higher, and licks his lips when he finds me naked underneath.

"Reign," he chastises.

Smirking, I spread my legs even wider for him, flashing my pussy. "Better get to work, baby."

"You are such a brat," he remarks, but it's soft as he yanks me down the seat. My head hits the leather as his talented mouth covers my pussy. His perfect tongue traces along my folds before flicking my clit, leaving me moaning as more cameras flash outside.

Dal struggles to get the car out of the crowd of paparazzi. Astro sits up front with him, and Cillian sits in the back with us, watching with a hungry expression. I meet his eyes as Raffiel dips his tongue inside me.

"Are you hungry, Cil?" I tease.

His hands fist on his thighs, and his eyes drop to Raffiel's head between my thighs as the sloppy sounds of him eating my wet pussy fill the car. My heart races as I groan, riding his face shamelessly.

"For you, always," he growls. "Tonight, I'll get you first."

"If I say so." I smirk, but it turns into a cry of pleasure as Raffiel bites my clit, punishing me.

"Bastard," I hiss, even as I tilt my hips, begging for more.

Chuckling against my flesh, he thrusts his tongue inside me once more, driving me toward the release I so desperately want and he promised.

"More," I demand huskily.

Cameras flash, but I know the tinted windows stop them from seeing inside of the car, not that I would care. I wouldn't stop him even if they could.

His head lifts from between my splayed thighs, his dark, dangerous eyes freezing me in the plush leather seat. "I live to serve you, Miss Harrow," he mocks.

"Then serve me, bodyguard," I mock right back. "Make me come before we get to the office or tonight, I'll ride every single one of them and not you. You can escort me and protect me at the party while your hard dick throbs, wishing you had served me better." Licking my bottom lip, I meet his eyes, my own filled with a dare.

"Don't they teach you never to taunt animals, rock star?" he purrs. "They might just bite you."

His head turns, and he sinks his teeth into my thigh. The sharp pain makes me yelp before his tongue rubs the sting away, and then he kisses up my thigh to lap at my pussy again.

My moans echo around the car, and Cil finally snaps, climbing over and turning my head. His lips crash onto mine in a searing kiss, his tongue mimicking the way Raffiel is tonguing my cunt. His hand slides inside the dress I'm wearing and he cups my bare breast. His expert fingers roll and tease my nipple into a stiff point as Raff nips my clit.

"So goddamn tasty, Reign," Cil whispers against my lips. "Now come for us. Walk into that boardroom with us knowing your cream covers your thighs. Your dirty little secret."

How could I do anything but?

Raff's mouth seals around my clit, sucking hard, while Cillian kisses me. He swallows my cry of pleasure as I tumble over the edge and into their awaiting arms. Ecstasy roars through my blood, one I only seem to find with them.

I sit at the head of the table in the boardroom once more. All the managers and shareholders—anyone with a bit of sway or importance in my career—sit around, listening for once. They seem to have learned, even my manager, William.

"So, how's the planning going for the album release and tour?" I ask after making them wait. A half empty coffee sits before me, thanks to Astro who made me one while I stared them down.

Pigs.

My guards sit behind me, trying to blend in. Part of me wants them to sit next to me and get their opinion on everything, but I know how that would look, and I've worked too hard to have these bastards think I depend on the will of a man.

Even ones I love.

So they sit behind me, protecting and encouraging me. Dal even promised to kill anyone who got out of line. They are so sweet.

"Good," William says, and one of the women clears her throat.

"Winchester." She nods. "Nice to meet you, Reign. I like the ideas you sent through for the album artwork and have booked Eamm Worcester, the photographer you like, to capture the images. I have also looked into scheduling each section of the album countdown like you wanted, and I agree, I think they would only help build anticipation. After this meeting, I will send you a detailed file for you to check out and ensure you're happy. As for the tour, we have elected cities and dates, as explained in the email you sent." More like a snippy voice message, but she's good, I'll give her that. She slides a sheet over to me. "This is for you to check over. We've given you the days you wanted off and leeway between shows so you don't burn out."

I was very specific about downtime. Tours are incredible but exhausting, and so far with my career, I have done back-to-back shows with travel between. Last time, it made me so tired, I was sick, which meant I couldn't properly perform for my fans. That's not something I want. I will still be doing one hundred and eight USA tour dates and a minimum of forty international, but I have time between to enjoy my life and ensure my health is top notch.

Scanning the sheet, I smile and glance up at her. "What's your position, Ms. Winchester?"

"I'm William's assistant."

Interesting. I look at my manager. "You're fired. I want her."

Her eyes widen, as does his as he sputters. He might have guided me since the moment I stepped foot in here, but he's stuck in his ways and he undermines me at every opportunity. I like her. She shows initiative, and she also took my wants and made them real without altering them for their own gain. She's fresh and new and clearly hungry.

She reminds me of . . . well, me.

"Miss Harrow," William begins.

"No, I don't want to hear it." I look at him. "You may help train her, but we all know you wanted to take more of a step back." I soften my voice. "I appreciate everything you have done for me, I do, and I appreciate your thoughts and help. I would still like you on my team but overseeing from a distance. If you still want to be in this world, then this is how you do it. Pass it on to the next generation. She is the future, William, and if you can't see that, then there is something wrong here."

I see the pain in his eyes. He knows I'm right.

"How about this?" I suggest. "You two both work on the tour and album and you can train her, and if you think she isn't the right fit after, we'll relook at it then."

He nods and glances at her. "I see her talent. You're correct about that." He grins. "When I met her, I knew you would get along and I still hired her."

Winchester smiles and turns to me, mouthing, "Thank you."

I shake my head. She did this for herself with her hard work. She doesn't need to thank me.

"I like this layout," I tell her. "Can I keep this copy?"

"Of course. I will also send a package of everything to your house to check over. I'll include my contact information with it in case you need any changes. I'm reachable day or night," she says.

"Good, then let's go ahead. I'm assuming we have contacted my dancers."

She nods once more. "We have confirmation from all but two, whom I will chase down this morning. They were all very grateful and thankful that you are trusting them again with your tour."

"Good, seems we're all set." I stand, and as I pass her, I lean in. "Word of advice? Don't kill yourself for the job, no matter how much you love it. Go outside every now and again and enjoy the world or it will pass you by. Trust me, you'll regret it if you don't." I glance up at my men. "You'll miss all the good."

She peers up at me.

"You'll figure it out. Thanks for all the hard work. You're going to go far." I sweep from the room, more excited than ever for what's to come. This is my year, and I plan to make the most of it. I want to give back to the fans who stuck with me through everything . . . and maybe make rock history.

FORTY-SIX

"**H**ow much time do you have before the party?" Astro asks, leaning into the doorframe of my bathroom where I'm floating in the huge spa tub. My toes and nails are freshly done and dry, my body is waxed all over, and I have a mask in my hair and another on my face. Still, he looks at me like I'm the sexiest thing he's ever seen.

Raff Jr. hurries over to him and smashes his nose into Astro's junk before hurrying to play with the others.

Grinning, I poke in the bubbles, stretching my legs out as I turn my head and rest it on the side to peer at him. "Depends on what you have in mind."

"You, always you, baby," he teases, stripping off his shirt and dropping it to the floor. My mouth goes dry as my eyes drop to his impressive chest. Smirking, he waits for me to check him out, and then he pushes his pants down and steps out of them, stripping for me. He lets me check out every hard inch of his body before he struts over and slips into the bath with me.

My legs float on either side of his waist as his hand lingers above my chest in the water. He's waiting for permission.

I smirk. "It's a good thing our fur baby left. We wouldn't want to scar him."

"Now that he's gone, I can do bad things to you," he teases, his lips hovering above mine. "Say yes, Reign. Tell me to fuck me."

I make him wait, torturing both of us as his eyes narrow. "I don't know . . ." I hesitate before laughing when he kisses me.

He huffs. "Don't be mean."

"Why? You like me mean," I whisper, sliding my lips across his chin and my hands down his abs, feeling him tremble against me.

"I like you any way I can get you, baby. Mean, nice, bratty, tired, I like it all," he admits, closing his eyes as he tips his head down to give me better access. Needing to see how far he will let me push him, I kiss along his neck and face, sliding my hand up his chest.

Unlike Raff, who has to be in control, Astro loves it when I play with him. He likes waiting for it, eager to serve, and that type of control over a man like this is addicting.

His golden skin shines brightly in the bathroom as water slides down it like a lover's caress. I know what Astro is capable of, yet despite all the power in his body, he relents to me, so I kiss him softly. "Astro, sit down," I tell him.

"Reign," he growls, opening his eyes, those bright orbs watching me carefully.

"Sit," I order as I slide out from under him, getting to my knees in the tub. He watches me for a moment before cutting back through the water and sitting at the opposite side on the ledge there. His thick arms spread out on either side of the tub, and he leans his head back as he watches me.

My eyes travel over him, drinking in every hard edge of muscle that Astro has. He was built for war and my pleasure, and I fucking love watching the play of his muscles, that slight smirk that always lingers around his lips, and the glow in his eyes. He's so fucking beautiful that sometimes, it hurts.

Moving closer, I run my hands up his hairy thighs, watching his eyes flare. "Reign." The way he says my name is like a prayer and a plea all at once, begging for me with one word.

Throwing my leg over his, I straddle his lap as I drag my nails down his chest lightly, watching as they slide under the water. He gasps and his eyes heat even more. Gripping his hard cock, I stroke his length as I refuse to look away from his dark gaze.

His lips part on a pant, and his hips lift slightly even as he tries to be good. "I never knew I could need someone so much," I admit truthfully as I slowly slide my hand up and down his cock. "Then I met you. Your fucking smile drives me wild, and I want to mess up your curly hair all the time. This body . . ." I lick a trail of water from his chest, up his chin, and to his lips. "It drives me mad. You were made for me, Astro. Weren't you?"

"Fuck yes." He groans as I release his cock and grip his neck, tilting his head back. "I've been waiting for you my whole life, Reign. Please don't make me wait anymore."

"Be a good boy and I won't," I tease, perching on his hard cock. He shivers against me, his eyes shutting in ecstasy just from that simple touch. Sliding a hand between us, I poise him at my entrance and wait. "Astro, look at me."

I wait for his eyes to open, and when they do, I slam down on his length, working every hard inch into me. Pleasure blooms in his eyes as he reaches out and grabs my hips. Water splashes around us at his clumsy moves as he helps me, his own hips lifting to bury himself deeper. When he's all the way inside, I stop moving, ignoring his urgings.

"Do you want me to ride you, Astro?"

"More than I've ever wanted anything." His eyes are half-mast as he stares at my chest. For a moment, I think he'll resist, but he jerks me forward, wrapping his lips around my nipple. My head falls back as he sucks and bites before turning his head and punishing my other breast. I can't think to torture him, my own pleasure demanding attention as my clit throbs.

He worships my breasts, sending an arc of pleasure to my cunt as I ride him slow and hard until we both moan. Our lips come together, my hands gripping his curly locks as his slide down my back to grip my ass.

As we fuck, the water sloshes around us, creating a whirlpool as we bite each other's lips. Pleasure and something much deeper pours from our kiss, our bodies working in tandem. My pleasure is his, and I swallow his moans as he kisses away my cries.

Breaking apart, we press our foreheads together, our eyes locked. "You're mine, Reign Harrow, from now until forever," he vows, his words hushed as he tilts me back, dragging his cock along the nerves inside me that send sparks shooting through me.

"Then you're mine." I grind down onto his length, reaching for the pleasure that's building.

"I always have been." He grins, thrusting up harder and making me cry out. "I was created to be yours, and I was lost, waiting until the moment I met you. My purpose. My destiny," he says, his words making my heart skip a beat. They are raw and beautiful and better than any lyrics I could write. "Now let's fall together, my love." His arms wrap around me, and his lips meet mine once more.

I fall.

How could I do anything but?

I cry my pleasure as he groans, shifting deeper as he explodes. He fills me with his love and release until we are locked together in the tub, unwilling to break apart as we kiss through it.

Here, in my house, I give myself permission to feel, to live, and find my happiness.

FORTY-SEVEN

She looks incredible, she always does, but this evening, I want to lock the doors and not let her out. She is a fucking goddess, and no one would be able to resist checking her out, never mind flirting with her.

What if she flirts back?

Am I allowed to kill them?

She's supposed to be single, and I'm not a fool. I checked out her past, so I know she would usually hook up at these types of parties. What if she does again? Am I expected to stand by and watch? I wouldn't, but when I meet her eyes as she walks toward me where I lean against the door, I lose my train of thought. Her hair is perfectly pin straight and curled in at the bottom, with one side braided back behind her ear to display her new ear tattoo and piercings up the shell, including a dangling anarchy symbol earring. Her lips are a deep red, which makes my cock hard, but it's the dress that renders me speechless. It's translucent and floor length, with crisscrossed mesh and sparkling diamonds. Her breasts are bare under the fabric, some diamonds covering her nipples, and her pussy is covered by a tiny scrap of black. She looks good enough to fucking eat.

I just stare, unable to help it as she comes toward me.

I know what the term shell-shocked means now.

She grins and kisses my cheek as she slides into the car, releasing me from her spell, and I suck in a deep breath, my lungs aching from the lack of oxygen.

Shaking off my desire, I hurry inside after her. Cillian sits at her side as Raff drives, and Astro sits with him. We always take turns, and I'm so lucky I get to sit in the back with her tonight.

My thoughts once more turn to what we're walking into. "What can we expect this evening?"

"Drinking, dancing, rowdy celebrities, probably drugs, and people fucking in the pool." She laughs. "Oh, and a whole lot of music."

"And you?" I find myself inquiring. "Will you be hooking up in the pool?"

Her eyes widen, her eyebrow arching. "Why, are you offering?"

"No, I just mean, I understand we can't go public, so if you're wishing to . . . to fuck someone else this evening, I would like a heads-up so I can let these idiots lead me away before I kill the person you touch."

She watches me carefully for a moment. "Dal, I don't plan to hook up with anyone," she tells me. "Why would I? I'm happy with what we have. Aren't you?" She appears shy, blushing slightly. "I know we haven't discussed what we are—"

"Baby," Raffiel interrupts, "if you think we are anything other than in a relationship, you're delirious. We share a bed, we go on dates, we fuck, and most importantly, we don't share, not outside of this car. You are ours, just as we are yours. Is that clear enough? If you wouldn't kill us, I would shout it for every single partygoer. I'd let them know you are our girl and not to bother looking. We don't play games, Reign, not like those before us, and we know what we want—you."

"Good." She grins. "I hate games. I never understood them. I'm yours, and you are mine. That's the deal."

"I have something," I grumble. "I thought maybe you could wear it. You don't have to if it doesn't match your outfit. I'm not good with female fashion but . . ." I pull the box out. "I just thought with this, you are wearing us on your body, so it's like a secret between us, and no one else knows what it means but us." It seems silly now, but her eyes widen, and she grabs the box from me before I can retract my words, opening the black case.

She stares, and I shift uncomfortably. "I'm sorry if you don't like it. I can exchange it—"

"Like fuck you will," she snaps, her eyes brimming with tears as they meet mine. "It's perfect. The most amazing gift I have ever received."

Tugging the slim silver chain from the box, she holds it up. Each point of the star has a jewel that represents our birth months, and in the middle is hers. She lifts her hair and turns. "Put it on me?"

"You don't have to, your dress—" I start.

"Dal, put the necklace on me," she demands, glaring at me over her shoulder.

Unable to deny her, I shift over and fasten it. She drops her hair and turns to me, holding the pendant. "It's perfect," she whispers. "I love it. I'll never take it off."

"Really?" I ask, unsure.

"Dal, it means the world to me. Not only did you get what type of jewelry I wear correctly, but you also went out and picked this without my help or me having to tell you. I love the idea of wearing a piece of you—all of you."

"Good." I nod, and she leans over and kisses my lips.

"Now you wear a part of me," she whispers as she sits back. "Let's go get drunk and dance way too much!"

The Dead Ringers' tour launch party is unlike anything I have ever been to before. Reign explained that they have an official one, but this is the unofficial one for friends and other artists, so basically a giant celebration. I'm a little pissed the man Reign hooked up with is here, but when we head inside, I see him staring longingly at another woman and let it go.

After all, I can't kill all of her exes, can I?

The huge house overflows with people, and I notice a lot of celebrities here, from rappers to actors. Hard liquor flows freely, and there are definitely some drugs. Every eye turns to Reign as she enters, filled with lust, hatred, or happiness.

They either want her or want to be her.

I don't blame them.

This is definitely a different world than ours. We are used to hunting through forests and slogging through mud, not overflowing diamonds and blaring rock music as people laugh and drink. It poses its own challenges, and I refuse to let my guard down with my girl here. She will have a good night, and I refuse to let anything else happen.

"Reign!" a drunk rapper calls, hugging her. "Damn, girl, looking fine."

"Thanks, Eight-two, great party."

"Isn't it? Tucker isn't here, though, so have a good night. Fool is in rehab. Shit, I might need a room next to him!" He laughs as he stumbles away, three women following him. She shakes her head, watching him go, but she does seem surprised about the news regarding Tucker.

Before I can ask her if she's okay, Trav spots her and heads over. "Reign!" He goes to hug her, but he meets our eyes and swallows, turning pale as he pulls back. "I'm so glad you came."

"Of course. I wouldn't miss this for anything. You know I'm your guys' biggest fan. Now introduce me to the famous Beck." She winks, and he offers her his arm. She accepts it, and he leads her through the crowd. Reign greets people as they go, accepting drinks that I take and pour out—the only way she's drinking is if we pour it.

You can never be too careful.

Trav approaches a sofa where three other men sit. I run my eyes over them and dismiss them as threats. They are the Dead Ringers, nothing more, but perched in the middle is a female. Beck, I am guessing. She's laughing at something one of them says, her eyes lustful as she watches them, and that does grab my attention.

"Travy." She grins when he joins them, and then she swallows when she sees Reign. "And Reign Harrow, Trav's booty call, I mean friend." Her eyes widen, and I see jealousy there as well as horror at her slip. She is too drunk to realize she said that out loud.

Reign just laughs. "Not a booty call anymore," she replies. "Just friends. You are the infamous Beck. It's nice to finally meet you, and I'm glad you fuckers got rid of that snooty bitch Kerry. She was a good singer but a horrible person," she remarks.

"So I've heard." Beck winces and stands. "I'm sorry. I didn't—"

"It's fine," Reign promises. "How about we get a drink?"

Becks nods, nervously glancing back, but Trav and the others just urge her on. It's obvious Reign means a lot to them, but so does Beck, and as Reign and Beck walk away, I watch all three of them stare at Beck's ass.

They all want her.

It seems we have more in common than we thought.

FORTY-EIGHT

She nods nervously and follows me. Beck is beautiful, but I knew she would be. It takes more than looks, though, for Trav to be obsessed, so she's clearly smart and talented, but I wonder what else. When we reach the bar, she steps up next to me, towering over me.

"Look, let me be blunt." Beck sighs. "I hate cat fights and jealousy. I'm not the type. It wasn't cool for me to call you a booty call. The guys love you. They say you're the coolest and that you're friends. I care about them and the band, so I think we should get along."

"I like that. I appreciate getting straight to the point. I hate word games and backstabbing. I've had enough to last a lifetime," I reply.

"I saw. Want me to cut a bitch?" Beck asks, making me laugh.

"No wonder they like you." She's perfect for them—brash, outspoken, slightly crazy, and obviously fucking talented. "Look, yes, I've slept with Trav—"

"That's none of my business," Beck interjects, swallowing. "We are just friends, bandmates."

"Sure." I nod. "But we haven't hooked up in a long time. I called him when I was lonely and hurt, but we didn't do anything, I promise.

I'm in a happy relationship with someone else, just don't spill that. I like my privacy now. So how about we start again? Hi, I'm Reign."

I hold my hand out, and she eyes it before smiling brightly.

"Hi, I'm Beck." She grins. "Nice to meet you. In fact, I even had your poster on my wall, so I'm kind of starstruck. I was worried about comparing—"

"No comparison here," I interrupt. "Talent is talent. The guys brought you on and they are the best. They obviously see that in you, so I have no doubt you're amazing." I glance around. "And this? This world takes some getting used to."

"Tell me about it," she grumbles, taking the shot and then staring at her beer. "Want to know a secret?" She leans in. "When I auditioned, I was working at a restaurant. I was nobody. This is . . . a lot to get used to. Does it ever get easier?"

"No." I grin. "But you find people who make it worthwhile and learn how to use it for your best interests."

"I know you always do. You make it look effortless," she admits, grinning at me. "Even that Tucker fucker, want me to kill him?"

I see Dal nod approvingly. "Not today. Now, how about we go back over there, get really fucking drunk, and I tell you all the guys' dirty secrets and embarrassing stories?"

"Sounds like a plan." Beck grins. "Hey, Reign, thank you." Her brows furrow. "This world is kind of lonely. I never know whom to trust."

"Trust me." I shrug. "I could use that kind of friend too, in all honesty."

"Then friends." She nods. "Now who else should I be worried about?" Hand in hand, we stroll through the party, and I can't help but grin at her. She's exactly what they need, and I'll admit she has this magnetism about her. She's just real, raw, and it's addictive. She has me spilling secrets without even meaning to.

She's going to be a fucking powerhouse, that's for sure.

I just hope the guys can handle that, but when I see them perk up when she returns, completely ignoring the groupies vying for their attention, I know they can.

I'm drunk as hell. I blame the guys and Beck for that. The girl can fucking drink. She even out drank me, which is a feat in itself. I lean against Astro while I wait for the bathroom, and he chuckles down at me.

"I need to pee so badly," I whine.

"I know, baby, one second." He holds me up.

When the door opens, he steps in, pulling me in next and sighing. I tug my dress up and hover over the toilet, groaning as I relieve myself. When I open my eyes, I see him watching me with a laugh.

"How sexy, right?" I wink.

"Very." He grins. When I'm done, I wash my hands, and he wraps his arms around me, looking at me in the mirror. "Having a good time?"

"The best," I admit. "I'm sorry. I'll slow down on the booze."

"Baby, drink all you want. We've got you. Just have fun and enjoy yourself." He frowns. "Why would we stop you from drinking?"

I startle at that. "Oh, um, Tucker said if I drank too much, I became embarrassing," I mumble.

"Fuck him. We aren't Tucker. Drink all you goddamn want. I'll hold your hair later." He helps me out of the bathroom and back into the party.

"There she is!" Beck calls. "How about a duet? They want to hear one of our new songs."

"Oh no, you guys sing it. It's your party—"

"Not a chance." She grabs my hand. "You sang with them for 'Dead to Me,' right? Well, do that one! Please, Reign, it would be the best moment of my life."

"You heard her." Raffiel grins. "Go on."

"Yes, I like him. Let's go!" Beck drags me to the outside area where there's an impromptu stage. Brilliant. I'm way too drunk for this shit.

She drags me all the way up the stage before letting go and sliding on a wicked black guitar. I borrow a spare green one that's similar to mine and step up to a mic as the guys prepare. "Alright, fuckers." Beck grins, speaking into the mic. "Tonight is a real treat. Rather than us boring you with all our music, Reign Harrow is going to sing with us. So for one night only, you're dead to us!" she screams.

The crowd gathers, screaming and chanting as I wink at Trav. Here goes nothing. I nod at Beck as the music starts up, and I try to remember my chords. It's been over a year, but it comes back like riding a bike as we play. When she starts to sing, I add in backup vocals until the chorus, and then I join in with her.

Swaying to the music, I let my voice ring out. I forget everything else as the booze moves through my veins, and when Beck heads over, shredding the guitar and singing, we share a mic. Grinning at each other, we work it, dancing and singing together.

When the song finishes, I glance over the crowd to see my men watching me. Blowing them a kiss, I tap my necklace, knowing they'll get the message.

I'm theirs, no matter what stage I'm on.

"How about another one?" Chase, the other lead singer, calls into the mic.

"Not for me, boys, this one is all you," I murmur as Kolton, the bassist, coos into the mic. "Dead Ringers, everyone, put your fucking hands up for the rock band of the fucking century!"

I clap as the crowd screams, and I bow to them as I head off stage. My guys meet me, and I lean back into Cillian's chest, uncaring who is watching, and when they start to play again, I grin up at him.

"Want to dance?"

"With you? Always?" Taking my hands, he twirls me around.

I let my heart beat to the music, swaying my hips as Cillian dances with me. The crowd surges around us until we blend in, just one of many. We become anonymous, and their hands slide across me possessively, tugging me into their bodies as they dance with me, using the cover to get what we all want.

FORTY-NINE

"**B**ut I want nuggets," I whine, pouting.

"No." Raff sighs, his arms crossed as he stands before the car door.

I lean into a smirking Dal, his hand gripping my ass. He said it's to catch me if I fall. He's such a sweetie. Astro is in the passenger seat, smirking, and Cillian is waiting to see who wins.

"Raffy," I whine.

I see him relax a little. "You don't need nuggets. You need water and sleep."

"You are so boring, isn't he, Dal?" I blink up at him. "You'd let me have nuggets, right?"

"Absolutely." He nods, making me point at Raff.

"See? It's just you!" I shout, stumbling with a laugh.

The sun is coming up, and the party is still in full swing, but Raff declared that I had enough when I tried to ride an inflatable unicorn down the stairs. How boring. He flung me over his shoulder and set me down in front of the car. My head spun like a son of a bitch, and it's his own fault that I threw up on his fancy, clean shoes—not that he seemed to care. He held my hair and rubbed my back, being all sweet, but now he's denying me the golden goodness of chicken nuggets.

How dare he!

He smirks. "In the car, Miss Harrow."

Groaning, I stumble past with Dal's help.

"And to think I thought I was falling in love with you," I slur as I smack his side. "I can't love a nugget denier."

"What?" he whispers, his eyes widening and his arms falling.

"You heard me." I nod. "Nugget denier." I hiccup and laugh. I'll probably regret this tomorrow.

"You're falling in love with me?" His whisper is quiet, and he stares at me for a moment before clearing his throat. "Astro, you drive. Take us to the nugget place."

I'm barely in the back when Raff reaches over and buckles me in, his hand dragging along my chest. I gasp as desire hammers through me, but he seems oblivious as he commands Astro to drive. I almost fall into Cil's lap with how fast he speeds away, and when I close my eyes, I must fall asleep because I wake up to a rough shake.

"Reign, you want nuggets, right? How many?" Grumbling, I open my eyes to see Raff staring at me. The bright lights of a drive-through shine into the back as he lowers his window. "Never mind." He grins as he turns to face the menu.

"What can I get for you?" the tired voice asks through the speaker.

"Nuggets," Raff replies.

"How many, sir?" the man asks in a monotone.

"We'll have them all."

"Uh, what?"

"All the nuggets you have. Baby, do you want anything else? A drink? A toy?" Raff questions, watching me hopefully.

"Ask for ice cream," Cil whispers.

I grin. "Ice cream."

"You got it, baby," Raff says seriously. "And all your ice cream too."

"Sir, it's a machine, and the machine is broken," the man comments.

"No, it's not. Do not lie to me. My woman wants ice cream."

"We don't have any. Please come around to the window to pay."

Grumbling, Astro pulls up to the window, and I watch as Raff leans out to the man.

"How much is it going to take to get an ice cream?" Raff growls.

The man's eyes widen as Raff pulls out a stack of bills and starts handing them over. "Uh, that should do it. Do you want any sauce? You can have whatever you want," the man squeaks, his eyes still on the bills.

"Baby?" Raff asks softly.

"Chocolate." Cil coughs in my ear.

"Chocolate please." I grin happily as Raff points at the man.

"You heard the woman, chocolate, and as many nuggets as you have. Here." He hands over more bills. "If you have it done in under two minutes, you can have the rest." Raff grins at me. "There we go."

"You're the best," I say dreamily, snuggling into his side.

"So pussy whipped." Astro grins, and I poke my tongue out at him. He returns the favor as we wait.

Not two minutes later, boxes and boxes of nuggets are handed over until they fill the back seat, and then an ice cream, dripping with chocolate sauce. Raff nods in approval and hands over the cash.

"I want one of those too." Raff points at an advertisement for their kid's meal that has a pink bracelet in it.

"You got it." A moment later, the worker hands that over, and Raff grins, turning to me.

"Here you go, baby."

Giggling, I rip open the packet and slide the cheap bracelet on.

"I love it. I'll never take it off." I hand the ice cream to Cil, and Astro pulls out of the drive-through.

"You little bastard," Raff grumbles but watches me worriedly as I kick my feet happily, doing a little dance as I stuff nuggets into my mouth.

"Now you can fall in love with me," Raff states as he hands me another sauce.

"Too late," I mumble around a nugget, but I get distracted as Cil grabs one. "Hey, mine."

"Babe, there are over thirty boxes here."

Growling, I grab it from his hand and shove it into my mouth.

"Get your own, I don't share food." I huff, ignoring his laugh.

Once I've eaten all I can, I cuddle into Raff's side, resting my head on his shoulder. His lips come down on my hair, and I hum happily in pure bliss—not too drunk and not too sober.

"Do you really love me, Reign Harrow?" he whispers, his heart racing. "If you do, tell me when you're sober. Tell me every day because I love you too, a whole fucking lot. I know you're super drunk right now, so first thing tomorrow morning, I will tell you. You can't deny it or ignore it like we know you will. I love you, Reign, and I refuse to let another day go by without you knowing."

"You're a softie." I giggle. "I knew it from the first moment I saw you. All big and brooding on the outside, but a softie inside, like an Oreo."

Raff sighs. "I am not like an Oreo."

"Oreo." I nod. "It's okay. I love Oreos."

"And we are home." Astro grins. "As amusing as this is—wait."

"What is it?" Raff demands, on high alert. He pushes me back into the seat, buckling me up as Cil turns to block the door with his back, and Raff does the same to his. What the hell do they think is going to happen?

"The front guard is flagging us down. Shall I proceed or fall back and allow you to speak to them?" Astro asks, his voice the calmest I've ever heard it. It sobers me up quickly as I scan them.

"What's happening?" I ask.

"Nothing, you're safe," Cil promises as Dal looks at Raff, and with a nod, he climbs out. The car locks immediately after he's gone.

"He shouldn't go alone!" I exclaim, leaning forward to see Dal approaching the guard. Cil tries to push me back but I ignore him, watching as Dal frowns at something and talks before heading back to the car.

The door opens and Dal grimaces. "You need to see this, boss."

"Stay," Raff commands. "First sign of trouble—"

"We get her out of here and fall back to the safe house, we know." Astro nods, his hands on the wheel.

Raff gives me a searching look before kissing me hard. "Stay," he commands, and then he gets out as well, meeting Dal around the front of the car. I watch them as they grow more agitated, and I can't take it anymore.

I know they want to protect me, but there's a sick feeling in my stomach that I can't ignore.

I push the door open. Cil reaches for me but I'm faster, and I make it around the hood when I hear them running after me. A hand catches my arm, but I wrench it free and don't stop until I'm by Raff. He hears me coming and turns to block my view.

"Get back in the car," he orders. "Now, Miss Harrow."

"Move." I meet his eyes. "I said, move."

He frowns, watching me carefully. "Please get back in the car, baby," he pleads. "I can handle this." The guard glances from me to him, but judging by the angry expression on Raff's face, I know this is bad and I need to know. I won't be able to let it go.

Whatever has him worried is scaring me shitless.

"Move," I demand, and he sighs, so I push past him, freezing at the sight before me.

Perched on a boulder next to the gate house is an open cardboard box addressed to me, and nestled inside is a bloody heart with a note stapled to the top.

Until I get yours, here is mine.

FIFTY

I grab Reign as she turns to throw up and haul her back to the car, turning to Dal and Astro who are the closest. "Stay with her." I shut the door on her pale, scared face, hating the helplessness I see in her eyes.

I move back to the guard, my nostrils flaring. "Who delivered it and when did it arrive?" I ask once more, my voice cold and laced with fury.

He stands taller. "By unmarked courier, not two hours ago. I have the receipt right here. I already called them, and they said it was dropped off at a shipping center this morning for special delivery. No name, paid in cash, and no cameras."

"Fuck's sake," I hiss.

"Why did you open it?" Cillian questions, glaring at the box.

"Something felt off, and since we are on high alert, I thought I should check all packages. Was I wrong?"

"No, not at all, you did great," I grumble, imagining if my girl had opened that. I don't know who this fucking bastard is, but when I find him, he's dead for putting that look in my girl's eyes when she was so happy and relaxed.

"Call the police," I command. "Lock this place down until they get here. I want answers, and I want the cameras online now!" I bark, beyond angry that this sick bastard managed to get this close to my girl again.

"Cil, with me. We check the house." The guard pales, and I nod. "I trust your skills, but I need to make sure before Miss Harrow goes inside."

"Of course. I'll call them right now, and I'll keep watch on the car."

"Thanks." I clap him on the shoulder as the gate opens, and Cil and I head to the house.

We don't leave a room or corner untouched, but just like I suspected, nothing has been disturbed and there's no one here. The new security measures are working and this bastard knows it, hence the delivery. He's playing it smart, and I hate that.

It also means he's watching. He could have even been waiting and watching when she saw the box, wanting her reaction.

We wave the car through, and I don't let go of Reign's hand until we are in the front living room. The windows are locked and shuttered, and there's only one way in or out. I station Dal at the windows and Cil and Astro at the door as I hand Reign some water.

Her hands are shaking, so I lift it to her lips as I crouch before her. "Sip, baby, you're in shock." A blanket drops around her shoulders, and I tuck it around her. "Do you want something warm?"

She shakes her head, lifting her eyes to mine. "Who is doing this, Raff?"

"I don't know, but I promise I will find out. This is good," I reply.

"It is?" She searches my gaze.

"It means he couldn't get in again, and he's getting bolder, which means he's more likely to make mistakes, but don't worry about any of that. It's our job to keep you safe, and we will never let anything happen to you."

"Why is someone doing this?" she whispers, tears filling her eyes. Each one that falls breaks my heart a little more. "What have I done wrong?"

"Nothing, absolutely nothing," I tell her, gripping her face and wiping the tears away. "They are sick, baby, that's all, sick in the head.

You did absolutely nothing wrong. They have, and they will pay for scaring you and making you cry."

"What do you mean?" she whispers.

"Baby, you forget who I am. Before I was yours, I was a killer. It's what I do. Do you really think any of us are going to let the sick bastard live, even behind bars, where he could be a threat to you?"

"Are you telling me you're going to kill him?" she asks, her voice hesitant. I stay silent, and she just blinks. "That's kind of terrifying and sweet all at the same time, but you will get in trouble."

"Let me worry about that, okay? Just breathe for me. You will always be safe with us around, and we aren't going anywhere. We know how to hunt and kill our prey, Reign, and this man has marked himself for death."

"Police should be here soon," Astro mumbles. "He's right, Reign. He fucked with the wrong people. There is a reason we are the best and why we did so much for our country. It's who we are, and we will become those people again so we never have to see you cry."

"But I don't want to lose any of you, and if—"

Dal comes to her side, turning her face to him. I see more emotion in his eyes than I have ever seen out of our psychopath. He doesn't feel. He never did . . .

Not until her.

"I haven't told you everything about my past, Reign, and now probably isn't the time, but you deserve to know. When I was sixteen, I killed my mother." She jerks, and he watches her carefully. He already told her that before, but the cool way he says it is sharp and sudden. "You remember me telling you she was a cruel woman who tortured me every day I was alive? She sold me for drugs and money. I was so messed up after it, they committed me. That's where the government found me. I was in a psych ward, labeled as a dangerous killer, but they saw those traits and thought they were good. They molded me into a soldier, an obedient little dog, and they used me over and over. The dead piled up around me and I couldn't escape, not until Raff, Astro, and Cillian.

"They brought a little joy into my life, and although I didn't know what it was, I stayed with them through our missions due to the bond they spoke of. My world was simple. Death was all I knew until you. You showed me what it means to be alive, to feel happiness, joy, sadness, and love. Death is easy for me, and I would kill everyone in this world to see you smile. I might have hated what became of me because of my past, but right now, I'm grateful I have the skills to keep you safe, so don't worry.

"None of us will ever get caught. Not with you on the line. We have a long life of you showing me how to live, and I plan to have that life with you, understand? Sometimes, though, you have to spill a little blood. This man, whoever he is, doesn't care about hurting anyone on the way to get what he wants, so neither will we. It's him or us. I choose us. I will do anything to protect that."

"Dal," she whispers.

"Shh, I see your heartbreak in your eyes. Don't. My life was dark and cruel but it led me here, and I'm thankful for that. I can't change my past, I can't change what I've done, but I'm going to spend the rest of my life trying to be the man who deserves you. The truth is, Reign, I don't care if I don't. I have no plans of ever letting you go, so let us do this. Let us protect you. I know you are used to doing everything alone, needing to be strong, but I've learned one thing from my brothers—everyone needs someone. You have to trust someone sometime, so trust me. Trust us."

"I do," she whispers. "But . . ."

"But what?" Cillian asks.

"What if something happens to you?" she blurts.

I bark out a laugh, as do the others. She frowns, but I can tell she's serious, so I swallow it back. "My love, we've dealt with terrorists, armies, warlords, and death every day. This one man isn't going to hurt us. Maybe we need to showcase some of our skills for you." I wink, flexing my arm as she grins. Astro smirks at my attempt to make her laugh as he strolls around.

"That's not how you do it." He rips his shirt off and starts posing for her. She giggles, and just then, the door opens and the police are escorted in by one of our guards.

"I'm so sorry, sir. We should have knocked," the guard mumbles as the four officers gawk at us and Astro, who simply grins.

"Just in time for the gun show—"

"Astro." Reign huffs.

Grinning, he puts his shirt back on as I take a seat next to Reign, and the officers hesitantly enter. A job like this could be a career maker for them, but it could also just as easily kill it.

Everyone knows what is at stake here, but I want to make it very, very fucking clear.

"Before we begin, know this is not the first attack. I'm sure you are aware, but this will not happen again. I want increased police presence around the house until he's caught."

"Of course, sir—"

"I wasn't finished."

The officer snaps his mouth shut, even as the sergeant looks at me incredulously for daring to order them around. If only they knew how high my friends went.

"Reign Harrow is your number one case right now, is that understood? If you allow this man to get close to her again, you will understand why our files are sealed, and yes, we know you searched after last time." I see the sergeant pale and know I'm right. "Good, so what do you have?"

"We ran DNA, but there weren't any matches. We have flagged it in the system in hopes it will match any new entries. There was some CCTV footage about a block away where we caught a man, six foot, well-built, in a dark hoodie running from the scene the night of. We are still trying to track his next moves. As for this evening, we will send the heart for analysis. I believe, like the others, it will be pig or cow. We are monitoring all credible threats to her security, and while we wait for new evidence, we will increase police officers like you suggested."

We continue to discuss our next moves. It will be easier if they are helping us. Either way, we will stop this man, and I won't risk Reign's safety over a pissing match.

When the police leave, I peer at Reign. "It's been a long night, my love," I mumble as she stares at the wall. "Let's get you to bed."

"I can't sleep," she whispers, so I lift her, taking her to my room. The others pile on the bed, surrounding her.

"Try for us," Astro begs. "Close your eyes. You're safe. Nothing will touch you here."

"You'll be here the entire time?" she asks.

"I promise." I never want to leave her again, not even to go to the bathroom, and my worry and promise to her wins. "Now sleep." She curls up between us as I meet Dal's eyes over her head.

I see death in his gaze.

There will be no holding him back now.

---

dal

Tonight, we are going hunting.

This man doesn't get to torment her for another day, and despite the police's assurances, I don't plan to let him live long enough to be arrested.

I meet Raff's eyes. My girl is between us, scared and unable to rest, and it stops now.

"Take Cillian," he mumbles. "Be back before she wakes up."

I can see how much it kills him not to come with us, but she's more important. Plus, we all know I'm the best hunter. He's ours, and when I'm through, he'll be begging me to carve out his heart and box it for her.

"I'm coming back, princess," I promise. "Sleep tight."

Kissing her head, I linger there for a moment before ripping myself away and striding from the room, Cillian on my heels.

The shipping store is easy to find, and we don't bother waiting for them to open. Instead, we let ourselves in through the back door, scaring the half-asleep clerk. He screams and scrambles for the phone, but I kick it out of his hand and smack him into the chair. "Stay and you won't get hurt."

"Please, I have no money."

"We don't want your money," Cillian replies, ever the kind one. "There was a package shipped to Reign Harrow."

"Oh god. I told the cops everything I know—"

"Tell us," I snap, my arms crossed.

He looks at me and balks. "It was a very late drop off, paid cash. We have no cameras. They are broken—"

"Describe him," I demand, "in detail. Now."

"He was tall, way over six feet, nearly seven, and he was wearing gray sweatpants with black and white paint splotches on them. He had a hoodie on so I couldn't see his hair, but I saw his face, and it was normal."

"Do better," I demand.

"Uh, he was white, bulky, and his nose was definitely broken in the past—not a looker, if you know what I mean—oh, and he had a tattoo!"

"Draw it," I snarl.

His hand shakes as he grabs a pen, flips over a receipt, and starts to scribble. He hands it over and I snatch it away, annoyed as I glance down. It's distinct. Nodding at Cillian, I turn and start to walk away, leaving him to smooth everything over.

"Forget we were here. If he ever comes back, call us." After delivering those parting words, he's at my side. "Lead?" he asks when I say nothing.

"It's a traditional tattoo, very distinct. I think if we show it to a few people, they will be able to direct us to where this person got it done and then to him."

"Good idea."

I was right. On our eighth shop, the eighty-year-old owner recognizes it. "Yep, I did that one many years ago. I don't usually remember because I do so many, but I remember that fucker."

"Why?" Cillian asks since I'm just glaring, hating being away from Reign for so long.

"Because he fucking skipped out on me. Here, I even have his picture in case he ever came back." Stepping behind the glass display case, she rips one of the photos off the wall and hands it over. The shop is small and in a run-down section of town, but she can obviously handle herself.

I take a picture of it and hand it back. "Thanks."

"He in trouble or something?" she asks.

"Or something," I admit with a cruel grin.

"Good. The bastard was rude. Now, I have to get ready to open up. Show yourselves out." She shuffles back to her station and we leave her to it, the bell ringing overhead as we head back up the concrete steps. The sign for Granny's Ink flickers on above us.

My feet just hit the sidewalk when my phone chimes, letting me know I have a match from facial recognition.

Pulling it up, I scan the list. "Arrested four times, burglary, DUI, domestic abuse, and assault. Last address is listed. Name's Michael Moore."

"Doesn't look the type, but then again, we are taught you can never be sure." Cillian sighs. "He's obviously a criminal."

I shoot him a look.

"But they usually have some sort of background with this kind of thing, right? Like stalking? Maybe she's his first victim. Fucker sure is smart though."

I ponder his words as we head to the address.

It's a run-down apartment building, and we get lucky. The bastard is smoking around back. It's almost too easy as we approach, one from each side, cornering him.

"I got no dope," he mutters, sparing us a look. The idiot is still in the same clothes.

Kicking out the bin he's perched on, I watch him fall, and without another beat, I smash my foot into his face. He screams as I crouch next to him. "You really fucked with the wrong people," I muse.

"I ain't fucked with nobody, man!" he yells. "Please." Cillian lifts him to his feet, only to drive his fist into his face and knock him back.

"You came after our girl," Cil hisses as he punches him again.

I've never seen Cillian lose his temper before. He's impressive.

"Fuck, Sandra was asking for it, man, I'm sorry. I didn't know she was married!" he cries.

Cillian is right, the fucker is smart, too smart to be this airheaded. "Stop," I instruct. "It isn't him."

"How do you know?" Cil pants, his knuckles split as the man groans at his feet.

"It's another dead end, a lead, nothing more. He knew we would follow it. He wanted us to. He's taunting us," I muse. "It's what I would do, watch you run around and laugh."

Crouching before him, I dig my fingers into his broken nose. "The package, who gave it to you?"

"The box?" he cries, and I release his nose as I nod. "Some weirdo. He gave me two hundred bucks to drop it off so I did. Why? What did the freak do? Fuck, I should have known. It was in the eyes, you know?"

"Describe him," Cillian demands. "The freak. Where did he meet you? Give us the money he gave you."

"I spent it," he says. I stab my finger into his broken nose again and he yells, "But I can tell you what he looks like!"

"You have exactly sixty seconds," I warn him.

"Glasses, brown eyes. Short, probably like six feet. Uh, brown— no, black hair, cut short. Dude looked like a professor or some shit, was in a suit with a waistcoat and a fucking pocket watch."

"We need more. Tattoos? Did you see a car? A name? Anything." That could describe hundreds of people in this city. We need something, anything.

"No, I'm sorry. He approached me outside of the bar I got kicked out of for trying to um, well, steal money. Offered me some bills to deliver a package. I knew I should have said n—"

"Which bar?" I demand.

"O'Donnell's over on Ridgemont."

Standing, I look down at him in disgust. "If he comes back to you again, call this number."

"Of course."

Cillian peels off some bills and drops them on him as we walk away.

I send a text to Raff to get into the cameras—that is, if there are any around there.

> Raff: Will do.
>
> Raff: Reign is waking up and asking where you both are.

"She's awake and asking for us," I tell Cil.

"Time to go home." I hate going empty-handed, but she's more important.

She has to be.

FIFTY-ONE

I managed to get some sleep, but now my head pounds from a mix of alcohol, lack of sleep, and shock, so Astro convinces me to stay in bed. I curl into his side as Raff works on his laptop. Eventually, Dal and Cillian come back. I don't comment on the blood on Cillian's knuckles, and I don't ask.

I know where they were, and I can't even say I'm sorry—not when they join us and I feel whole and safe since the first time I woke up.

Cuddled into Dal's chest, with Raff Jr. draped across me, I watch the subtitles of the news report. *"Police were called in the early morning to rock star Reign Harrow's house once more. You might have remembered a week or so ago that there was a break-in. Well, it seems there has been another incident. Could this be a coincidence, or does Reign Harrow have an obsessed fan? So far, there have been no comments from her management or Reign herself, but we hope everyone is okay."*

Turning it off, I push up. "I need a bath to wash the feeling off," I mumble.

"Beck called this morning to check on you. I told her you would call her back," Raff says softly.

"Thank you." I kiss his head as I pad into his bathroom, adding salt and bubbles to the water that he's started to keep for me. As the tap runs, I lean back into Cillian who follows me in, and he wraps his arms around me.

"Are you okay?" we ask at the same time, making us laugh.

"I'm fine. Don't you worry about me, love."

Closing my eyes, I lean back into his warmth until the bath is full enough.

"Arms up," he murmurs roughly. I lift them and feel him settle his big hands on my hips before peeling off my stolen shirt, leaving me bare. Taking my hand, he helps me into the bath. When my eyes open, I watch him strip and climb in behind me, tugging me back into his arms. His hard cock presses against my ass, but for the first time ever, I ignore it.

I need his comfort more than anything else.

My eyes close as I relax in his hold. When his rough hands start to caress me, I open my eyes to find him washing me. Tears form once more as he gently cleans every inch of me with such care, it almost makes me ache. Have I ever been treated so well? So kind? It's in every touch.

After lounging in the bath for way too long, Cillian helps me out, drying me off before I do my skincare routine and makeup, needing that layer like armor if I am to face today. Dressing in a white dress and heels to give myself an extra boost of confidence, I head downstairs to meet the guys. I have to speak to the press and police today so I need this edge.

I need them.

I've just accepted a coffee from Astro when my phone rings. Raff hands it over, and I check the caller ID before picking up.

"Hello?"

"Reign, I'm so glad you're okay. There's been an emergency meeting called at our office. It's in one hour. Can you make it?"

It's clear I don't have much choice. "Sure, see you then." I meet the guys' eyes, knowing they are already wondering what's happening.

"It was Will. They want a meeting in an hour," I tell them, my head tilting as they share a look.

Sitting in the stuffy boardroom, I take strength from my guys surrounding me, knowing they will protect me. The cameras outside were insane, and there were so many questions. After giving a brief statement, I feel drained. All I want to do is go home and curl up with my guys and let them make it better.

I can't and won't though. I won't let this sicko win, so instead, I sit here while a room of suited males and females discuss the situation like it's a PR move and not really happening to me.

"Let's get an update of where we are at, shall we?" Will suggests.

"Well—" I begin.

"Oh, sorry, Reign, I know this must be hard. I was talking to Mr. Walker." Frowning, I turn to look at Raff. "Please sit, all of you."

They leave my back, head around the table, and sit stiffly in the chairs.

"Now, we know you have been doing a stellar job of protecting Reign, after all you came highly recommended or we wouldn't have hired you, but you were hired for this exact job—to stop her stalker."

"I'm sorry. What?" I blurt.

Heat flashes through me, followed by cold. I almost shiver, my heart clenching like it knows something I don't.

My eyes go from him to Raff, my heart skipping a beat before racing.

"Oh, well, you see, Reign, yes, we knew about the stalker. You get a lot of threats, and while you were away, one got particularly bad. When you came back, we hired them since we were worried. They were to report on the stalker—"

"You knew?" My accusation hangs in the air, and my eyes go to Raffiel, Astro, Dal, and Cillian. "You knew I had a stalker and never told me? Moreover, you lied to me?"

"They were doing their job. Please don't be angry, Reign. They were supposed to report back—"

"On my life," I spit, knowing what he's trying to say. I feel betrayed. Raff won't even meet my eyes.

My heart aches so much, I bend slightly to try to ease it, my stomach rolling. I trusted them, and all this time, they have been keeping secrets. I don't care if it was for my well-being. They knew how I felt.

It's my life, my choice. I should have been told.

They lied to me.

"Well . . ." Will coughs. "A little, just so we could—"

My ears ring as I stare at the four men I thought I knew.

The four men I stupidly fell in love with.

I thought they were different. I always knew they were here on the board's orders, but they never once told me about the stalker. If they lied about that, what else are they lying about? What else have they told the board, the very men who want to use me for their own gain?

Fuck!

I let them into my house.

I let them into my heart.

I gave them everything—my pain, my loyalty, my body.

They betrayed it.

They are nothing but liars like every other person in my life.

My heart breaks, that foolish organ crumbling into a million pieces, and I struggle to breathe. I try not to let it show, my leg shaking as I fight the urge to run far and fast just like I did last time.

I'm always the fool, aren't I?

I told myself I wouldn't trust anyone, wouldn't give them my heart and let it be broken again, and here I am, right back in the same situation, letting someone else smash it to smithereens as their lies come to the front.

I am such a fool.

It hurts so much, I feel like I'm dying, and even as I force a smile for Will, it quivers, but I refuse to falter and break here.

I can't, not even as I feel tears burn my eyes.

They lied to me, and that's all that matters. I feel filthy for letting them touch me, every memory of us turning sour as I stare at them. They knew my past and chose to keep things from me anyway.

They get nothing more of me.

Not a single fucking one of them.

Fuck them all.

Worst of all, fuck my stupid breaking heart.

FIFTY-TWO

I feel like I'm going to be sick. Reign won't even look at me. She's pale and hurt. I see it.

I wanted to tell her from the beginning but I didn't, and now it's like a train wreck. I watch her close down. All that joy, happiness, and hope we slowly brought back into her life disappears. Her eyes turn cold and hard, just like when we first met her.

I watch the woman I love rebuild herself into someone I don't recognize, all because of our stupidity and desire to protect her.

At first, they asked us not to tell her, but then I couldn't. She was just getting her life back together, and I didn't want to uproot it again. I made a stupid decision.

I stare at her, unable to look away. She doesn't even glance at us, her gaze firmly on the head of her label. She's my obsession, I live for her, and her denying me her attention is killing me.

"Miss Harrow," I say softly, and she flinches but doesn't look at me.

I lay my hands on the table, leaning closer. "Baby," I plead, "look at us, please." She continues to avoid looking at me, but I see her shoulders hunch. "Baby, please, we would never hurt you, I promise. You have to listen to our reasons."

"My love, he's not lying. We would never hurt you. I'm so sorry, please."

The others try, all of us pleading and interrupting the meeting.

She continues to sit there without even glancing at us, as if we are below her.

Reign acts as if she has forgotten we exist when she is the center of our world, and I can't even blame her. We broke her heart and her trust. We knew the consequences of our choice, and I can already see her running away from us, but this time when she leaves, she will take all our hearts.

"Are we done?" she asks, completely ignoring us. Her tone is hard and cold.

"Yes," he responds, and she stands without even looking at us. If I let her walk out that door, we are done forever. I will never see her again.

I'll lose her.

"Reign," I yell, ignoring the whispers and looks. I push away from the table and stand. Cillian catches me around the waist, and security holds us back as we try to go after her. "Baby, look at me! I'm sorry. Look at me! Please fucking look at me," I scream. "I love you!"

"Reign!"

She doesn't look back once.

FIFTY-THREE

Scrambling past the men, I race after Reign. She's facing forward in the elevator as the doors shut.

"Reign! Wait!"

I feel her eyes on me as she reaches over and presses a button, and I watch as the doors shut in my face. I slam into them before turning, looking for the stairs. We can't let her get away.

We can't.

"Give her some space," Raff orders, but his voice shakes.

"Space? Not a fucking chance. You know her. She will—"

"Gentlemen, please join us."

I look around Raff to see the board. Raff's expression is hard and he grips my arm, dragging me back into the room, but I feel the tremor in his muscles. He isn't as unaffected as he seems.

God, I rub my chest as I slump into my chair. My gaze goes to her empty seat and I remember the agony in her eyes as she looked at us with disbelief and then heartbreak. It killed me. I wanted to rip my chest open and give her anything just to gain a moment to explain.

How did we get to this from the bliss of this morning?

"Well, from what we just saw, it confirms a few rumors. You have crossed the line. A relationship is prohibited with a client. You are all fired," Will states.

"Do you think we care?" Dal snaps. "How could you do that to her—"

"I thought she knew."

"You made us sign a contract that prevented us from telling her about the stalker," Cillian hisses. "We never reported to you about her life, but we couldn't tell her the full truth, and now she's alone with a stalker—"

"We'll handle that. It's no longer your concern." The doors open. "Security will escort you out."

Thrusting my chair back, I push past the muscle and hurry to the elevator, my brothers with me. As we descend, I count down the seconds I'm away from her.

"What a fucking mess," Raff says. "We'll sit her down and explain—"

"You think she'll listen?" Cillian snaps. "In her mind, we betrayed her just like every other person and she isn't wrong. We lied to her. We never told her the full truth. We should have when the stalker—"

"We had no choice," Raff reminds him.

"Don't use that as an excuse to make yourself feel better. We broke her trust and her heart, and Reign Harrow doesn't forgive or forget. You know that better than anyone. We've lost her, and I will never forgive myself or you."

The doors open, and Cillian storms out.

Is he right? Have we lost her?

"Come on, Havier," I beg. "You know us. You have to let us through."

"I'm so sorry. I can't. Orders." Havier winces. "I really am sorry."

"Orders from whom?" Raff asks. "They don't control her house—"

"From Miss Harrow herself. In fact, she told me to, uh . . ." He blushes. "To let you know your stuff will be outside within the hour and to never come here or contact her again. Her words."

"Please," I implore, barely able to speak around the lump in my throat, my chest aching so much I can't breathe. "Just one minute, that's all I need—"

"I can't afford to lose this job. I have a baby and another on the way. I'm really sorry."

"Was she okay?" Dal asks quietly.

She took a taxi, which we know because we came back in her car, and Raff reluctantly hands the keys over to the unsure guard.

"She was . . . She seemed angry," he admits.

Dal nods. "Anger is good."

"How is anger good?" I round on him. I don't even realize I'm rubbing my chest until his eyes drop to it. Turning away, I kick the post. "Reign! Reign!" I scream, ignoring the cameras. I hear the gossip, but I don't fucking care.

I can't lose her.

"Reign, please!" I scream. "I know you can hear us! Just give me one minute!"

"Come on, man, this isn't the way." Raff wraps his arm around my chest and tugs me back when it's clear she isn't coming down. "Don't make a scene that will hurt her more. We'll find a way to see her, but not like this. I promise, Astro, I'll fix this."

Shrugging off his arm, I glare at him. "You can't fix everything, Raff." I turn and walk away, knowing if I stay, I'll break down. I'd camp right there and scream her name until she came for me, but he's right. That would hurt her more.

I've hurt her enough.

Fifty-Four

"Reign!"

Pressing my back against the front door, I cover my mouth to muffle my sobs. I held it together all the way home despite feeling the burn in my eyes. I don't even remember arriving, but as soon as the front door closed behind me, I slid to the floor and cried.

How could they?

Raff Jr. whines at their voices, his cold nose digging into my skin as he covers me protectively, understanding I'm upset and wanting to make it better.

My head drops back, hitting the door. I want to scream, but I know they will just come in after me, so instead I choke on my pain, hunching as I hear them fighting to get to me. It hurts so fucking much, and it hurts even more that all I want is for them to hold me and kiss it better.

Can you die from heartbreak? It sure as fuck feels like I can.

The organ clenches and refuses to beat, spreading agony through my chest to my entire body, as if the pain of their betrayal is carried through my veins.

"We'll be back." The promise is almost whispered.

Cillian.

Even his voice sends a fresh wave of agony through me as tears fall in uncomfortable streams down my face, my lip trembling as I try to hold it in.

Pulling out my phone, I check the cameras they installed and see them walking away. Part of me is hurt that they are leaving so easily.

Am I that easy to get over and forget? Was it just a job?

Part of me is glad they left, but part of me wants them to make it better like they always do. I'm confused, and it hurts so fucking much.

My entire life implodes around me again, the one I rebuilt from ashes and promised to protect.

I crawl to my knees and then stumble to my feet, then I storm to the control room, remembering what Cillian showed me. I turn off the servers, the cameras, so they can't see into my house.

They don't fucking get that right.

Anger consumes me alongside pain, blinding me to anything else. I find myself in the kitchen, and I swipe a bottle of vodka, ripping off the cap and downing some.

The burn lights me up and enhances my anger as I wander through my empty house. Every room is a reminder of them. The kitchen where we ate every morning. The living room where we had movie nights. Their bedroom . . . My bedroom.

At the doorway to my room, the bottle hangs from my limp fingers as I look around, remembering the way they made love to me. How could they? How could they look me in the eye and make all those promises while lying?

"Fuck them!" I shout, throwing the bottle. It hits the light and shatters. Screaming, I swipe my hand across my side table, watching it all fall and shatter. Storming to the bed, I rip at the sheets.

When I come out of my fit of rage, I'm in the middle of my destroyed bedroom.

Sobbing, I pull at my necklace and toss it into the destruction. I go to rip off the bracelet, but for some reason, I can't, and that only makes me cry harder.

I feel myself spiraling. I feel the need to run, to get far away where they can never hurt me again.

I don't want to lose myself like last time. Whimpering, I crawl through the mess, cutting my knees until I find my phone, dialing blindly.

"Hello?" the voice answers.

"I need you," I beg.

"Well, shit." Beck whistles, leaning into the doorway as she surveys the mess. "I respect the anger." Carefully stepping over glass, she slides down the bed to sit next to me. I look like a fucking mess, but she was the only person I could think to call. "I would say you are okay, but you aren't. What happened, and who do I need to kill?"

Lifting the bottle, I take a drink. "They lied to me."

"Who did?" she asks before her eyes widen, no doubt realizing my usual followers are nowhere to be seen. "No fucking way."

Her disbelief makes it worse, sending another wave of agony through me.

"Way." I hand over the bottle. She takes it and drinks before wiping her mouth. "They lied to me this whole time. I loved them, Beck. I let them in. I told them things not even Tucker knew, and it was all a lie."

"Fucking assholes, want me to kill them?" she snaps, dead serious.

I snatch the bottle back and down more. "No, I just want to forget. I want to be numb. It's selfish and dumb, but I didn't want to be alone. I'm so tired of doing everything alone."

"I'm glad you called. I can't help with the pain, but numbness and forgetting? That we can do." Standing, she offers me her hand. "Come on, Reign. Fuck those dumb, hot idiots. Let's get you hammered." I look up at her and place my hand in hers. She yanks me to my feet and winces. "We have to do something about your face first. You look like someone punched a panda."

I bark out a laugh despite myself, and she grins.

"There she is," she whispers, squeezing my hand in reassurance.

"Don't let them win. Don't you fucking dare, Reign." I flinch, and she holds my hand tighter. "Get even, get angry, and get over them. Do whatever the fuck you have to do, but don't let them win. It might feel hopeless now, but you're not alone, and remember there is always a way out."

"I love them," I admit.

It's the first time I've said it out loud.

I should be happy, but I'm just numb.

"I know, and that's why it hurts so fucking much, darling. Love always does because we give them power to destroy us, and when it happens?" She swallows, tears welling in her eyes. "It feels like you can't breathe, like you can't possibly go on, but you can. You place one foot in front of the other. Breathe. Fight. Hit. Make a mess. Do whatever you have to so you can keep yourself going and give yourself a fucking reason to live, but don't you dare give up. I can't handle that again."

I nod, swallowing back my tears. She's right. Fuck them. I won't run this time. This is my life and my fucking world! Fuck them and their lies. I'm Reign fucking Harrow.

Nobody gets to break my heart unless I let them.

I'm back, baby.

FIFTY-FIVE

"Okay, thanks." Raff looks like shit. His hair is a mess, and his suit is rumpled. His eyes are red, but he won't let us stop. He's trying to hunt down the stalker so he can't get to our girl while we aren't there.

Our girl . . . I guess she isn't anymore.

We can't even see her.

My fingers twitch with the need to check on her. She belongs right here with me. I need the weight of her in my arms. I can still smell her on me, and I never want to bathe again.

All I want is her.

Unlike me, Raff has turned his pain into determination.

Astro is lost, and Dal is quiet.

I'm angry and so fucking hurt. I don't deserve to be because I did this to her. I don't deserve to hurt, but god, I do.

I hurt so much, I don't know how I'm not bleeding from a thousand cuts.

"We can keep going on to the next—" Raff scrambles to answer his phone as it rings, hope in his eyes.

"Baby—oh, uh, hi." He frowns, putting it on speaker.

"I just thought you should know your girl is here and she's a mess.

Don't you ever tell her I told you. Fix whatever you did," Trav snaps and hangs up.

Raff frowns. "He sent me a location. Do you think he's telling the truth?"

"I don't care, do you?" I retort.

"No, let's go get our girl," he says, striding to the car.

We follow, and my heart races the entire drive. What if she kicks us out? What if she's hurt? I need to know. I need to see her, just for a moment, even if she hates us. I can't breathe without her.

The party is massive. We blend in, looking like hired security, as we circle the property, trying to find our girl, until we follow the music. I come to a stop in the entrance of the huge mansion, where the foyer has been turned into a dance floor.

In the middle of the crowd is Reign.

No matter what, just like when I always see her, my thoughts evaporate, my heart screams in happiness, and I'm gobsmacked by her beauty.

Her head is thrown back, and her eyes are closed. She's wearing nothing but a skimpy, translucent dress and she looks incredible, but she's so fucking drunk, and I know it's because of us.

A man grips her hips, grinding with her to the music, his touch lustful and possessive.

Someone is going to die tonight.

He is touching what is ours.

I hear a scuffle and glance back to see Raff trying to restrain Dal. "Cil," he snaps.

Dal's eyes are black, and I've never seen him look so dangerous. Astro helps Raff as my eyes go back to Reign to see her taking the man's hand and slipping through the crowd.

My entire body goes cold. Jealousy and pain roars through me as she starts to head upstairs with him. Their intentions are clear.

Snarling, Dal shoots past me. Fuck.

I run after them, racing upstairs and seeing him round the corner. When we find him, he's kicking down the bedroom door. We hurry inside to see her sit up, and the shirtless man on top of her glares at us.

"What the fuck, bro?" he snaps.

"Get out, bro," I mock. "Unless you want him to kill you." I tilt my head to Dal.

The buff golden boy looks at Dal before paling at what he sees, and he immediately flees. We let him pass us before making a barrier again.

"Are you okay?" Astro asks like a lovesick puppy as she stands, glaring at us like we're strangers.

"Yes, Reign, are you okay?" I spit, my jealousy taking over. How could she do that only hours after being in bed with us? "Not even a few hours and what? You're going to fuck us out of your system? Look at yourself."

"Fuck off," she snaps at me. "Why the fuck are you even here?"

"For you," Astro whispers, his eyes filled with tears.

"For what's ours," I say since Raff is silent and Dal is twitching with the need to kill the man who touched her.

The bitter laugh she lets out makes me flinch.

"Not yours," she says, directing her rage at us, and it's wrong, but it makes me hard. Feeling her anger is better than feeling her pain.

"No?" I step toward her, and she steps back. I keep going until she hits the bed and I pin her there. "Want me to remind you how you begged for our cocks?" I'm being cruel, but I can't seem to help it when I notice her smeared lipstick and drooping top.

She let him touch her.

"So that's it, huh? We make one mistake and you go back to drinking and fucking around to feel something." My head snaps left from the slap, and then pain slams through me. I roll to the side, covering my cock and balls she just kneed, and fall off the bed. Nostrils flaring, she tugs her top up and turns her glare on us.

"This is my fucking life. Don't make the mistake of thinking you have any say in it. I fucked you, and we had a good time. It was nothing more. Don't forget your place," she sneers cruelly, lashing out just like I did.

God, how did we get here?

I want to go back and start again, but even then, I wouldn't trade what we had for another shot. I don't want to forget everything we shared.

"Reign—" Raff holds up his hands.

"It's Miss Harrow to you, Mr. Walker," she spits.

"Miss Harrow," he whispers lovingly. "Let's just talk. We'll sober you up, and you can hear us out—"

She goes toe to toe with him. "No, I don't want to hear you out. In fact, I don't want anything except for you to get the fuck out of my life and never come back. Is that understood? I'm not your fucking mission, Raffiel. I'm not something you can achieve or fix. This—" She gestures between us. "Whatever the hell it was is over. It's dead. I'm a goddamn rock star, and you're a killer in a cheap suit. Go back to your world, and I'll go back to mine."

"You're our world," Astro says sadly.

She swallows, and I see her resolve weaken just for a second before she steps back. "Then get a new one. I don't want to see you again. You are worse than nothing to me. You're just another person who used me. Don't worry, I'll make sure to put it in a song."

Raff shrinks back, flinching in pain, clearly thinking we've lost her. I stumble to my feet, but Dal steps before her, blocking her exit.

"Move," she demands.

He meets her eyes, and she stares back.

She is the one person in the world who is safe from him.

"Either kill me or move," she hisses. "Those are the only things you're good for."

He takes an audible breath, the only sign of his agony, and then steps aside.

"Good little dog," she sneers before storming out, leaving us staring after her.

"So this is what pain is," Dal whispers, watching her. "I don't fucking like it. I don't like it one bit. How do you survive it?"

I don't know.

I really don't.

FIFTY-SIX

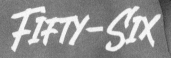

"**D**al." Raff races after me, and when I feel him reach for me, I duck under his touch and spin, slamming my hand out. It hits his chest, and he flies back with a grunt, his ass landing on the street. He doesn't even try to fight back. He just sits there, looking up at me with sadness in his eyes.

The moon shines down on the empty street, the music from the party pumping to us even here, rumbling under my feet, and somewhere in there is my girl.

My life.

My very fucking reason for breathing . . .

She looked at me like everyone else did, like the shroud had finally been pulled back and she saw the beast inside. Her lip curled in disgust, and I saw the pain in her gaze, but all it did was rip me apart.

My body has been used, abused, and tortured and I have stood against it all, but one look, one sentence from her, and I'm dead.

I'd take war over this any day.

If this is living, I don't want it.

It hurts too fucking much.

"Dal," he repeats. "Just stay calm."

He thinks I'm going off the rails, ready to kill everyone, but he's so very wrong. There is no anger, only a pain I can't understand nor survive. It's too much, and the emotions are too strong.

"I can't live without her," I say, suddenly understanding. "She calms the storm, and without her . . ." I stumble away from Raff. "I can never go back. I'm not him, not the killer, and now I'm not the man who loved her either. I'm . . . nothing."

"Dal," he repeats slowly, getting to his feet.

I see the others racing toward us. I'd left swiftly, unable to look at her without feeling everything she did—disgust, rage, and hurt.

I did this. I knew the pain she felt, the loneliness, and the scars she bore, and I still let us lie to her.

I begin to spiral back into that dark place where nothing hurts, and I feel nothing but hopelessness. It seems easier just to give up. Her life would be better without me. She wouldn't hurt anymore. Even my brothers would be better off without me. They wouldn't have to constantly worry about what I'm doing or monitor my actions and words and shelter me.

No, this world would be a much better place without a beast like me.

Isn't that what she meant?

"I won't hurt her anymore. I won't," I state calmly. "My mother was right. This world would be better off if I were never born." I step back and into the path of the truck I saw coming out of my peripherals. Its brights splash across me, and for a moment, I'm cleansed of all the pain. I'm free.

A honk splits the air, and as I close my eyes to welcome oblivion, a hand grabs mine.

One touch holds me to this world and all that darkness parts, letting me see how foolish I'm being.

I was a fool. I can't give up, not now, but it's too late.

I feel the air as the truck swerves and hear the squeal of its tires, and I know it's going to hit me. My eyes open and meet wide, terrified ones I've gazed into a million times—eyes that made me understand love.

My Reign.

She glances at the truck then to me, and something hardens in her gaze as I gape at her.

A firm yank tugs me into her waiting arms, and the truck barrels down on us. Now we both stand in its path. Her arms wrap tightly around me, her face pressed to my chest, ready for the hit.

She came for me.

She saved me.

No!

She can't die like this. With a burst of energy, I throw us as far as I can, turning midair so I land on my back, grunting as I hit the hard sidewalk. The truck avoids us by inches and skids to a stop down the road.

For a moment, all I hear is my racing heart, and then yells invade the silence.

"Dal!" Raff, Astro, and Cillian are all shouting. "Reign!" They rush to us, checking us over, but she pushes their hands away, shaking in my arms as she sits up.

"Reign?" I murmur. The sound of my voice seems to break her out of whatever stupor she was in.

"You're okay, you're okay," she says, running her hands over me. "You chose to live. You're okay." She meets my eyes, and I see tears splashing down her face. "How could you? How could you do that to me?" Her fists pound against my chest. The sharp pain feels so good. It reminds me that I'm alive. How could I ever miss the beauty in the sweet agony? "How could you ever try to leave me? You selfish bastard! How could you do that?" she screams, hitting me.

I feel something hit my cheek so I touch my face, and as I pull my finger away, I see a teardrop.

I'm crying.

"Reign," I rasp.

"You bastard!" she screams, hitting on me. "You selfish bastard." Her sobs cut into her words as she collapses against my chest. "How could you let me lose someone else? Haven't I lost enough? How could you?"

Crying with her, I hold her tight, understanding for the first time that emotions are not easy to control but they mean we're alive.

"I'm sorry. I'm so sorry, Reign," I murmur, shame filling me.

"You fucking bastard," she sobs, pulling away.

"I'm sorry. I'm sorry," I repeat. "I thought you were better off without me. It was just a second, but I was so stupid. I'm so fucking sorry."

She scoots away from me, wrapping her arms around herself.

"Reign," Raff says, shaken. "Are you okay? Please, baby."

"What were you thinking?" Astro roars at us. "You," he seethes at me before turning to Reign. "And you. What were you thinking?"

"I wasn't," she whispers, her eyes on me. "I couldn't let him die, but I can't forgive you either."

A shadow falls over us, and we all glance up to see a terrified-looking Beck.

"Reign, are you okay?" Beck asks, shooting me a watery glare as she takes Reign's hands and pulls her to her side. I watch Reign shake in the embrace, her eyes on me.

"If you ever want me to forgive you, you will never pull something like that again. Do you understand, Dal?" she snaps.

Nodding stiffly, I watch as Beck glares at me and leads her away.

"I'm going to make sure she's okay." Cillian shoots me a look. "If you ever pull something like that again, I'll kill you myself." He smacks my back. "She needs you, brother. We need you. Don't ever forget that."

"It was just all too much," I admit. "It hurt too much, and then I realized it would stop. No more pain, no more worry, no more nightmares—"

"And you'd be dead," Astro roars. "Then what? We'd be in pain, filled with shame and guilt until it killed us. Did you think of that? Did you even care, you prick?"

I shake my head, hanging it in shame.

"Enough," Raff barks. "Cil, take Astro and make sure they get home okay." I hear them stomp away, and Raff strokes my hair.

"Let it out, brother. It's okay, you're okay, and she's okay." My tears fall silently as he holds me. "God, Dal, death is never the choice. Never, do you hear me?" I lift my head and meet his glassy eyes, watching his tears fall for me. "Think of those you would leave. Astro, Cil, me . . . Reign. It would kill us. You wouldn't hurt, but we would for the rest of our lives. Think of everything you still have to do. No matter how fucking dark it seems, brother, there is always a way out. You are too fucking strong to give up."

"I regretted it immediately," I admit, "but I didn't think I could stop it. I'm sorry, Raff. I really am."

"I know." He sighs, wrapping his arms around me. "Promise me you won't do it again."

"I promise," I vow. I would never hurt my family like that.

When he pulls back, I see the shadows in his eyes, and I know I put them there. He doesn't believe me. I need to regain his trust as well as Reign's. Shame battles with my determination.

He's right. There's always a way out, no matter how bleak it seems.

There is so much to live for, and even in the darkness, there is a light switch . . . a hand.

She was mine, and I promise to always be hers.

FIFTY-SEVEN

The bright lights of the truck flash in my mind, as does the look in his eyes—regret.

Groaning, I sit up, giving up trying to sleep. Beck left after getting me settled, but this house is just too quiet and big without them, even with Raff Jr. close on my heels, as if protecting me in their place. Not to mention, my mind won't stop whirring.

Dal tried to kill himself.

Guilt is eating at me. Is it my fault? Of course it is. He made the decision, but it won't stop me from blaming myself, and it's making me feel sick to my very core. I didn't even think as I ran to him. I had to stop him. I might still be angry, but I can't live in a world without him.

I love him, and it fucking hurts.

It's not the moment of heartbreak that hurts the most. It's in the stillness after the fact. It's in the days after, when you repeat their words in your head over and over so much, they don't seem real. You remember their touches and their looks. You question everything from the start, and you torture yourself until you can't sleep or eat. All you think about is the constant pain, and within that stillness is when you truly break.

That's when you realize just how strong you need to be to survive.

They say heartbreak can't kill you, but I beg to differ. I wrap my arms around myself to hold myself together.

My house is too quiet.

My heart is too jagged and broken to work again.

No, the moment of heartbreak isn't the worst. It's what comes after.

It's trying to heal from a pain you can't fix. No doctor or medication can make it go away. No one else can see it, but you can feel the open wounds. You can only numb yourself for a little while, but when the quiet comes, it will return.

The truth is, I crave it because it means I'm still alive.

Pain has always been my constant companion, in a sense, because heartbreak has been with me since I was born to a mother who didn't love me enough to stay. I had a father who hated me enough to hurt me and a brother too innocent for this world. I even had a fake fiancé who was too blind to care. Yes, I know heartbreak well, and in a sense, we are old friends.

Along with the pain is anger. They did this to us and destroyed what we could have been. Dal almost killed himself, and I'm so mad that he could be that selfish.

The emotional turmoil is too much, and I find myself in the one place I feel safe—my studio. I'm curled up under a blanket, my guitar on my lap like a shield. I hold my phone in my hand, open to the group chat.

The last message is from them.

> QueenB: Okay, which of you idiots used all my fancy body scrub?

Cillian: Definitely Astro, babe.

Raff: Which one? I can run out and get you more.

Dal: What is body scrub?

> Astro: I deny everything. However, if you happen to notice that my skin is silky smooth, I demand a lawyer.

> QueenB: *Laughing emoji.*

Swallowing against the heartache, I hover my thumb over the keyboard, debating asking if they are okay, but then I remember I'm not supposed to care anymore.

I want to tell them this house is too big, but I don't. I try to close my eyes and sleep when my phone suddenly vibrates. I scramble to answer it, hope choking me.

"Hello?"

"Reign, darling, are you okay?" The female voice is soft and worried.

"Who is this?" I ask, slumping when I realize it's not them.

"Astro's mom, Gloria. The boys called and told me everything. They are worried about you but didn't want to hurt you, so I called."

"They asked you to?" I murmur.

"No, those idiots beat around the bush. I called because I was worried and wanted to make sure you are okay. Are you?" she asks, her motherly voice making tears fill my eyes once more.

"No," I rasp.

"Oh, sweetie." There's a thud. "Get your old ass up and pack the car. We are going to the city."

"Wait, what?" Astro's father mumbles in the background, and it makes me grin despite everything.

"The car," she says exasperatedly, like it's straightforward.

"Woman, it's five in the morning. Go back to sleep." There's another thud. "You know, I heard divorces aren't that expensive anymore."

"Don't tempt me," she hisses. "Sorry, Reign. Carry on, love, what can I do?"

"Nothing, thank you. So . . . they told you everything?" I settle back, strangely comforted now that she called me, even if she is Astro's mom.

"They did. The idiots. When I see them, I'm going to smack them blue. I'm so mad at them, Reign, so mad for you. I know they will have their reasons, they aren't cruel for the sake of it, but that doesn't make me less angry and hurt for you. Do you need me to come to you?"

Swallowing, I allow her words to flow through my mind. Their reasons . . . They kept saying that and I didn't give them the time of day. Was I wrong? No, they lied to me, used me, and hurt me. I'm allowed to feel upset. No matter their reasons, they made the wrong choice. She is right though. They aren't cruel for the sake of it.

"Reign, do you need me to come? Say the word and we are there. You are family now, and that means everything. They may be my sons, but I care for you a great deal," she murmurs.

"No, thank you though. I really appreciate the offer and your call," I admit. "I was feeling very alone."

"Well, you aren't. You're family now too, and family doesn't let each other hurt alone. Why don't you come stay here for a little while?" she asks hopefully.

"I don't want to run, not again. I need to face this, but I really am thankful. I think I'm going to try and sleep now . . . Mama?" I whisper. After all, she is the one who insisted I call her that before we left their house.

"Yes, my love," she murmurs.

"Will you make sure they are okay?" I ask.

"Of course, now get some sleep. I'll call you tomorrow. Good night, Reign."

"Good night." I hang up, cuddling the phone as my eyes close, exhaustion finally winning out.

I hate the kitchen the most. It's too fucking empty.

I try to fill it with music, but it doesn't work, so I stop going in there. Food turns up, all my favorite dishes, and there are no names, but only one set of people could get it to my door without anyone seeing. Flowers sometimes accompany the meals as well as little love

388

notes I can't bear to read. I swim, I try to write, I clean, and I pace. I don't think I would even be looking after myself if it wasn't for Raff Jr. I have to cook and play with him and that brings me a little joy in the darkness. When I can't stand being in the house anymore, I call the new guards I've been assigned. They've clearly been given strict rules and don't enter the house unless necessary. They also don't speak or even look at me as they escort me to the car.

"Where to, Miss Harrow?" I startle at his voice. It's wrong, strict, and cold. It's not purring and familiar.

Clearing my throat and my obsessive thoughts, I force a smile. "To the studio please." The album is ready to drop any time, but maybe working will help keep my mind off them.

He doesn't respond, and I sink back in my seat, pulling my shades over my eyes. The cameras beat at the car, and I have flashbacks of similar nights, of the guys laughing as they touched me where the cameras couldn't see, and I have the insane urge to run away from all the reminders, prying eyes, and pain.

My phone vibrates, and to distract myself, I scroll through the notifications.

One catches my attention.

> Unknown: See you soon.

I delete it and instead focus on the texts.

> Beck: ARE YOU ALIVE?

> Beck: DO I NEED TO COME AND SAVE YOU?

> Beck: KOLTON JUST WALKED IN ON ME GOOGLING HOW TO KILL SOMEONE.

> Beck: WAKE UP, BITCH.

> Beck: Why all caps? Shit, sorry.

Grinning, I type out a response.

> Reign: Who are we killing and what was his response? I'm alive.

Beck: About time. We are killing your exes, obviously. He was on board. We are on our way to Home Depot to get clear containers and shovels.

> Reign: I have questions . . .

Beck: We watched a program, Santa Clarita Diet, and figured we could do it that way, but we are open to suggestions.

A moment later, a picture comes through of Beck and the band holding up chainsaws, and I can't hold back my snort.

> Reign: I like your thinking, but shouldn't you guys be packing for tour?

Beck: Boring, fine. Text me later, hot stuff. The offer for murder remains open.

> Reign: Got it, cutie.

Shaking my head, I navigate through my other messages, ignoring the group chat of the guys, which hasn't stopped since this morning. They are determined, I'll give them that. I stop at one from Tucker.

Tuck: Saw the news. Hope you're okay. I'm always here if you need anything, even just a familiar ear to talk to.

> Reign: Thanks.

The group chat, called Reign's Boys, has a new notification, and at first I want to delete it without looking, but I can't resist punishing myself. I don't read the ones before it, unable to handle that yet, but I peer at the newish text.

> Raff: Dal is sleeping. He's okay. Reign, I know you probably won't respond, but please be okay, just let us know that at least. I'm begging you. I'm so sorry, baby. I hope one day you understand why, but if not, please know we love you. Don't run from this world again, not because of us. We will wait for you forever if that's what it takes. We won't ever give up on you.

I swallow my pain. He hit the nail right on the head after all. Didn't I think of running again?

I shouldn't respond. God, I'm a glutton for punishment.

> QueenB: I'm okay.

There, that's all I say and then I shut it, ignoring the chat as it blows up with their responses. We pull into the underground parking garage at the studio, so I guess the new guards aren't taking any chances. I wait for them to open the door, a habit, and they sweep the surrounding area. When the door opens, I slide out.

"Thanks," I say softly.

A nod is all I get. Rolling my eyes, I blow out a breath and head to the elevator with them in formation around me. It's ridiculous, really—

Bang-bang-bang.

I duck, the sound of gunfire loud and distinct.

"Contact!" one of the guard's screams. "Back, car, go!"

An arm wraps around me and tugs, keeping me down as we spin, but not before I see one of the guards drop with a shout, blood blooming on his chest. "Shit, shit, man down, let's go!" the one holding me barks.

Whimpering, I run with him, stumbling in my heels as everything seems to slow down as the *pop-pop-pop* of the gun gets louder. When I glance back, I see more of the guards falling as they protect our backs, their guns out. Spinning forward, I drop my bag and phone and almost fall.

The guard yanks me up and we round the car. He pushes me to it as he opens the door, but my eyes widen when a masked man in a suit rounds the car, calmly reloading. "Behind you!" I scream, but it's too late. The guard turns just in time to get a bullet in the head.

My scream rips free as he spins from the force, his open, unseeing eyes haunting me as they meet mine and he falls against me. I push him away as his blood covers me. Whimpering, I manage to get free and scramble back on my hands and knees as the man in the mask tilts his head and watches me.

It's silent.

There are no screams or voices.

They are all dead.

He killed them, and I'm next.

Oh god, I'm such a fool.

"Please," I implore, piercing the deafening silence.

"You beg prettily." A computer voice comes from the mask. "Do it again."

"Please, please, just let me go. I have money."

He laughs, and it's haunting. "I don't want your money, Reign." He crouches before me as my lip trembles. He uses the gun to tip my chin up as I cry, fear coursing through me. "I want something much more valuable—you."

Sirens split the air and my eyes widen. His head turns to the garage entrance. "Damn it, two minutes early. I guess our time is cut short—" I take my chance, refusing to die on my knees, and bring my hand down like I was taught. I snap his wrist, the pain making him recoil and drop the gun. I take the shot and kick off my heels as I scramble to my feet and run for the slope, making sure to zigzag.

"Reign!" the voice roars.

I run faster, but when he skids to a stop before the slope, I swerve, knowing I'm not going to make it. I race down the line of cars and duck behind one, covering my mouth as I hide.

The sirens are getting louder.

"Reign, Reign, Reign, that wasn't very nice, and you'll pay for that," the voice calls, getting closer. "Where are you? Duck, duck, goose . . . Boo!" He pops around the car, and I kick out with a scream.

He catches my foot and uses it to drag me out. I try to claw my way under the car, breaking my nails, but it's no use.

He drags me out, kicking and screaming.

Flipping me over, he presses the gun to my chin once more. "Time to go, Reign. Remember, I'm always here. This is going to hurt. A lot." My heart stops, and just when I think he's going to leave, he lowers the gun and presses it to my side.

There's a sudden sharp pain and my eyes widen.

No!

He shot me.

Shock slams through my body as he lays me back, tucks the gun away, and watches me for a second before whistling and strolling away. I blink up at the gray ceiling of the garage, my hands slipping by my side.

Why are they slipping?

Lifting my head takes great effort, but it allows me to see the blood covering my fingers. Blinking slowly, I cover my side, and agony surges through me.

Oh god, he shot me!

I'm going to die. Fuck, I can't die, not like this.

With shaking hands, I rip off my shirt as I hear yelled words and boots rushing my way. Gripping it in a ball, I press it to the wound and slump back. "We have her!" a voice calls as several bodies surround me. "Shit, she's shot. Get an ambulance!"

"Captain, we have eight bodies here, as well as the ten that were taken down by her other guards at the distraction point at her house. The door is swinging, in pursuit of the suspect," comes down the radio.

"Hold on, Reign," a soft female voice says from behind a mask. A hand grips mine, covering the wound. "Just hold on, they are on the way. Talk to me, okay?"

"Where are they? They should be here," I whisper. "Please, where are they?"

"Who, Reign?" she asks.

"Raff, Astro, Cil, Dal—" I cough. "Where are they? I want them." I feel tears sliding into my hair as agony takes over. "Where are they?

They promised to protect me," I whisper as my head rolls to the side, everything going fuzzy.

"No, don't you fucking dare. You stay with me, you hear? They are coming. Raff, Astro, Cil, and Dal are all coming, so you just hold the fuck on, Reign!"

It's too late.

I'm swallowed by the waiting darkness, their names on my lips.

FIFTY-EIGHT

A steady beep invades my unconscious brain, pulling me out of the darkness and into a numb, unresponsive body. It's harder than it should be to force my eyes open, and when I do, I have to blink to bring the room into focus. It's done in whites and cream, with some brown curtains pulled shut over a window.

Everything is soft and luxurious, but not even that can hide the hospital machines and charts.

Why am I in a hospital?

My mind is blank. I turn my head slowly with a wince, spying the closed brown door and the window with the blinds drawn. I try to call out, but my voice doesn't come. I cough, attempting to clear my throat. "Hello?" I croak.

I twitch my fingers, and with great effort, I manage to slide my hand over the bed. I find a buzzer and hit it. I wait, allowing myself to come to, and with each passing second, my body starts to come back online. I don't feel any pain or anything though.

Did I fall?

Did I hit my head?

The door opens, and a nurse and doctor rush in. "Miss Harrow." The doctor smiles. "You're awake."

"What happened?" I whisper.

The nurse hurries to my bedside and slowly adjusts the bed to sit me up. I'm still mostly lying down, but she lifts a glass with a straw and I sip, swallowing the water. She takes it away after a few. "Not too much, you'll make yourself sick."

"How are you feeling? I'm Dr. Ramos, your attending physician. If you need anything at all—"

"What happened?" I frown, glancing between them. "I don't understand why I'm here."

They share a look, and Dr. Ramos's smile turns sad. "Miss Harrow, you were shot."

What?

"Not to worry, though, because we removed the bullet, and you were lucky. It missed anything vital. It was just a bleeder . . ."

I watch his mouth move as my ears buzz. I was shot?

Everything comes back and I gasp.

The guards.

The masked man.

I try to sit up.

"Please, Miss Harrow." The nurse gently presses against my shoulder. "You need to rest; your body needs to heal. You are on some strong pain medication at the moment and you're safe, so just lie down."

"I'm not safe. Did the police catch him? The man?" I demand.

"Why don't you sleep, and we can talk after?" Dr. Ramos suggests.

"I can't sleep while he's out there." I frown as something hot runs through my arm. "Nurse?"

She's pressing something. "Sorry, sweetie, you're going to hurt yourself. You're safe, I promise. Now sleep, and when you wake up, we'll let the police in to talk to you."

"No, wait," I slur. "Please, I'm not safe—"

It doesn't matter.

The meds kick in, swallowing me again.

"Shh, you're going to wake her up, you idiot," comes a familiar, stern voice. "Damn it, Astro, turn off the TV."

"But it's the finale," he whines. "It's not like she's watching it."

"He's not wrong," I mumble, opening my eyes. There's chaotic movement, and I flinch when I realize there are four identical worried faces peering down at me. "Jesus, that's terrifying."

"She's talking to you." Cil nudges Raff, who smiles brightly, but there are shadows in his eyes.

"You're awake," he whispers.

"Yeah." I grab the bed rail and sit up. They instantly swarm me, fluffing my pillows and straightening my blankets before sitting on the chairs surrounding the bed. It's clear they have been here a while. I wonder how they got in, but nothing will stop them. "Don't let anyone lie to you, being shot sucks," I joke.

"It does." Dal nods. "Even more than stabbing."

I blink at that, unsure what to say. "Did they get the guy at least?" I scan their faces. "They didn't, did they?"

"No, he got away in the madness, but don't worry. We would have been there, Reign. You have to know that, but he tricked us. We thought you were at the house, and we were ambushed by ten very well paid mercs. It was a distraction, and by the time we got rid of them and tracked you, you were en route to the hospital. I dropped Raff Jr. at Emma's for the meantime. He's upset but okay," Raff explains.

They didn't abandon me. I should have known better, but not even they could have predicted what would happen.

"How can I not worry?" I grumble. "The guards . . . Are they . . ."

"They didn't make it, any of them, but they did their job," Raff replies.

"I need to make an announcement. I need to reach out to their families with my condolences and pay for the funerals—"

"Shh." Astro takes my hand. "That can wait. You need to rest. You've been through a lot, and healing is all about good energy."

"Not this shit again." Cillian groans, even as he grins at me.

Swallowing, I look at them, some of the pain coming back. When I was shot, I wanted them, and although my heart softens knowing they have been at my side protecting me, I'm still hurt. "Why are you here?"

They all flinch. "Why wouldn't we be here?" Dal retorts.

"I told you I didn't want to see you again."

"You were shot," Astro says sadly.

"That doesn't change—" I don't know why I'm arguing. I feel safer with them here, but my own damn pride won't let me admit it.

"We could have lost you," Raffiel snaps, and my mouth closes. "We needed to see that you were okay, Miss Harrow. We had to. Please don't make us leave just yet. I know you're mad—"

"Don't. I'm too tired to deal with this right now." I tug my hand from Astro's, worried I'm too comfortable. It's almost impossible to remember why I'm hurt, the drugs making me sleepy. "Just, please leave for now, okay? I just want to sleep."

"Reign," Cillian begins.

"Please," I demand, meeting each of their eyes. "I need some space. I'm tired." I close my eyes, sliding deeper into the bed. Looking at them hurts, but what scares me the most is how right it feels to have them here despite everything.

There's silence, and then Raff speaks. "Okay, Miss Harrow, we'll leave for now. We'll be close if you need us, just tell them to call." When I don't react, I feel him move closer before lips press to my head, making me jerk. "Sleep well, Reign, and trust us."

My eyes open as I watch them file out and the door shut.

What did he mean by that?

Turning my head away, I focus on the window where it's dark outside, running his words through my head. My first thought upon seeing them was joy. I felt safe. For a moment in that garage, I didn't think I would ever see them again. No matter what happened, I still love them, and the idea of never saying goodbye hurt.

I know they left, and I let time pass as I stare out of the window, running over everything, from the feeling of the gunshot to watching those guards die to my heartbreak.

Can I truly not let them in? Even after everything?

I hear a creak and sigh. "Please, Raff, I just want to be left alone." There's nothing but silence until something tugs on my arm. My head jerks to the side and I freeze.

A man in a doctor's coat stands next to me, his smiling brown eyes hidden behind thick-rimmed glasses. He looks smart and kind with a soft smile, but something makes me uneasy. "Who are you? Where is Dr. Ramos?" I demand. "Hey, what are you doing?" I try to move away as he pulls out a needle and sticks it in my arm.

"Don't worry, Reign, everything will be okay now. I told you I'd be here, didn't I?"

"What?" I slur as the room starts to spin. "What did you give me?"

"Just a sedative to keep you calm so you don't injure yourself further while I get you into the car. It's okay. I've got you now. I'll save you from them, then it will just be you and me."

"Wait, stop." I reach for the buzzer, but he pulls it away, tugging the bedding back and sliding me to the edge. My body is limp. I can't even seem to muster up the energy to scream as he tugs my gown down. Tears slip from my eyes but luckily, he carefully pulls on a sweater dress and tugs it down before kneeling and putting some shoes on me. I slump forward, and he catches me.

"Shh, I've got you. I know you were calling for help, calling for me, and I've got you now. You're safe. They'll never have you again. It will be us forever."

"You're crazy," I mumble.

"Don't be rude, Reign, not after everything I went through to get you here and for my plan to work. The idiots are out chasing my dummy leads right now, so it's just you and me. I'll keep you safe forever now. No more cameras or being forced to sing, no more Tucker or your backstabbing friends, no more bodyguards taking advantage of you."

"Why are you doing this?" I ask. I don't know how he understands my words, but he does.

"Because I love you." He frowns at me. "Just like I know you love me too. Don't you remember when we first met?"

I slump farther, and he catches me. "I'll remind you later, but for now, let's go." Lifting me into his arms, he carries me to the door and into the hallway, my head lolling as I call for help, but it's empty at this hour and the floor is private. Whimpering, I feel tears streaming down my face as he carefully positions me in a wheelchair.

"Don't cry, Reign. Everything will be okay now." Wiping away my tears, he starts to whistle as he wheels me down the corridor to the elevator. He strokes my hair as my head slumps to the side, the sedative taking full effect even as I try to fight it.

This is it.

I'll disappear forever.

I'll never see Beck again. I'll never get to watch movies with Astro, cuddle with Cillian, fight with Raff, or sing with Dal. I'll be trapped with this crazy bastard until he kills me.

They'll think I ran again.

The doors open and I blink, sure I'm seeing things. "Hi there." Astro grins, aiming a gun at the man behind me. "It took you long enough. I was starting to get bored."

There is a click, and when my head lolls farther back, I see Dal behind the man, holding a gun to his head. "It really did take you too long to take the bait," Raff remarks as he and Cillian circle us. He has the nerve to wink at me.

Wink!

"You really aren't as smart as you think," Cillian comments.

"She's mine," the man hisses. "Mine! Fine, arrest me, but I'll still come for her—"

"There seems to be some misunderstanding. We aren't cops, so we don't care about laws, only her. You won't get the chance to hurt her again." Raff raises his gun, and I jerk as the shot rings out. The wheelchair slides forward and spins so I can see the man fall.

There's a bullet hole in his head.

Dal steps up to him and fires two more into his chest before grinning at me. "We have to be sure."

"Don't worry, you were always safe," Cillian promises. "Now let's get you back to bed. I'm guessing the drug is kicking in. Fucking moron couldn't even get her without sedatives."

I open my mouth, but nothing comes out. Raff crouches at my side, covering me with his suit jacket. "Sleep, Reign. We've got you."

FIFTY-NINE

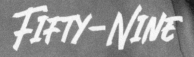

We refuse to leave Reign's side, even for questioning, so they do it in her room. We've earned some goodwill since we saved the hospital from a major lawsuit if Reign was kidnapped on their time—not to mention the cops who were supposed to be outside of her room but took a break.

There is also our history. After a few phone calls, the body disappeared, so they have nothing they can hold us on.

My eyes cut to her once more, so small and frail in the bed as she sleeps off the sedative. She is going to be pissed when she wakes up, and my lips curve at the thought.

"Once more please."

I arch my brow at the cop, and he clears his throat. "Just once more please."

"We followed the leads and found out who her stalker was. It was only a matter of time until he acted. Unfortunately, we found it too late, thinking the attack was at her house. When she was shot and brought to the hospital, we found it suspicious. There was no way he would shoot her unless he meant to. We figured it was his plan—get her alone and isolated, thinking she's safe, and abduct her. We found traces of sedatives at his house, along with a badge for this hospital. Then, we simply bided our time." I cut out the parts where we illegally hacked the systems and went to the morgue.

I'm sure management will spin this in their favor at some point, but I don't care. She's safe, she's alive, and now we can work on healing her body and heart. We aren't letting her go; we never were. We just needed him to think we had so he would act.

"We searched his place as well. It's obvious he has been stalking Miss Harrow for some time. We even found this." He hands over a photo, which was obviously taken off a camera. In it, the man smiles widely and stares adoringly at Reign, who is smiling into the camera, and behind her are more fans who are all lined up. It looks like a meet and greet. "Our detectives think she showed him some kindness and the obsession started from there. He warped his life to match hers and made it seem like she was something to him. We also found tickets for a boat. He was planning to take her far away. You saved her life. I think you need a promotion or a pay raise," the man says.

"Her safety is all I need," I murmur as I stand. "Thank you, officer."

"Um, of course." He hurries to his feet, knowing he's being dismissed. "My sergeant will want to speak to her when she's feeling better. We can come to her, of course, but until then, if there's anything else, anything at all, don't hesitate to call us." He hands over a private number, and I nod.

Astro escorts him out and blocks the door.

There are fans and cameras lining up outside, and the news stations are covering this around the clock, so much so we yanked out the plug for the TV. Reign is resting, and that's all they need to know.

Moving to the bed, I take her hand and kiss the back of it.

"Come back to us, baby. We're waiting."

We were right. Her management spins it as their plan, from firing us to the public scene outside her house to us rescuing her. We don't care, since it doesn't matter to us who gets credit. They can call us heroes, but all I care about is being her hero.

Shaking my head, I turn off the TV once more. Reign is still sleeping hours later. The doctors think she had a stronger reaction to the sedatives because of her wound and the meds she was on.

When her eyelids flutter, I almost jump for joy.

Her eyes open as she groans. She struggles to sit up, so I catch her and sit her up slowly. I don't wake the others who are finally sleeping. It's been days since they got any rest.

"He's here—"

"Shh, you're okay. Calm down. Breathe for me," I tell her.

I place her hand on my chest, forcing her to feel my breaths until she slows her breathing to match mine. "That's it. You're safe. He's dead, Reign. He can't hurt you anymore. You're safe. Say it with me."

"I'm safe," she whispers. Despite her volume, the others wake up.

They surround her, speaking too quickly for her to keep up, and I can tell it's overwhelming her. "Give her a second," I demand, and they fall silent. "Are you okay?"

"I . . . Fuck, I don't even know what to say except thank you." She looks at us. "For not leaving, for being here, for saving me . . . I don't know what he would have done to me had you—"

"Shh, don't think of that." I squeeze her hand.

Nodding, she looks down, and I don't like the silence.

"Reign?"

"I'm grateful . . ." She trails off, and when she lifts her head, there are tears in her eyes. "But overwhelmed. I think I need you to leave." I can't help the reaction I have to that, and she swallows hard, looking at us. "Just for now."

"Reign," Astro says.

"Reign, look—" I start.

"Please, Raff, so much has happened. I'm grateful you stayed and that you saved me, but I need to process. Just give me some time, okay? I'm not saying forever. I'm just saying for now."

I hate that.

The last thing I want is time away from her. I almost lost her once.

I can't lose her again, but I nod, knowing if I push this, I could lose her forever.

She looks like a cornered animal.

She feels trapped.

The last thing I want is for her to bolt, but as we gather our stuff and I watch her carefully, I have a feeling that's exactly what she plans to do.

"Okay, just for a little bit, but we aren't going anywhere, Reign, and you will hear us out. This isn't over, Miss Harrow. You are ours, don't ever forget that."

SIXTY

I can't face the cameras, questions, and people. I can't do it. I can't even turn my phone back on after it blew up the first time I did.

What do I do? I do what any coward does. I run. I discharge myself with their advice and medication and I manage to arrange a car to pick me up around back, thanks to the hospital who clearly wants to avoid any bad press. Once home, I pack a bag, and then I'm on the road before anyone even realizes I've been here.

I leave the city lights and all the trouble behind.

I never should have come back, but then I wouldn't have met them and I wouldn't have fallen in love.

I wouldn't have found my sound again.

Right now, my regret mixes with my hope, and it's too much for me to handle.

I hit a familiar road, one I took all those months ago, and like then, my heart is broken, so I escape to the same place I did before.

I need to figure out what I'm going to do next.

Is this the end of Reign Harrow, or just the beginning?

I settle in for the two-day drive, planning to drive right through, racing from my worries and my heart, from them, not knowing if we can ever be together again.

"I wondered when I would see you again." The familiar southern drawl settles all my nerves and I collapse in my seat.

The two-day drive was long. I parked in my car and kept my face hidden. The gunshot wound hurts, but I've had worse in my past, and I keep it clean and dressed and take the medication, so that's all that matters.

My eyes are drawn to the view around us, making the last few days all worthwhile.

My seat faces the dock and water, and I look out at the view that healed me. This place brought me back to life and gave me reason to fight. Turning my head, I meet the blue eyes of the woman who gave me this place.

Vinette.

Wrinkles crowd her smiling eyes, her tiny eyebrows gray in her age. Her lips are tilted in a crooked smile, and her gray hair is curled back away from her face. She wears a perfectly pressed sundress, her body both lithe and muscular even now.

One look and I want to cry and laugh. "You knew I'd come back?"

"I'm not a fool, Reign Harrow."

My eyes widen. The whole time I was here before, she never once called me by my full name. I never even told her what it was. I liked being anonymous here. I liked being just Reign.

She grins like she knows my thoughts. "I always knew who you were, child, even then. I have a TV." She winks.

"Then why . . . ," I whisper.

"Everyone comes here for a reason," she murmurs. "Me included. I had a feeling there was a reason you ran to this tiny town, so I left you alone." She looks at me sadly. "Are you okay?"

"No, not one fucking bit," I admit, my lip trembling as tears form in my eyes. I stare back out at the water, gripping the arm of the chair.

Nothing has changed here. Not the tiny road signs, the dirt roads, or the way the water touches the sky as if kissing it.

It makes my heart unravel and the tears fall.

As usual, Vinette lets me work through my thoughts, never pushing. I rented the cabin, which is behind us, when I first ran away. Something about this town called to me when I drove through it—call it fate or just an empty gas tank, but I stayed a night. That night turned into two, then three. Something here made me relax, and then one morning, I saw Vinette out here, enjoying the sun in the space between the cabins, and I just sat down. The one I rented used to be her daughter's.

We didn't speak for a week. We just enjoyed the peace together.

When we did, though, she always saw the truth and had a way to help me deal with my thoughts and feelings. I came for the peace, but I stayed for her wisdom and friendship—one that didn't ask for anything, that didn't need anything, that just gave.

"I thought I was so strong," I say, and as usual, the words pour out. When I glance at her, I try to blink away the tears. "I thought I was so fucking strong, but I feel so weak. I fell in love, Vinette. I fell in love so hard and they were perfect, everything I'm not. I thought I could be what they needed, and that I wouldn't need to depend on them, but all my bravado and talk, the great rock princess, Reign Harrow . . ." My gaze returns to the water. It's so calm, unlike the raging in my heart. "And I'm still the scared little girl hiding in the dark from her father, unable to protect my little brother."

"Reign—"

"I couldn't even keep myself safe. I couldn't even fight back when he came for me. They had to save me time and time again and I let them. I let them hurt me and lie to me because I was so desperate to be fucking loved, to feel safe and protected because I'm so fucking weak."

"Have you finished?"

I snap my mouth shut and glance at her.

"No offense, Reign, but that's bullshit."

My mouth drops open. It's the first swear word I've ever heard her use. "What?" I stutter.

"You heard me, child. It's bullshit. Everyone needs someone sometime. No one is ever as strong as they pretend to be. Everyone fears something. You are so much more than that scared little girl." Taking my hand, she squeezes it. "It wasn't your job to save your brother, Reign, and it wasn't your fault he died. You need to forgive yourself, child, because we both know he does. You were a kid, Reign."

I bite my lip, tears rolling down my cheeks.

"And you grew up into an amazing woman. A kind one. One who brought me breakfast every morning, who helped me make sweet tea because she knew it was my absolute favorite. Who helped Ned from down the road fix up his roof because his back hurt without complaint. It's not great public acts that make us, Reign, but the small ones. They show who we are, especially when your life isn't in front of a camera. I know you. You are a brilliant woman. You're smart, talented, beautiful, kind, loving, and yes, you've been hurt. You let it harden you, but you were growing and learning. Don't ever call yourself weak again. It is not weak to retreat. It takes great strength to acknowledge you're struggling and pull back to deal with it. Reign Harrow, this world is a complicated place, and as for love, there is nothing more complicated than that, but I'm betting those men never once cared that you leaned on them. I'm betting they loved it because they love you. How could they not? It's time, Reign."

"Time?" I mumble.

"The birds still sing, Reign, the sun still rises, and the world still turns. Everything moves on, and yesterday is forgotten, so why can't you forget? Move on, Reign. It's time. You left that little house and the bodies behind a long time ago, but it's time to get up now and walk out that door. It's time to forgive yourself." She pats my hand. "Stop making excuses about why things won't work and stop running at the first sign of trouble to protect yourself. Everything else will fall into place. Our place in this world isn't always what we thought it would be, but from the happiness I saw on my screen, I would say you found yours. Fight for it, whatever that entails."

"I don't know if I can," I admit, looking back at the water. "It would be easier just to disappear and forget."

"It would," she concedes. "But that's the coward's way out and you are not a coward. Not like me."

"Vinette." I frown, looking at her.

"I never told you my story, Reign, but I think it's time." She settles back, her eyes on the water and a sad smile on her lips. "My true name is Vinette Wilson." The name is familiar, but I don't know why. "I was a ballerina, one of the best in the world for a great many years. It seems like a lifetime ago. I never thought I could love anything as much as I loved dancing. Being on that stage brought me to life. It wasn't about the applause or the money or the skills. I felt free when I danced across that stage."

"Vin, I had no idea," I whisper.

"Many don't. I buried that life a very long time ago. It was better to let go than to let it rot me from the inside out, but even now, a part of me yearns for that stage. Don't let it do that to you, Reign. Time isn't always kind, but I'm getting ahead of myself. The night before my big performance, one that would have put me in the history books, I was attacked by someone I knew. He was the stage director. I knew he wanted me, I had even flirted to get what I wanted, but that night, something broke inside me. When it was over, I just lay there, like a broken marionette, as he left and told me to warm up for my performance tomorrow. I didn't tell anyone. I didn't report it. I should have, but I was a coward, Reign. I ran, and I didn't stop running for a very long time, not until I got here and saw that old cabin. I made it my home, and then I found out I was pregnant.

"My daughter was born from his attack. I hated her at first. I wanted to get rid of her, but the first time I heard her cry, I knew the truth. She was all mine, and it was my duty to protect her at all costs. No matter the path that brought her to me, I could choose my future, and I did. It wasn't what everyone else would have chosen, but it was mine and it was a happy one. I always regretted never telling anyone, though, never standing up. I always regretted never going back and showing my daughter how to stand up for herself. I cut off my old life but it never left me, and neither did my love for performing. Something like that . . . we are born with it, Reign. We are born to do it. No matter what happens, you have to be true to yourself. I wasn't for a very long time. It was only when I lost my daughter to cancer ten years back that I started to realize how cowardly I'd been. I hid from my gift, my passion, and my past. I don't want you to grow old and be regretful of what you could have had. I don't. Trust me, it's not nice. I wouldn't wish it on anyone. I can't change my life, and I wouldn't because I got to love so deeply it will never leave me, but I can't let you run from yours like I did mine. Shit happens, Reign, horrible fucking shit, but it's how we deal with it that makes us who we are. I'm not saying don't cry and not to be angry at the world, but don't give up on it."

"Vin," I sob, my heart breaking for the woman who became my rock without ever letting her own cracks show.

"Look." I follow her gaze to the birds on the water. "They know they could be attacked, yet they still flock to the water. We are those birds, Reign. Do we flock and soar high in victory, or do we fall and sink to the bottom? That's our choice in life. We make it what it is. I made my place, and now it's time you make yours. You're always welcome here, but I don't want your sad eyes here again. I want those happy ones on my screen. I want to watch you shine—maybe because I'm a selfish old lady who wants to see a woman succeed when no one else thought she could. What I'm trying to say, Reign, is live so big you scar this world with your brilliance. Love so hard that at the end, you're not scared. Don't go meekly into the dark. Fight it with everything within you. I know you can, if you are brave enough to forgive and to . . ."

"Move on," I whisper.

"Move on." She nods, glancing over at me with a smile. "Now, I'm betting those four men who have been watching us for a long time are the ones you love, no?"

I turn and find them waiting before the cabin, protecting me. Part of me knew they would follow me. Deep down, I knew they wouldn't let me go. Did I test them by bringing them here?

Is Vin right? Am I finding excuses to sabotage my own happiness by thinking I don't deserve it because of my past?

"Yes," I croak as I stare at them.

"It's your choice, Reign. Stay and live with regrets or forgive and move on."

I look at her, searching her gaze. "I'm so sorry for what happened to you, Vin, but you are not a coward. You had the strength to bear a child born from hate and destruction and love it so much that even now, I see her with you. You are not a coward, Vinette. You are a strong, brilliant woman who took a lost woman and gave her a shoulder when no one else would, and I will never forget what you did for me." Standing, I smile down at her, and she kisses my hand and pushes me.

My decision is made, one I already made deep down.

I will forgive them and stop running.

Everyone makes mistakes, and I know the one they made was out of loyalty for me, and maybe if I hear them out, we might just have a chance at something brilliant—something I'm unable to live without.

"Go, Reign. Be brilliant. Be what you were born to be."

I smile as I turn to them, and it only grows.

Walking around the chairs, I head toward them.

Even now, I see the hope in their eyes, hope I'll come home to them.

For a second, I'm brought back to the moment I first met them, knowing even then they would change my world. I wasn't wrong, and I thank a god I don't believe in for that.

For them.

We can solve anything if we are together, and I'm very tired of running. Vin is right, it is my choice, and I choose them.

I start to run, needing to get there quicker, and the smiles that break out across their faces only make me move faster. They meet me half-way, wrapping their arms around me.

"I missed you," I admit. "I forgive you, and I missed you."

"We missed you too," Raff replies, pulling away. "I love you, Miss Harrow, and know this. Listen carefully. We'll never hide anything from you again. I promise we did it to protect you. We want the best for you. I'm not saying we won't make mistakes, but I swear if you give us a chance, we'll never let you be alone again."

Some might say I gave in too easily, but if a man is willing to kill another to keep me safe, then I would be a fool not to forgive them. We're new at this, but I have no doubt that what he said was true.

They kept a secret, which was wrong, but they did it with good intentions.

It's time to let go of the past.

It's time to start fresh.

Life is too fucking short not to.

"I love you too." I kiss Raff deeply and turn to Astro. "And I love you." I kiss him, wiping away his tears as I turn to Cillian. "I love you." I kiss him before turning to Dal. "I love you, my beautifully flawed protector." I kiss him deeply. I let them hold me, my voice soft. "We need to talk and discuss what happened, but I'm all in if you'll have me. You made mistakes and so did I. I shouldn't have shut down, shouldn't have run away just because it was easier. I should have fought."

"It doesn't matter now. All that matters is that we are together," Astro says, staring into my eyes, and just like that, I forgive them.

Humans are flawed beings, but holding onto the hurt will only make me bitter and lonely. I have a chance at a love so deep, it will scar my world, and this, like Vin mentioned, is worth fighting for no matter what.

"You are our life," Cillian says, squeezing my hand.

"Our reason for living," Dal adds.

"I don't plan on changing though," I start, needing them to know. "I'll still be a pain in the ass."

Astro smirks. "Our pain."

"Baby, we never wanted you to change. We love you for who you are," Raff promises.

"Okay then." I snuggle back into their arms, where I should have been all along.

Sometimes things need to break apart to come back together, and when they do, their flaws are what make them shine with beauty. Those imperfections make them unique, one of a kind.

Just like our love.

I vow in that moment to never hold myself back from them again. I'll tell them I love them every day, and I won't be scared of it anymore because I know wherever I go, they will follow.

I let them hold me as the sun shines down on us, and when I pull back, I'm crying and grinning. "Take me home?"

"Anything you ask, Miss Harrow."

SIXTY-ONE

It will take us a few days to get home, not that we are in any rush. We use the time with Reign, without anyone else prying, to heal together. For the first night, we stay in a rural hotel on a lake with hardly anyone around, and as I approach the firepit they sit around, my eyes are drawn to my girl. She has on one of our oversized sweaters and her leggings, but she looks so beautiful that I just stare for a moment.

Reign loves deeply, and I know we are damn lucky she forgave us.

Finding my seat at her back, I hold her in my arms as the others joke and laugh. This is the happiest they have been since she walked out of that boardroom. I know we still have a lot to talk about and work through, but that will come in time.

For now, this is all I need.

Our job as her bodyguards might be over, but as her lovers, we will be at her side until death calls us home. Where Reign Harrow goes, we go.

A few hours later, I lift her into my arms. "It's late, and you need rest."

The others quickly agree, and we work as a team to get the room organized. We sweep it for bugs and cameras and then push the beds together. Once she's showered, I clean and redress her wound for her and give her medication before she crawls into the middle of the bed. I turn off the lights, and we all pile in around her, protecting our heart.

It isn't long before snores fill the air, and I move closer.

I hold her in the dark while the others sleep, watching her lashes crest over her cheeks as she sighs. "Thank you for forgiving us. We'll never hurt you again."

"You better not," she whispers with a wicked grin, and I smile.

"There's my girl."

"Raff," she whispers later.

"Yes, Miss Harrow?"

"What happens now?"

"Whatever you want. It's your life. We are just along for the ride," I promise.

"You'll stay?"

"Like you could ever get rid of us." I almost snort. "We didn't need this job, Reign. We took it because some deep part of us knew it was important. I never could have guessed how much, but it's time to settle down at your side, where we belong."

"Okay." She grins, her eyes fluttering open. "Because I still have a whole lot of trouble I want to get into."

"Oh, I have no doubt about that, my little anarchist." I kiss her lips, savoring every moment. "Good night, Miss Harrow."

"Night, Raffy."

---

cillian

Reign is tired, but she refuses to rest when we get home. The only way I can get her to relax is to lie next to her on the daybed out back, trapping her in my arms. A lot has happened over the last few weeks, so I let her lapse into silence, just happy she's back in my arms where she belongs. I know Raff has hurried away to pick up our fur baby, knowing she needs him right now. Plus, he belongs here, in our home. With us.

"If you want to talk about what happened," I begin. She went through a traumatic experience. We are used to it, but she isn't.

"I'm okay." She snuggles closer, but she must feel my questioning glance because she sighs. "Really, I am. I always felt like I was waiting for something bad to happen, but now that it finally has, I'm relieved. I can get on with my life, and that's all I want. For now, I just want to be happy. Can we?"

"Of course." I bend my legs, getting settled, and my shorts ride up.

"What's that?" She pushes my shorts up and gasps as I grin.

The new tattoo is still healing, but her lyrics are easy to pick out. "Cillian." She stares at me.

"We are forever, Reign Harrow, and I wanted the moment you realized you loved me on my skin for just as long." Her eyes widen, and I chuckle. "I might not be a lyrical genius, but I know a love confession when I read one."

Giggling, she traces it with her fingers as she leans into my side. "I never thought we'd be here again. I thought it was over." She lifts her head as my heart clenches. "Even when I was hurt and angry, I missed you. I missed you so much, it made it hurt more."

Kissing her head, I hold her tighter. "You will never miss us again. We aren't going anywhere, and we'll earn your forgiveness every day for the rest of our lives."

"Deal," she whispers as I kiss her head.

"And my skin is your notepad anytime. Cover me in your lyrics, Reign, like my heart is covered in you."

SIXTY-TWO

One week later . . .

Reign is having nightmares. It's why we are standing in an opulent office downtown. She has spoken to us about what happened, but I suggested she talk to someone else as well. I hate that I can't fight her demons in her sleep, and I want to help in any way I can, so when she suggested we come together to face our demons as a team, I could do nothing but agree.

Apart from her nightmares, Reign is doing good. She's healing well with a private doctor, who checks on her every day. We wait on her hand and foot and spend time together, making up for lost time.

She speaks to Beck and Jack almost every day. Even Winchester comes by, and they get on as if they have known each other for years. Her management isn't happy we're back, but Reign put her foot down in a way that had us all jerking off in the shower—she basically called us hers and told them to get over it.

With the way the press is eating up her story and desperate for any image of her, they have chosen to give her whatever she wants. Plus, it means free security, and they can't argue with that, even if we answer to her and not them.

"Please sit." Dr. Wright, or Andie, as he told us to call him, gestures to a couch.

It's a hard habit to break, but I sit down for her, letting her take my hand.

"This must be a little weird, huh? Two people with different traumas." Reign grins shyly.

"It is a little unusual doing a session like this," he admits with a friendly grin.

"Well, we have never been normal." She giggles, the sound making my heart fly. I felt nothing until I met her, and then I felt too much, but now I wouldn't change these feelings for anything, even the pain that comes with it, because they are hers, just like me.

If she wants me to bare my soul to this man, then I will because I will do anything to make her feel better, and if he crosses us, I'll simply cut out his heart.

"Why don't you tell me what brought you in today?" he begins.

I look at Reign and smile. "Love," I admit. "Love brought me here."

---

astro

"Ma, I know, please stop," I beg as she rants down the phone.

Raff Jr.'s barking makes me grin as I glance outside to see him chasing Dal around happily, filling the house with joy and life.

"So help me, boy. You lock that shit down before she gets away again, I mean it. Oh, and make sure to eat properly. You looked skinny in that picture they captured yesterday at the beach."

Chuckling, I lean against the kitchen counter, snacking on strawberries. "Will do, love you."

"Love you too. Tell the boys and Reign that I said hi." She hangs up.

Reign strolls in like I summoned her. "Hey, hot stuff."

"Hi." I peer at her as she steals a strawberry, and since I have the opportunity, I tug out the box I carry around everywhere with me.

I slide it across the counter, and Reign tilts her head. She picks it up as she swallows. "What's this?"

Her voice trails off as she opens it and sees the emerald ring inside.

I put it in a new strawberry-shaped box, but it's the same ring. "I know you're not ready for this yet, but I need you to have it. When you are ready, you can put it on."

"Astro," she whispers, staring at the ring.

"Reign, I have been in love with you since the first moment I laid eyes on you. Ring or no ring, you're mine and I am yours. Don't feel pressured—" I gape when she takes the ring out and slides it on her finger.

"I guess I should get you guys one." She winks as she kisses me. "Oh, and tell your mom hi back."

"You . . . I . . . You . . ." I stop sputtering as a wide grin takes over. Gripping her tight, I drag her into a deep kiss, careful of her wound. "Oh, Reign Harrow, I'm going to love you to death."

"You better." She smirks. "Now how about we pull that prank on Cil—"

I stare at her, watching her mouth move but hearing nothing. I can't help the flutter in my heart or the tears in my eyes. She is so goddamn beautiful, but it's more than that. It's in her heart, her soul.

Reign Harrow is someone this world needs, and she is also someone I need. She took a broken joker boy and loved him when nobody could.

"Well, what do you think?" she asks, and I realize I've just been staring at her.

"Whatever you say, babe," I croak, and she grins.

"Come on." She holds out her hand, and I lay mine in hers, letting her lead me anywhere.

I'd follow Reign Harrow to the ends of the earth and beyond.

SIXTY-THREE

I take several weeks to rest, and the guys drive me crazy. They never leave me alone, and at the end of my break, I'm ready to face the music—literally.

They moved back into my house like they were made to be there, and they were. This time, there are no contracts. They aren't here as my bodyguards, but I don't think I'll ever get rid of them in that aspect. They are here as my boyfriends, and nobody gets to judge or know.

My life is my own, so screw what anyone else thinks.

Swallowing hard, I face the closed door of the press room. They aren't here to tear me apart, but to put me back together. It seems in my absence, the truth about my attack came out and it only made my reputation that much more infamous, but it's time for the truth to come from my lips.

A hand touches my back, and I glance up with a smile. "Are you ready, my love?" Astro murmurs.

"Ready." I nod as Raffiel opens the door. Dal and Cillian are already waiting, and each take a hand and help me onto the small stage with the table and mics. They even pull out my chair, making the crowd laugh before they stand by my side.

They never let me leave their sight.

Clearing my throat, I hide my shaking hands and smile brightly. "Hi, everyone, thank you so much for coming out. I won't be taking any questions, but I have a statement to read. I hope that's okay." Sitting up taller, I gaze out over the room that would have previously paralyzed me with fear—fear of what they might say—but let them say what they will.

I know the truth.

Those who love me also know the truth, and that's all that matters.

"As I'm sure you all know by now, I was attacked. A man opened fire on me and my heroic guards, who sadly lost their lives." I choke on their names as I list them and have to take a deep breath before I continue.

"Those are the names of those who lost their lives in regard to the attack, not the assailant. We will not immortalize him. I survived, but at the hospital, the man found me once more—a man, I have learned, that was stalking me for a very long time, who has broken into my house and terrorized me for a little over a year. The only reason I am here today is because of the four men standing at my side. They saved my life." I take a deep breath. "I'm healing, and I have no plans to run away again," I tease, making them laugh. "This is my life, and it felt important to share the truth. This happens to women across the world all the time. I want them to know they are not alone. No one should live with a stalker. So, for everyone asking, no, he did not kill Reign Harrow. He did not stop me. He only made me more determined to be who I am. For all of those people watching right now with dreams in their hearts, a wonderful woman recently told me to forgive myself and to shine brightly, and that's what I plan to do.

With her permission, I begin to speak.

"I won't let an insane man, whose name I won't ever voice, dull that. I am alive, my scars will heal, and I have learned just what I'm capable of, so instead of talking about him, let's talk about something much more important—my album," I joke, and others laugh. "No, let's talk about the Vinette Wilson Fund." I glance at Raff who nods. They helped me start this. "Vinette Wilson was a ballerina when I was a child, and one night, she was attacked in a place where she was supposed to be safe, so for every silenced woman out there, for those still suffering days or years after an attack, I'm starting this fund. It's a safe haven, without questions or judgment, just survivors and understanding. If it's been a day, a year, or fifty, anyone is welcome to come and share their story, if they wish, or just find some peace like she offered me. Please keep the men who saved my life and their families in your thoughts and prayers and give them the privacy they need to grieve what has been lost. Thank you."

I wave as I walk off stage, my men with me.

The press might never know who they truly are to me, but that doesn't matter to me or them.

We know what we have, and I'll protect that until the end.

My very own family.

"Where are we going?" Vin grumbles. "I can't believe you kidnapped me. You told me we were going to dinner, and that was over three hundred miles ago."

"Shh." I tug her after me. "Breathe, Vin, remember to breathe." I pull her blindfold up, keeping her hand in mine as I move to the side. She gasps. "The original stage burned down with the building, but it has been rebuilt." I glance at her as she stares out at the empty seats of the theater she was meant to perform in all those years ago. Vin gave me my dream back, and I want to give her hers. "I want you to reclaim your legacy on it—not for a crowd or for him, but for you. One last dance, Vinette Wilson, and I would be honored to be your audience. I don't want you to have any regrets, not even at the end."

"I don't think I can do it," she whispers. "I'm not that girl anymore. I'm a weak old lady—"

"You are a wise woman. Close your eyes, Vin, and feel the music. Take yourself back and give into that passion one last time. Follow your dream." The guys start the music for me when I step back, and I cover my heart as I wait.

She turns to me, her eyes red, but when the music flows, I see the years melt away. She's unsure at first, but she closes her eyes and feels it, and slowly, her hand starts to move. I cover my mouth, watching as she lets go.

She moves gracefully across the stage, twirling and dancing, but it isn't the beauty in her dance that makes me grin widely—it's the smile of pure happiness that curves her lips.

It's the smile of a dreamer.

Taking my guitar from Dal, I sit and start to sing as the music slows. She stumbles and whirls to face me, but I just grin, and when there's a break in the lyrics I wrote, I nod and continue singing.

She's unsure, but this song's just for her.

It's slow and filled with love, heartache, pain, joy, and regrets, and there are ups and downs, just like with life. It's Vin's song and always will be.

When it's over, she meets my eyes, grinning from ear to ear. "Thank you," she mouths.

"Thank you, Vin. Now take a bow," I reply, and when she turns around, she bows with a laugh. My guys and Beck clap and whistle for her. Flowers rain from above as she laughs and bows, and I can't help but feel so full, I might burst.

I wanted to track down the man who attacked her, I wanted justice, but the truth is, that was my selfish wants. She never wanted that. All she ever wanted was to finish her dance and say goodbye to her dream.

Vin never wanted revenge, just a second chance, and I can understand that.

Under the falling petals, she has just that, and I'm right there with her.

SIXTY-FOUR

Three weeks later . . .

I am officially cleared by the doctor. I didn't tell them that was the reason I went for the checkup or why they had to wait outside, but it puts my plans in motion as we head home. As we drive, they innocently plan tonight's meal and choose a movie like we have every evening while I've been healing.

Once in my room, I put my necklace back on, one I never should have taken off. My fingers slide over the cool metal before dropping to the cheap bracelet I couldn't bear to part with.

"You know it has a tracker in it, right? That's how we found you." I jerk around at Cil's teasing voice, even as my mouth drops. "Raff added it one night while you were sleeping. Don't tell him, he thinks he's slick like that."

"I should have known." I chuckle. Rather than feeling controlled or held back by that, it makes me feel loved and protected. Without it, they never would have found me. Who knows what could have happened then?

They saved me in more than one way.

His arms wrap around me as I hold the necklace and turn my eyes to the city beyond. I have answered so many questions and taken part in so many interviews since the incident, but I refuse to give them any information on my private life. Some are speculating that I'm dating someone, but the truth is, they don't get to know.

These men are mine, and I plan to keep them that way.

I know who is important now, who I need, and it's these four men I love and the true friends I've made. Beck, who often stands up for me in interviews, has become my biggest supporter, and she wants to bring down the patriarchy together.

In time, we will, but right now, rather than fucking over the men in my life, I want to fuck them.

It's been too long since I've had them inside me. I miss it, but more than that, I need it with a ferocious desperation that borders on obsession.

Grinning evilly, I kiss Cil's arm and slide from his embrace. "Let's go for a swim. I'll get changed and meet you down there."

"Sounds good. Swimming will be good exercise." He kisses my cheek on the way out. "I'll tell the others."

I hurry as I shed my clothes, leaving nothing but the necklace and bracelet on before redressing. I blow a kiss into the mirror and turn to leave to find my bodyguards.

They are already in the pool when I make it downstairs, and I don't stop until I stand at the edge where they stood all those months ago. They smile at me, their eyes filled with love as they wait for me.

"Hey, Miss Harrow, do you want to play?" Astro calls teasingly.

"With you? Oh, I want to play alright," I purr, and I watch their eyes darken as the sun kisses their bodies.

"Let's start our forever the same way we started, shall we?" I open the robe and let it drop to the ground.

I'm naked, just like the day they met me, and I dive into the pool, knowing they will follow me.

I come up and slick my hair back as they swim to me. Raff reaches me first, tugging me into his arms. Desire ignites in his eyes even as he resists it.

"Miss Harrow," Raff warns, but I cut him off, kissing him quickly.

"The doctor said I'm fine, so fuck me, Raff. Remind me whom I belong to while everyone else clambers to own me. Remind me who is mine while everyone fights for it." I pull away with a smirk. "Fuck me here, where we met, like we all know you wished to that day."

"Reign." Dal reaches for me, and I swim backwards with a grin.

"I'm an artist." I smirk. "So inspire me."

"Softly." Raff finally caves. "No matter what that doctor says, we won't hurt you, but we'll never leave you wanting. We are here to cater to your every need."

Astro dives under the water, coming up before me, and his lips press to mine. I taste chlorine and sweetness, which is all him. A body presses to my back, and I turn my head, kissing them blindly.

He tastes dark and smoky, so I know it's Dal, his brutal kiss leaving me breathless as their hands slide over my body. Astro dunks under the surface, and I feel his lips press to the scar of the bullet wound.

They said they could eventually fix it with plastic surgery, but I told them to leave it. It's a reminder for me.

Feeling Astro kiss it so sweetly brings tears to my eyes, but then I gasp as he presses one between my legs and resurfaces, tipping me back. Dal catches me as my legs spread on either side of Astro, then more hands join, holding me up for them to feast on.

Cil and Raff lower their heads, and Raff swoops in to kiss me hard while Cil kisses along my chest until his tongue lashes my nipple. I groan into Raff's mouth as Astro's lips slide up my legs, tasting the water before he kisses my pussy.

I jerk from how sudden it is, the sun and my desire overheating me as I lift my hips for more.

"Relax, Miss Harrow, we have you," Raff says as Dal tips my head back and kisses me, and Raff slides down, wrapping his lips around my other nipple.

The juxtaposition has me groaning, and when Astro's tongue thrusts inside me, I hand myself over to the pleasure they provide.

Every inch of my body is touched and tasted.

Astro's tongue fucks me, thrusting in and out, while Raff and Cil suck on my aching nipples and Dal kisses and bites my throat. It's been too long. I come so quickly, Raff chuckles.

"I love how much you need us," he growls, kissing over my racing heart as Astro licks up my release before dropping my legs. Dal catches them and rubs his huge cock against my ass.

Cil moves before me, holding my legs open for them.

Dal slides me against his hard cock before pressing inside me, pulling out as Cil thrusts in. They fuck me together, softly but determinedly, their hands holding me still so I can't hurt myself.

There, under the sun, before the city filled with cameras and nosy assholes, they make love to me while my others watch on protectively.

I kiss Cil and then Dal as they fuck me until I come again, dragging them with me. Cil fills my cunt while Dal splashes over my pussy and thighs.

Pulling me from their arms, Raff spreads me across the pool's steps, the water lapping at my side and back as he moves between my spread thighs. He drags his cock over my messy pussy and kisses me as he slams into me.

I cry out loudly, uncaring who hears.

"Astro, take her mouth and keep her quiet," Raff orders, and my head is turned as Astro forces his cock deep into my mouth. I swallow around his length as they slowly fuck me.

My back arches, and my hips lift to meet his thrusts as he bends and kisses the bullet wound.

Astro's thrusts speed up, and I know he's close. Raff notices, and he tilts my hips, hitting that spot that has me seeing stars. When Astro groans, spilling down my throat and over my lips, I splinter once more, dragging Raffiel with me.

He roars my name as he fills me, burying himself deep as he comes.

When I come to, my heart is pounding and I have to force my eyes open as I relax back into the water.

"I knew the moment I laid eyes on you that you would be mine, Miss Harrow. Sorry it took so long for my heart to catch up," Raffiel whispers.

"I'm not." I smile, reaching for them. "That day changed my life. No matter what brought us together, I'm thankful for it. My life has never been so perfect, and I can't wait to spend the rest of our lives together."

Wherever I go in this world, I know they will be with me.

My bodyguards, my loves.

After all, I'm their rock star.

"You are too right." Cil smirks, making me realize I said that out loud. "And long may she fucking reign."

SIXTY-FIVE

Two months later . . .

It's album release day and everyone I love is here—Astro's mom and dad, his sister and nephew, Beck, the Dead Ringers, Jack, and Winchester. Even Vin is here. Everyone who supported me is under my roof, anxiously awaiting the moment it drops, the moment my life starts for real and I become Reign Harrow the rock star once more. It's nearly midnight, and I'm pacing anxiously, Raff Jr. following my every step like he always does. A bandana that one of my men put on him proudly reads, "My mummy is a rockstar!" My men watch me with nothing but love in their eyes. The last two months have been crazy in the best way. I have never been so happy, and my privacy has been respected. The world gets what I show them, but my men get everything from me. I don't hold anything back anymore.

I glance at the countdown, aware just how raw this album is.

My label said it has so many preorders and saves, more than they've ever seen before, but I know that means nothing. I poured my heart and soul into those lyrics, and it's my comeback album.

It's my reinvention, so I need it to do well.

"Baby." Raff grins, and I dance out of his outstretched hands as the clock hits zero.

"We are live!" Winchester shouts. She has been invaluable during this experience, and I can't wait for her to join me on tour.

I turn back to the screens. To the left are the number of downloads, and to the right are the social media feeds. I wait nervously to see what my fans will think. Arms wrap around me as I stand here in my home, which is open to everyone now because we don't hide who we are.

Either you like it or you don't.

It's my fucking life, and I won't hide it or lie.

"It's going to be amazing," Dal whispers. "Have a drink, princess."

I do.

And one more.

And one more.

I must have fallen asleep at some point because I wake to a scream and fall from the sofa. "*Rolling Stone* is calling it the best album of the decade! Reign, you did it! Everyone loves it! You already have six songs in the top ten. Holy fuck!"

"What? That's impossible—"

"Not for you. Congratulations, Reign Harrow, the revolutionist!" Beck yells. "My goddamn hero and the sexiest bitch on the planet."

Laughing, I take the drink she offers, uncaring what time it is. "I did it?"

"You did it, no one else," Astro replies. "Just you, Reign. I'm so proud of you. Look at you."

As my loved ones celebrate, I sit back, surrounded by love and laughter, and I smile.

My gaze goes to the ceiling. "For you, baby brother," I whisper. "We did it. I hope you're proud."

A hand grabs mine. "Dance with me!"

Laughing, I down my drink and allow them to pull me back to the living.

I allow myself to be happy.
I give myself a reason to live.
Even when it's not easy.
Even when everything seems like it's against me.
And it is so worth it.

I will never forget the woman who taught me to fight, to revolt, to be loud, crazy, and to follow my dream.

They call me an anarchist, but the truth is, I'm just living.

Just as Vin carved a path for me, I will carve a path for everyone who comes after me, and I'll have some fun doing it.

Surprisingly, the most saved, anticipated song is the one I never unveiled until now, ready for the world to meet my brother. He will be immortalized, and when thousands sing to it, they will remember him with me.

They will love him with me.

I always thought reaching the top was all I wanted, but I was wrong. This was what I wanted—the joy from performing and the happiness of crawling into bed with my loves.

My life with them is just beginning, and I can't wait to follow its path.

My life has never been easy, but it's been fucking glorious, and before the lights dim and the outro plays, I will scar this world with my dreams, with my music, until the very end.

EPILOGUE

"*Scandal has shaken the rock world once again, with Beck Danvers' surprise departure in the middle of a Dead Ringers performance at Warped Tour. Beck, the new lead singer, was on a sold-out world tour with the infamous bad boy band when she suddenly stormed off stage and didn't reappear. So far, three dates have been canceled, and there's no news from the band—*"

"*Beck Danvers, the drama queen—*"

"*Dead Ringers, who are no strangers to drama, have once again made headlines with spoiled singer Beck Danvers. The mysterious new lead singer landed them in hot water—*"

"*The question is, will the band ever recover from this? Will Beck Danvers come back for one last melody, or is she rebelling?*"

Scoffing, I turn the TV off and recline on the cheap motel bed. If they only knew the truth about me.

If they only knew Beck Danvers doesn't exist.

If they only knew I was a fraud, just like my bandmates know now.

about k.a. knight

K.A Knight is an USA Today bestselling indie author trying to get all of the stories and characters out of her head, writing the monsters that you love to hate. She loves reading and devours every book she can get her hands on, and she also has a worrying caffeine addiction.

She leads her double life in a sleepy English town, where she spends her days writing like a crazy person.

Read more at K.A Knight's website or join her Facebook Reader Group.
Sign up for exclusive content and my newsletter here
http://eepurl.com/drLLoj

also by k.a. knight

THE FALLEN GODS SERIES *PNR*

Pretty Painful

Pretty Bloody

Pretty Stormy

Pretty Wild

Pretty Hot

Pretty Faces

Pretty Spelled

Fallen Gods - the omnibus 1

Fallen Gods - the omnibus 2

COURTS AND KINGS *PNR RH*

Court of Nightmares

Court of Death

Court of Beasts *coming soon..*

FORBIDDEN READS *(STANDALONES)*

Daddy's Angel *CONTEMPORARY*

Stepbrothers' Darling *CONTEMPORARY RH*

LEGENDS AND LOVE *CONTEMPORARY*

Revolt

Rebel *coming soon..*

PRETTY LIARS *CONTEMPORARY RH*

Unstoppable

Unbreakable

FORGOTTEN CITY *PNR*

Monstrous Lies

Monstrous Truths

Monstrous Ends

DEN OF VIPERS UNIVERSE STANDALONES

Scarlett Limerence *CONTEMPORARY*

Nadia's Salvation *CONTEMPORARY*

Alena's Revenge *CONTEMPORARY*

Den of Vipers *CONTEMPORARY RH*

Gangsters and Guns (Co-Write with Loxley Savage) *CONTEMPORARY RH*

STANDALONES

The Standby *CONTEMPORARY*

Diver's Heart *CONTEMPORARY RH*

Crown of Stars *SCI FI RH*

AUDIOBOOKS

The Wasteland

The Summit

Rage

Hate

Den of Vipers *(From Podium Audio)*

Gangsters and Guns *(From Podium Audio)*

Daddy's Angel *(From Podium Audio)*

Stepbrothers' Darling *(From Podium Audio)*

Blade of Iris *(From Podium Audio)*

Deadly Affair *(From Podium Audio)*

Deadly Match *(From Podium Audio)*

Deadly Encounter *(From Podium Audio)*

Stolen Trophy *(From Podium Audio)*

Crown of Stars *(From Podium Audio)*

Monstrous Lies *(From Podium Audio)*

Monstrous Truth *(From Podium Audio)*

Monstrous Ends *(From Podium Audio)*

Court of Nightmares *(From Podium Audio)*

Unstoppable *(From Podium Audio)*

Unbreakable *(From Podium Audio)*

Fractured Shadows *(From Podium Audio)*

SHARED WORLD PROJECTS

Blade of Iris - Mafia Wars *CONTEMPORARY RH*

CO-AUTHOR PROJECTS - *Erin O'Kane*

HER FREAKS SERIES *PNR Dystopian RH*

Circus Save Me

Taming The Ringmaster

Walking the Tightrope

Her Freaks Series - the omnibus

STANDALONES

The Hero Complex *PNR RH*

Dark Temptations *Collection of Short Stories, ft. One Night Only & Circus Saves Christmas*

THE WILD BOYS SERIES *CONTEMPORARY RH*

The Wild Interview

The Wild Tour

The Wild Finale

The Wild Boys - the omnibus

CO-AUTHOR PROJECTS - *Ivy Fox*

Deadly Love Series *CONTEMPORARY*

Deadly Affair

Deadly Match

Deadly Encounter

CO-AUTHOR PROJECTS - *Kendra Moreno*

STANDALONES

Stolen Trophy *CONTEMPORARY RH*

Fractured Shadows *PNR RH*

Burn Me *PNR*

CO-AUTHOR PROJECTS - *Loxley Savage*

THE FORSAKEN SERIES *SCI FI RH*

Capturing Carmen

Stealing Shiloh

Harboring Harlow

STANDALONES

Gangsters and Guns *CONTEMPORARY*, IN DEN OF VIPERS' UNIVERSE

OTHER CO-WRITES

Shipwreck Souls *(with Kendra Moreno & Poppy Woods)*

The Horror Emporium *(with Kendra Moreno & Poppy Woods)*

find an error?

Please email this information to thenuttyformatter1@gmail.com:

- *the author name*
- *title of the book*
- *screenshot of the error*
- *suggested correction*

Printed in the USA
CPSIA information can be obtained
at www.ICGtesting.com
LVHW052253271023
762316LV00003B/3